To my wife, Sandra; our four children: Adrian, Suzanne, Elizabeth and James; our nine wonderful grandchildren: Jerome, Ona, Joy, Hamish, Annabel, Holly, Maisie, Imogen and Henry.

Mike Walsham

MONIQUE

AUSTIN MACAULEY PUBLISHERS™

LONDON • CAMBRIDGE • NEW YORK • SHARJAH

A CIP catalogue record for this title is available from the British Library.

ISBN 9781528921398 (Paperback)
ISBN 9781528921404 (Hardback)
ISBN 9781528921411 (Kindle e-book)
ISBN 9781528963428 (ePub e-book)

www.austinmacauley.com

First Published (2019)
Austin Macauley Publishers Ltd
25 Canada Square
Canary Wharf
London
E14 5LQ

A close friend for many years, Paul Yeates, gave me invaluable help on the formatting of submissions to publishers. Other friends and family members have urged me to write this novel for nearly four years.

Many thanks must go to Bill Patterson for his help with the cover design and to my granddaughter, Holly, for the time she spent assisting with the design in the latter stages.

Chapter 1
Early April 1940

As the fully laden train of twenty wagons started to move slowly out of the siding, he shovelled more coal into the furnace, as instructed. Artur Selmer had been working as a fireman with the burly German senior driver/engineer, named Hans, for a month. Hans was in his late forties. He was a tall, well-built man with a shock of fair hair and a florid complexion. His sleeves were usually rolled up when he worked on the train that revealed strong, muscular arms. He liked his *steins* of beer when off duty, but this affected his waistline. He had originally been employed by one of the private state railway companies in the 1920s, but had been selected to join the newly reorganised authority, the *Deutsche Reichsbahn (DRB)*, in 1937.

Hans was a full-paid member of the National Socialist Party and was proud of having been given the responsibility of ferrying high quality armour for the Reich. His family lived in a village near Leipzig and he would be allowed a week's leave after this trip. His two young sons would be celebrating their seventeenth birthdays during the time he would be at home, and they would have been members of the *Hitler-Jugend* for nearly three years. One of the twins was destined to be transferred to the SS as a result of his attitude and commitment to the Party. Hans was very excited to be going home after four weeks of work. He looked forward to being with his attractive wife, Heidi, and to be updated with what the family had been up to during his absence.

Artur was thirty-one years old. He had all the correct papers to substantiate his position. He had a Danish passport specifying he came from the village of Løgten, northeast of Aarhus, in Jutland. He had a Nationalist Party member's card showing that he currently lived in a village near Munich. He also had a German passport linking him to a small village near Munich. He had sharp blue eyes and a good head of straight, fair hair. He was lean and fit after all the training he had recently been through as a British agent, but was about 4″ shorter than Hans.

Artur had learnt German from his governess, Helga, who came from Munich. She was only nineteen years old when she had been taken on by his mother soon after he had been born – his mother was not at all keen on babies at the nappy stage. Helga adored Artur and was never far from him, singing German lullabies and talking about her little sister, Ingrid, who she hoped Artur might meet one day. Artur enjoyed all the attention he received at this early stage of his life and was quick to learn all that Helga taught him. Artur's mother would only speak Danish to him and talk to him about her family and the family's farm animals back in Denmark.

Artur had to be careful with his Danish that he had learned from his mother as she came from a village inland from the coastal town of Rungsted, north of Copenhagen. There were significant differences in pronunciation and the use of words from these two parts of Denmark – Jutland and the east of Sjaelland – and would be easily detected by anyone who was familiar with the language. Danish was not likely to be needed by Artur until he completed this current assignment with his planned escape through Jutland back to England.

Even after only six months since the outbreak of war, Artur was already on his second operation as a British agent into mainland Europe, but this one was much longer and more dangerous. His superiors thought it a very risky assignment for such a new, inexperienced recruit; one that required Artur to use his initiative, to be clear-headed at all times about the objective and to trust nobody. He was, as a result, given much less than a 50-50 chance of being successful and less than one in a hundred chance of escaping capture and returning to England safely. He was, however, very confident of his own abilities and his general Arian appearance could be of significant assistance, not to mention his language skills.

Artur worked well with Hans; he initially had a shaky start but now he was trusted as Hans' assistant and had worked hard on his relationship with him. Artur had a natural ability of making people feel at ease with him, especially in this situation where he was not really a German national, but a very fluent and competent German speaker. His aptitude for making people laugh was used to great effect with Hans, who enjoyed poking fun at the English and how they didn't stand a chance of winning the war against the Germans this time around.

About ten days earlier, in one of Hans' favourite bars with the *steins* flowing so freely, Hans had told Artur that he had received information from one of his sons that Germany would soon walk into Denmark and thence into Norway. Artur was aware from his occasional coded communications with London that Hitler and his Chiefs of Staff were in a dilemma as to whether the army should occupy the neutral countries of Norway and Denmark, or march into and occupy the Low Countries. Hans confirmed that Hitler favoured the former because the much needed Swedish iron ore for armament manufacturing was coming from the Norwegian port of Narvik during these harsh winter months. In addition, France and Great Britain wished to persuade neutral Norway and Sweden to let them take their troop ships into Norwegian and Swedish waters in order to give support to the Finnish resistance that was fighting the Russians.

London would be very interested to hear what Hans had told Artur, and knew that it was classified information that had been carelessly given to him that evening. Artur had listened to every detail so he could relay it to London at his next opportunity. One of Artur's many strong points was that he had trained himself to make a beer last very much longer than most other people, and yet give the impression that he was getting drunk. Hans even apologised on behalf of the German army and hoped none of Artur's family in Jutland would be caught up in the skirmishes that were bound to occur. That reflected the trust that Hans had in Artur; it wasn't the first mistake that Hans had made and it would probably not be the last.

It was early April 1940. The weather had been bitterly cold over most of mainland Europe during January, especially Germany, Scandinavia and the Low Countries of Belgium and the Netherlands. Snow still lay around and, earlier in the day, the pale grey clouds suggested more was to come. It transpired to have been one of the coldest winters on record, with temperatures reaching as low as −40 °C in some places. It was not nearly so cold now.

Artur had been operating trains with Hans for the last four weeks on a route from the Daimler-Benz engine manufacturing plants near Stuttgart to the assembly plants for the Messerschmitt Bf 109 fighter planes in Regensburg, in the east of Germany. This time, however, the train was carrying tank engines and would make a diversion to the tank assembly plants of Krupp-Grusson at Magdeburg, southwest of Berlin. The route would go via Nuremberg and on to the relatively new line to Berlin. This change of plan had only been presented to Hans a few days earlier, but fortunately it didn't affect Artur and his fellow agent, Gerhart's plans as the split in the line to take the train to its new destination was a long way east of Stuttgart, beyond the place where the sabotage of the rail line was due to occur.

As the train increased its speed, Artur went over in his mind what he had organised with Gerhart over the last two weekends. They had earlier obtained detailed maps of the rail route from outside Stuttgart to

Magdeburg and had identified a stretch that went through a wooded area east of Milmersdorf, just over half way between Stuttgart and Nuremburg.

As far as the senior driver, Hans, was concerned, all seemed to be going normally. The train was travelling at night and was expected at its destination just after dawn. It was Tuesday, and Artur had not been in touch with Gerhart since their final planning meeting on Saturday, apart from a coded message received on Monday night saying all was still OK. The receiver was now in its case inside a sack hidden back at the station; he would collect it in due course.

Artur looked at his watch to check the time: another twenty five minutes to go before the zero hour. He opened the steel door on the left of the cabin and looked outside for some minutes to try and identify some landmarks. He had rehearsed this part of the exercise each time he had travelled on this route over the last four weeks. This, therefore, seemed quite a normal thing to Hans that Artur did, but this time it was for real. The train clattered over a level crossing, past a village, and then suddenly he realised that he recognised the small station of Sachsen. This gave Artur a jolt. He carefully looked at his watch and saw they were two and half minutes ahead of schedule.

Artur turned back from looking out of the train and told Hans that he would shovel in another load of coal. Artur looked briefly at the locomotive's dials to see that all was in order. He took up the shovel and gathered up a load for the furnace. As he fed the fire with more coal, he looked under his left arm; he saw Hans was looking away from him at the darkened countryside going past. In one swift movement, Artur turned and hit Hans hard over the head with the shovel. Hans fell to the floor; Artur hit him several more times until he was sure he was unconscious. He checked Hans' pulse and thought he must be dead, but he spent no more time investigating. He put down the shovel and pushed Hans' body towards the opening of the cabin. *'Wow, he really is heavy'*, thought Artur, wondering if he could get Hans out of the driver's compartment as planned. One last big heave and Hans slipped out into the cold night air onto the snow-covered side of the track. Artur gave a big sigh of relief, quickly looked out of the cabin to his left and just managed to see Hans disappearing from view. Suddenly, he realised that time had quickly passed by. He looked at his watch and there were only a few more minutes to go.

Gerhart had planted the explosives on the track just before 10 o'clock that night. He had double checked that all was still primed and in order, twenty minutes before Artur's train was due. The devices had been placed in a number of old bicycle pumps, attached to each rail with three foot long slow-burning fuses. As arranged, Gerhart lit the fuses ten minutes before the train was due and retired quickly up the slight embankment and behind a tree to await the blasts. It seemed an eternity before the flash lit up the night sky for a few seconds. Gerhart hoped nobody of any importance had heard the explosions as he went and examined his handy-work. He found the rails had been blown upwards just where the fish plates had been a few moments earlier. He was satisfied that the speeding locomotive would be derailed and that the wagons carrying the valuable tank engines would career off the track and into each other with great force. He quickly left the scene and moved towards where the train was coming from. He needed to be well down the track to avoid the wagons when they came off the track and away from where the armed guards would be searching for the saboteurs. He also needed to be close to the rendezvous point that he and Artur had agreed on.

With five minutes to go before the train was expected to hit the booby trap set by his fellow agent, Artur very slightly increased the speed of the train. He then prepared himself to jump from what would become a driverless train. He hoped the train's increasing speed would not alert the armed guards that were positioned at intervals in the wagons, but that was a risk he had to take. He saw the faintly lit signal box in the distance as he stood outside the cabin on the footplate. As the train passed it, he slightly increased its speed again, checked that his leather satchel containing all his papers, and some primitive tools, was securely fastened to his torso. He counted to ten: *Six, seven, eight, nine, ten: Jump!* he said to himself, almost out loud.

Artur had practiced the escape from the train a dozen times during training, but nothing could really compare with the real thing. He hurled himself as far as he could into the darkness, away from the moving train and over the low fence, curling himself into as tight a ball as possible. He tried to prepare himself for the impact in the snow, but he glanced off a tree at speed. He had instinctively covered his head with his hands to protect it, at the same time clinging to his precious satchel. He landed heavily on the ground that was only lightly covered with snow, rolling some distance in the same direction as the train. He hit his head on a boulder and suddenly came to rest, his limbs all in a bit of a tangle.

Eventually, Artur opened his eyes very slowly. He felt very cold as he lay in the snow. He couldn't move easily, but he managed to move his head enough to see a young woman standing near him. She was in her twenties, he thought, and had a very kindly disposition. She seemed to be in strange clothes that hung loosely about her delicate frame. When she saw his eyes open, she gave a kindly smile and said some words to him in a language that he hadn't heard before, but something deep in the back of his mind told him that he could speak back to her. The woman knelt down beside him. She had a large sheep skin coat over her arm and gently laid it over him to keep out the cold and handed him a goat skin water bottle. In her language, she told him to take a drink and not to worry about anything. Artur understood and instinctively did as he was told but still didn't really know what was happening. Was he dreaming or was this for real, he thought to himself, and yet this woman seemed very familiar.

After a while, Artur tried to raise himself into a sitting position, but the woman gently rested her hand on him and told him to relax for a little longer. Artur felt his memory coming back and was anxious to meet up with his accomplice and get out of the area as the enemy would be searching everywhere, very thoroughly. But firstly, he had to know who the woman was, why she had helped him and why she was there.

"I have to meet a friend who will be wondering where I am," he said, in a language which seemed to come so naturally to him.

"Don't worry," she said, in the same language. "You will be safe with me."

"But who are you? You seem very familiar to me; what is your name and why are you here?"

"My name is Marie and we were intimate friends a very long time ago. You were one of the chosen few that left the Cathare fortress of Montségur to hide their golden treasures in a cave not far from Usson."

"Hang on a moment. I haven't been involved in hiding any treasures and where is Usson anyway? All I think I know is that I've just jumped from a speeding train that is carrying supplies for my enemy, the Germans."

"I'm sorry," she said. "It's my turn not to understand what you are saying."

With that, his head suddenly became very painful and throbbed. He collapsed onto his back again and fell into a deep sleep.

Chapter 2
Mid-March 1939

Andrew Williams had been identified as a potential agent early in 1939. He had been in a City of London pub with some of his friends from the bank after work. He was a clerk on the foreign exchange desk and had worked at the same bank for over twelve years. He wasn't very keen on the job and had shown little ambition, which was probably why he hadn't yet been promoted to senior clerk, even if he did have the aptitude and good connections. He did, however, enjoy the bank's social activities, such as the Hockey, Cricket and Rifle Clubs.

Andrew didn't know it at the time, but he and some of the others who still remained in the pub had been joined by a recruitment officer, Charles, from the Special Intelligence Service (SIS). They very much enjoyed each other's company and, as was his wont, Andrew broke into jokes about the Germans and the French, in fluent German and French. Some of the songs that they sang were known by a few, but Andrew had a knack of changing some of the words which sent everyone into hysterical laughter.

Around 10:30 p.m., a small group split away from the rest and moved on to a night club that Andrew recommended. At this stage, Charles asked Andrew to contact him before the end of the week on a phone number that he gave him. The guard on the club door warmly welcomed Andrew and his friends, and they were directed to a vacant table not far from the piano. They were getting more and more outrageous with their stories and had ordered more drinks until, quite suddenly, Andrew got up and went over to talk to the pianist. At the end of the number, Andrew swapped places with the pianist and started playing and singing some of the popular numbers of the day, changing the words every now and again to make them very risqué and hilariously funny. He also sang a few of the German army marching songs, again cleverly altering some of the words. Most stood up with a Nazi salute and a finger across the top lip, mimicking Hitler. Everybody joined in where they could and there was a lot of laughter. A little while later, when he was back at the table, he glanced at his watch and noticed how late it was getting and excused himself rather hurriedly to the others. Needless to say, Andrew knew he was going to be in his wife's bad books, yet again, for failing to contact her about his being late home and not arriving until the early hours of the morning.

Andrew phoned Charles a few days later and they arranged to meet at the Oxford and Cambridge Club in Pall Mall after work the following Tuesday. Andrew knew the Club quite well as he had met some of his old school friends over the years at the Club as they had gone up to Oxford or Cambridge after leaving school. Andrew checked in with the Commissionaire and was told that Mr Charles Compton-Browne was awaiting his arrival in the main bar. After a few pleasantries and having ordered drinks, they retired to a table where they would not be overheard or interrupted. Following a laugh about the previous week's enjoyable time at the pub and the club, Charles asked a few questions. Andrew was not often very open with people he didn't know well about his past and his family, but he seemed to relax with Charles. He explained about his Danish family connections, his German governess and his French-speaking school friend with whom he used to spend summer holidays in Bruges and near Lille in Northern France after the Great War. That's why he had such fluency in a total of four languages.

They spent just over an hour together, with Andrew doing most of the talking about his life, family, interests and the imminent possibility of a war in Europe. He looked at his watch and he was concerned about the time. He asked to excuse himself as he had a wife who was seven months pregnant. He needed to get home at a reasonable time as he was still very much in his wife's bad books from the week before. Charles quite understood Andrew's situation and thanked him for his time. They arranged to meet again the following week, but this time at Charles' office in St James', where he wanted Andrew to meet his 'Chief'. Before they parted company, Charles explained to Andrew the importance of his not telling anyone, including his wife and family, about what they had discussed and where they would be meeting next time.

The weather was very cold at the weekend: a light covering of snow on the ground but clear, blue skies all around. Andrew arranged to meet a good friend of his on Saturday and go shooting in the nearby fields in NW Sussex, not far from where Andrew lived. Andrew's black Labrador, Max, had been fully trained for this type of exercise and he welcomed the opportunity of going out with his master, especially as he noticed that he was taking his favoured 16-bore with him – this meant hunting, not just walking.

Andrew collected his friend, Brian, at 11 o'clock on Saturday, and drove to the entrance to Hill Farm. Andrew knew the farmer at Hill Farm well and he was permitted to walk quite freely over his land and shoot rabbit, hare or pheasant, should he encounter any. Nonetheless, Andrew never took his farmer friend for granted and had phoned him just before calling Brian to make sure it was still all right to walk over his land on Saturday morning.

The two of them trudged over the frozen snow for over an hour, keeping their eyes skinned for any rabbits or hares. Max had raced up and down the other side of the hedgerows hoping to frighten animals out into the open for the men to have a shot at but, rather disappointingly, nothing had ventured out in the crisp, cold conditions.

They returned to Andrew's car and drove to a pub in a nearby village known to both of them: the Royal Oak. They knew they could get a good pint, be greeted by the jolly publican and warm themselves in front of the roaring fire in the Public Bar. The conversation had mainly centred on the developing situation in Germany, the imminent birth of his first born, due in May, and his wife's attitude towards his recent late home-comings. It was at this stage that Andrew found it very difficult not to tell Brian why he was in bad favour with his wife and about his recent meetings with Charles. He knew he would eventually have to confide in someone and it was most likely to be Brian, but probably not until after his next meeting with Charles.

Andrew's sister-in-law and brother-in-law had come down for the weekend, so he needed to be back from the pub in time for a light lunch. Having them down for the weekend would be helpful to his wife and would take his mind off his meetings with Charles and, more particularly, the next meeting with Charles' boss during next week. He and his brother-in-law, whose company he really enjoyed, managed a walk on Sunday with Max before a hearty roast lunch and a snooze for everyone in the afternoon. Nonetheless, time still went very slowly and he couldn't stop himself from thinking over what the next meeting with Charles might involve. He had slept little at night since the last meeting and had often disturbed his wife with his tossing and turning. He left by the usual train for London on the Tuesday and excused himself to his wife for not knowing what time he might be back that evening, but would phone when leaving London. He told her that he had an important after-hours meeting with his manager, Mr Beckett, who had only set it up on Friday of the week before.

Andrew left his office promptly after work on Tuesday and took a cab to the road in St James' next to the one given to him, just as Charles had said. He waited till the cab was out of sight before turning into the correct road given in the address. He found the house number and knocked with the highly polished brass knocker. A few moments later, the door was opened by an attractive young brunette, probably in her twenties, with a welcoming smile and sparkling hazel eyes.

"Mr Williams?" she enquired knowingly, before Andrew could say anything.

"That's who I am," said Andrew, smiling back at the young lady at the door.

"My name is Helen. Mr Compton-Browne is expecting you. Please go up to the first floor; his office is on the left."

Andrew thought he would rather spend more time chatting to Helen than going to a meeting, but he was expected and it was important to arrive at the appointed time.

"Thank you," said Andrew, casting a glance at Helen and giving her a wink of his eye that made her blush just a little.

On the first floor, he straightened his tie and smoothed down his hair with his right hand. He looked to his left and knocked firmly on the door marked 'C. Compton-Browne Esq., MA'. A familiar voice told him to enter and, as he opened the door, he saw two other men in the room as well as Charles.

"It's good to see you again, Andrew. Thank you for coming to my office. You found the address easily enough did you, old boy?"

"Thank you, Charles, yes I did."

"Let me take your coat, Andrew. I would like to introduce you to my 'Chief', more usually known as 'C', and a colleague of mine, James Wilder."

They all shook hands and looked each other in the eye with a rather forced smile as they mentioned their names. C was quite a bit older than the other two and he didn't look in the best of health, occasionally attempting to take a deep intake of air into his lungs. C wore a tweed suit with what looked like a college tie and a blue handkerchief falling out of his top pocket. Andrew noticed that C's brown shoes were well polished and thought his own black ones were not to the same standard. He hoped nobody would notice.

Andrew glanced around Charles' office, trying not to look too nosey; the coat and hat stand that now had an extra coat on it; there was a large knee-hole desk with a leather top that faced him opposite the door he had come in, mostly covered with neatly piled papers; a pen-and-ink stand plus a photo that he couldn't properly see; two telephones, one of which was red. There was a separate square table to the left side of the window on his right on which was an ashtray with several stubbed out cigarette ends. He didn't think Charles smoked so he assumed they must be C's dog-ends. There was a large picture of the King on one wall and an equally large picture of a college chapel that he recognised to be King's College

Chapel, Cambridge, on another wall. The wooden floor round the outside of the room was well polished and there was a large rug covering the majority of the floor.

Andrew, Charles and James took their seats. C decided to slowly walk about the room with one hand behind his back and a cigarette in the other. A silence came over everyone in the room that seemed to go on for many minutes. C looked quite serious. He glanced at Andrew a few times as he wandered round the office and muttered a few things to himself. He took a deep drag on his cigarette – held in his left hand Andrew noticed – and spluttered a little as he did so.

The silence was then broken by Charles giving a slight cough. He proceeded to brief C and James with what had transpired between him and Andrew during the weeks before; firstly in the pub and then at the O&C Club. He retold a couple of Andrew's amusing anecdotes about the Germans that he had heard whilst in the night club and they all laughed, except Andrew, who felt a bit embarrassed to hear them again. It was quite apparent to Andrew that they already knew most of what Charles was saying – except the jokes – and it was all being used as a gentle entrée to the discussion that would follow.

There was then another slight pause before C asked Andrew if he knew anything about the Secret Intelligence Service and its importance, particularly during times of war.

"No, sir," Andrew replied.

"As I'm sure you are fully aware, Williams, the situation in Europe, especially with what this rogue Hitler is doing, is getting very close to war. Not only did his armies march into Austria last year, but a few days ago Czechoslovakia was occupied by the German Army. Hitler is now saying that Czechoslovakia no longer exists except as a part of the German empire.

"The British and other world governments are well aware that Czechoslovakia is a major manufacturer of machine guns, tanks and artillery of a very high quality at the Skoda factories; very useful to Hitler's desires on further German expansionism. Where will Hitler go next: Poland, Western Europe? Not that I'm saying England will get involved but, if push comes to shove, we might have to support our Allies, such as France and Poland, should Germany start to threaten them or their interests. Even our Prime Minister has made our country's position quite clear so we have to be prepared for the worst; do I make myself clear?"

"Yes, sir," replied Andrew. "But, pardon me for asking, how does this involve me, sir, a humble bank employee in the City of London?"

"People like you, Williams, are very few and far between in England. Charles here just happened to stumble over a person who seems to speak

German and French like a native, plus the more unusual language of Danish, not to mention English," C said with a slight chuckle, at the same time stubbing out his cigarette in the ashtray on the small table by the window.

"In addition, you have had a very good schooling and you have considerable charm; I think you would get on well with most people. You look very fit and you are in your very early thirties. You enjoy your Bugatti cars with like-minded people and have spent many a weekend with some of them at hill climbs and rallies over the last few years, with a moderate amount of success. You have excellent eyesight and you can shoot like a marksman, having won several shooting tournaments since 1926 at the bank."

Andrew looked very surprised on hearing details of his recent activities and his perceived character.

"Don't worry, Williams, we did some careful research into your background, talents, family and friends before we asked you to meet us today. We probably even know your shoe size!"

Andrew tried to smile, but he was troubled about how much of his background they had delved into and seemed to know about.

"Have no fear, Williams, anything we find out about you will be a closely guarded secret. If we discover anything untoward, we will of course discuss it with you first to see if it's true. I'm sure there is nothing hidden and no skeletons in the cupboard, so to speak," C said with a wry smile.

"Let me get straight to the point, Williams, and not beat about the bush," said C. At this time, C was looking out of the window through a gap in the curtains to the darkened street below. He had his hands in his jacket pockets. He then turned round, straightened himself as much as he could and faced the three men, focussing on Andrew.

"My department, and others in the various Services, is often looking for possible new recruits and no more so than at this time of tension in Europe. At present, as I said a moment ago, we are not on a war footing YET," he stressed, "but, we must prepare ourselves for what seems likely to happen in the not too distant future."

"Please excuse my interruption again, sir, but I have been employed by my bank for more than twelve years. I am about to be a father in the next couple of months and need to be near my wife."

"I quite understand what you are saying, Andrew." C had cleverly introduced a much more relaxed and informal manner by using Andrew's first name and it made Andrew feel a little more at ease with the situation.

Charles then chipped in and said, "We have one or two ideas that we would like to put to you. If you don't like what we say, or you feel it's not your scene then you are free to go and we will part amicably; nothing more will be said about these meetings."

Before Andrew could say anything, C continued on from Charles' points.

"My department and my predecessors have been selecting, training and sending out into the field, young men like you – and some young women too – on special missions for many years. They have often been asked to go to European countries that require fluency in one or more languages. Some of these 'agents', as we call them, link up with local nationals, carry out surveillance operations and report back to my department. In the present climate, my people are only away for a few days at a time, but I can foresee this would be for a much longer period, should the situation in Europe worsen.

"Obviously, before anyone becomes an agent, there is a training program that is spread over a number of months that can be designed to suit each trainee's needs. It is conducted at our special training establishments in the south and north of England and in Scotland by highly qualified instructors. Men like you would learn about unarmed combat, the use of weapons such as pistols, radio communications, the Morse code and the use of coded messages.

"In your current employment position, you would be expected to take two days off every other week, which we would agree directly with your employer. Until now, no employer has refused to cooperate once we have clearly explained everything to them. As far as your wife and family are concerned, they will think that you are going to the office as usual or on a management training course, probably requiring an overnight stay each time or the occasional weekend.

"How does that sound so far, Andrew?"

"I feel very flattered that you think I could fit in and be trained to be one of your 'agents', as you call them, but I'm still concerned about how I will deal with my wife's pregnancy in the next two months and my new life as a father?"

"Quite so, Andrew, I understand fully. If all goes according to plan, you will not be commencing your training until late May or early June at the earliest anyway. As you can imagine, your employer has to be contacted and persuaded to release you for the periods mentioned. But before that, you will have to undergo a very thorough medical check carried out by our special medical team. You will be required to sit with linguists in all three of your foreign languages to see how fluent you really are and they will ascertain whether or not you need any extra tuition or instruction to bring any of them up to a higher standard. There will be a requirement for character references. Once you've been through all these assessments and we have concluded that you are suitable for the Service, we will have decided how and where you might be involved with our intelligence team. There will then be a number of different forms to be completed, assuming you want to continue with what we have in mind.

"Does that make you feel a bit better about things?"

"Yes, sir, it does. But there is still one important question I want to ask. I don't think my bank will grant me, or your department, two days off every fortnight without reducing my salary, so how do I afford to live?"

"That's a good point, Andrew. I would like James here to deal with that."

Andrew looked at James Wilder. They gave each other a brief smile and he nodded politely as James stood up. James looked a little nervous and unsure of himself in his rather unkempt flannels and scruffy sports jacket. His tie was rather too bright and it had a mark below the untidy knot where he had obviously spilt something. He wore horn-rimmed spectacles that were probably very strong as his eyeballs looked quite large when looking at him.

"Thank you, C, it will be a pleasure," he said as he stood up to address Andrew, without really looking at anybody in particular. "It's all very simple, Andrew. I assume I may call you Andrew?"

"Of course," replied Andrew with a smile.

"Thank you," said James and continued. "During the assessment and training period, whether the bank continues to pay your full salary or not, the Service will arrange to pay you a daily rate equivalent to what you are currently receiving, plus an extra 10%. You will also be covered for all expenses, including travel, until you become a full member of the Service. By the way, we will reimburse your expenses that you have already incurred before you leave this evening. How does all that sound?"

"Well, that certainly seems more than generous, but as I'm sure you must realise, I'm going to find it very difficult not telling anyone what I'm involved in and where the extra money is coming from."

C then took another cigarette. He lit it. He turned to Andrew and smiled at him.

"Sorry, Andrew, I should have asked earlier, would you like a cigarette?"

"No thank you, sir, I don't smoke."

C put his silver cigarette case back into his jacket pocket and placed the lighter back on Charles' desk.

"Andrew, all our recruits have been at the same stage as you and have said exactly the same sort of thing. It's part of why we are considering you. We are very certain that you will find a way to play your cards very close to your chest and act accordingly. The important thing is to appear to everyone you meet as though all is normal, but you must quickly learn to trust no one with information about the Service, listen carefully to everything you hear and report back to your Service contact any concerns you might have. Of course, I should emphasise that you will not become a full-time member of the Service until England has declared its intention to be at war with Germany. This situation may or may not occur but, if or when it does, your employment with the bank will cease."

Andrew was very surprised by C's last sentences, but started to feel a sense of excitement in his stomach.

"With that, unless you have any further questions Andrew, I believe we should finish this meeting. We have very much enjoyed meeting you and feel you could be a very useful and important asset to the Service, should the Country's situation alter. Please think carefully about all we have talked about and contact Charles again in the next two weeks with your decision. Does that give you enough time, Andrew?"

"Yes, sir, I think it does, but there is a lot to mull over."

They all stood up, shook each other's hands and there were thanks all round for the time spent together. James asked Andrew if a 'fiver' would cover his expenses to which Andrew showed some surprise, but accepted, albeit with some reluctance. Charles helped Andrew on with his coat and opened the door for him to leave the office. Once outside the door and before going downstairs, Andrew hesitated as he could just make out some of the conversation between the three Intelligence Service officers. Each of them had said they had found the meeting very useful and that if Andrew's languages were as fluent as Charles had suggested to them, Andrew could eventually be employed in extensive undercover work for C's department, once war in Europe was declared.

Andrew came down the stairs in a bit of a dream to find Helen waiting to open the front door for him.

"Good night, Mr Williams. Have a good journey home."

"Thank you very much, Helen. I didn't realise I had been in the meeting for so long." He gave Helen a broad smile and disappeared into the cold night air.

Andrew headed for Victoria station, but fortunately remembered to phone his wife from a call box after checking the time of the next train; they were usually every half an hour at this time of the evening. His call was received very coldly by his wife. She complained that as she had felt hungry, she had already had her supper and would probably be in bed before he returned home – it was already 8 o'clock. She asked him nothing about how his meeting had gone. She seemed to be in another one of her moods that might last a day or two.

Andrew thought that, under the circumstances, he needed a drink. He went into the station bar and ordered a pint of beer. He needed to reflect on the meeting and how it might change his life completely. He was very excited by the prospect of doing something so different from his boring banking job later in the year, even with the possibility of war.

Hardly any lights were on when Andrew arrived home shortly before 9:45 p.m. He tried to make as little noise as possible, but Max heard him and excitedly ran to him from his basket at the end of the hall. Andrew thought the dog ought, at the very least, to have a short walk round the garden before he looked in the kitchen for something to eat. He didn't feel like much, but knew he should have a sandwich or some cheese before turning in.

After walking his dog around the garden, Andrew sat in the kitchen and mulled over the evening's meeting with C and what this might do to his life. He tucked in to some cheese and cracked open a bottle of his favourite red wine. What was really difficult was not being allowed to discuss any of what was going through his mind with anyone – not even with one of his close friends that he knew he could trust implicitly. *I desperately need to speak to someone before the end of the weekend, if possible, but who should it be?* He thought to himself.

In his mind, he went through all of his friend's names, not in any particular order: *Peter – I've not known him for long but I know he would understand my predicament and be trustworthy; Jack – he would give sound advice and I've known him for over fifteen years; Harry – a good friend but liable to spill the beans after a scotch or two; Phillip – a man of sound intellect and strong morals who would look at the bigger picture; and then there's Brian – always a good listener and known by me since our childhood.*

It has to be Brian, Andrew said to himself with great relief, almost shouting his name out, but quickly remembering the time of night and that the kitchen was just below his wife's bedroom. He knew Brian was the right choice. He would arrange to see him sometime over the next weekend. Andrew finished his wine, stoppered the bottle, washed up the glass, put away what remained of the cheese and went very carefully upstairs. After cleaning his teeth and donning his pyjamas, he slipped under the sheets next to his sleeping wife, pleased with his decision and equally pleased that he hadn't woken her. He quickly fell into a deep sleep.

Andrew awoke bright and early and brought his wife a cup of her favourite tea plus a biscuit. She still hadn't forgiven him for his late arrival home as she mumbled a sort of 'Thank you'. Andrew asked her how she was feeling and if she had a doctor's appointment in the next couple of days.

"I told you at the weekend that I had to see the doctor on Wednesday, and that's TODAY," she said in a cross manner.

"I'm sorry, dear, but there's been a lot going on at the office recently, it slipped my mind. Will you be able to get someone to go with you or can you manage on your own?"

"If I can't get Barbara to come with me, I'll have to manage on my own, won't I?" she said in a very resigned fashion.

"I seem to remember the appointment was at 11 o'clock, but if it had been late afternoon, I could have got home early to go with you myself," said Andrew.

"You've not been home by 6:30 p.m. or any earlier for the last three weeks so why should I expect you back early today when I need you to be?" she said, almost spilling the last of her tea. "You had better get off to the office and let me sort out my day for myself. Will you be late again or can we have supper TOGETHER tonight?"

"I'll tell you what, why don't we go out for supper at The George & Dragon tonight? I'll book a table for 7 o'clock, so that it's not too late for you to get an early night."

"Oh, all right," she said. "I suppose that will make up for a few of your late evenings. Perhaps you can also tell me what these office meetings have been all about."

Andrew knew this was going to be raised at some point or other, so he had better have some good answers prepared. He kissed his wife gently on the forehead and hoped she had a satisfactory appointment with her doctor.

"I'll be back home by 6:30 p.m. tonight, in good time to get to the pub for a nice meal."

"I hope so," she replied. "As I said a moment ago, I'm looking forward to hearing all about those office meetings, if that's what they were."

Chapter 3
Wednesday, 3ʳᵈ of April 1940

Artur suddenly woke up; he felt very cold and his legs ached as well as his head. At this point, he had no idea how long he had been lying in the snow, but he knew he had to get away from where he was lying, and quickly. He looked around him and remembered the kind woman, Marie. It was difficult to see very far and she wasn't anywhere to be seen, but the sheep skin was still there, over his torso and the top of his legs.

Artur jumped to his feet. *How did this sheepskin coat get here?* He muttered to himself. *It looks like the one that is supposed to be in the hut with the other one for Gerhart.* He realised he should waste no more time and wrapped the sheep skin around his shoulders; he was feeling very cold and shivered as he gained his composure. He was relieved to notice that his satchel was still over his right shoulder. He checked its contents and everything was there that should be. He stood next to a tree and listened carefully for a few moments. He could just make out distant noises and voices of someone shouting out orders, probably to make contact with the commander stationed further up the line to update him with the state of the train. The railway line was to his right so he turned about and started to walk in the opposite direction to the distant voices.

It was difficult to see exactly where he was going, but he made sure the railway line on his left was not more than forty metres away from his chosen path for the time being. He noticed in the snow that he was walking in the same direction as another set of foot prints: smaller than his and with no discernible tread marks. *That's very strange*, he thought, *who on earth could be walking through the forest at this time of night? And they seem to have been made quite recently. Whoever it is, I need to be very careful that this person doesn't hear me.* This troubled Artur so he paused for a few seconds, but he couldn't hear any sound anywhere near him. *Of course*, he thought, *the snow might be muffling the sound of each step on the ground.*

Gerhart had heard the sound of the engine and wagons careering off the rails into each other and blocking the track. He knew the sabotage had

24

been successful, but this was twenty minutes ago. He hoped Artur had jumped off the train and not injured himself, especially with the speed of the train and the frequency of the trees at the track side. They had arranged a rendezvous at a small hut in the forest some fifteen minutes from now so he made speed to be there before Artur, as agreed in their plan.

Gerhart had a tiny torch to help him find his way, but he had only used it occasionally until he walked straight into a tree. He just managed to prevent himself from letting out an expletive that could have been heard by someone as much as a kilometre away. He had badly bruised his nose and forehead. He was sure that blood was coming out of his injuries, but he had to press on regardless. He walked more slowly now, stopping every forty steps to listen out for any noise around him; he used his torch more often but with a great deal of care. He reached the hut five minutes before the allotted time; more by luck than good judgement, he reckoned. As he was about to enter the hut, he noticed a set of prints coming from the opposite direction, smaller prints than his and having no real shoe tread marks. *Funny,* he thought, *they certainly don't look like Artur's; whose can they be? In any case, they're coming from deep in the woods towards the hut from where Artur would be coming from.*

Gerhart was now very worried. He removed his pistol from his coat pocket, cocked it and listened for a moment for any sound coming from within the hut. Nothing! He looked about him and searched the ground near the entrance door that was on the left of the hut; the prints definitely went into the hut. He took a deep breath and very carefully raised the catch on the door. He opened the door a fraction, expecting someone to rush out and apprehend him, or even shoot him. Nothing! He eased the door open and peered in with the light of his torch. Nobody! Everything was as he expected it to be, as he scanned round the inside of the hut. *Hang on a minute*, he said to himself, *there's only one sheepskin coat and we definitely brought two here at the weekend!*

Gerhart glanced at his watch with the aid of his torch: *Artur should have been here by now,* he muttered to himself. The arrangement was that he should wait no longer than five minutes after the rendezvous time, after which time he should proceed to the next meeting place that was just under two hours walk through the woods and the fields in a direction that would take him well away from the railway line. He grabbed the remaining coat; he knew he would need it for the next few days, especially as the weather was still very cold. After he had had a further look round the hut, he closed the door and reluctantly, but purposefully set off for the next meeting point.

Meanwhile, Artur realised he had insufficient time to reach the first meeting point at the hut where he had to link up with Gerhart. He knew he had to forget about the woman in his dream – if it really was a dream – if he was to meet up with Gerhart at all and not be captured. He pulled out his torch and compass, as well as the roughly sketched map that they had produced when they were last together. He quickly plotted a bearing to the second rendezvous and estimated he would be at the second meeting place in just less than two hours as long as he didn't encounter any more problems or deeper snow than what was around him now. He calculated that he must have been asleep for twenty-five minutes. He left the other footprints. He knew he needed to hurry, but his head still ached and his right leg was feeling very stiff.

Chapter 4
End of March 1939

Andrew asked his boss if he could have a quick word with him as soon as he got into the office.

"As you know, sir, my wife is expecting our first child in less than a couple of months and she is due for an appointment with her doctor this afternoon. I do obviously realise that we are very busy these days leading up to the end of the financial year, but I would very much appreciate it if I could leave early today to be with her."

"Well, I suppose so, Williams, but I can't really let you go until 4 o'clock at the earliest."

"That's extremely kind of you, sir. I'll make up for any lost time by working a couple of times in the lunch-break."

"That's a good idea, Williams. Thank you for the suggestion. By the way, how is your wife coping with her pregnancy? The first one can sometimes be a bit nerve-racking, even with a lot of support from the family, but your family don't live close-by, if I remember correctly?"

"Thank you for your concern and you are quite right, the family are not nearby. In addition, it doesn't help that she doesn't get on very well with the family members on my side. She does, however, have some really good friends who live in neighbouring villages and they keep in touch with each other."

"Friends are sometimes more help than close family. As they say: 'You can choose your friends but you can't choose your family'. This could well be true in your wife's case, Williams," he said with a slight smile. "Do let me know if you need a bit more time off nearer the time as we shall be well past the Financial Year End by mid-May."

"Thank you sir, I'll keep you or your secretary posted with any developments."

Andrew felt greatly relieved with his boss' pleasant attitude about leaving early, especially as he could sometimes be very negative towards husbands whose wives are with child.

Andrew kept his head down during the day and only every so often did he do a bit of clock-watching. What he was more preoccupied with was the other part of his life that nobody else knew about – *yet*. He had to speak to Brian at the weekend, but he felt he needed to spend a couple of hours with him in a quiet, private place, probably over lunch. Andrew's other concern was what sort of cock-and-bull story he was going to dream up that his wife would believe and also would satisfy her curiosity. This time, he knew he had to give a plausible story that didn't bear any resemblance to the truth. She usually viewed stories that he had told her on other occasions with a huge amount of suspicion, but she never wanted to prolong any discussion for very long. Hopefully she will be quite tired after the doctor's examination, will be thinking more about her pregnancy and looking forward to its conclusion. What Andrew did know was that he would wait for her to raise the subject of his recent lateness first and try to detect her attitude.

The 5:15 p.m. train left Victoria on time, but as it stopped at most of the stations, Andrew had time to mull over some of his thoughts. He arrived home by 6 o'clock and was welcomed quite warmly as he entered the house – most particularly by Max, who thought it was his lucky day!

"Hello, dear," Andrew said. "How did you get on with the doctor today? Did he have nice things to tell you?"

There was a muffled voice of his wife coming from upstairs that seemed to say that she hadn't quite heard what he had said. Andrew went quickly up to the landing and repeated what he had said.

"Oh, it went very well; I went with Barbara. Afterwards, we went and had a bite to eat at the Royal Oak."

She came out of their bedroom towards Andrew on the landing and Andrew thought she looked really rather glamorous, all things considered. The smock was a variety of blues, matching her eyes and covering her bulge very discretely. She had a heavy, dark blue cardigan over her arm and she carried her special black handbag.

"The publican was very friendly and he told us he'd seen you and Brian the other Saturday lunchtime. You can imagine my surprise; you never told me that's where you had been."

"Sorry, I thought I'd told you I was meeting Brian and going for a walk with Max. I assumed you would have guessed we would go to the Royal Oak; after all, it is one our favourite watering holes."

"Oh, never mind, let's be on our way. Did you book a table?"

"I'll just quickly change out of this suit. Yes, I phoned up at lunchtime and I got the table near the open fire. I thought you might like that as it's still quite cold and the snow hasn't all thawed away yet. I heard today that there might be more on the way, but you can't trust what the weather forecasters say these days.

"Has Max had a walk this afternoon? If not, I'll take him out after we get back."

"No, I walked round the garden with him, but he did at least do his business so he should be alright for an hour or two."

They went in her car as it was a saloon with a heater that worked. The George & Dragon was only fifteen minutes away so they weren't too late for their booking. Anyway, Bill, the publican, knew them well and had kept the table that Andrew had asked for, even though others had tried to take it over.

"Good to see you again, Mr Williams, and your good lady. I must say you're looking really well; pregnancy is obviously suiting you! Shall I take your coats?"

"Thanks, Bill. By the way, I don't want someone pinching my car keys from my coat pocket this time. It's a long walk home and not too many cabs around in the country, especially in cold weather."

"Don't you worry; I'll take them out of your pocket and keep them behind the bar till you're ready to leave."

"Excellent idea, Bill! I hope there isn't an extra charge on the bill for this special service," said Andrew rather loudly, followed by a noisy laugh.

"Come on, Andrew, don't make such a fuss. You've made everyone look at us when they came out for a quiet supper and a drink."

"Sorry, dear. I see the menus are already on our table and you can probably see the specials menu on the wall from where you are. What would you like to drink?"

"I'll just have a half of ginger beer shandy, please, with a bit less beer than is normal. I don't want the baby getting more excited than usual tonight. He disturbs me enough in the night as it is."

Andrew was quite surprised by his wife's light-heartedness, but was sure it wouldn't last very long. The evening meal went well and they had a brief chat with some friends of theirs who had come in for a quick pint before heading off home. By about 8:30 p.m., Andrew settled up with Bill and they thanked him for a most excellent supper. On the way home, Andrew's wife brought up the subject that he had been expecting all along.

"So, tell me, Andrew, why these late nights recently? I'm very eager to hear what it's all about. You're not keeping secrets from me are you?"

Andrew told her that the very late night was because of one of his office colleague's recent engagement. They went to a pub after work and he was persuaded to go with a few of them to a club afterwards. The other two times were because his boss had wanted to talk to him after hours about some possible management courses he wanted Andrew to go on in the summer. He was cleverly preparing her for what might happen later in the year, but wasn't sure she'd swallow it.

"So you might get a promotion at last, will you?"

"It's possible," said Andrew, "but it's not likely to be until the end of the year; and who knows what state the Country will be in by then."

"Do you really think there might be a war in the near future?" she said in a rather worried tone. "Knowing you, and your friends, you would want to join up at the earliest opportunity and where would that leave me and our small baby?"

Andrew was half expecting this, but he tried to placate her.

"Don't worry, dear, it might not come to anything. Nevil Chamberlain and his Government have got their fingers on the pulse. They're mostly pacifists anyway, except for that Churchill man, who keeps on about the Germans and preaching gloom and doom."

"I hope you're right, but you can't help wondering when the news bulletins paint such a terrible picture of the changing face of Europe. How is it that Hitler gets away with taking over Austria and then marching into Czechoslovakia? Surely the allies can give Hitler a stern warning that 'enough is enough'? Can't our Government tell Hitler that any more aggressive moves against any other nation in Europe will be considered an act of war?"

She had a good point, thought Andrew. *At least we've got off the subject of my late nights, and she thinks I might get a promotion! I seem to be taking on the character of a deceptive spy already by telling half-truths to satisfy the recipient.*

The rest of the week went well at home and he arranged to meet Brian for Saturday lunch at the Red Lion, a pub they didn't normally visit and a bit further from their respective homes. It should allow them to talk quite privately. Andrew told his wife this time and she seemed to accept his reasons for meeting Brian, even though they weren't the real ones. She was still on a bit of a high about Andrew's possible promotion.

Andrew was up early on Saturday, and as the weather was a bit more spring like, he went out with Max for a good walk over the neighbouring fields. The walk helped to clear his thoughts for the lunchtime chat with Brian, but he was still a little hesitant about how much he should tell him. On his return home, he gave his wife breakfast in bed and took her the newspaper; the *Daily Sketch* was her particular favourite.

"You were up early this morning, dear; are you feeling alright? Don't forget you're meeting Brian for lunch today," she said, to Andrew's surprise.

"I'm fine, thank you. I did wake early, but I thought it such a nice morning, after all the cold we've been having recently, that I'd take advantage of it and get out with Max. It saves you from having to take him out later this morning."

"Won't you be taking Max with you to the pub? You usually do and you know how much Brian likes to see him."

"Not this time, no. It is very likely Brian will bring his dog and he and Max don't always get on well. Anyway, Max will be company for you while I'm out."

There were still a couple of hours left before he needed to leave for the pub, so Andrew put on his boiler suit over his walking clothes and went out to the garage to tinker with his car – his pride and joy. He checked the oil level, tyre pressures, radiator water level and so on. He clambered underneath to check the exhaust pipe fastenings, the handbrake cables and looked to see if any more oil had dripped from the engine into the metal tray on the floor beneath it. He hadn't used the car for a few weeks, so after he had completed the thorough examination, he gave it a good wipe down with a damp chamois.

When Andrew returned indoors, he found his wife up and dressed in a brightly coloured, loose-fitting frock.

"That looks nice, dear. Is it new?"

"Yes, it is. I bought it when I was out with Barbara the other week. She recommended a shop not far from the doctor's and she picked out this frock to try and cheer me up."

"What a good idea of Barbara's. I would suggest, however, that even though the sun is shining, the weather is still cold so you would be advised to wear a cardigan or coat if you should venture outside."

"It's good of you to say that, but please don't fuss; I'll be fine."

Andrew looked at his watch and decided it was time to get ready and go and meet Brian. He was beginning to feel quite apprehensive about the meeting and how much he should tell Brian.

"I'll just pop upstairs and change into my sweater and trousers. Then I'll be off. Is there anything you want me to bring in for the weekend, or have we everything we need?"

"No thank you, I did a small shop on Wednesday. Be careful how you go, and give my love to Brian."

"Will do! I hope to be back at about 3 o'clock."

Andrew put on his heavy outdoor jacket, gloves and peaked cap – the keys were already in the car. He went by the shortest route to the Red Lion pub that took him only twenty minutes. He wanted to be there first, if possible, so he could gather his thoughts.

Andrew greeted the man behind the bar and asked if he could use the table in the corner by the window as he was expecting a friend to join him.

"No problem," said the barman. "What would you like to drink? I'll bring it to you."

"A pint of your best bitter, please."

Andrew sat down at the table, took several mouthfuls of beer and watched for Brian to drive his car into the car park. Sure enough, only ten minutes later, Brian arrived. Andrew stood up to greet him.

"Good morning, Andrew. What a grand day."

"Hello, Brian, glad to see you. Tell the barman what you want to drink and come and join me. No dog I see?"

"No, I was out earlier with him and so left him at home."

The two chatted easily for a while about nothing in particular.

"So, Andrew, here we are at the Red Lion that we don't use very often and you want to tell me something very important. What's this all about? I'm all ears and ready to listen."

Andrew took a long gulp of beer. He started by telling Brian that what he was going to tell him was for his ears only. He also told him that he had been emphatically instructed not to talk to anybody, but he desperately needed to talk to somebody that he could trust, even if he was going against what he was told.

Andrew started at the beginning and how he'd met this guy at a pub in the city. He moved close to Brian and very quietly spoke to him about the meetings and the operation that he was being asked to join. He left nothing out, except he didn't mention any of their names. Occasionally, because Andrew was being careful about how loud he was speaking, Brian had to ask him to repeat a few things. When Andrew had finished, he told Brian once again that he must not talk to anybody about what he'd just told him.

"My goodness me, that is quite a story, Andrew. Before I ask any questions, I'd better get a couple more pints. Are you having the same again?"

"Yes please, Brian. We'd better order something to eat too so can you toss over a menu?"

Andrew felt a great weight had been removed from his mind as he perused the menu choices; he just hoped Brian wouldn't spill the beans. Andrew was very partial to rabbit and as they had rabbit pie on the menu, that would be his choice.

"Thanks, Brian, cheers! I'm settling for the rabbit pie. What are you going to have?"

Brian went for the steak and ale pie and settled back at the table with the beers after ordering the food.

There was a moment's silence. Each of them had taken a few swigs of beer; Brian wasn't sure what to say next.

"I suppose you've heard the news on the wireless about the latest situation in Spain? Franco has announced that the Republican Armies have surrendered and that the Nationalists are the victors, ably supported by Germany and Italy, of course?" said Brian.

"I knew who had been giving support to the Nationalists, but I certainly didn't hear about Franco's announcement. I've had rather too many other things on my mind lately to listen to the news."

"Of course, I quite understand. But this situation could quite easily bring war in Europe a lot closer and make your decision to join the SIS a lot more important."

"As I said before, please keep your voice down and don't mention who I might join. I'm already nervous about having spoken to you in the first place. I don't want anyone else to overhear anything.

"Sorry to appear a bit dictatorial, old man, but it's extremely important that this information remains only with you and me."

"I quite understand. Mum's the word!

"I really am very honoured that you feel you can trust me with all this, but what do you seriously think you want to do with your life, especially with the imminent arrival of your first born? By the way, how is your lovely wife?"

"She's up and down, Brian. You know her as well as I do, really. But that aside, I am humbled by the people I spoke to and at the same time excited about the prospect of doing something quite different from working in a boring old bank for the rest of my days. Mind you, if war does come to Europe, what better way can you think of making a contribution to our nation's future?"

They were almost caught in mid-sentence as the pretty young waitress arrived with their meals. She gave a lovely smile as she placed the different dishes at the correct places.

"Thank you very much, Anne," said Andrew, looking at her with a broad grin.

"How did you know my name, sir?" she said rather coyly.

"It's written on the tag attached to your left breast!"

"Oh, so it is; silly me."

All three of them had a good laugh and Anne asked if they required anything else.

"Brian, would you like another drink? How about a bottle of red?"

"Oh, why not? Might as well be hung as for a sheep as a lamb!"

"What red do you recommend, Anne?" asked Brian.

"We've just got in a nice French Haut Medoc," she said. "1935, I think. It might be a bit pricey."

"Never mind that, it sounds excellent, doesn't it Brian? One of those and two glasses, please."

As the waitress left them, Brian and Andrew had a quiet chuckle to each other. Andrew wondered when Anne might be going off duty and if she needed a lift home. He was beginning to feel quite light headed and it wasn't just the booze that was affecting him. He was so relieved at sharing his story with Brian. He wasn't asking Brian to help him make a decision; he'd already made up his mind for himself.

The wine duly arrived. It tasted so smooth and went so well with their main course. Not much was said as they tucked in to their meals and drank the wine. Eventually, Brian paused; he knew he had to be the first to say something.

"I know you said you can't tell your wife any of this or what you're going to be doing, but how are you really going to handle things with her? She's not stupid you know and she does have a very suspicious mind. You no doubt remember that cock-and-bull story you dreamed up to get yourself out of a very sticky situation after staying the night in London with Helen? Each time you're late home, she must wonder about you. After all, you do have a bit of a reputation!"

"Look Brian, I'm on a bit of an easy wicket really and she is so well off with me that she dare not question me too many times. Anyway, the point is, my lips are sealed as far as what I do is concerned. She will definitely not know the truth of what I'm doing; it's more than my job is worth. Only you will know; no other friends of mine will know anything. I will just have to make stories up. The simple truth is, if you keep near to the outline of the real story and not divulge the details, all should be OK. I'm already beginning to behave and sound like an agent without any of the training!

"That was a great meal, Brian. Shall we finish the wine and have a coffee?"

"That's a very good idea, Andrew. By the way, there is one last question, if I may: what happens if you are captured or killed whilst on active service with this group? She'll surely find out, or be told by someone what you've really been doing?"

"Apparently not. According to the people I spoke to, I will be enlisted into one of the services, but will be working for the group I have been speaking to; not all the time, mind you, but when a particular job needs to be done. As I told you earlier, I will have signed the Official Secrets Act so my lips will be sealed, probably for the rest of my life. It will be like living a double life!"

"Bloody hell," said Brian rather too loudly. "Rather you than me, old boy. Mind you, your languages will help and you've always been a bit of an independent type who can think on his feet. Probably ideal for the job really and that's why you've got as far as you have with these people."

The coffee arrived and they finished the last of the bottle of red.

"Do you want anything else to drink, Brian?"

"I'd better not. Good Heavens! Is that the time? I've got to take the dog out when I get home and it still gets dark a bit early, even with fairly clear skies at present."

"You've no idea how helpful it's been to tell you what's been going on in my life recently. It feels as though a great weight has been taken off my shoulders. I can't stress enough, though, how important it is for you to stay *shtum* about what I've told you. In any case, it might never happen. I might fail the medical, or the bank might not release me; you just never know, do you? By the way, I'll pick up the tab, OK?"

"That's very generous of you, Andrew, and thanks for sharing your secrets. Do let me know how things go, won't you? Give my love to your lovely wife and hope all continues well with her pregnancy."

"Thanks, Brian, I'll do that."

Andrew went to the bar to pay the bill and thanked the landlord for an excellent lunch. He asked if the waitress was still around as he wanted to give her a couple of bob.

"She's just getting ready to leave, actually, so you can give it to her yourself when she comes through in a moment. She wants to catch the 3 o'clock bus and it leaves outside the pub in about five minutes."

"Where does she have to go as I could give her a lift if I'm going the same way?"

"You'll have to ask her as she's usually met by her boyfriend at the other end."

The waitress came through from the back and looked even prettier in her yellowish-orange frock, with her brunette hair brushed down to her shoulders. Andrew helped her on with her brown coat and asked her if she would like a lift in his car rather than catch the bus.

"I'm sure it'll be out of your way, won't it? I'm catching the bus that goes to the left outside the pub."

"Look, here's a few bob for looking after us so attentively and I'll gladly take you to your destination, if that's alright?"

Anne looked at the publican and he mouthed to her that he thought it was alright, but it was really for her to decide.

"Alright then, that's very kind of you, thank you."

They all departed for the car park having said their goodbyes.

"You had better wear this scarf," said Andrew, leaning into his car and handing her one of his wife's from under his seat. "As you can see, I've got the roof down, even if it is still early April. I wouldn't like you to catch a chill now, would I?"

Andrew and Brian shook hands and said they would be in touch again in the next week or two. Andrew opened the passenger door for Anne and made sure her frock wasn't caught in the door as he closed it.

Andrew turned left into the road outside the pub whereas Brian went to the right. Anne thought Andrew was driving a bit too quickly, but she hesitated to say anything as she was quite enjoying the experience – never having been in a Bugatti before. The bus journey would have taken over three quarters of an hour whereas Andrew could have taken only twenty minutes if he hadn't taken the route through the woods. It was a deliberate ploy of Andrew's to ensure that he got to know a bit more about Anne and her life before she was dropped off at her destination, just as the bus was arriving. Anne's boyfriend was there to meet her and looked very surprised to see her being chauffeur-driven home in such a beautiful car. He helped her out of the car and glared at Andrew with a rather jealous look. Andrew thought he was a nice looking chap, but a bit too young for her by about six years. They said their farewells with Anne thanking Andrew for the wonderful drive in his lovely motor car.

Andrew sped off, waving to the pair of them as he went.

I wouldn't mind seeing her again, he thought to himself. *How come she isn't engaged or married already? I'll find out a bit more next time, maybe.*

Andrew drove quickly home via the short route and arrived just after 4 o'clock. He put the car in the garage and suddenly remembered that Anne still had his wife's scarf.

I've at least got an excuse to see her again. I must try and see her next Saturday when she leaves at 3 o'clock from the pub.

He went into the house and, after hanging up his coat and cap, went through to the lounge. His wife was on the sofa and had lit the fire.

"You're a bit later than I expected," she growled.

"So sorry dear, didn't really notice how quickly the time went. Brian and I seemed to have a lot to talk about, and he sends his love by the way. He hopes you're coping well with the bump!"

"The bump indeed! That's not what Brian would have said, I'm sure. Anyway, what did you two have so much to talk about when you see each other nearly every other week?"

"Oh, you know, the possible promotion at work, the situation in Spain and its possible effects on the rest of Europe. That usual sort of topical stuff that's all in the news," he lied.

"That's not like you. You're not usually interested in that sort of thing. You usually want to discuss cars, dogs, holidays, clubs, girls, and so on."

"Would you like some tea, dear?" he said, trying to change the subject.

"That's a nice idea, Andrew. Do you think you can find the cake in the tin above the fridge? I fancy something a bit sweet."

Andrew strolled into the kitchen and found all the tea things, as well as the cake. He was in a very jolly mood and thought about how he could get back to see Anne next weekend. He was quite pleased with a possible 'catch' but he knew he mustn't get too carried away; he had had his fingers burnt before and also had the odd disappointment.

Chapter 5
Wednesday, 3ʳᵈ of April 1940

Artur plodded on through the light snow, stopping every hundred yards or so to listen for any noises, particularly voices, just as he had been instructed. He set off again with a bit more purpose, but he missed his footing – probably an old rabbit hole – and fell over on his side. It reminded him of the bruise he had received from hitting the tree after he had jumped from the train. He lay still and thought he heard distant voices coming from the direction of the railway line. He got up rather unsteadily and moved on a bit more quickly. Anyone intent on trying to find the saboteurs would only need to follow his foot prints in the snow.

After another half an hour, Artur paused for a drink of water from his metal canister. He was about to exit the wooded area so he checked his compass and looked at his watch. *I'm going to be late for the second rendezvous. Where the hell has all the time gone?* He looked very carefully to his left and right through the gloom. He just picked out a hedge about forty metres to his right that went away from the woods. He stayed a few yards inside the woods until he was close to the hedge. He set off down the left side of the hedge for about fifty metres, scuffing up the snow as he went to make it appear that a number of people had gone in that direction. He saw a gap in the hedge, but went past it for about twenty metres before doubling back. He carefully broke through the small gap and walked as briskly as he could on the other side of the hedge for ten minutes before stopping and listening carefully. Being on the right side might help him avoid being seen by anyone coming out of the woods, if they had followed his tracks.

Artur knew he still had a long way to go before reaching the next meeting place, but he heard men's voices again, this time a little nearer than last time. He felt he was making reasonable progress, but was now worried he might be caught.

I wonder where Gerhart is, he said to himself. *Has he reached the disused barn and checked out the getaway motorbike?* Artur tried to break into a gentle jog, but his limbs were tired and they ached from the impact with the ground after his escape from the train. He quickly glanced at his compass with the aid of his torch and checked the sketch to try and guess how much further he had to go.

Meanwhile, Gerhart had made swift progress and could just see the outline of the barn that hopefully still housed the French registered Peugeot 250 motorbike. Artur and he had haggled with a middle-aged French farmer near Saverne, a few miles west of the German border. The farmer had bought the bike in 1935, and although he was loath to part with it, he didn't want it to get into the wrong hands if the Germans should invade France. The beauty of this bike was that it had good lights. Artur had fitted a soft seat on the pillion so that both could get away together even if the pillion rider would still be a bit uncomfortable. They had filled it with fuel and had inflated the tyres a little above the recommended pressure. Both he and Artur had licences to drive bikes, but it was Artur, with his mechanical know how, who had checked the bike out and ensured it was serviceable. That, however, was more than ten days ago, before they had blown up the railway line.

Gerhart ran the last eight hundred metres to the barn, but stopped just before it, behind a tree. He was very wary of any movement, even at 4 o'clock in the morning. He was, after all, in a country that was, for all intent and purposes, in a warlike state with all peoples of Europe. The barn was in a corner of a field and both were still covered in a fine layer of snow, added to which, it was a bit frosty in places so footsteps might be heard from a distance away. After what seemed like an eternity, he carefully and slowly moved towards the barn door that was slightly ajar but not open enough for him to enter. He pulled out his flick knife. Gerhart was nervous, but controlled himself as he opened the door inch by inch. He switched on his torch and crept inside. There was a sudden flurry of activity as a chicken shot past his leg – half flying, half running – and squawking loudly to get outside. Gerhart was relieved but startled, and hoped nobody in the small house about 100 metres away had heard the kafuffle.

After getting his breath and composure back, Gerhart went into the barn and searched around for the bike. There it was, just as they had left it, covered in several sacks. What a relief! The keys had been placed in a paper bag on a narrow ledge on the opposite side of the barn from the bike. He fingered around where he thought they'd been left only to find that they were further to the right. *Funny,* he thought, *did someone move them? Maybe it's my forgetfulness.* He took down the bag, took out the keys and put them in his inside pocket for later use. He put away his knife and looked at his watch. *I suppose Artur is alright and if so, he should be here very soon,* he remarked to himself.

Artur was getting more tired. He stopped and listened for any sounds of possible followers. Nothing. *Perhaps they've given up the chase and headed back to the stricken train? I certainly hope so.* Artur set off again only to miss his footing again and fall into a ditch. *Shit!* he exclaimed, *How did I miss that? Just keep your eyes skinned, you idiot!* He clambered out and brushed most of the muck off his sheepskin coat with his cold hands. Before he set off again, he checked that he still had everything with him that he should have. For quite a while, he felt nearly 100% again. He crossed another ditch with ease this time, and to his surprise he was in the field that had the disused barn on the far side. As he set off, he noticed some footprints in the snow coming from his left. *Those must be Gerhart's, they're not military boots so can't be any of Hitler's mob from the train.* He felt elated at the thought of meeting up with Gerhart again.

Gerhart was aware of a noise outside the barn, drew his pistol and cocked it in readiness.

"Who goes there?" he said rather softly but firmly in German.

"It's Artur, you silly bugger! Stop pointing that thing at me and put it away."

The relief on each of their faces would have made a real picture as they embraced inside the barn.

"Come on, Gerhart, let's look at that bike and get the hell out of here before someone finds us. We can talk about our experiences later when we have more time. Have you got the keys from the shelf?"

Gerhart handed Artur the keys just as Artur was removing the sacks covering the bike.

"Looks much as we left it," said Artur. "We ought to start it in here to muffle some of the sound, but let's open the barn door wide so we can quickly wheel the bike out before we make our getaway."

It was obvious that Artur was in charge. He did what was necessary to the bike to ensure a first time start. With the ignition on, he checked the lights both front and back. He didn't want to be stopped by anyone because of faulty equipment. Artur unstrapped his satchel, took out his German driving licence and passport, and placed them deep inside the pocket of his fleece.

"How are you feeling, Gerhart? Are you ready for the off? I'll do the first stint until we need to stop the first time for fuel – probably about 150 km after. We had better get used to using kilometres instead of miles. It will probably be best if we cross over the Rhine west of Karlsruhe. The border goes down the centre of the river south of Neuburg so once we are over on the other side, we will be close to French territory, agreed? It will be a long haul so we will need to sleep for a few hours somewhere during the day before Karlsruhe."

"You are right, Artur. Shouldn't we look at the map that we stored in the pannier to see the alternative border crossings?"

"Good idea."

Artur switched off the bike's lights and took out his torch. They laid the map on the ground and went on hands and knees. They decided to face the door in case a casual, nosey visitor should venture in.

"Fortunately, this map is quite a detailed one. This is where we are," said Artur. "And this is where we need to get into France. That means we can cross at one of these three places," and he pointed them out on the map.

"We've got a full tank of fuel so we shouldn't need to stop more than twice until we get close – unless we are stopped by police or the military, of course – but we'll cross that bridge when we get to it."

Artur folded up the map, gave it to Gerhart and told him to put it in his pocket for easy access. Gerhart picked up Artur's small suit case that had been behind the bike that contained a few clothes; he knew he would have to hold on to it during their journey

"I suggest we have a drink of water, have a pee and prepare ourselves for the next part of our adventure. And may God give us good fortune!"

"I certainly second that, old chap. I'll get the gloves out of the other pannier and the two pairs of goggles."

After completing all the preliminaries, Artur turned on the ignition. The engine started at the third attempt with plumes of smoke coming out of the exhaust and he wheeled it out of the barn. Gerhart attended to the door so it didn't look any different from before, although he couldn't easily disguise the footsteps in the snow. Artur pushed the bike to the road, switched on the lights and checked that everything was in order. He and Gerhart climbed aboard and they set off down the road in a westerly direction, with Gerhart clutching the suit case as best he could.

Chapter 6
April 1939

All the papers that weekend were full of the situation in Spain with pictures of General Franco outside the Spanish Parliament buildings in Madrid proclaiming a victory for the Nationalists in the Civil War. Andrew didn't usually get a Sunday paper nor listen to the news on the wireless, but this was different.

"You don't normally get a Sunday paper or read any paper quite so avidly. What's so different about today?" asked Andrew's wife.

"This Civil War has been going on for three years," said Andrew, looking over the top of the paper at his wife. "People who had been neighbours for years were fighting each other; family members have been killing people of the same family. Even if Europe goes to war later this year, there is nothing worse than a Civil War. Nobody really knows who their enemy is, who can be trusted and who cannot. It's just terrible."

"What has suddenly made this situation of so much interest to you when you've had other occasions to get anxious about, such as the terrible bombing of the Basque town of Guernica by the German airplanes, just over two years ago?" she asked, rather pointedly.

Andrew put the *Sunday Dispatch* paper down on his lap and looked at his wife.

"I suppose there are a couple of reasons really. One is that the Germans seem to be looking for more countries to invade and, sooner or later, England and their allies will have to say 'Enough is enough' and declare war. Secondly, and probably more importantly, our situation is about to change in less than two months with the birth of our first child. I know one can't turn the clock back, but it might not be a very good time to bring a youngster into the world."

"As you say, we can't put the clock back, but it should be a happy occasion for us to look forward to, assuming the birth goes according to plan."

"You're right, of course, and the sooner the baby arrives the better it will be for both of us, most particularly for you."

"Thank you, dear," she said. "But what has really brought this interest on? If, for the sake of argument, we should declare war on Germany, would you join up? Have you already spoken to our friends about what you and they would do? Brian, for instance. You only saw him yesterday, so did you discuss the possibility with him? You told me when you got back that you'd spoken about the situation in Europe so the topic must have come up. "

"No. Not in so many words."

Andrew felt he was starting to get into difficulty, but he was suddenly let off the hook when his wife let out a squeal, saying that the baby was very active and was making her feel very uncomfortable.

"I think I'll just go upstairs for a bit of a lie down, if you don't mind. Maybe you ought to take Max out for a walk before the weather changes while I rest."

"That's a good idea," said Andrew, with some relief.

Max seemed to sense some activity and came into the lounge from his basket in the hall, wagging his tail furiously.

"OK, Max, let's go for a walk before it gets dark."

Andrew collected Max's lead, donned his walking clothes and left the house by the front door.

That was a narrow escape. I must be more careful how I react and what I say on those occasions in future, he said to himself, as he set off down the path opposite his house's drive.

Andrew walked briskly in the cold, late afternoon air. His thoughts were at sixes and sevens, but he had at least made his mind up that he would phone Charles on Monday morning and start to get the ball rolling. He couldn't tolerate the indecision any longer.

Andrew caught his usual train on Monday morning, and he was relieved that his wife had had a comfortable night after such a disturbing afternoon and evening. It had put her in better spirits as he left the house for the railway station.

He thought he would phone at about 11 o'clock, and make the call from one of the small offices that was not currently in use – Mr Jordan was away visiting another branch office this week. At just before 11 o'clock, he strode into the office, closed the door and asked the switchboard operator for an outside line.

"Please could I speak to Mr Compton-Browne?"

"Could you tell me who's calling, sir?" the telephone operator replied.

"My name is Williams, Andrew Williams."

"Just a moment, Mr Williams. I'll check to see if Mr Compton-Browne is available."

43

There was a pause on the line for what seemed like an eternity and one of Andrew's work colleagues looked through the window of the office that Andrew was in and gesticulated something. Andrew rather annoyingly intimated to him that he was on the phone. The colleague seemed to understand just as the operator came back to Andrew.

"Sorry to keep you waiting, Mr Williams, I'll put you through to Mr Compton-Browne straight away."

"Thank you very much."

Once he was put through he said, "Charles, is that you? It's Andrew here."

They went through a number of introductory remarks for a few minutes about the weather, Andrew's wife and the end of the Spanish Civil War.

"Charles, I'm going to get to the real point of this call. I think it's important that I meet you somewhere soon as I've made my decision. I know it's short notice, but can we meet for a quick chat and a drink today, say 6 o'clock?"

"You'd better let your wife know this time!" Charles retorted. "That will be fine with me."

"I know my wife will be out this afternoon and early evening with a friend, but I'll let her know I'll be home about 8:30 p.m. anyway."

"That's good, Andrew. Let's meet at that pub near the Apollo theatre, next to Victoria Station. You know the one I mean?"

"Excellent choice, Charles, I'll be there. I'm looking forward to seeing you again."

"Likewise, Andrew. Bye for now."

Andrew hung up and wandered out of the office to his desk. His colleague came over and apologised for interrupting his call and told him that his wife wanted him to call her as soon as he could.

Andrew called home about half an hour later, after he had gathered himself together and calmed down following his call to Charles. It wasn't as important as his colleague had made out, but she needed to tell him that she would be spending the night at Audrey's as it would be too far to drive home that evening. He would have to find his own supper of cold meat in the fridge, or eat out. She would see him the following evening. And, yes, she was feeling fine.

The day went by very quickly, but Andrew arrived five minutes late at the pub. He cursed himself for being unpunctual and apologised to Charles, who, of course, had arrived ten minutes early.

Andrew quickly relaxed, knowing that he didn't have to clock watch as he often had to on previous after-work 'meetings'.

"So you've made a decision then, Andrew. Will I be surprised? You've come to this decision on your own and not discussed anything with anyone else, not even your wife or your best friend?"

"No, I haven't," he lied, looking Charles directly in the eyes as he said it.

"I have thought long and hard about everything you and C have told me. I would like to be considered to work with your organisation." Andrew was extra careful not to mention the name of the organisation in a public place, like the pub.

"Very good news, Andrew, and you have understood all the ramifications that this decision entails?"

"Yes, I have, but I've still got to go through all the tests, provide references, and complete the training."

"I don't suppose, Andrew, that you'd mind coming back to my office now to complete some of the paperwork. It would save a lot of time?"

"What a good idea. As it so happens, my wife is staying out tonight so I have no deadline for getting home tonight. Let's do it before I change my mind!"

"Excellent. Let's finish our drinks and go to my office. We can always have another one later on."

Charles hailed a taxi and they arrived at his office near to St. James', where Andrew had been before. Unfortunately for Andrew, the receptionist had already left before they arrived. Following Andrew's call in the morning, Charles had anticipated Andrew's decision and had prepared all the papers for him to read and sign. It took a good hour to go through everything, and some of the more important documents would have to be countersigned by C the following day.

"Well, that's the major part concluded for the moment. Do you have any questions, Andrew, before I take you out for a bite to eat?"

"As you might expect, one of my real concerns is how the organisation will approach the bank? Who will you be contacting and what if they don't want me to be released?"

"It's a good question, Andrew, but I'm sure you will not be surprised when I tell you that your bosses are already aware of our operation and the sort of people we look out for. In fact, one of your colleagues at your branch is also working for us and has been for a few years now. This is for your ears only, but he spent some time in Spain during the Civil War on several occasions, finding out how much the Germans were supporting the Nationalists and with what sort of armour."

Andrew tried not to look startled at this revelation and tried to think who it might be.

"That will certainly make your job easier if they already know a lot about your setup. They probably won't be surprised that I've been approached, especially as the list of my language skills is on their files."

"If that's your only question for the moment, I suggest we retire to one of my favourite restaurants for some supper."

Charles and Andrew spent a very convivial and relaxed evening together in the restaurant of Charles' choice. As he was told he wasn't paying, Artur chose as a main course a rare filet steak with vegetables – it would go very well with the Burgundy. It seemed as though a great weight had been taken off Andrew's shoulders and, not only that, he didn't have to rush home or make excuses for his late evening out. Charles also seemed in a happy frame of mind, perhaps because he had persuaded Andrew to make what will be a complete change in his life.

At the end of the evening, Charles took Andrew by taxi to Victoria station. During the drive, Charles said that not much would seem to happen for a few weeks as the forms had to be seen by a number of senior people and countersigned. Andrew's bank management would be contacted and invited for a meeting, probably with C and the Head of Intelligence.

Andrew got home just after 10:30 p.m., and he thought some fresh air would help both him and Max. He took his torch and he walked one of his short but more usual walks that started with the pathway to the side of his house, through light woods and by the side of fields.

On returning home, Andrew decided to have a brandy and listen to some of his favourite dance music records on the radiogram – a selection of Teddy Wilson and Roy Fox from his big collection of 78s suited his mood. He particularly enjoyed Wilson's *As Time Goes By* and Fox's *Things Are Looking Up*. He felt pleased with himself for his evening's work, and even though he didn't feel tired, he knew he should turn in and try to get some sleep.

The next few days were fairly normal for Andrew at home and the office, except that Brian called him on Thursday – the day before Good Friday – to see if he would like to spend a couple of days the weekend after Easter with some of their friends down in Devon, probably near Ilfracombe. Andrew thought it would be a good idea as there wouldn't be too many more occasions to get away before the baby was due. He would have to check it out with his wife first and get back to him. He'd see if his sister-in-law would enjoy another trip down for the weekend; it would be company for his wife.

"I know it's a week away, dear," Andrew said to his wife, "but Brian called me and has asked if I would like to join him and some of his friends down in Devon for the weekend after next. How do you feel about it? Could we ask your sister to come down so you wouldn't be on your own?"

"At the moment, I don't see a problem, but I do have another hospital check-up on the Wednesday after Easter. Depending on the results of the examination, it should be alright. I'll ring my sister in any case and ask her to come down; we can always cancel her coming if I'm not up to it and you're going to be here. Is that OK?"

"Sounds like a good plan. Brian and the others will quite understand if I have to cancel going to Devon at the last minute."

Andrew felt quite excited at the thought of going away for a few days; it would allow him to take his mind off the big decision he had just made and be able to give the Bug a good run after the long winter.

Brian was pleased with Andrew's response and his plan for the following weekend. It all sounded like good sense. Brian noticed a much more relaxed attitude in Andrew, more like his old self, but didn't want to mention anything as he half guessed the reason.

Over the Easter weekend, Andrew tinkered with his car and made sure it was in good shape for the trip to Devon at the end of next week, even if he did end up by not going. He took it out for a spin and, as it was Saturday and nearly lunch-time, he decided to visit the Red Lion, where he met Brian a few weeks before and the time when he leant Anne, the waitress, his wife's scarf. *She might be there today*, he considered excitedly, *but I'll only have a pint.*

The pub was quite busy as he drove into the car park, but there was enough space for his Bugatti. He wandered into the bar and was immediately recognised by the waitress, who smiled and blushed a bit as Andrew smiled back and greeted her with a peck on her cheek. She slipped away with the food she was carrying for some of the customers so Andrew managed to catch the eye of the barman and ordered a pint.

Andrew stayed standing at the bar as quite a few people were going to their tables for their meals and there was more space there. He turned round to see if he could catch Anne's eye again, but she ignored him as she was so busy serving food and going backwards and forwards to the kitchen. After about twenty minutes, when Andrew was ordering his second pint, Anne came over to his side, slipped his wife's scarf deep into his trouser pocket and turned to go back to the kitchen. Andrew just managed to grab her arm before she left and she turned round to face him. Her eyes were bright and shiny and she had a naughty look on her face.

"I thought you might have been in a week earlier," said Anne. "I've been carrying the scarf around ever since you let me borrow it."

"Do you go off duty at 3 o'clock today as usual to catch the bus?"

"Yes, but I'm due to go on to Redhill today where I will be meeting my boyfriend."

"As much as I would like to take you to Redhill today, I'm only expected to be out for a short while before returning home for lunch," Andrew said very disappointingly. "I'll try to come in here in two weeks' time, after lunch at about 2:30 p.m., and maybe we could go for a drive afterwards when you've finished work. How does that sound to you?"

"That's fine by me," said Anne. "Don't forget to bring a scarf for me to wear, will you?" she said with a smile.

"No, I won't, but have something warm to wear in case it's cold weather. I look forward to seeing you in two weeks."

Andrew downed his second pint and went to his car in the car park. He drove home quickly so as not to raise any suspicion with his wife.

"Oh, that's good timing, dear. I've just made a light lunch. Is the car going well now?" said his wife.

"All seems to be running well. The little run out allowed me to test everything out very satisfactorily, thank you."

Andrew and his wife had lunch and when she had gone upstairs for a rest, he took his dog for a long walk. He needed the air to clear his head.

Chapter 7
Wednesday, 3rd of April 1940

Artur and Gerhart made good progress in the first hour and the bike coped well with two people on board. The plan was to get as close to Heilbronn as possible before stopping for fuel and something to eat. They made sure the bike wasn't over stretched, so they kept the speed down to sixty km per hour, where possible. They had started off at about 5 o'clock, it was still dark and would be for almost the next two hours. They had been going for about 100 km when Artur suddenly felt very tired. He had had no real sleep since getting on the train the previous evening and, what with the effort of getting to the barn and the concentration needed to ride the bike in the dark, he had to stop. He pulled over off the road and down a track for a short way so they wouldn't be seen.

Gerhart had been aware that something was not quite right.

"I'm absolutely knackered," said Artur. "I have to get some sleep for about an hour, then you can take over. You keep watch and also listen out in case you hear any traffic passing our way. Don't wake me unless it's absolutely necessary, understood?"

Almost before Artur had finished his sentence, he lay down where there was the least amount of snow with his head on his satchel and was asleep. For a moment, Gerhart did nothing but just stare at Artur. He knew that Artur was going to rely on him at this tricky time. Suddenly, he pulled himself together, took his pistol out, checked it and leaned the bike up against a nearby tree, out of sight of the road. He walked carefully and cautiously towards the road. He looked left for about two minutes and then right for about the same amount of time.

Fortunately, Artur had chosen to take a route on a minor road for the moment, Gerhart said to himself. *There shouldn't be much traffic passing here and it's still dark. We haven't seen many vehicles of any type for ages; just the occasional delivery lorry when we were on the major road.* He thought he nodded off for a few moments, just as he was thinking things over, but it was for longer. He was wakened by a faint noise in the distance from his left; it seemed to him to be the sound of heavy vehicles, not one but quite a few. His heart jumped and he listened more intently. *Wow, it seems like a large convoy coming this way. I'd better move the bike and the suit case into those bushes but I won't wake Artur unless he wakes of his own accord.*

Gerhart completed his tasks as the thunderous sound of the vehicles got nearer and nearer. There were some trees not far from the road that he could lie near to, but he decided to go behind the one near the bushes where the bike was instead. The lights from the leading trucks were getting very close and the sound was almost deafening, and still Artur didn't move. Fortunately, Artur was hidden from the road by some large bushes, so he wouldn't be seen by anyone in the convoy unless they deliberately came up their track.

Gerhart stood very still as the first vehicle passed the entrance to the track they were in. He guessed it was moving at about 40 km/h and was closely followed by eleven others of a similar type. They were heavy armoured half-track personnel-carrying trucks, a sort of tank with a machine gun pointing slightly to the side. Gerhart recognised them as *Sonderkraftfahrzeug (Sd.Kfz 231s)* special purpose vehicles from pictures he'd been shown in England during training. *Probably on the way to the French border near Saarbrucken,* he thought.

The commander of each vehicle looked straight ahead out of his turret. Only once did one commander, near the rear of the convoy, glance towards the track to his right but he saw nothing of consequence.

Some minutes after the last vehicle passed, Gerhart came from behind the tree and went to where Artur had lain, but to his surprise he wasn't there.

A voice from the bushes by the roadside startled Gerhart.

"Why didn't you wake me when the convoy was approaching, you silly bugger?" It was Artur, of course, and he was right, as usual.

"You were sleeping so soundly, I thought it best to leave you where you were. I'm not surprised you woke up, the din was extraordinary. Did you see them all?"

"I certainly did and I'm glad none of the commanders spotted us; we'd have been in deep shit if they had. Hopefully, no more convoys will come our way for a while, so I suggest we both try and get some sleep before setting off again. It should give enough time for the convoy to get a good way ahead of us. We had a lucky escape and we'll probably need more lucky moments in the next couple of days."

They both awoke at about the same time, around 8 o'clock. It was light and they were pleased they had hidden themselves further down the track and off to the side behind bushes before they turned in. It was very unlikely someone walking or driving down the road while they were asleep would have noticed anything.

Artur was up first and was busy checking the bike. It seemed to be in good order and hadn't suffered from the journey – so far. Artur occasionally had superstitious tendencies and he talked to the bike as if it were a person, thanking it for all that it had done for them and hoped it felt well enough for the next stages of their journey. At the same time, he smiled broadly and stroked the petrol tank very gently and slowly with a cloth. It didn't purr but if it could, he was sure it would have done.

"Right then, Gerhart, are you ready to take over? We will need some fuel soon, so it's always advisable to stop at the first place that's open and fill up. Are you OK with that?"

"Absolutely. Let's be getting on our way."

The road was getting a little busier now as people were setting off for work. Most of the snow had melted, but it was difficult on some of the sharper bends where the road was still icy in the more sheltered parts. On the outskirts of Heilbronn, there was a small petrol station on their side of the road that had just opened. They pulled over and a man came over to them with eyes wide open.

"Haven't seen one of those Peugeots for a while; nice bikes," he said with a western German accent. Artur did the talking and spoke back in a deliberate broken German accent with a hint of French thrown in. The man understood Artur wanted the tank filling up and the tyre pressures to be checked.

"You don't look like my usual customers, especially in those sheepskin coats," said the man with a grin, as he filled the tank. "Where are you off to at this time of the morning?"

"My brother and I have been to see our mother, who lives east of here and who's very unwell. Our father died quite a while ago when they lived in France and, as she's German, she decided to move back nearer to her sisters. We left early in the morning and are hoping to get back to our home in France before nightfall," Arthur said, at the same time pointing to Gerhart. "It was she who insisted on us wearing these coats. You know what mothers are like, especially towards their sons!"

"You had better take great care," said the man. "There are a lot of troop and armoured vehicle movements going on north and west of Heidelberg. The news suggests something big is about to happen, but they're not being very specific. Hitler controls the media, you know."

Artur knew he'd said far too much to the man, but he thought it better to make up a half-believable story rather than raise suspicions in the man's mind by being uncommunicative. *You never know who or what he knows*, he thought to himself. Artur thanked the man for his concern, paid him and slipped a bit more into his hand for checking the tyres. The man smiled at Artur and Gerhart as they got back on the bike. As soon as the bike was out of sight, the man went back into the office, rang up the payment on the till and picked up the phone.

Artur was driving again now and after a few kilometres, he turned down a narrow lane and stopped some 300 metres from the main road behind some bushes.

"We had better look at the map and see if we need to change our plans. I didn't like the look of the man at the garage and I said too much to him about where we'd been anyway, and these sheepskin coats didn't help," said Artur. "At some point, we must try and find something else to wear and ditch the sheepskins. It wasn't in our plan to wear them on the bike, but they did keep the cold air out."

They laid the map out over the bike's seat and studied the Rhine river crossings very carefully.

"I think we'd be better off trying to cross the river near Karlsruhe. There are a number of bridges further north, but the French border is nearer than if we went via Mannheim as we originally thought. Once we're over the Rhine, we are going to be splitting up: you going over into France and with me heading to the north for Denmark. Unless, of course, we get into any kind of trouble. Do you think that's still the right move, Gerhart?"

"Yes, you are probably right, Artur. A suggestion might be that as we get past Karlsruhe, we look to cross at the first bridge that isn't controlled by the police or the army. As you know, when we were planning our escape route in England, I favoured staying together until we were in France and then going our separate ways. I still think this would be a better plan."

"OK, Gerhart, that's a good idea. Let's do that, but we can't believe that we'll continue to have no trouble so we had better split up once we're in France; it's safer that way and makes good sense. "

Artur folded up the map and they returned to the road going west, looking out for the signs to Karlsruhe.

Chapter 8
April 1939

Not much of importance happened during the week after Easter. Andrew's wife had a satisfactory check-up on the Wednesday, and she seemed to be in good humour knowing that her sister was going to be with her for the weekend. Andrew prepared a list of things he needed to take to Devon and had a look at the map to remind himself of the route. Brian phoned on Thursday evening to check that Andrew was still able to go away and was pleased when he said that he could.

"As I think I've mentioned to you, we're planning to go to Parracombe and we'll probably stay in the same pub that we've stayed in before. You remember the one, I'm sure. We stayed there last year and we nearly got chucked out for making so much noise; you were playing the piano and all of us singing songs well after midnight."

"I certainly do remember, and there was that single woman staying there who joined us and knew all the words. It should be fun as long as the landlord doesn't refuse to let us stay again."

"It's OK, Andrew, I've already booked four rooms and the landlord's fine about us staying. He said he'd prefer us to stay rather than have four empty rooms.

"By the way, we're not leaving until Saturday morning, probably trying for an early start at about 8 o'clock, if that's alright with you?"

"That's fine," said Andrew. "If it's alright with everyone, I'll bring Max so it won't mean my wife will have to worry about taking him out."

"I think everyone expects you to bring him, under the circumstances, and he's usually so very well behaved, so it won't be a problem."

Friday came and went with Andrew carrying out final checks on his car and storing vital tools, oil, jack etc. in the area behind the passenger seat the evening before departure. He decided he would fill up with fuel again in the morning. He gave Brian a final call at about 9 o'clock, and everyone was ready for the off the following morning.

Andrew was up bright and early, and took Max for a good walk so they wouldn't have to stop too many times on the way to Parracombe. He kissed his wife goodbye and hoped she'd have a relaxing weekend with her sister, who was due to arrive later that morning. They were all at Brian's house by 8 o'clock and they got a good number of miles under their belts before stopping for lunch at about midday, having had a 'pit stop' around 10:30 a.m. They left after lunch and arrived at the Fox and Goose in Parracombe before 4 o'clock. After they had checked in and, as the weather was quite fine, they couldn't resist driving down to the sea at Lynmouth via the 1-in-3 hill from Lynton. Andrew nearly came a cropper before the bottom of the hill when taking a bend too quickly, but once there, they took a walk along the promenade to stretch their legs and breathe in the sea air. Back at the pub, they had a few pints before a hearty supper, followed by some games of darts, cricket being the most popular one. Everybody was in good spirits and knew that Andrew probably wouldn't be able to make another weekend away until well into the autumn, what with his baby due in a few weeks from now.

After an excellent breakfast and with a fine day ahead, plus 'tops off', they decided to drive along the 'B' road to Wheddon Cross and down to meet the A39 west of Minehead. The next section towards Barnstaple gave them the opportunity to go hell-for-leather up Porlock Hill. After a stop on the edge of the moors and with wonderful views to the sea, they gave Max a good long walk and returned to Parracombe for a few pints and an early lunch.

The drive back to Sussex was a bit more eventful. Driving a different route back, Andrew's car had a puncture in the front nearside tyre as they were driving at speed on the long, straight road from Stockbridge. Andrew wrestled with the steering wheel whilst at the same time trying to reduce the car's speed by changing down through the gears. He almost brought his Bugatti under control, but at the last minute it careered off to the left and the front dropped into a ditch. He had been leading the way so all those behind him just had to watch at what seemed like a slow-motion film.

Everyone stopped and came running over to where Andrew's car was, to find that he had been thrown out of the car onto the edge of a field. He just lay there, laughing his head off and shouting, "Silly bloody car! Why can't it do as I want it to?"

They all then suddenly shouted at Andrew and asked him where Max was. They looked inside the passenger well where he'd been lying; they gently lifted the car in case he was under it; they looked up and down the ditch in which the car was resting; they looked into the field where Andrew was, but all to no avail. Then, to everyone's surprise and relief, Brian saw Max hobbling along the road from the direction they had just driven, making some strange squeaking sounds. It would appear that he must have leapt out of the car as Andrew was trying to control it and landed badly on one of his legs. Brian examined Max while the others attended to Andrew, who very fortunately had only a few cuts and bruises. They then examined the car and, as it was quite heavy, it needed all of them to lift it out of the ditch and put it upright on the verge. It looked very sad as it stood there leaning down at the front. There were dents and scratches on the passenger side, but otherwise no major damage and the spare tyre on the back looked to be unaffected by the car's off-road experience.

They got to work on changing the wheel and then Andrew sat in the driver's seat. The car wouldn't start at first but after a few attempts, it fired and there was a great cheer from everyone. Andrew carried Max to the passenger well and after a few checks on the wheels and exhaust system, they set off, this time at a more sensible and leisurely pace.

Andrew got home around 8:30 p.m. As he went through the front door, followed by Max, who limped quite a lot, he shouted to his wife, "Hello, dear, I'm home safe and sound."

There was a muffled 'Hello' from upstairs.

Andrew's wife came down to the lounge just as he was attending to Max's leg.

"Is there something the matter with Max?" she enquired.

Andrew turned to greet his wife whereupon she let out a squeal.

"What on earth have you done to yourself? You look a real mess and you've cut your cheek quite badly in two places."

Andrew told her about the puncture and some of the details of the incident, and how Max had jumped out and hurt his leg.

"But you could have been killed. You must have been driving much too fast for the accident to have happened in the first place. Was anyone else involved? How's the car? Poor Max; he does look a bit shaken, and his leg! It's not broken is it?"

"No, it's not broken, just badly jarred from when he landed on the road. It's fortunate that he's not more badly injured, I agree, and the same applies to me."

Andrew returned to attend to Max's leg and he thought it would be sensible if he bandaged it up until the vet had given his opinion and assessment of any further real damage. He asked his wife if she would fetch the bandage from the downstairs cloakroom. When she returned, he asked how her weekend had gone with her sister coming down, and apparently all had gone just fine; she'd had no real discomfort except a bit in the night.

Max ate his meal. Andrew poured himself a large brandy, a soft drink for his wife and they sat down together on the sofa. He told her some of the things that they had done over the weekend and that it would probably be the last time he could do something like this until the autumn, with the baby due in a month's time.

At about 9:30 p.m., Andrew went out to the kitchen to prepare a few sandwiches and fetch another drink for the two of them. He checked on Max in the hall. He gave him a gentle stroke; he didn't get up but just looked up at his master and flapped his tail a few times against the side of his basket. Andrew hoped there was nothing more sinister that might be wrong with Max than just a sprain.

Shortly after 10:15 p.m., they felt in need of some sleep, so they shut up the house and retired upstairs to bed. Andrew lay there thinking: all things being considered, it had been great fun over the weekend. He wondered when he might have the same sort of fun again in the months to come, or, bearing in mind the changes about to occur in his life and the likely developments in Europe, it might never be possible for it to happen again.

The days went past without anything special happening, except a visit to the hospital for his wife. Andrew asked his wife if she could take Max to the vet on her way back from the hospital and have him checked out. As Andrew had suspected, it was a nasty sprain and the doctor advised to keep his leg bandaged for another week.

At the weekend after the trip to North Devon, Andrew attended to his damaged car, but there was only so much that he was able to do – it looked very sad in its current state. He had arranged with the local garage to collect the car on Tuesday, the 25th, and have the bodywork attended to. He was told that the car would probably be out of service for ten days, but they would let him know when it would be ready for collection.

Andrew hadn't had the chance to visit the Red Lion and see Anne again – yet! He found waiting for news from Charles a real challenge and at one point felt like giving him a call to get an update, but decided against it. He thought it better that he devoted more time on getting home at a reasonable hour every evening and being on hand for his wife, who seemed to be getting more and more anxious and uncomfortable with each day. She wasn't sleeping too well, but was more comfortable and relaxed when sitting in her favourite arm chair.

On the 4th of May, in the morning, Andrew was called into Mr Beckett's office. For many months, Andrew would clearly remember it was a Thursday – a very significant Thursday too. The manager told Andrew that he'd had a call from a Mr Charles Compton-Browne who wanted Andrew to phone him at his office during lunch time. The manager said he probably knew what it was about as he had had conversations with Mr Compton-Browne's superior, C, a few weeks earlier. Andrew was told that he had his permission to use the phone in his office so that he wouldn't get any interruptions. Almost immediately, Andrew felt very excited, but tried not to show it.

"It's alright, Williams, you can relax. We know you've got a lot on your plate at present. How is your wife bearing up, by the way? Not long now is it before the birth of your firstborn?"

"No, not long at all, sir. Probably only a few weeks to go. As far as my wife's concerned, it can't come soon enough."

"Please give her my best, won't you? Nothing worse than a long labour, so I'm told!"

Andrew then left his manager's office, looked at his watch and saw it was only an hour before most people would be going for their lunch, including Mr Beckett, his manager. He found it difficult to concentrate on any work, but fortunately he had a couple of urgent items to attend to that would help to pass the time.

At just before 1 o'clock, Andrew's manager left his office. He came over to Andrew and told him that his office was now available for a couple of hours as he had a business lunch to attend.

Andrew didn't want to rush in as soon as the office was free, so he waited until 1:15 p.m. Andrew picked up the phone, expecting to hear the switchboard operator's voice, but his manager had arranged for a direct outside line. Andrew dialled Charles' number and got his secretary, Helen.

"Could I speak to Mr Compton-Browne, please? He should be expecting me."

"Who's calling, please?" asked Helen. Andrew didn't recognise her voice.

"It's Williams, Andrew Williams."

"Oh, Mr Williams, how nice to speak to you again. Are you keeping well?"

"Yes, thank you, I'm very well. I didn't recognise your voice."

Andrew thought of continuing the conversation with the lovely Helen for a bit longer but decided against it.

"I'll put you through, Mr Williams; he's expecting your call."

Andrew and Charles spoke for a good ten minutes about various things, including the developing situation in Europe. Charles then asked if Andrew could meet him after work on Friday to talk about the next steps in joining the Intelligent Service.

"Do you mean I've been accepted?" said Andrew, very excitedly.

"So far, so good; still quite a long way to go though.

"The next thing is to get a medical arranged, but I'll tell you everything when we meet tomorrow. How about the pub near Victoria Station, where we had a meeting before?"

"That's fine by me," said Andrew. "I can make it by 6 o'clock, if that's alright with you?"

"Perfect. Now I assume you have a passport and perhaps some spare, recent passport photos you can bring along, plus your birth certificate and a couple of names of possible references?"

"I'll see what I can dig out," said Andrew. "Until tomorrow."

"Fine," said Charles, and the line went dead.

Andrew continued sitting in his manager's office for a good five minutes, pondering over his call to Charles. *What on earth am I letting myself in for?* He thought to himself. *I hope I can find everything that Charles wants.*

Andrew got home in good time. He greeted his wife, who had had a restful day with a friend, and he disappeared into his study, followed closely by Max. He searched the top drawer of his desk and found his passport. Nearby was a small paper bag and he saw there were four passport-sized photos in it. He opened a box file labelled 'Personal' and found all the documents that Charles had asked for. *Thank goodness I'm quite well organised, for a change,* he thought to himself. He put everything in an envelope and placed it in his briefcase.

"What are you doing, Andrew?" said his wife from the lounge.

"Nothing, dear, just getting ready to take Max out before I get some supper."

"Don't worry about getting supper, I prepared enough for us when I got lunch for Barbara and me. If you're out for only half an hour with Max, I will have it ready on your return."

"Alright, I'll not be longer than twenty five minutes."

Andrew ran upstairs and quickly changed out of his city clothes into his casual shirt and trousers. He put on a sweater and went back down to the hall. He took Max's lead from the hook in the hall, changed into his walking shoes, put on his jacket and cap and went out with Max. He went across the road and up the path on one of his shorter walks. All the time he was thinking about the planned meeting with Charles the next day and how it might affect his life. He had already decided on his two references: Brian and his manager at the bank. He hoped they would be acceptable to Charles and the Intelligence team.

Andrew had got back home early, but Max had hoped for a longer walk as he slouched into his basket. After taking off his outdoor clothes, he wandered into the kitchen to give his wife a hand with the supper things. They would eat in the dining room, she had said.

The conversation was easy, unlike some evenings; Andrew knew he had to tell his wife that he'd be late back home the following day.

"I hope you don't mind, dear, but one of the chaps from the office is leaving and some of us are having a drink with him after we finish work. He's been at our branch longer than I have, but he and his family are moving to a branch in Manchester. He asked for a transfer because his wife's parents need assistance and his wife is their only child. Very good of the bank to help them like this, don't you think?"

"Goodness me! Who'd want to move to Manchester of all places?"

"But your brother and his family live up north and you like going there."

"That's very different. They live in the countryside, north of the Manchester area," she said rather smugly.

"Anyway, I shall be a bit later than normal tomorrow," Andrew repeated.

"You don't normally tell me when you will be late home, so I suppose I should be pleased with your consideration to me."

"I just thought that as you are so near to having our child, you ought to know a bit more about what I'm doing so you don't have to worry. By the way, has the doctor said when you will be admitted for your final examination? It's less than a week before the baby is due."

"Nothing is precise when giving birth to a baby, particularly when it's one's first."

Andrew wasn't sure where this discussion was going so he got up from the table and started to clear away the dishes into the kitchen. Anyway, he thought his wife would start asking too many questions that might be difficult to answer.

After everything had been cleared up and stacked in the kitchen, they sat down in the lounge. Andrew thought they ought to find out the latest news so he put on the wireless, much to his wife's annoyance. The main item described how Germany was very soon likely to formalise its 1936 Rome-Berlin Axis agreement with Italy. If Germany went ahead, it would make the British Government very nervous. It considered that as war against Nazi Germany was a possibility, approval should be given to bring back conscription for all single males, aged 20 to 22. This would bring in nearly a quarter of a million men for military training.

"Well, at least you're not in that age bracket," said Andrew's wife.

"No, I'm not, but if matters get worse later in the year, I can see call-up being brought in for older men, probably up to 40-year-olds."

"Let's hope it doesn't come to that. I don't want to be fending on my own, particularly with our baby."

There wasn't any more really to be said by either of them, particularly as Andrew knew, almost with certainty, that he would be involved in some kind of activity in the not too distant future. Andrew switched off the wireless as it was getting too depressing for his wife and she felt the need to get some sleep.

On Friday morning, before he caught the train to London, Andrew double checked the contents of his briefcase, making sure he hadn't left anything behind that might be vital for his meeting with Charles. He had told his wife that he should be back by about 9 o'clock and that, if she felt tired or he was a bit later, she should go to bed before he got back, to which she agreed.

Almost on the dot of 5:30 p.m., Andrew left the office for the pub. This time he was there before Charles.

"Good to see you again, Andrew. Sorry it's been so long since I was last in touch, but the business with Germany has focussed all our attention, as well as dealing with your application forms."

"Not a problem, Charles. I know you're a busy man and that the security of the nation rests on the Intelligence Services' agencies."

"What will you have to drink, Andrew? Oh, and I nearly forgot to ask, how is your wife, it can't be long now?"

"She's getting fed up with the bump. She doesn't get a lot of rest, even at night. The little blighter is very active and kicks out a lot. It's due next week so I'll have to be on hand at a moment's notice. She has a good friend who is on standby during the week days, which is very helpful. If she should go into labour during the daytime, she'll contact the doctor and me."

"That's good. It helps you and her if there's a trusty friend on call. Shall I get you a pint?"

"That would be fine, Charles. Thank you."

Charles got the drinks and they settled down at a table away from the busy bar area – it was a Friday evening after all. Nearly an hour went by in what seemed like no time at all, so Charles asked Andrew if he'd like a snack at the nearby restaurant so long as Andrew had enough time.

"That would be a nice suggestion," said Andrew. "I'm not expected back till 9 o'clock or a bit later. My wife thinks I'm at an office colleague's leaving do."

With that reply, they gathered up their papers and walked to the restaurant round the corner from the pub. They had a light meal as they continued talking over the next stages of Andrew's application, once the administration department had copied all the documents that Andrew had brought with him and those that he had signed, witnessed by Charles.

"I think we're almost there Andrew. Do you have any further questions to ask?"

"Just how much does my bank manager know about what's going on?"

"As I said a few weeks back, he is in on the recruitment process and there is one other employee at your branch that is already signed up with the Intelligence Services and you won't even know who he or she is. Only one other branch of all the banks in London has someone signed up to the Service. The next step is to get you a thorough medical from one of our doctors. Probably, a Dr Freeman will send you a letter to your bank. Fill in the form and arrange for him to see you as soon as possible. Once the results are received and deemed acceptable, and I have no doubt they will be, I will contact you about a training plan. Does that sound alright with you, Andrew?"

"That's fine by me, Charles. It sounds as though I won't be undergoing any training until June at the very earliest?"

"That's about right. By which time, your child will be a month old, I suppose? Please let me know when the happy event has occurred, and I wish you and your wife all good wishes. Please contact me if you have any concerns, but I'm sure you're doing the right thing by working with us."

Andrew looked at his watch and to his surprise it was already 8:30 p.m.

"Good Heavens! I'm sorry to break things up, but I must get the next train that leaves at 8:50 p.m. Thanks for the meal and everything that you've helped me with."

The two men shook hands warmly and smiled at each other. Andrew left the restaurant for the train home and Charles paid for the meal, thinking to himself that the Service has probably enlisted a very competent, loyal and dedicated agent.

Chapter 9
Wednesday, 3rd of April 1940

As they got nearer to Karlsruhe, their pulses were starting to race. It had been over forty five minutes since they had filled the bike up with fuel. No sooner than they had thought that all was going well for them when the engine started to cough and splutter and it had begun to rain. They were on the outskirts of a village and could see in front of them, as they rounded a left hand bend, a small *gasthaus*. The bike stopped altogether, and so Artur pushed it with Gerhart walking behind with the case. They suddenly felt very conspicuous in their sheepskins. Artur stopped walking and turned round to talk to Gerhart.

"When we get to the *gasthaus*, we'll have to pretend that we are French and we'll ask them if they can help us with our troublesome bike. Get out our French passports and keep the German ones somewhere safe. I'll go into the *gasthaus* while you stay outside with the bike and keep a sharp look out for any trouble. Hopefully the manager will allow us to bring the bike through the side entrance and into the courtyard at the back, out of sight of passers-by. If you should be alarmed by anyone or any army vehicle should come into view, blow the whistle once for a short while."

Artur went in through the entrance door and pressed the bell on the reception desk. He didn't shout, but asked quite loudly if anyone was there. An attractive lady in her late 30s came from what looked like the kitchen. She smiled sweetly at Artur as she said, "*Bitte*?"

Artur greeted her and smiled at her. He spoke clearly but slowly in French about the problem with the bike and whether or not he could get help. The lady appeared to understand Artur, but excused herself as she returned to the kitchen. A few moments later, she came back to the reception area followed by a man wearing a white apron and wiping his hands on it as he walked towards Artur with a quizzical look on his face.

Artur again explained his position with the bike and told him that he and his brother needed to get back into France. The man spoke back in very broken French and said that his brother ran a small garage on the other side of the village and what he doesn't know about engines is not worth knowing. He suggested that the bike be brought round into the courtyard away from the road and that while they were having a coffee and a piece of cake, he would ask his brother to send his young apprentice down to collect the bike.

Artur thanked the man and excused himself so he could go and tell his brother what was going on. Just as he was going out of the door and towards the road, he heard the whistle being blown by Gerhart. Artur froze and followed the direction that Gerhart was pointing. A number of troop-carrying vehicles were about 600 metres away and coming into the village from the way they had entered only a few minutes earlier.

"Gerhart, without rushing, get the bike into the back courtyard, take off your sheepskin coat and put it with mine, together with the goggles behind the bike. Return to the front of the *gasthaus* and walk calmly into the reception area where I shall be waiting for you."

Gerhart did as Artur had told him, and in a short while was standing by him in the reception; he put down the case. The man greeted Gerhart and ushered the two of them into a small dining room that was laid out for breakfast. As they entered the room, troop vehicles started to thunder past the window overlooking the road. A few people, who were having breakfast, as well as those that had just arrived, stopped and stared at the convoy. Artur was careful not to show too much interest, but did count twenty vehicles with probably as many as twenty army personnel in each.

Gerhart and Artur sat at the table furthest from the window and their coffee and cake duly arrived. After some ten minutes, a young man entered the room and introduced himself – in German – as the apprentice at his father's garage. Artur pretended not to understand too well what he was saying just as the boy's uncle arrived and explained everything in German to the young boy. The man said, in his broken French, that the boy would take the bike to the garage and phone in about an hour to give him an update. Gerhart gave the bike's keys to the boy and he was told the bike was in the back courtyard. Once the man and boy had gone, Artur told Gerhart in French that they must not only exercise patience, but also be on their guard regarding their security.

Suddenly, Artur remembered that the panniers contained important maps, papers and other essential items. He jumped up from the table, leaving his satchel with Gerhart, and just managed to catch the boy as he was wheeling the bike up the road towards the garage. Artur excused himself for startling the boy and pointed to the panniers. He told the boy very slowly in French that he needed the pannier contents so he could plan the reminder of his route back to France once the bike was fixed. The boy realised from Artur's sudden appearance that he needed something from the bike. They smiled at each other and after a few moments, Artur had taken all that he needed and the boy went on his way.

I hope I haven't left anything of real consequence in the panniers, Artur thought to himself. He returned to the *gasthaus'* breakfast room and sat down in front of Gerhart, somewhat relieved that he'd remembered about their things.

"Is everything OK?" asked Gerhart.

"I hope so," Artur replied. "As soon as we've finished our coffee, I think we ought to pay up and wander down the road looking for a shop for new coats. I'll ask the man and he might know of somewhere."

Artur paid the bill and asked the man if he had a bag to put the panniers' contents into and he duly found one under the counter. The man offered to look after the bag whilst they went to the shop and Artur agreed. The man had been very helpful, but he didn't think they'd find anything at the only possible shop up the road on the left. The rain had eased off as they walked along the road; getting some fresh air was what they really needed.

"I wonder what's wrong with the bike," Gerhart said.

"It's probably only some muck in the carb. I could have fixed it by the roadside, but we did the best thing by pushing it to the village and avoiding being seen by the army convoy."

They found the shop but there was nothing suitable, just as the man had thought. They wandered around the village trying to pass the time before the boy might call about the bike. They returned to the *gasthaus* and told the man that he was right – nothing suitable. The man then disappeared and returned with two lightweight rain jackets. He asked them to try them on for a possible fit. One was rather large for Gerhart and the other a bit small for Artur. The man said they'd been left by some guests a few weeks ago and as nobody had come back for them, he offered them to Artur and Gerhart. Artur was not prepared to let them be given as a gift so he handed the man a few notes. At that moment, the phone went.

"Good news," the man said. "The boy says the bike is now working properly again. Only dirt in the carburettor, I think he said. He'll be bringing it back in a few minutes and you can pay him then."

"I thought that might be the problem," said Artur, slowly, in his broken French accent. "By the way, is it possible for us to stay the night here? We can share a room. We are really tired after our journey and we've some way to go before we get home."

"Of course," the man said. "Please, can I see your passports, I'll give them back to you a bit later? Would you like to go to your room and freshen up after the bike has been returned? If so, my wife will make sure that the room is ready and that there's plenty of hot water for a bath, if you would like one."

"That sounds too good to be true. Thank you," said Artur. "But I would prefer to have the passports back before we are shown our room, if that's not a problem?"

The boy brought the bike back; Artur paid him and gave him a bit extra for his efforts. Artur took the bike round the back into the courtyard and managed to find something suitable to put over it. He located the sheepskin coats and put them under some odds and ends in an outhouse. He put the goggles into his newly acquired jacket pocket.

Hopefully they won't be found for a while, by which time we should be in France, he mumbled to himself.

On returning to the reception area, Artur was handed the bag containing the panniers' contents together with the passports, and he and Gerhart were shown to their room containing two beds. Artur decided to lie on the bed that was nearer the door and he contemplated their next move whilst Gerhart used the bathroom along the corridor. When Gerhart returned, Artur was already asleep.

During the afternoon, they chatted quietly about the derailment of the train and Artur mentioned his mishap with a tree after he'd jumped from the train. He also told Gerhart about the strange lady who had brought him the sheepskin coat from the hut, and the weird but recognisable language that she spoke. Neither of them could explain that episode. Anyway, they thought they'd been really lucky so far to avoid being on the road when the convoys passed. They had an early supper and decided to turn in at about 9 o'clock, ready for an early start the following morning.

In the middle of the night, they were awakened by a lot of shouting going on down in the reception area. Artur was immediately alert. He crept over to the door, unlocked it and carefully opened it to listen to what was going on downstairs. It appeared that a couple of German army officers were asking the man if he'd seen two men on a bike wearing sheepskin coats during the previous day, heading for the direction of Karlsruhe. The man categorically denied seeing anyone of that description, but it did not convince the officers. One of the officers appeared to hit the man hard in the stomach because he seemed to crash to the floor, moaning, and still denying any knowledge of the men they were looking for.

"We have information that suggests their bike broke down not far from here yesterday morning," one of the officers shouted. "We think they came here for assistance and a coffee and we want to search the premises."

"But I have guests who are sleeping and they won't want to be disturbed in the middle of the night," the man said as he was given another punch.

Artur looked at Gerhart, who was now standing next to him, and they both knew that they could be in great danger if they didn't do something, and quickly. They very quietly put the rest of their clothes on and Artur slung his satchel over his neck and shoulder. They also put on the rain jackets that the man had given them. They remade the beds and tidied the room as well as they could so that at a quick glance it looked as though nobody had been in there. Artur carefully drew the curtains and looked down to the road below to see the officers' staff car outside. The engine was still ticking over and he could just make out the face of the young driver. Artur picked up the bag containing the items from the panniers and led the way out of the room. He locked the door but left the key in the lock. Gerhart followed with the suit case as they turned right towards an emergency stairway at the end of the corridor that they had found earlier in the evening.

There was more shouting coming from the reception area and it appeared that the officers wanted to search the rooms. The officers came bounding up the main stairs, followed closely by the man, still exclaiming about his sleeping guests, just as Artur and Gerhart had started down the emergency staircase that led into the far end of the dining room. Artur and Gerhart stopped and listened; they took out their revolvers and cocked them and saw it was just after 3 o'clock in the night. With all the noise going on upstairs, they crept along to the reception desk and took a quick look outside. The car was parked near the dining room window, so they weren't noticed by the driver as they looked through the door of the main entrance. Artur turned to Gerhart and very quietly said that they ought to avail themselves of the vehicle outside that the officers had kindly left on the road. Very fortuitously, the officers had left their hats on the reception desk so they put them on as best they could and walked out of the *gasthaus* towards the car with their pistols in their pockets. For a moment, the driver thought they were the real officers and this gave Artur and Gerhart just enough time. The driver quickly got out of the car and ran round to open the nearside rear door without really looking at the men. Artur took his gun out and said very firmly to the driver in perfect German, with the gun stabbed into his side, to do exactly as he was told if he wanted to stay alive. Meanwhile, Gerhart jumped into the back behind the driver's seat and Artur pushed the driver round to the front and into the car. At this point, Gerhart took over and had his gun pushing into the back of the driver's neck, giving Artur enough time to get into the passenger seat with the bag of maps and other belongings.

"Drive the vehicle away as though you have the officers in the car. Do nothing to draw attention to us or you'll be shot. Do you understand?" said Artur, leaning towards the driver, who was now sweating a bit. The driver nodded and glanced through the right side of the windscreen to check if his real charges were coming out of the main door of the *gasthaus,* but they weren't.

"We want you to drive to the other side of Karlsruhe and go over the first bridge we come to across the Rhine. After we're on the other side, we will give you further instructions."

Artur turned round to Gerhart and gave him a wink.

"Let's hope we've got a head start on those officers," Artur said in French, a language that he hoped the driver didn't know.

"That was a narrow escape. We were fortunate the officers left their hats on the reception desk; it just gave us a moment of credibility," said Gerhart, who was now sitting back in his seat. He straightened his hat and tried to take on the persona of a German officer, even without a great coat.

The driver did as he was told and drove through Karlsruhe and west of Mühlberg, towards the road bridge – the railway bridge being to the north of the road bridge. There were no guards as they crossed but on the far side, Artur could see some armed soldiers on each side of the road.

"Listen very carefully," Artur said, very firmly. "Drive gently to the other side of the bridge and flash your lights as we get near to the guards to indicate that you want to drive straight on. Do not do anything silly because I shall be sitting back in my seat and saluting the guards as we pass them. The guards will think we are your real passengers."

They thought the guards recognised the car because they all stood to attention and gave the Nazi salute as the car passed them. Just as they believed they were clear, Artur looked in the wing mirror and saw that one of the guards was gesticulating something that suggested there might be a problem. *Perhaps it was because I was sitting in the front passenger seat,* Artur thought to himself. Before the guards could really do anything, Artur told the driver to head for Landau.

Once they were some 10 km west of the bridge, Artur told the driver not to go more than 50 km/h so as not to draw attention to themselves. Artur felt sure that word would have been passed by the stranded officers to a command post in Karlsruhe by now, telling them that their car had been stolen. Artur asked the driver how much fuel the car had and was told that it was still over half full.

They arrived at Landau just after 5 o'clock. Neither Artur nor Gerhart relaxed during the journey and in particular when driving through the villages and towns. They were always looking out for army trucks or policemen who might try to apprehend them, or even shoot at the vehicle.

"Gerhart, will you sit forward and keep close to the driver while I look at the map?

"Don't try any funny tricks," Artur said to the driver in German. "I need to look at the map with my torch."

Artur rummaged in his bag and found the map he was looking for. He soon identified Landau and saw the road he wanted to take to reach the French border.

"Continue towards Zweibrüchen which will take about one and a half hours. Just before Zweibrüchen, I will give you further instructions. Is that clear?"

The driver nodded but said he needed to relieve himself.

"We drive through a wooded area in about fifteen minutes and we will be able to pull off the road and stop somewhere," Artur replied.

After a while, they came to a wooded area. The driver was told to drive slowly and look for a track into the woods. They found a track to the right after a couple of kilometres, drove slowly up it and the driver turned the car round to face the way they had come in, just as Artur had instructed him.

"Now, don't try any funny business, so get out of the car and do what you need to do. My friend will be right next to you with his pistol to make sure you don't make a false move. When you've finished, get back into the car and be ready to drive off."

Just before the driver got back in the car, Artur asked him if there was anything in the boot.

"Nothing of any importance," said the driver.

"Open the boot and I'll decide if it's important," replied Artur.

The boot was opened by the driver and Artur shone his torch around inside. Amongst other things, there were lengths of rope, some automatic rifles, boxes of ammunition, two army great coats, two pairs of boots, a box of hand grenades and a holdall.

"Nothing of importance, you said! Close the boot lid and get back in the driver's seat. Let's get a move on."

They drove on and after forty minutes, Artur started looking for the turning for Althornbach and Hornbach.

"When we get to the middle of Hornbach, there is a branch in the road going to the left, more of a track. Go down it for 2 km and pull off to the left side of the track, into the woods."

The track was quite bumpy, but they found the track off to the left and went into the woods. Artur had thought this area was right for crossing the border as there were no bunkers near here and therefore less likelihood of being caught.

"Gerhart, you get out of the car and when you've taken the rope out of the boot, get the driver out. I'll gag his mouth with the cloth from the glove box and you tie his hands behind him and then down to his legs."

All was done as Artur said, although the driver put up a bit of a struggle when he was pushed to the ground and finally tied to a tree.

"There's also a holdall in the boot so put some of the hand grenades in it together with the bag with the maps and so on. You carry the holdall and I'll take the case. We had better put the officers' hats in the boot too. We'll have to leave the rifles and great coats, so lock up the car. Throw the keys as far as you can into the woods once you've checked that we have all that we need for the next part of our escape."

Artur and Gerhart stood still, facing the track with the car behind them for a few moments and listened for any sound of a vehicle or voices, once the car was locked. They were startled by a noise of something moving in the woods behind them but they thought it must be a deer or a boar, or so they hoped. They moved slowly forward to the track and turned right. They walked for about seventy metres before crossing to the other side.

"There is a lightly wooded area and then a few farm buildings about 100 metres further on to our left. They are in France and I don't think there's a fence or a wire between the two countries at this point, but we'll soon find out."

They tiptoed very slowly forward and stopped every few yards to listen for any sound. Nothing. Artur very briefly looked at his watch with his torch and saw it was 6:30 a.m. *It's amazing how time flies when you're enjoying yourself,* he thought to himself.

As they went past the first cottage that was about 40 metres from them, a light went on in what looked like the kitchen. They stopped dead still in their tracks, daring not to breath; as it was quite cold their breath might be seen, even in the dark.

"There's a farm track to the right of the cottages that will take us to the village of Schweyen, if my map is correct. But as we'll be in the open when we walk along the track, you should set off first, I'll cover you and I'll follow in five minutes," Artur said. "Is that OK with you, Gerhart?"

"That's fine, Artur. Let's get going. The sooner I start, the sooner we'll get to Schweyen."

After the five minutes were up, Artur set off in pursuit of Gerhard. It wasn't easy to see Gerhart but he could just about hear his steps. The track meandered its way between open fields, past another cottage and eventually came to the southern edge of the village where Gerhart stopped, waiting for Artur to arrive.

"What should we do now, Artur?"

"It's only a small village and as it's so near to the border, some of the people will very likely be German or supporters of Germany. We need to get further into France, so we'll head for Breidenbach which is a small town about 5 km away from here. There are some woods not far down the road so we ought to hide in there for a while and get some sleep. Is that alright with you?"

"Sounds a good idea to me," replied Gerhart, who was beginning to feel very tired.

Sure enough, in less than 2 km, they came to some woods on the left and followed a track well off the road. It didn't take long for the two of them to settle down and fall asleep only to be awoken by the noise of a car going along the road towards Schweyen.

Chapter 10
Saturday, 6th of May 1939

The weather on the weekend following Andrew's meeting with Charles was fine and warm. He got out into the garden for only the third time since the beginning of April, and he noticed how quickly the weeds were growing. He spent most of Saturday morning attending to the vegetable patches which would be completed by the gardener when he came on his regular weekly visit on Tuesday.

Andrew and his wife sat out in the warm sunshine with a drink before having a light lunch. She felt the baby's arrival would not be many days more, and decided to take a nap in the afternoon. Andrew took Max for a walk while she slept and worked over in his mind how things might be for him over the coming months. When he returned home, he phoned Brian and asked him if he'd be free to meet him for a drink just after midday the following day. He replied positively and they agreed on meeting at the Crooked Billet for a change.

Andrew's wife slept badly on Saturday night and thought she might be starting labour. As well as that, the baby had been very active and had kicked so much that she thought it might burst out of her stomach. Andrew felt so concerned that he asked her if he should cancel meeting Brian for a drink, but she said she'd phone Barbara and see if she could come round for a couple of hours when he would be out. Barbara was only too pleased to help and arrived at 11:30 a.m.

Andrew's wife had agreed for him to use her car. He left Max in the hall, ran outside, jumped into her car and arrived at the pub just after 12:15 p.m., having driven very fast.

"How are things, Andrew? You look like you've seen a ghost."

"Barbara has had to come to the house and be with my wife as she had such a terrible night last night and got very little sleep."

"One blessing is that it can't be long now before you'll be a father and your wife will be out of all this discomfort. I'll get you a pint and we'll go outside in the warm sunshine for a while."

The warm, still spring air allowed Andrew to relax, and the beer tasted very good too. They chatted about the weekend away in Devon and Andrew told Brian that Max seemed fine: no repercussions after his jump from Andrew's moving car. Likewise, Andrew's bruises and scratches were clearing up well and he hoped to pick up his car towards the end of the week.

"So, my dear friend, what is on your mind that you need to speak so urgently to me about?" enquired Brian.

"I met this chap from the Intelligence Service the day before yesterday after work. I submitted all the documents he had asked for and signed all the papers he put in front of me. I was asked to provide two references and I gave him your name and address. I hope you don't mind; after all, I hadn't even asked you if you would do it for me."

"My dear fellow, I am delighted to be of help. I've given a couple of references for people before, but will they ask any particular questions?"

"All I know is that you will receive something in the next week or so. There will be forms with questions and you will be asked to answer them honestly and to the best of your ability. There will then be a section where you have to describe my character and personal attributes."

"Do I tell them that you're a bit of a womaniser?" said Brian with a laugh. "Sorry, it was a joke really."

"I shall ignore that remark," said Andrew rather seriously. "Once you've completed it all, you will be told to return the forms in the stamped addressed envelope provided. The address on the envelope will be to a third party that will review your replies and forward everything to someone at the Intelligence Service offices. The third party might write to you to ask for clarification on any answers you've made, or anything else that you've written. Is that OK?"

"Of course it is, Andrew. I will be only too pleased to help, you know that. Now, don't you worry. You've made your decision and it's the right one. You have my complete support and backing on this and you can trust me to say nothing to anyone about what you've told me. Just relax. Remember, you told me they said you could back out of this commitment at any time you like but, in the meantime, I know you will give it your best shot. The sort of thing you will be asked to be involved in is right up your street."

"Thanks, Brian, for that; it is very reassuring. Let's have another pint and drink to our futures and to whatever life might ask of us."

Andrew drank down his beer and went inside to the bar to get two more. He felt a great weight had been removed from his shoulders. He couldn't wish for a better friend to have confided in.

The pub was busy, even for a Sunday lunchtime. After ten minutes, Andrew returned with the beers. They drank each other's health and wished each other all good fortune with whatever the future might bring them

"It was at Prep school that we met, wasn't it, Andrew? Then we went to different Senior Schools but still managed to keep in touch because we used to live quite near to each other. We occasionally met up when we were at home on holiday. Do you remember, you called me early one summer day and asked if I'd like to go on a camping holiday to the Lake District? We stayed near Thirlmere and walked over the hills to… What was the name of the place? Anyway, you got rather sunburnt that day and your mother was very cross with you when we returned home."

"Rosthwaite," said Andrew. "I remember that holiday very well. We went via Blea Tarn and you fell in and were soaked for the rest of the day."

They continued to reminisce about that holiday when they were in their late teens. Suddenly, Andrew looked at his watch and found they'd been talking for quite a while, and it was time he was thinking of going home.

"I must go now, Brian. I'm really glad we had this chat."

"Me too, Andrew. Keep me informed of your wife's progress. Let me know if there's anything I can do to help."

They shook hands, said their goodbyes and went their separate ways. Andrew managed to get home by 2:15 p.m. and so was in his wife's good books; Barbara got away a little earlier than expected.

"How's Brian? Did you get a sandwich, or have some lunch when you were at the pub, Andrew?"

"No, I didn't. Presumably Barbara got you something so is there any of it left?"

"There should be enough so go and have a look in the kitchen."

Andrew did as was suggested. He found enough for a snack and tucked into it in the kitchen. His wife came and joined him after a while and put her arm round his neck as he sat at the kitchen table. She told him that she thought their child would be born very soon and that she would get the doctor to call on Monday.

"That's a very good idea, dear. Didn't he say some while ago that he thought it was due on the 16th and that's Tuesday next week?"

"Yes, he did. I think I'll go and lie down for a bit. Have you got all you need?"

Andrew said that he had.

All was well for the rest of the day, and both Andrew and his wife had a good night's sleep. Andrew went to the office as usual, feeling very perky and pleased with himself after speaking to Brian. It had helped him considerably; he felt at ease with life. All he wanted now was for the baby to be born.

Just after 3 o'clock in the afternoon, a phone call came through to his manager's office and Andrew was ushered in rather anxiously by Mr Beckett's secretary.

"I don't think there's anything too much to worry about, Williams, but someone has just phoned to say that your wife had a fall at lunchtime at home and she has had to be taken to hospital. By all accounts, your doctor has been to the hospital and has given her a thorough examination. My secretary has the number you should ring so I suggest you do that right away."

"Oh my goodness! Thank you for the message, sir, I'll go and make the call. Did the person who called leave her name?"

"I don't have it, but my secretary may well have taken it down. You may use the spare office as you will probably like to make the call in private."

Andrew thanked his manager and left his office. He asked the secretary for the phone number and went into the spare office to make the call.

"Hallo? This is Andrew Williams here. I've been asked to call because my wife has been taken to hospital. Who am I speaking to, please?"

"It's me, Barbara. Everything is alright with your wife and there appears to be no damage to the baby, the doctor says."

"What on earth happened, Barbara?"

"She was going into the kitchen to get a drink and your dog ran in front of her and her feet were taken from under her. She fell to the floor rather heavily, but fortunately she didn't hit her head on the corner of the sideboard. I don't think you need to rush straight home, but you ought to go and see her this evening. As you will probably guess, she's been admitted to Horsham hospital."

"Thank you so much, Barbara. I am assuming that my wife struggled to the phone and called you after her fall?"

"That's right and I went straight over after calling her doctor."

"I am very grateful to you. Very many thanks."

Andrew rang off and decided he should update his manager with the situation. He was told that if he wished to leave early then he was free to go. Andrew finished some of his business that he had been in the middle of dealing with and left the office just after 4:15 p.m. He thought it would be best if he went home first and used his wife's car to get to the hospital; he would then have transport to get back home again afterwards.

As soon as Andrew got home, he let his dog out into the garden while he changed into something a bit more casual. After Max had come in, he gave him some food and drove off to the hospital. On his arrival, he found a sister who told him in which ward he could find his wife and that it was alright to visit her for no more than half an hour.

"Hallo, dear," said Andrew. "I came as soon as I could. Are you feeling alright now?" He leant over and gave her a kiss on her cheek, then sat on the side of the bed.

"It was so stupid of me. I should have watched what I was doing. It was Max who got in my way and I hadn't seen him. I'm sorry you had to leave the office early."

"Never mind, as long as you and the baby have not been affected by the fall, that's all that matters. What did the doctor say?"

"He was very good. He came to the house and did an initial examination. He thought it would be best if I was admitted as a precaution. After all, the baby's actually due a week from tomorrow so I might as well be here, he said. He and the senior sister then did further, more thorough tests. I think the fall might have hastened labour, but I'm very comfortable at the moment."

"It's all a great relief and thank goodness Barbara could come round so quickly. Is there anything you need me to bring you as you probably left the house in a bit of a hurry?"

"You could bring me a clean nightie and my dressing gown. I remembered to bring all my toiletries. When do you think you will come again?"

"Unless you need these things urgently or if you go into labour, I'll come at the same time tomorrow; OK?"

"That should be fine, thank you. I believe Barbara is coming tomorrow afternoon so if there's any change, I'll get her to ring the office."

"Fine. Now you get a good night's rest and not worry about anything except you and the baby. You're in good hands here and you've got a good doctor."

Andrew said farewell to his wife; he gave her a couple of kisses and left the hospital. He was greatly relieved that she looked so chirpy and relaxed. He got home, made himself some sandwiches and listened to the radio for about an hour before turning in.

Andrew was up bright and early and, as it was a fine morning, he went out with Max. He thought he should phone Barbara and ask her to let Max out into the garden in the afternoon before going to the hospital. Once in the office, he briefed his manager about his wife and he was allowed to leave early each day until the baby was born. It was a very thoughtful gesture.

Tuesday came and went without anything of note occurring, but a phone call came through the following day to Andrew in the office that his wife had gone into labour. He left just after lunch and reached the hospital late afternoon. He was allowed to see his wife for a short while, but was then ushered into the waiting room. A nurse came to see him after about an hour and explained that it might be best if he went home and they would call him when his wife was closer to giving birth. She gently warned him that it might be a difficult birth as the baby seemed to be quite big.

At about 3 o'clock in the night, Andrew heard the phone ringing and rushed downstairs to answer it – *It can only be the hospital,* he said to himself.

"Hallo, Williams here. Yes, I'll come over straight away. Do you need me to bring any things for my wife?"

Andrew was given a list. He dressed, collected the things into a small case and drove to the hospital.

"I'm afraid you can't see your wife yet," said the night nurse. "The doctor and nursing staff are with her and the baby's due very soon. If you want to rest, you may use this ward over here. We will let you know when the baby is born as it might be a tricky birth."

Andrew went into the ward, took off his shoes and lay on the bed. The next thing he knew was the nurse coming in.

"Congratulations Mr Williams, you have a son."

Andrew shot out of bed and embraced the nurse which made her blush a bit.

"That's wonderful news. Can I see my wife and baby now, please?"

"Of course you may, but remember your wife had a very difficult labour and she needs a lot of rest before she can come home. He was over 9lbs!"

For the remainder of the week and all weekend, Andrew was on cloud nine. He was a very proud father. All the people at the office, including his manager, took him out to the pub after work on the Friday – he was terribly late home. He had told Brian and they went on a bender on Saturday at lunchtime that lasted till closing time at 3 o'clock, so much so that he was in no fit state to go and visit his wife. That meant he hadn't been to the hospital since he saw the two of them on Thursday morning; she was not pleased at all. He had phoned Charles, and he sent a card to his wife congratulating her on the birth of her son, as though it were from someone at the bank. He had also spoken to his mother and his wife's father, her sister and brother-in-law and others.

After all the drinking and celebrating that he'd been doing over the last three days, Andrew decided he was going to drastically change his drinking habits. His wife and young son were brought home by the doctor on Friday of the following week, so at least Andrew would be around for the weekend. His wife's father couldn't come down to the house but spoke to her on the phone. For every day of his wife's first week at home, Andrew got back early from the office. His wife thought he was a changed person, taking his responsibilities very seriously, although he didn't change nappies. His wife was still rather weak in her first week at home, so it was fortunate that Barbara and another friend, Pat, could call round most days to give her any help she needed. The maid, Edith, used to come in only once a week, but during these early days and until the end of June she came in on Mondays, Wednesdays and Fridays.

During the second week at home, Andrew and his wife discussed who they should choose as Godparents – they had already chosen a name for the baby: he was to be called Alfred Frank Williams. The favourite for both of them was Brian, but they argued at length over the other two. Andrew wanted his brother and his wife whereas his wife wanted her sister and brother-in-law. Eventually, the latter two were agreed on.

In the early part of the first week of June, Andrew received a letter at the office from Charles. It stated that references had been received and the forms had been duly completed by the referees. It was a bit of a surprise to Andrew as he'd almost forgotten about the Intelligence Service, what with the arrival of his son and all that had entailed. Charles suggested they should meet on Friday after work at the O&C Club, where they had met previously. Andrew wrote a reply of acceptance instead of phoning him. Andrew told his wife that he needed to be late home on Friday and she readily agreed.

"You've been getting home so early for the last two weeks and been so attentive that I can hardly deny you a night out once in a while, can I dear?"

Andrew was pleased that she didn't make things difficult for him; in any case, her sister and brother-in-law were coming for the weekend and that was usually enjoyable for all concerned.

Andrew duly left the office on Friday, and made his way to the O&C Club. He was ushered into the bar where he found Charles talking to a man at a nearby table. Charles saw him and immediately got up to greet him, offering him his hand.

"My dear Andrew, very many congratulations on the birth of your son. I trust all is well with him and your wife?"

"Yes, all seems well, thank you, Charles. And thanks for the card, it was much appreciated."

"Come and meet a colleague of mine," said Charles, who led Andrew to the table where the man was already standing. "Andrew, this is Peter Fortescue; Peter, I am pleased to introduce you to Andrew Williams. He's just become a father to a boy so he's very happy with life, as you might expect."

The three of them smiled and talked about the early days of fatherhood for a few moments. Charles then asked Andrew if he'd like his usual pint of bitter, but he stressed that he would only have a half. This caused Charles to frown a bit and look sideways at Andrew before moving to the bar for the order.

"There you are, Andrew. Don't tell me that fatherhood has made you alter your drinking habits, has it?"

"No, not really, but for the first few days after the baby's birth, I went quite mad and I feel it's only right to cut back a bit."

"As long as you've not changed for ever, that's alright with us, isn't it Peter?"

Peter nodded and smiled at Andrew. Charles then spoke to Andrew about the next steps he will be asked to take towards being accepted by the Intelligence Service.

"As I have mentioned a couple of months ago, we need to send you on a few courses: physical training, weapon handling, map reading, unarmed combat and so on. Peter heads up training programs and he will explain what is involved, in which order you should take these courses and where they are situated. Over to you, Peter."

Peter went into quite a lot of detail on the aspects of each course and commented that, initially, Andrew would only be away for a day at a time.

"I'm sorry to butt in, Peter, but I just ought to mention that your manager at the bank has given us the go-ahead to allow you to do this training, as long as it's no more than three days every fortnight. He fully endorses your suitability for a role in the Service. Back to you Peter."

Peter carried on from where he had left off by mentioning basic signalling, Morse code and the use of radios.

"My goodness, Peter, is all of that really necessary before I'm accepted into the Service?"

"Oh no, I'm assuming you will already have been signed up before all of this training."

"Andrew, I have to say," said Charles, "that for all intents and purposes, you are all but signed up. We only want you to have a medical and you're in."

"Oh, I see," said Andrew, a little nervously. He'd been taken a little bit by surprise by this information. "I have to say that I was going to mention to you that I've not heard from Dr Freeman yet concerning the medical."

"I'm very sorry he hasn't been in touch yet, but what with the imminent birth of your son and the fact that he's been away on holiday, it's not been possible to set up a date for your medical. I only spoke to Freeman this morning, knowing that I would be seeing you today, and he has given me a couple of dates for you to consider."

Charles drew out his diary and read out the dates on offer.

"I'll take next Friday, 9th June, if that's still alright? No doubt you'll tell me where and what time?"

"That's great news, Andrew. It will need all the afternoon at his surgery in Clapham."

Charles handed Andrew a piece of paper with Dr Freeman's address and phone number on it and he scribbled the appointment time on it too.

"Well, that covers the medical. Peter, did you want to leave anything with Andrew about some of the training courses and the optional locations that we use?"

Peter fumbled in his briefcase and brought out an envelope marked SECRET & CONFIDENTIAL, for Addressee Only. Andrew noticed that his name was already on the envelope.

"I think you'll find everything you need in there. When you've decided to start the program, give me a call and I'll arrange the first three courses to fit in with your availability," said Peter.

Andrew put the envelope in his briefcase and gave a big sigh.

"I just have to pass the medical, then the fun starts!" he said with a big grin. "I can't wait. Thanks Peter, for all the material."

"There's only one more thing," said Charles. "I shall need you to sign the Official Secrets Act forms before you go on any courses. Could you meet me at my office in St. James' next Tuesday, the 6th, at lunchtime? It will only take a few minutes."

"Fine by me," said Andrew, already thinking about the lovely Helen, Charles' receptionist.

They all stood up and prepared to leave. They shook hands and thanked each other for their time. Andrew left Charles and Peter in the bar, and once Andrew had left, they talked about Andrew and the likelihood of his being a good agent in due course.

Chapter 11
Thursday, 4th of April 1940

After the car had passed going towards Schweyen, Artur looked at his watch to find it was 11 o'clock and that they'd been asleep for over three hours. They obviously needed the rest, but they now felt very hungry.

"I suggest we go back to the road and start walking towards Breidenbach. We'll have to try and hitch a lift. It's a big risk but it's our best chance of getting away from the border area," said Artur.

"If we're really lucky, we might even be in town in time for some lunch," said Gerhart, with a wry smile as he patted his stomach.

They picked up their gear and set off for the road. They turned left and walked on the right hand side of the road. After about fifteen minutes, they heard a vehicle coming from the direction of Schweyen. They stood by the side of the road. Artur thumbed for a lift but the car went straight past. They felt very crest fallen, but they then noticed that the car had stopped further ahead of them and started to reverse back towards them. They ran to the vehicle and Artur went round to the driver's window that was wound down. He spoke in French as he asked the man if he was going to Breidenbach. The man replied in the affirmative, but also asked what they were doing so near to the border.

"Why do you need to know?" said Artur rather cheekily.

"I was listening to the radio this morning," said the man, "and there was a report about two men who were on the run having apprehended some senior German officers' driver and their car during the night. I just wondered if you were the ones, or if you knew anything about the incident?"

Before Artur answered, he looked into the car and noticed that the man had a rifle on the passenger seat. He realised that the man had spoken good French, but with a strange sound to some of his words which made Artur suspicious. *Was he a German sympathiser that lived in Schweyen?* thought Artur. *Why did he know about the German officers? Had he been listening to a German radio station on purpose?*

Artur made a hasty decision and quickly brought his pistol out of his pocket and pointed it at the man's face.

"Why were you listening to a German radio station this morning?" Artur demanded.

"What you will not realise," said the man, rather curtly, ignoring Artur's threatening approach with his pistol, "is that there is a distinct possibility that France will be invaded, and very soon. If that's the case, I want to get my family out of this area and down to my brother's place in Gray, near Dijon. If things got really bad after that, we could slip into Switzerland where my mother-in-law lives. I was listening to the radio for any hint that I could detect in the newsreader about Germany's intentions when I heard about the theft of the officers' vehicle in the night. The military thought it was likely to be by those who had been involved in the train derailment two days ago. The SS is on the hunt for two men. Any knowledge of their whereabouts should be immediately reported to the military commander in the area. Also, the location of the stolen vehicle and its driver was urgently needed."

"You do understand," said Artur, "that if I think you could still be a German informer and that you are lying, I will have no hesitation in shooting you. So tell me more about yourself and quickly too."

Just as the man was nearing the end of the account of his situation, both he and Artur were aware of the noise of another vehicle coming towards them and being driven very quickly. At this point, and with the man's attention being diverted to the oncoming car, Gerhart jumped into the passenger seat, picked up the man's rifle and pushed it into the well in front of him before the man could do anything.

"Do you recognise that vehicle?" said Artur. "If so, who's driving it?"

The man looked at Artur and his gun.

"Yes, I do. He has a small farm north of Schweyen very close to the border. He's a German Jew and his name is Kurt Bernstein. He is in his mid-fifties and lives with his mother. He has no children and he's not married. He usually minds his own business and will not stop, but might wave at me as he passes by."

Artur was starting to believe the man but he wasn't 100% sure. He wondered how much the man might tell anyone else of his encounter with Gerhart and him, although all that he had said sounded plausible.

The other vehicle passed the man and, just as he had predicted, Kurt waved to the man but didn't smile or slow down to see who the two men were with him. This seemed to convince Artur of the man's credibility; he relaxed and put his pistol away.

"OK. I think I believe you and your story but it might take a bit longer before I can trust you," said Artur. "We want you firstly to drive us to

Breidenbach and take us to a café where you are known. After a meal, you'll take us to Nancy, which is only 130 km from Breidenbach. You will pretend that you have known us for a long time, when we all knew each other in a village near Dijon – somewhere like Pesmes, for instance. We haven't seen each other for over ten years. Even though we will argue over who pays the bill, you will insist and here's something towards it. You will refer to us as André and Gérard. Is that understood? And what is your name?"

The man seemed to relax a little also and said his name was Phillipe. He agreed to Artur's instructions, but said he would have to get fuel in Breidenbach. He beckoned Artur to get in the back of his car and to leave Gerhart in the front. Artur gave him more money for the fuel, which he pocketed with a somewhat grumpy "Thanks". Nobody said anything until they saw the village sign saying 'Breidenbach'.

"Not far from here, on the left, is the 'Auberge du Village'," said Phillipe. "I am well known there as I go for a double espresso at least three times a week and this is one of my usual days. We will sit at the bar and you can order something to eat; the *plat du jour* is often good value for money. They might even have rabbit, if you like that sort of thing?"

Phillipe parked his car half on the pavement and they entered the café. There was a lot of chatter and Phillipe was greeted by nearly everyone: some he shook hands with and smiled at, a few others he embraced. He introduced André and Gérard to the manager and, just as Artur had instructed, he said that André and he were friends from some while back in Pesmes. The manager smiled and shook their hands, but Artur thought there was a suspicious look in the manager's eye. He started asking Artur questions about Pesmes, but Artur racked his brain and was able to respond quite satisfactorily. He asked Artur if he knew where the *Mairie* was, on the left or the right down Le Grand Rue, because he couldn't quite remember. Artur helped him by saying that he thought it was on the right, a little way before the church. The manager smiled and nodded his agreement, but Artur felt it was a trick question and that he knew where it was all along.

Meanwhile, Phillipe had been talking to some of his acquaintances and there was occasional laughter. Artur and Gerhart ordered the *plat du jour* with Artur choosing the rabbit as main and Gerhart the fish. They moved to a table by the window. When their meals arrived, Phillipe joined them. He asked them if they'd like another beer to go with their meal, but they declined with a smile. At the end of the meal, Artur and Phillipe discussed rather loudly about which of them was going to pay the bill; eventually Artur gave in and Phillipe went and paid it – just as they had planned. Artur and Gerhart went up to the bar, shook the manager's hand and thanked him for an excellent lunch. The manager's eyes followed them out of the door and, by moving to the left side of the bar, he could see them getting into the car. Artur and Gerhart were in the car first but, as Phillipe was about to get in, he turned and saw the manager looking his way. He gave the manager a smile and waved at him with three of his fingers clenched and the index finger and thumb sticking upright. The manager nodded in an understanding way. Artur saw none of this.

Phillipe drove a bit further into the village, turned into a petrol station and filled up with fuel. He took quite a time in the office and that concerned Artur, especially as there were no other cars in the garage. Eventually, Phillipe returned to the car and apologised for the delay. Apparently the man in the office had talked to him about the news bulletin that had mentioned there being a lot of troop movements in northern Germany and near the border with the Low Countries.

Having gone back on themselves for a few kilometres, they turned left and drove off towards Nousseviller and then Sarreguemines, just inside the border. It was just after Sarreguemines that Artur began to feel sick with a terrible pain in his stomach. *It was that bloody rabbit,* Artur thought to himself.

"Phillipe, can you pull over, I feel I'm going to be very sick in a few moments."

Almost as the car stopped, Artur was out of the door and depositing his lunch on the grass; several times he wretched his guts out.

"I reckon that man at the bar arranged for my food to be poisoned. I didn't like the way he looked at me anyway," said Artur.

"Are you feeling alright after your fish, Gérard?" said Artur to Gerhart.

"Yes, I'm fine, André. Maybe you were just a bit unfortunate and it wasn't deliberately poisoned."

"I think he's a Nazi sympathiser," said Phillipe. "I should have gone to the other bar, but I didn't think he'd give us a problem and certainly not anything like that."

"I think I feel a lot better for having got rid of that lunch so we had better press on for Nancy," said Artur. "I'll sit in the front, if you don't mind, Gérard? Are you OK with that Phillipe?"

Phillipe nodded his head in agreement. Once they were all in the car, they continued on their way towards Château-Salins, keeping to the minor roads at a leisurely pace. They had just passed Kreuzhof when they were suddenly overtaken by a large black car that seemed to be on a mission.

"According to my map, Phillipe," said Artur, "there's a road crossing this one in the centre of Grostenquin. Turn right there and then the first turning left; that road will then join the one we're on now, but stop at the T-junction before we turn into it. We'll wait there for ten minutes."

"Why do we need to do that?" said Phillipe. "There's no crime in a car overtaking us, is there?"

"You obviously didn't recognise the occupants," said Artur.

"The one in the passenger seat was the owner of the Auberge in Breidenbach, where we had lunch, or whatever you'd like to call it. I thought there was something untrustworthy about him when we were in his bar, and then there was the business of me being sick. The back seat occupant, I didn't recognise. There wasn't really enough time to get a good look at them, but they seemed to be very interested in us. I'm not sure who the driver was.

"Phillipe, do as I ask and stop for a full twenty minutes. We'll see if anything develops."

Phillipe stopped the car just before the T-junction, turned off the ignition and looked at his watch. Artur got out and walked to the junction. He half hid himself as he looked to his right so he could see any vehicle coming from the village of Bertring. He stood in position for a good ten minutes, and then wandered back to the car. Just as he was about to get back into Philippe's car, there was the noise of a car coming from Bertring that sounded as though it was being driven very carefully in second gear.

"I seriously think the car that overtook us contained people who were looking for us and, as we didn't proceed through Bertring, they have come back looking for us," said Artur.

"What do you want to do now, André?" asked Phillipe in an anxious tone.

Artur explained that as soon as the car, if, of course, it was the one that overtook them, has passed the end of the road and round the bend into Grostenquin, he should edge out into the road, turn right and make speed for Morhange. Then, just after the road goes over the railway line, he should bear to the right and then first left so that they would be facing the main road again. He should then wait for any possible further developments.

The large black car slowly passed the road they were parked in. Artur just saw the colour and size of the car, but fortunately the occupants wouldn't have had a good siting of them because a delivery truck passed in the opposite direction and obscured their view.

Phillipe moved the car out to the road. As they looked left, they saw the black car go round the bend into Grostenquin.

"We were very lucky with that delivery vehicle interrupting their view of us," said Artur. "But once they've searched around the Grostenquin area, I'm sure they'll realise that we've duped them and they'll be after us again in double quick time. They might even have set up a road block with some accomplices after Morhange. Remember also, we are still not very far from the German border."

"Let's make a run for it, Phillipe. Put your foot down once we're through Bérig-Vintrange. According to the map, there are a couple of good long stretches of road totalling about 25 km before we get to Château-Salins," Artur instructed.

Phillipe went as fast as he could, but after about ten minutes, he saw the same black car in his mirror that they had seen drive slowly past the end of the road in Grostenquin.

"I think we're being followed," said Phillipe, "and the car is catching us up really quickly."

Artur looked round and saw the black car gaining on them. He scrambled into the back seat and told Gerhart to get in the front with Phillipe. By this time, the black car was within 50 metres of Phillipe's car.

"When I give the signal, slam your foot hard on the brake but try to keep the car going in a straight line," said Artur. "The driver of the black car is likely to try and avoid hitting us and, if we take him by surprise, he will either try to overtake us or swerve sideways, and perhaps go off the road. It very much depends on how quick his reactions are. I will try and get a shot at one of his tyres.

"Are you ready, Phillipe? On the count of three, brake hard then accelerate away. One, two, three," Artur boomed out.

Phillipe did as instructed and, apart from a slight wobble, he kept the car straight. The black car swerved to avoid colliding with the back of Phillipe's car and was almost sideways on. Artur leaned out of the window and took several shots at the front tyre with his pistol. The tyre exploded, causing the car to become unstable; it rolled over, left the road and its speed took it into the ditch, bonnet first. By this time, Phillipe had accelerated away from the stricken car, but he'd been looking in the mirror for too long. His car was half across the oncoming carriageway and, as he looked forward again, he saw a truck coming round the bend and directly towards him with its horn going continuously.

"Oh, shit!" shouted Phillipe, as he wrestled with the steering wheel. Phillipe's car was now on the wrong side of the road, but the alert truck driver saw a possible opportunity of going on the wrong side of Phillipe and turned the wheel to his left. There was then a terrible, metallic screeching sound as the two vehicles scraped past each other at speed, ripping off the passenger side wing mirror of Phillipe's car. Artur had been looking out of the back window on the passenger's side at the black car's graceful drop into the ditch when he suddenly realised what was happening in front. He just managed to bring his head into the car as the two vehicles scraped past each other.

Much to Artur's surprise and relief, Phillipe had now very deftly steered the car onto the correct side of the road and had brought it to a halt to gather his composure. He looked in his mirror and saw the truck stop near the black car in the ditch. Two of the men in the black car were struggling to get out of the car but it appeared that the driver had been injured. When the truck driver came over to offer help, one of the men drew a pistol and shot him. The other man, with a great deal of difficulty, dragged the driver out of the window towards the truck. Artur thought the man who fired the pistol was the manager of the Auberge, but he didn't recognise the other men.

"Are you alright, Gérard?" said Artur. "Let's face it, you were closer to the truck than you would normally wish to be!"

"I've felt better but I'll survive!" retorted Gerhart.

"Well done, Phillipe, for avoiding the truck, but the fun isn't over yet. Sorry about the state of your lovely Citroën Traction Avant, but let's get the hell out of here as fast as we can. This car of yours ought to be able to outrun the truck, even after they've got it turned round. The only problem might be that, if they get near enough to us, they'll probably start shooting at your car or ramming it."

Phillipe had drawn a few deep breaths and set off again, paying great attention to his position on the road and looking out for oncoming vehicles. They went through Morhange unhindered, although a few people on the pavement pointed at the damage to the car as they went past. After the village, the road went through countryside and was quite straight. Artur kept looking back through the rear window for the truck that he felt sure would be following them, but he didn't see it. After about six minutes or so, Phillipe said with some alarm in his voice that the steering was beginning to feel rather heavy and was starting to pull the car to the right.

"We've probably got a slow puncture," said Artur. "Do you have a spare and a jack, Phillipe?"

Phillipe replied that he had.

"If you can manage it, Phillipe, according to the map, the road skirts Dalhain and then you'll see to your right a small wooded area. There should be a track off this road and, if that's the case, turn up it and then left into the woods. There should be sufficient shelter for us to change the tyre without being noticed by anyone coming along the road."

Phillipe slowed the car down a little and did as instructed. He managed to turn into the woods, but the steering was getting very heavy. They all got out of the car and before starting on the punctured wheel, they inspected the damage to the passenger side of the car.

"Oh, my poor car!" said Phillipe. "I haven't had it very long. I bought it with some money left to me by my Granny, who died just under two years ago."

"Never mind, Phillipe, it can be mended, I'm sure. Let's get this wheel changed and be on our way."

They struggled getting the flat tyre off because the car was too low for the jack to go under. Two of them just managed to lift the front of the car high enough for Phillipe to get the jack underneath. They changed the wheels and put all the tools they had used back in the boot. Just as they were doing so, they heard a truck coming fast along the road from the direction of Morhange.

"I bet that's them," said Artur.

At the same time, a police van went quickly past in the opposite direction. Artur just caught a glimpse of the truck and he was sure it was the same one. He didn't see the occupants so he hoped they hadn't seen them or Phillipe's car in the woods.

"I don't think they will come back this way looking for us. Apart from anything else, someone might have seen what they did to the truck driver and with the police being at the scene any minute, they wouldn't risk it. So, as it's the middle of the afternoon and after all that excitement, I suggest we get as comfortable as we can in the car and close our eyes for half an hour or so."

The others agreed with Artur; they got into the car and settled down for a well-earned rest.

Chapter 12
Saturday, 3rd of June 1939

Andrew enjoyed the weekend at home with his wife's sister and brother-in-law, and they helped a lot round the garden. On Sunday, his wife had started to get in the habit of feeding the baby and then lying out in the warm, early summer sun. Her sister and brother-in-law had left before lunch. In the afternoon, Andrew went to his study and opened the sealed envelope that Peter had given him.

This shouldn't be too bad, he thought, *the locations of most of the training establishments are not that far away so I should be able to get home easily afterwards.*

After reading most of the material, he put it all back in the envelope. His desk had a drawer with a lock on it so Andrew put it there with his other personal documents for safe keeping. He went outside and found his wife at the end of the garden, dozing.

"Hallo, dear," she said. "Could you see if the baby is alright and not in the sunshine, please?"

Andrew saw that his son was awake so he picked him up out of the mobile, wicker-work cot and held him to him, making cooing noises and tickling him under the chin.

"I've just thought, Andrew, do you know where the camera is? I'd like to take one of you holding our son."

"It's in the lounge, on the table by the window. Here, you hold him while I go and fetch it."

Andrew was back in a moment. He put his son in his arms again and his wife took a couple of snaps with the house in the background.

"They should be nice photos for the album. I'll finish the film during the week and get them developed."

Andrew started to wonder how many more relaxing weekends there might be similar to this one, especially with the possible imminence of a war with Germany. He had read only two weeks ago that Germany and Fascist Italy had ratified their alliance in Berlin and it was labelled by the

Italians as the Pact of Steel. The German Foreign Minister had also signed a Non-Aggression Pact with Estonia and Latvia.

"Shall I get some tea, dear?" said Andrew, trying to take his mind off a possible war situation. "I think I noticed some rather nice chocolate cake in the fridge earlier on. I'm sure you would like some, you're quite partial to chocolate, aren't you?"

"That's a good idea, Andrew; I could do with some tea and cake."

Andrew disappeared into the house and found all the things he needed for tea outside. He cut two hearty pieces of cake and even managed to find a couple of napkins.

They enjoyed the tea outside, and there were some occasional gurgling sounds coming from the cot that amused them both. Soon after the tea things had been cleared away by Andrew, his wife took Alfred indoors to change him and prepare to feed him. Andrew came back out into the garden. He saw his neighbour in his garden and they exchanged a few pleasantries about the weather and Andrew's new-born child.

After a very enjoyable but different weekend, Andrew resumed office work on Monday and mentioned to his manager that he would need to take Friday afternoon off in order to have a medical. As this discussion was in the privacy of his manager's office, they could openly talk about Andrew's entry into the Intelligence Service and how he had his manager's blessing.

On Tuesday, Andrew slipped out of the office and went straight to see Charles in his St. James' office. When he arrived and pressed the bell, he was surprised that it wasn't Helen, but some older woman who let him in. Andrew tried not to look too crest fallen but when he was in Charles' office and after signing all the papers – in triplicate – he asked where the lovely Helen was, only to be told that she'd got the day off to visit her sick brother somewhere in Suffolk.

On Friday, immediately after lunch, Andrew took a train to Clapham Junction then a taxi to Dr Freeman's surgery. He only had to wait five minutes before he was called into his room. He was greeted by a man a bit shorter and rounder than himself, with a round smiling face and a full black moustache. His greasy hair was also dark with a deep parting.

"Hallo, Andrew. Please come in and sit down next to my desk. Now, I've been asked to give you a full medical and send off the results to this company," he said and showed Andrew the address, but it meant nothing to him.

"To start with, I want you to strip down to your underpants and we'll take things from there."

Dr Freemen went through everything very thoroughly, noting all the results on the form provided.

"Well, Andrew, I can honestly say that I've not met many men more fit than you and your eyesight is incredible, not to mention your lung capacity. I will have no hesitation in proclaiming you in A1 condition."

"Thank you, doctor, that's really good to hear."

Dr Freeman signed all the forms and asked Andrew to countersign them. The doctor then completed his invoice and placed everything in the self-addressed envelope provided.

"I think that's about everything, unless you have any questions?"

Andrew said that he had none and ended by thanking him for his thoroughness and for finding nothing untoward wrong with him.

"It's a pleasure, Andrew, and I wish you all the best. This medical test must be for something very special as I've not been asked to conduct such a series of tests on anyone for some years."

Andrew shook the doctor's hand and left his surgery for home. He was well pleased with the preliminary results that the doctor gave him, but not really surprised. He knew in his heart of hearts that he was in good shape. He managed to get home about the same time as usual, so he didn't have any explaining to do to his wife as to where he had been.

On Saturday, he rang Brian and asked if he was available for a beer at lunch time the next day. They arranged to meet at the Crooked Billet this time as they weren't very well known there and he had something special to talk to Brian about.

They both arrived at the pub's car park at exactly the same time. Brian jumped out of his car and came over to Andrew.

"My goodness, your man has done an excellent job in repairing your car. When did you get it back?"

"Oh, a few weeks ago now, not long after my son was born."

Brian wandered around the car, touching the panels and running his hands along the paint work. He stood at the front and looked down the side panels and drew in his breath.

"Wow, Andrew, that's as good as new. You must be so pleased with the result. Did it cost the earth?"

"Yes, I am very pleased with how it's turned out and no, it didn't cost as much as I thought it might."

They went inside and Andrew bought a pint for each of them and they went outside again into the garden.

"The main reason for meeting is that we've been thinking about Godparents for my son, Alfred Frank Williams, and we'd very much like it if you would agree to be his Godfather."

"My dear, Andrew, nothing would give me greater pleasure. I should be delighted."

"That's settled then. My wife and I are also pleased that you have accepted. The second thing is that I have finally had my medical test for the Service, signed all the papers plus the Official Secrets Act forms. I am, for all intents and purposes, a member of the Intelligence Service."

"What excellent news. I was going to tell you that I had received the forms and returned them duly completed and signed as your referee. Where do you go from here?"

"I have to arrange training courses over the next few weeks, or even months, in various disciplines. Fortunately I don't have to travel too far in the early stages, so I should be able to keep my wife in the dark as to what I'm doing.

"By the way, you no doubt heard that Germany and Italy have endorsed their alliance in Berlin. The Italians call it the Pact of Steel. What do you make of that?"

"I think we are one big step nearer to being at war with them. It seems as though we have no alternative."

"I agree. The only thing that worries me is: are we properly prepared for an all-out war? After all, everyone knows that Germany has been rearming since 1936, making planes, tanks and sophisticated armour under the guise of something else, and denying it. We wouldn't stand a hope if we were invaded."

"I am totally with you on that, Andrew, but if we have the Empire and US resources on our side, we should be able to beat them, don't you think?"

"I'm not sure about the Americans. Look how late they left it to come in on our side in the 1914-1918 war. They always think that Europe is such a long way from them that they can't be bothered to get involved. I reckon they would only involve themselves if any of their territories was attacked."

"You could be right, Andrew, but I hope you're wrong. I really do. Anyway, so much for our thoughts on the way of the world; let's drink a toast, once again, to your newly arrived son, Alfred."

They stayed for another twenty minutes, talking about various things of common interest and then parted for their respective homes. Andrew got home in good time for lunch and it was the first time since his wife had come home with Alfred that she had made the main Sunday meal. His son was in the wicker cot in the garden having already had his lunch. They sat in the garden in the afternoon next to the cot and Andrew tried to contemplate his next move with the Service, the future of his family and that of his country.

Chapter 13
Thursday, 4ᵗʰ of April 1940

Artur was the first to wake and, to his great surprise, he found it was after 5 o'clock; he couldn't believe it. He got out of the car and inspected the tyres; they all seemed OK. He wandered down to the road and stood behind a tree. He looked left and right for a good five minutes and only saw a few vehicles, mostly going towards Morhange. He wondered if the body had been identified and if the car had been taken from the ditch to a garage nearby.

"André, where are you?" shouted Phillipe, who was now out of the car but looking towards the woods.

"Keep your voice down, Phillipe. I'm just by the road watching for any suspicious vehicles."

Phillipe turned around quickly and walked with some haste over to Artur. Gerhart was also awake and out of the car, stretching himself. When they were both beside him, Artur told them that they should stay by the woods until it was dark, just to be on the safe side. Phillipe didn't like the idea as he was supposed to be back in Schweyen by 7:30 p.m.

"My instructions were that you take us to Nancy, to which you agreed. I've given you more than enough money for the petrol, so what's the problem? Because of what we have encountered this afternoon, you might not even be back in Schweyen until sometime tomorrow, but it's only about 50 km to Nancy from here."

Phillipe tried to argue with Artur, but he got nowhere. Artur told them that they would leave at 6 o'clock and, if there were no more hold ups, they could be in Nancy by about 7 o'clock.

During the waiting time, they studied the map that Artur had taken from the bag and they considered places where they might be ambushed between Château-Salins and Nancy.

"Unless they know we are going to Nancy, they are very likely to be waiting for us either in the village of Château-Salins, or this side of the village," said Artur. "Do you both agree?

"The only way they would know is if you said anything, Phillipe, to the Auberge manager or the man at the petrol station."

Phillipe fidgeted a little and looked down at his shoes rather sheepishly, indicating to Artur that he must have said something to someone.

"So who did you say something to and what did you say, Phillipe?"

"Well, I didn't really say anything to anyone."

"What do you mean, you didn't really say anything?" retorted Artur. "Just remember, Phillipe, we only need your car, we don't really need you so you had better tell us the truth."

As he said that, Artur pulled his pistol out of his coat pocket and cocked it.

"It all happened so quickly, André. The man at the garage was filling up the tank with petrol and he asked me why I needed it filled to the top. It's a bit unusual as I normally only have twenty or thirty litres. I then just happened to say that I needed to go to Nancy."

"That's it then, Phillipe. You told him exactly where we were going. Is he a friend of the bar manager?"

"Of course, everyone in a small village like Breidenbach knows everyone else, particularly those running small businesses. I'm really sorry," he said pleadingly. "I really didn't think, it wasn't deliberate."

"OK! The damage is done, but I bet you anything you like, that he phoned the bar manager and told him your destination. Then, when those men came to the bar asking after Gérard and me, and the bar manager, being a German sympathiser, set off in pursuit with them. It all fits together now."

"As I have already said, I'm really very sorry, André. What should we do now?"

"For God's sake, stop bleating Phillipe. Pull yourself together man."

Artur put his pistol's safety catch on and returned it into his coat pocket. There was a noticeable expression of relief on Phillipe's face.

"Look, it's close to 6:30 p.m. now, so let's get on our way and hope we don't encounter any more problems before we get to Nancy."

They all got into the car with Artur sitting in the passenger seat again. He was watching Phillipe carefully, but he didn't think he would try anything silly, certainly not for a while anyway. They came out of the wooded area to the road and, as it was cloudy, it was starting to get dark. No traffic had gone in either direction for about half an hour. They turned right towards Château-Salins and picked up a good speed. They drove carefully just past the centre of the village, looking for the sign to Nancy that should go off to the right. There was a slight air of nervousness in the car as they looked for the turning, with Artur occasionally turning his head to the left for the sight of the truck that might be awaiting their arrival. He was hoping that the two and half hours that had passed since they last saw the truck might have made them give up the chase, but he knew he could not assume that.

To the relief of all of them, they had successfully negotiated the route through Château-Salins. They allowed themselves to relax as they headed for Nancy that should now only take them about forty minutes. They were approaching Champenoux and the fairly tight bends in the village centre when they were flagged down by someone waving a very bright torch. Artur reached into his pocket for his pistol and cocked it in preparation for a problem. He noticed a truck across their carriageway and was sure it was the one whose driver was shot. There were two men by the truck and then there was the flag waver, who looked like the bar manager. Gerhart had acted quickly and had tucked himself down behind the front seats and covered himself with the rug that had been on the back seat.

"Get out of your vehicle and get your hands up," said the bar manager, who didn't appear to have a gun, but pointed the torch into Phillipe's eyes.

Phillipe jumped out of his car with his arms aloft, but Artur waited to be dragged out. The man came round to Artur's door, pulled it open and tried to grab Artur by the scruff of his neck. Artur was having none of it and stayed in his seat. The man called for assistance and one of the other two men came forward. It was difficult for the two of them to get a hold of Artur's clothing or his arm as he was wriggling and struggling in his seat. Artur wasn't sure if the other men were Germans, but he was certain that he wasn't going to get captured.

Artur relaxed a bit and allowed himself to be dragged a little way out of the car head first. He had managed to get his feet against the driver's seat that was further forward than his and, as his legs were bent, he suddenly, and with all his strength, launched himself out of the car. This surprised the two men and they fell to the ground in a heap with Artur on top of them. He put his pistol against the head of the bar manager.

At this point, Gerhart was out of the car and pointing his pistol at the man next to the truck some 20 metres away.

Almost at the same time, Gerhart and Artur shouted at the men.

"Don't try any funny business or all of you will be shot," said Artur in French, as Gerhart walked quickly towards the man by the truck. By this time, Phillipe had dropped his arms to his side and gone to fetch his rifle from his car.

"Right, you men, why do you have an interest in us?" said Artur, now standing, with his foot on the neck of one of the men by the side of the car and who was on top of the bar manager.

The man near to Artur spoke to them in German saying that they had been ordered by the Gestapo to find them because of their possible involvement in the train derailment on the line from Stuttgart a few days ago, and the abduction of the German officers' car and driver from outside the village *gasthaus* east of Karlsruhe.

"What makes you think we were involved in such a daring act?" asked Artur, this time speaking in German.

"Your travels have been noticed by many people along the way and have been relayed to the Gestapo. We are acting on their behalf. We were told to find you, capture you and take you back into Germany for interrogation. They eventually found the officers' car and the driver, and he told us you had crossed the border into France in the direction of Schweyen."

Just as Artur was thinking of what to do next, he hadn't noticed that Phillipe had slowly come around the back of the car towards Artur.

"Drop your gun, André, or I'll have no option but to shoot you."

Artur turned to face Phillipe and saw intent in his eyes. He was no longer the bleating individual any more, but a determined person with plenty of spirit. Just as Artur was about to drop his pistol, Gerhart had turned and taken a shot at Phillipe, who screamed and grasped at his wounded shoulder as his rifle flew into the air. Knowing that he'd saved the situation for the time being, Gerhart turned his pistol back onto the man next to him.

A couple of cars had come slowly past the back of the truck away from Champenoux, the occupants staring and trying to understand the situation. Gerhart waved them on their way and they reluctantly obeyed his gesturing. At the same time, he kept his pistol pointing at the man, fully alert to the fact that he might try to disarm him.

Artur ordered the two men out from under his foot to walk to the roadside and sit down with their hands behind their heads. He told Gerhart to search the man at the truck for any firearms or knives and to get him to join the other two men at the roadside. Gerhart was then instructed to go and pick up Phillipe's rifle and to search the rest of the men. A pistol was retrieved from each of the Germans and a pistol plus a knife from the bar manager.

Artur turned his attention to Phillipe.

"Have you got any rope in the boot of your car?"

"Yes, there are several pieces."

"Gérard," said Artur in French, "while I keep watch over these men, get the ropes and tie their arms behind their backs. Once you've done that, remove their footwear and throw them as far as you can into the field behind them. Phillipe, regardless of your injuries, you are to sit next to these men and also have your arms bound behind you."

It was a painful process for Phillipe, but after a struggle, his arms were tied behind him. When all was done, Artur manoeuvred the truck so it was parked by the roadside facing the village. He got out of the cab and shot the two nearside tyres and put the keys in his pocket.

"Gérard, if it's alright with you, I'll drive and you can navigate. Now that all these men know we were intending to go to Nancy, we had better change our plans and head for Epinal," said Artur, loud enough for them all to hear.

"Thanks for the use of your car, Phillipe, but if you hadn't been so foolish in telling the garage man that you were going to Nancy, we wouldn't have had all this trouble and you wouldn't have had a wounded shoulder."

Artur and Gerhart got into the car with their unexpected arsenal of weaponry in the boot and drove through the village towards Nancy.

"Our destination, Gerhart, will not be Epinal but Neufchâteau. We ought to be there in less than one and a half hours. We'll find a small hotel for the night. I'm sure we'll get a well-earned rest, especially if we have a nice meal. What time is it now?"

"It's after 7:30 p.m. If it takes one and a half hours to get to Neufchâteau, it might be too late to get a meal and a room."

"You are right. We'll have to take a chance and stop on the west side of Nancy for the night. What are your thoughts, Gerhart?"

"I agree," said Gerhart, studying the map with his torch. "Let's make for Toul. There should be an Auberge or a small hotel, and we could make it before 8:15 p.m. with any luck. We also ought to think about getting the tyre repaired whilst we're in Toul, don't you think?"

"Well remembered, Gerhart old boy. We should get it fixed tomorrow before we drive any further."

They made good progress through Nancy, even though Artur found changing gear a bit difficult with the lever coming out of the centre of the facia. They found Toul without any difficulty and headed for the centre of town. The centre was built in a circle, with shops, cafés and a few banks round the outside and a fountain in the middle. They saw Le Central Hôtel to their right; its outside lights were still on and they could see a few people in the restaurant. Artur parked the car outside – leaving Gerhart to keep watch – and went in to the reception. The receptionist was very obliging and was able to offer a twin room overlooking the town centre as requested by Artur, and, as a bonus, he could park the car round the back for no extra charge. He was told that the kitchen closed at 8:30 p.m. so if they wanted a meal, they would have to be quick. Artur thanked the lady, took the room key and went to the car.

"We're in luck, Gerhart, and we can also park the car round the back and out of sight of any nosey parkers!"

They quickly put the car in the parking area round the back and out of sight, so nobody would notice the terrible dents and scratches to the nearside of the car. They put all their possessions in the boot and went smartly into the restaurant, which was now almost empty. They enjoyed a relaxing meal – all the time speaking in French – and retired to bed just after 10 o'clock.

Chapter 14
Tuesday, 6th of June 1939

Andrew received a letter at the office that was marked CONFIDENTIAL and ADDRESSEE ONLY. He was fairly sure it would give him a list of dates for the first three or four courses that he was to attend as part of his training. He hoped they would be spread out over the next two or three months but, knowing the Service, it will more likely be within the next two.

He read the attached letter and then saw the list of dates. The first course was at Bisley for weapons training in the middle of June, the second course was at Aldershot in Surrey for fitness training in early July and the third was in southern Hampshire a few weeks afterwards for map reading, radio communications and Morse code. The letter also mentioned unarmed combat and training of 'endurance under interrogation' for August with no dates scheduled yet.

Andrew read everything again very thoroughly during his lunchtime, and he couldn't help himself thinking over the dates during the rest of the afternoon. He knew he needed to speak to his manager about attending the courses and he'd do that sometime tomorrow. He left the office on time, and he thought he would somehow have to find a way of coding the dates and courses in his diary, just in case someone started looking through it.

"Hallo dear, I'm home," he said loudly as he went through the front door. There was a distant voice coming from the kitchen, but it wasn't his wife's so he wondered what was going on. He went through to the kitchen to find Barbara standing over his wife who was sitting on a chair near the kitchen table.

"Is there a problem, Barbara?"

"Oh hallo, Andrew. Your wife has had a fall outside as she was carrying Alfred back from the wicker cot only about an hour ago. Alfred is fine but your wife is rather shaken. She phoned me so I called round straight away. She's had a cup of tea and fed the baby, but she says she feels a bit sore round her tummy. I think it all started with her being out in the sun and it was rather hotter than she was expecting. You know how much she dislikes the heat."

"You are so kind to have come round, Barbara. We're very lucky that you live so near; you always seem to be available too!"

Andrew gave his wife a hug and asked if she was feeling a bit better and was there anything else that she needed.

"No, thank you, dear. Alfred is upstairs so perhaps you could bring him down to me and I'll give him a bit more food shortly. Barbara, many thanks for coming over. Now that Andrew's home you may leave if you like."

Barbara said her goodbyes and after Andrew had seen her to the door, he went upstairs to fetch Alfred only to find that he was asleep, very peaceful and quite oblivious of everything. Needless to say, Andrew gently picked Alfred up and carried him downstairs. He was still asleep when he got back to the kitchen and he handed the baby over to his wife.

"Would you like me to make some supper, or have you already prepared something during the day?"

"As you rightly guessed, I made something during the day and it's in the larder covered with a lid. It'll need warming up, and I bought some vegetables when I was out this morning. As you know, Edith doesn't come on Tuesdays but I called her this morning and she came round for an hour. I was able to leave little Alfred in her capable hands."

"Are you sure you should be out on your own so soon after having the baby? After all, it wasn't an easy birth and you were in the hospital for a week before being allowed home."

"You are right, but I just needed to get out into town for a bit of a change. The doctor called last week and he said I was recovering well and that I could drive if I felt up to it."

"But please, don't go overdoing things, you don't want any complications to arise. He was only born about three weeks ago. Maybe it was a combination of the sunshine and the effort of going out that caused you to fall. Do take good care of yourself."

Nothing further was said, and so Andrew got on with preparing supper while his wife dealt with the baby. Andrew suddenly remembered that he'd left his briefcase in the hall so he went and put it in his study behind a chair. Max saw him coming and thought he was going to take him for a walk, but instead he let him in the garden to go round on his own. He would call the dog in later just before they sat down to supper.

Andrew went to the office the next day, but was rather concerned about his wife as she'd had a restless night due to some bruising to her side as a result of her fall. He arranged to phone her before lunch to find out if the doctor had been able to visit her. She said that he hadn't but was expected in the afternoon. When Andrew got home, he was pleased to hear that there was nothing really to worry about and the doctor had given her some pain killers that would help her sleep better at night. If things hadn't got better after the weekend, she was to call him again as she might need to have an X-ray at the hospital.

On Saturday, as it was a nice sunny day, he thought he would take a run out in his car, and have a pint at the Red Lion and hopefully he might find Anne on duty. He'd cleared it with his wife and said he would be back for a late lunch. He felt he needed some air to try and think through the courses he was going to be attending during the next few weeks.

The good weather had brought a lot of people out and the pub was heaving. He knew he wouldn't get much time to speak to Anne, but he went in with some hope. It took him a while to reach the bar but fortunately the barman saw Andrew and came over to him and greeted him warmly with a firm handshake.

"Good to see you again. How are you? I hear you are now a father; how are the mother and the baby boy?"

Andrew was a bit surprised to think the barman knew so much about his life, but he told him that all was fine and that all his family and friends were very pleased for the Williams. He ordered a pint and when the barman had his back turned he looked around for Anne but couldn't see her. The pint duly arrived.

"You're very busy today. I suppose the good weather has brought everyone out?" said Andrew.

"Can't complain; it's all good for business. If things get crazy in Europe in the next few months, business will no doubt take a bit of a nose dive."

The barman excused himself from further conversation as he needed to serve other people, so Andrew went away from the bar area towards the garden. As he was going through the door, he noticed Anne coming towards him with a handful of plates and cutlery. His heart gave a bit of a flutter and he smiled broadly at her. He held the door open for her and she seemed to deliberately brush against him as she went past.

"As you can see, we're very busy today, but I should be able to speak to you in about fifteen minutes," she said with a broad smile

She disappeared inside and Andrew felt elated as he wandered over to the only vacant table in the sunny part of the garden. He sat down and thought about his first course and his trip to Bisley in a week on Tuesday. He wondered how he should get there, but really the only way was by train up to Clapham, then down to Woking and a cab to the shooting range. He didn't have to be there till 9:30 a.m. so he should manage it quite easily.

He was mulling over the different types of shooting that he might have to be tested on when a gentle voice interrupted his thoughts.

"Hallo Andrew, how are you? You haven't been around here for a few weeks so is everything OK?"

Andrew stood up when Anne arrived and they smiled at each other warmly.

"Everything is just fine, thank you. I have been meaning to come here to see you but it's been a bit hectic over the last month, what with one thing and another. Anyway, I'm here now and I'm pleased to see you again."

"Look," said Anne, "I haven't got much time today and I expect you have to leave fairly soon too, but I don't work every day here so perhaps we could meet up after you finish work one evening?"

Andrew thought quickly and asked her if Tuesday next week would be a possibility.

"Yes, I think that would be good for me. Where would you like to meet? Is there anything in particular that you would like to do?"

"Shall I meet you where I dropped you off to meet your boyfriend a while back, say 6 o'clock?"

"I look forward to that. Do you want my phone number in case you have a problem?"

Anne wrote her phone number on one of the slips of papers she had in the pocket of her waitress' uniform.

"That's settled then."

Andrew stood up and gave her a broad smile. He gave her a kiss on her cheek and they said goodbye.

Gosh, he thought, *I really hope I don't have to stay too long at Bisley that Tuesday; perhaps I should drive and then I won't have to come back via Clapham which otherwise might take up valuable time to get to her place by 6 o'clock*

Andrew downed his pint and drove home. He wasn't late and as it was still a sunny day, they had a light lunch in the garden. His wife was still in a bit of discomfort, but certainly the pain killers were helping her to sleep better at night. Alfred, of course, slept through the night now so he didn't add to the problems.

"Now that we've agreed on the Godparents, don't you think we ought to look at possible dates for Alfred's Baptism?"

"I'll get my diary, dear, and see if there's anything brewing that we should avoid."

"There ought not to be," said has wife, rather crossly. "It's going to be a weekend anyway."

Andrew got up from his chair and went inside to fetch his diary. His wife already had hers so she had presumably prepared for this discussion beforehand.

"I suppose we ought to go for a weekend at the end of July or early August," she said. "So how about either the 30th or 6th? We would obviously have to check with the vicar as well as the family, and Brian, before firming a date."

"They are both fine for me, so could you call the vicar tomorrow and I'll speak to Brian this evening. We should really alert the family this evening too, just in case some are taking a holiday. I'll speak to mother this evening and you could call your sister and brother-in-law, plus your brother and sister-in-law from Lancashire? That would then cover the main people."

"That's a good idea, dear. I would like to ask Barbara, especially as she's been so helpful to us recently, and one or two others of my particular friends, like Pat. No doubt you'd like to ask Peter and his wife, Doreen, plus Jack and Margaret? Plus Edith, to help the caterers and tidy up afterwards."

"Yes, that would be nice. They're always fun to have around. I suppose you want a tea back here afterwards?"

"Yes, I really would. If it's not a nice day, we can always come indoors. Let's hope the vicar is available for a 3 o'clock service. I will phone the caterers that did a Baptism tea for Pat about a week ago and see what they can offer."

It seemed to Andrew that most of the ideas had been discussed and agreed upon. Early in the evening, he phoned Brian; he and his wife were available for both dates and would pencil them in his diary. Andrew's wife's father was free for both as were her sister and brother-in-law and they would bring father down with them. Andrew's mother was away, according to her live-in maid and wouldn't be back until the middle of the week.

That all done, they sat down for a drink and sandwiches and cheese, once the baby had been fed and put to bed.

Chapter 15
Friday, 5ᵗʰ of April 1940

They had a really good night's sleep after a somewhat exhilarating day and awoke feeling very refreshed. The breakfast was simple and typically French, but was more than adequate after such a good meal the previous evening. Artur asked the man on reception about a garage to get the tyre mended and was told there was one on the road to Colombey-les-Belles, going south out of Toul. The wireless was on in the reception area and, as it was a news bulletin, Artur stayed for a moment to listen to it with the receptionist.

"Is this a local news bulletin or the national one?" enquired Artur.

"The international news has already been broadcast, so this is now the local one from Nancy."

'Sometime during yesterday afternoon, a car was found in a ditch near Champenoux and a man's body lay near it; apparently he had been shot,' said the newsreader. *'If anyone has witnessed anything or knows anything about this incident, would they please get in touch with the central police station in Nancy.'*

"My goodness," said Artur, "with all that's going on in Europe at present, is this incident really worthy of being broadcast?"

"We're quite parochial in this part of France and, not being far from the German border, this sort of incident could be related to the German war effort. By the way, didn't you say you'd driven from the east of Nancy to get here? Maybe you saw something near where the newsman mentioned?"

"As it happens, I don't recall saying anything about where we'd come from. In any case, I wasn't asked when I registered for the room. Incidentally, what did the international news mention? Presumably, Germany's intentions to take over more of Europe?"

Artur was successful in diverting the subject from the local news as the receptionist looked very serious, tutted a few times and nodded his head.

"I think trouble is brewing for France and probably some of the Scandinavian countries too. The German army and the Luftwaffe are just too powerful for the British and French Expeditionary Forces. If Germany invaded the Low Countries and entered France from that direction, the British Forces could be surrounded and might have to surrender."

"That's a very good point," said Artur. "That could be a disaster for over 400,000 allied men."

On that rather worrying note, Artur decided they ought to be on their way. He expressed his thanks and said he would find the garage to try and get his tyre repaired. The receptionist bid farewell and wished him a good journey.

During all this, Gerhart had gone to the car with the suitcase and the bag, and was waiting for Artur to arrive. He'd looked round the car and thought the damage to the passenger side was worse now that he'd seen it in daylight. At least the passenger door opened and closed alright, even if there was no wing mirror. The rear bumper was drawn back at a bit of an angle and the rear nearside tyre had a few scratches on it, probably from the trucks bumper as it went past.

Artur came round the corner to the Hotel's parking area and saw Gerhart carrying out an inspection.

"Do you think we'll make it to Dijon, or should we 'acquire' another car?" said Artur with a glint in his eye.

"I think we should be OK but we ought to watch the rear nearside tyre and not go too fast. The man at the garage who might fix the punctured tyre will no doubt notice the tyre in question and recommend we buy a new one."

"He can recommend all he likes. We'll just have to be careful. In any case, when we get the tyre in the boot fixed and if a problem develops with the rear tyre, we'll be able to change it."

No more was said about the rear tyre, so they got into the car and drove out of Toul towards Colombey. Gerhart was driving and Artur was looking out for the garage. He easily saw it and told Gerhart to drive towards the entrance of the maintenance area where there were a number of cars waiting. Artur jumped out of the car and went into the office where a man was seated and who was on the telephone. Artur waited, and when the conversation had finished after a couple of minutes, he smiled at the man. He explained that he'd been recommended to call in by the man at the Central Hotel in Toul and that he had a spare tyre with a puncture. The man went out of the office towards the car and he noticed the damage to the nearside panels.

"My goodness," he said. "What happened there? You're lucky the front wheel wasn't damaged as well."

"You are right, of course, but it's the tyre in the boot that I would like to get fixed, if possible, please."

Artur was just about to open the boot when he remembered that all the guns, knives and hand grenades were in there and he wasn't sure if they were properly stowed in the bags.

"Just a minute, I'll get the key," said Artur.

Artur went to the driver's door and as he opened it, he whispered to Gerhart about the arms being in the boot, as well as the flat tyre.

"It's alright," said Gerhart. "While you were paying the hotel bill, I put everything in the bags. They will not be seen. The wheel is on top of the bags and can be lifted out without affecting anything else."

"Phew! That's good thinking, Gerhart; saved by the bell, as they say!"

Artur took the keys from the ignition and pretended to unlock the boot with one of them.

"There it is," said Artur, pointing inside the boot and lifting the wheel out for the man to inspect.

The man bent down and ran his hand round the wall of the tyre, both the inside and outside. He then slowly rolled the wheel along and looked at the tread with a great deal of care. Suddenly, he stopped and smiled to Artur.

"There, the usual sort of thing: a nail through the tread."

"That's a relief. Will it take long to fix it?"

The man scratched his stubbly chin and ran his grimy, greasy hand through his hair.

"I suppose you'll be wanting it today," he joked. "I've got a lot on, as you can see, and I'm a man short today, but for you, it'll take half an hour. It will probably need a new inner tube too."

Artur shook the man by the hand and smiled broadly in a charming manner, that only Artur knew how to do. The man rolled the wheel away to the maintenance area and told one of his youngsters to stop what he was doing and get on with repairing the gentleman's tyre.

The tyre was duly repaired and a new inner tube was needed, but no other problems were found. The wheel was taken to the boot and Artur put it inside. He paid the man and thanked him profusely for attending to it so quickly but, once again, the man tutted at the damage to the car's nearside telling Artur that he ought to get it fixed. Artur just smiled and told him it wasn't a priority.

They were on their way again, having taken the opportunity to fill up with petrol whilst the tyre was being repaired. Artur told Gerhart to head for Langres and then to Gray, with the final destination of the day at Pesmes, some 220 km away. Artur hoped they could stay for the weekend with someone he first met in Paris in 1931, but who moved to Pesmes in 1934. He told Gerhart that he last visited her in Pesmes in 1935.

They stopped for refreshments just south of Langres for about an hour and were in the vicinity of Pesmes by 4:30 p.m. Artur racked his brain to remember where the house was. He seemed to think the road they were on would come in from the north, as they had been through Gray. There would then be a sign to the village and they would turn right, round a right-hand corner, into the centre of the village square. Artur surprised himself at the accuracy of his directions and he told Gerhart that the woman's house was down on the right on the opposite side to the church. They parked in the main square and after locking the car, they walked to the end of the square and down Le Grand Rue towards the church and past the Mairie on the right.

It all had come back to Artur and little had changed in the five or so years since his last visit. He was suddenly very uncertain about knocking on the door and how he was going to explain to her why he was there and what he was doing in France during these difficult times. He hesitated and stepped back from the door and moved towards the church, beckoning Gerhart to follow. He told Gerhart that this woman will want to call him Andy and that he will introduce him using his agent name of Gerhart. He said to Gerhart that to stay for three or four days at Monique's house before escaping from France was very necessary, but that they had to take great care with what they say. He knew Monique wouldn't delve just for the sake of it and would just be pleased to see them.

Artur went back to the door and gently but firmly wrapped the knocker twice and waited. It seemed an eternity before he heard any noise from within the house. His heart was thumping hard in anticipation and he was just about to knock again when a window opened upstairs and a woman's head popped out.

"Who is it, please?" the woman said in French.

Artur recognised the voice and looked up to the woman, but before he could say anything, she shouted out a welcome in French.

"My dear Andy! How nice to see you after all these years! I thought I would never see you again after you got married. Don't run away, I'll be down in just a moment."

"My goodness," exclaimed Gerhart. "She's a beauty. How and when did you meet her?"

"I'll tell you later, if Monique doesn't tell you first."

The front door opened and Monique ran out and embraced Artur; she then kissed him on both cheeks.

"Oh, *mon Dieu* Andy, you look wonderful, you are still as beautiful as I remember," she said in broken English, and smiling from ear to ear as she looked at him. "And oo is your 'ansome ami?"

"His name is Gerhart and he too speaks French if you want to revert to your native tongue. Do you have anyone staying with you or can we go in doors, please?" Artur rather nervously had looked about him, hoping that people nearby in the village might not notice the two strangers who were calling on Monique. He couldn't be too careful.

"Oh, I am so sorry, I forgot my manners for just a moment," she said in French. "Please go inside. Don't you have any luggage?"

"We have some things in the car, but we didn't want to bring them to the door until we knew you were at home."

They walked into the comfortable sitting room and after Monique had shut the front door, she joined them. Her bright blue eyes flashed at Gerhart and then at Artur; she had attractive creases at the sides of her eyes that appeared when she smiled. She beckoned them to sit down but she continued to stand.

"How long can you stay, Andy? Why are you suddenly in Pesmes? Are our two countries not at war with Germany? Have you not been called up for active service like many others? Does your wife know you are in France?"

"Dear Monique, so many questions! Only a few can I answer for the moment, but one I can answer straight away: is it possible for us to stay until next week or do you have your parents coming down?"

"Sadly, my parents died a couple of years ago, so you can stay for ten days if you like?"

"I am so very sorry to hear about your parents. I remember meeting them when I came here in 1935 and they seemed very well then. No, ten days will not be necessary but till early next week would be very helpful."

Gerhart thought he hadn't seen Artur so animated and relaxed for a long time. Perhaps the person sitting in front of him was the reason. Maybe Artur thought he was safe in Monique's house for the moment, where nobody would find the two of them.

While they were all indoors, enjoying each other's company, a couple of inquisitive locals saw the Citroën parked in the square. They had a close look at it. There weren't many cars in the square and so the Citroën stood out, not only because of the crumpled nearside panels but also the different number plate from the local ones; they had seen the car arrive earlier and two men get out. They weren't 100% sure, but they thought they had seen a Citroën like it in the village about a year ago. Where had these two men come from and why were they in Pesmes? They thought they would ask the garage owner in the morning if he could identify the registration plate for them.

Chapter 16
Monday, 12ᵗʰ of June 1939

On Monday, Andrew's wife didn't feel any worse from her fall and the pain killers were giving her a good night's sleep. She didn't phone the doctor and would leave things till the end of the week. She did, however, phone the vicar and agreed on arrangements for Alfred's Baptism on 6ᵗʰ August. She phoned her friend, Pat, and she gave her the phone number of the caterer that she had used.

The week went by for Andrew without too much of note, except for writing to Charles telling him about the dates for the various courses he had arranged. Also, he told him about the medical that he'd had the previous week and that he thought it went well.

Andrew phoned his mother on Thursday evening. She'd had a good holiday in France at a friend's villa in Antibes and felt very refreshed. She noted the date of Alfred's Baptism and said she was looking forward to it. She said she would come down on the Saturday and stay for two nights at the Cross Keys to save his wife from making up beds, especially for her. A likely excuse: she didn't like staying because she wouldn't get the same service as she would at a hotel.

On Saturday morning, Andrew and his wife wrote all the invitations to Alfred's Baptism and they confirmed to the caterer what their needs were. They felt very pleased with their efforts, so Andrew suggested they go out for lunch on Sunday. He had heard that the Six Bells in the neighbouring village was good, so he made a reservation for 12:30 p.m. He mentioned that they would be bringing their baby with them and he told the manager that he would not give any problems to the others in the dining room as he will have been fed before leaving home.

Sunday evening came and Andrew reckoned it had been a good family time at the weekend. His wife really enjoyed going out and Alfred had behaved himself, so much so that the manager complimented them on how quiet he had been. In addition, they were both very pleased that all the invitations were ready to send off. Andrew started thinking about the trip to Bisley for the weapon training course and wondered if he really would have time to meet Anne at the agreed time.

On Monday evening, Andrew told his wife that he would be back home late on Tuesday because there was a special office meeting after work and he wasn't certain when it might end. She found it difficult to accept, but inwardly she hoped it might be something about his promotion. Andrew quite often drove his car to the station so when he said he would be doing that on Tuesday, it didn't come as a surprise to his wife.

Andrew was up early on Tuesday morning to check that he'd got all the necessary papers for the weapons' course. He also secreted an old pair of trousers and shirt into his car together with an old pair of shoes. He knew from previous visits that the men at Bisley wouldn't want him in a suit all day. He left home only a little earlier than normal and made good progress to Woking, and remembered his way to the Bisley ranges. He arrived at 9:15 a.m., just ahead of his appointed time.

Andrew stopped at the entrance barrier and a uniformed soldier came out of his sentry box to greet him.

"Good morning, sir, can I help you?" said the sentry.

"Good morning, my name is Williams and I'm expected this morning for weapons' training."

The sentry looked down the list on his clipboard.

"Have you any means of identification please, sir?"

Andrew handed him his passport that he had fortunately remembered to bring with him.

"Thank you, sir."

The sentry examined the passport and checked his list again.

"Ah, yes sir, your name is here. Please sign against your name and I'll fill in the time and your car registration number. A very nice car too, if I may say so, sir."

Andrew took back his passport and duly signed his name. He thanked the sentry for his comments about his car.

"You are expected to report to Hut B about 100 yards down on your left, sir. I will phone Sergeant Baxter to tell him that you are on your way. You may park in front of the hut. Do you have any questions, sir?"

"No, I don't. Thank you for your help."

The barrier was raised and the sentry saluted Andrew as he went through and he parked in front of Hut B. He took out his holdall with his change of clothes and went in through the hut door.

"Good morning, Mr Williams. My name is Sergeant Billy Baxter, but you can call me Billy. I have the pleasure of being your instructor for today. I notice you're in a suit so I assume you have a change of clothes in your holdall?"

"You assume correctly, Billy."

"Very good, so if you would like to follow me, I'll show you to the changing room. Can I call you Andrew or Andy?"

"Andrew will be fine. Thank you, Billy."

Andrew was shown where to change and he returned to the front room of the hut where Billy was waiting for him.

"Now," said Billy, "before we start, I need you to sign this form, please. On the form is a list of the weapons that you could use but we'll go through the list and choose those that are the most appropriate for your needs in a minute. Please sign at the bottom of the page next to where your name is written in capitals."

Andrew looked down the list and was very surprised at the items on it; most of them were way beyond his requirement. Billy went down the list with Andrew and told him that he had been advised to test him and/or familiarise him on pistols, rifles and machine guns. He told Andrew that he will be shown how to handle each type, how to fire it at a standing and moving target and also, probably most importantly, how to maintain it and clean it after use. He said there would be a break for lunch in the canteen of about an hour and that, all being well, he should be finished and ready to leave by 4:30 p.m.

"What sort of weapons are you used to using, Andrew?"

"I have two sporting guns of my own: a .410 and a 16-bore. I have also used other rifles when shooting in the bank competitions."

"Excellent! Do you fire in both the prone and the standing positions or just standing?"

"Obviously, when I'm out walking with my dog, a pheasant or a rabbit might suddenly appear so I have to be prepared to fire in a standing position with either foot to the front. At the bank, all the competitions are in the prone position."

"Any experience with pistols, Andrew?"

"Only once did I fire a pistol that belonged to a friend."

"Do you clean and maintain your own rifles?"

"Yes, I do. I have pull-throughs and plenty of 4 by 2s, plus light grease."

"You are much more experienced with weapons than I was expecting, so let's go over to the firing range."

They walked about 100 yards to the ranges and entered through a door in the middle of a long wooden building. A few other people were at the left hand end so Billy took Andrew to the right. He handed Andrew a rifle and went through its firing mechanism and handed him some cartridges. He asked Andrew to take up a prone position and prepare to fire four rounds at the 50-yard target in his own time. Billy went to the telescope at the side to inspect Andrew's shots. The first shot was to the right of the bull's eye in the eight ring so he adjusted the sights a few clicks. The next three shots were in the bull's eye, just off centre and still a little to the right.

"Very good, Andrew! By the way, you are aware that I have to record every single shot you make and all the results must then be sent away?"

"Yes, I am, Billy. Still, thank you for telling me."

Billy put Andrew through his paces with the rifle and then he started on the pistol; he brought up the torso target at thirty yards away. He explained the proper stances depending on the type of target. He then got Andrew to start off facing backwards and on the count of three to turn and fire at the target. He also fired from a prone position at targets different distances away. After every other group of shots, Andrew was instructed to clean the weapon.

All these exercises and target shootings took most of the morning, so they cleared everything up and locked away all the arms. They went off to the canteen for some lunch; quite a few people filed into the canteen as it was just after 12:30 p.m. Billy apologised for the lack of choice on the menu and hoped Andrew would find something he liked. They chatted very easily during the lunch break after which they went to a different hut for the machine gun training and target shooting. This was all new to Andrew and he wondered on how many occasions he might be required to handle such a weapon. Anyway, he was expected to fulfil the training so he happily went along with it.

When they reached the hut for the machine gun training, Billy mentioned that they had very few classes on machine guns as Bisley was primarily for pistols and rifles. However, he showed Andrew the heavy and light weight machine guns. He explained that as the light weight gun was more likely to be the one that Andrew would be expected to use, he would focus on that one. Andrew was shown how to strip down the gun and how important it was not to touch the barrel after shooting as it would be very hot. Everything was covered in great detail and Andrew was given the opportunity to fire the light weight gun at several targets.

All this activity took most of the afternoon up to 3:30 p.m., and Billy seemed very happy with Andrew's results. Once everything was completed, they went to the admin office to complete all the paperwork. Andrew examined all his marks and hoped the Service would also be happy with them.

"Well, Andrew, I am pleased to tell you that you have come out with an 'A' rating over all the weapons you have fired today. If you exclude the machine guns, which obviously you are less familiar with, your rating would be 'A+' or marksman+. Does that seem to be a fair assessment to you? "

"I am very pleased, Billy, and thank you very much for all your excellent instruction, without which my grades would have been much lower, I'm sure. I very much appreciate your time."

Andrew looked at his watch and was amazed that it was after 4:30 p.m. He asked Billy if he was free to go as he had to be somewhere else by 6 o'clock. Andrew went back to change into his city clothes and shook hands with Billy before driving out of the gate.

Chapter 17
Friday, 5th of April 1940

"It is so wonderful to see you Andy, I really can't believe it. You have no idea, Gerhart, but I've only seen Andy once since we first met in Paris in 1931. Andy and some of his friends came over to watch England play France in the rugby international. It was taking place at the Stade Colombes in early April. We and some of my friends from University were near to where Andy and his friends were. It was a very close match and France won by only one point: 14 to 13, if I remember correctly. It was only the second time that we had beaten England in the five nations' championship since we first entered in the early 1900s. The French crowd was very excited, of course."

"I told you Monique might well tell you how we met before I got a chance," remarked Artur, with a finger pointing at Monique and a typical smile.

"But Andy, the match was only the start of it all. We all went back into central Paris and called into nearly every bar that we came to. We sang and danced and ended up at *Le Moulin Rouge*. You managed to get to the front with me and a few others, and you made very rude comments about some of the girls' anatomy! Anyway, I think we should have a drink. After all, we will have four days to reminisce and have some laughs. I have a bottle of white wine in the kitchen that is quite cool so shall we have that?"

"What an excellent idea, Monique. In the meantime, can I use your bathroom, please?"

"Of course, you know your way around my small house."

Monique went out to the kitchen for the wine and Artur went upstairs. He took a quick look around the rooms; she'd had them newly decorated since his last visit. There were three bedrooms on the first floor, one of which was the main one with its own wash hand basin, and one main bathroom. The main bedroom of Monique's overlooked the road and that was presumably where she'd seen them after he had knocked. Artur wandered down the stairs and into the lounge just before Monique came in with the wine.

"I heard you walking around upstairs, Andy. Do you remember much or does it look different?"

"I like the way you've decorated the upstairs. It's so bright and cheerful, just like you."

"Forever the flatterer, Andy! Would you open the bottle, please and pour out the wine? I'm sure Gerhart will feel he's been waiting too long," said Monique, as she looked at Gerhart with an engaging smile.

They all toasted each other's health and drank to the future of their countries. They chatted for almost an hour and finished the wine.

"I have to ask you if you mind going out for a meal as I haven't enough provisions to make supper at home tonight. I thought we might eat at a new restaurant that has recently opened. It's owned by a couple of brothers and their families; they intend to make it a hotel as well. It's on the main road going through the village, before one reaches the bridge over the river. They have a rule that diners have to be at the restaurant by 8 o'clock. So, I suggest I show you the rooms upstairs and you can get your things from the car. Then you can tell me why you're in France and what you are doing here in Pesmes."

Artur knew these questions were going to be asked sooner or later, so when he was out at the car with Gerhart, they talked about what they should say, or, more likely, what Artur should say. They considered several scenarios but only one was going to satisfy Monique: something near to the truth. When they were at the car, they realised that they had very little to fetch: the holdall with all the items from the panniers and Artur's small suit case. Each of them had only one change of clothing and a minimum of toiletries. While they were searching for items in the boot, they wondered how they should conceal the arms that they had accumulated. Gerhart suggested they should wrap them in the rug, so he got it from the back seat. Artur was relieved to see his satchel on the floor in front of the passenger seat; after all, it contained all his documents and papers. They collected all the maps and together with their clothing, put them in the holdall that they had taken from the German officers' car.

"Right," said Artur. "I think we've got all we need so let's put everything else in the boot so it's out of sight, and lock up."

By the time they got back to the house, it was close to 7:30 p.m. Monique was upstairs changing so Artur and Gerhart ran upstairs to the landing.

"Andy, if you could use the room at the front and Gerhart the room at the back. I've put towels in both bedrooms. If you want a bath, there's plenty of hot water, but remember that we ought to be at the restaurant by 8 o'clock."

Andy mouthed to Gerhart that he'd have a bath in the morning and Gerhart said likewise. Andy freshened up, quickly shaved and he told Gerhart that the bathroom was now free.

They were all downstairs at 7:50 p.m. and decided they should leave right away. They walked to the restaurant so they crossed the square and down the steps to the main road. The restaurant was on the other side of the road. Monique went in first and she was greeted very warmly by the lady of the house.

"How nice to see you, Miss Monique, and today I see you have two very handsome escorts."

"I am indeed very lucky. I'm sorry I didn't book a table, but I'm hoping you have space for us tonight, perhaps near the window?"

They were ushered to the table for four by the window in the back room and were told that they didn't expect many people. They had a most excellent meal, and at about 9:45 p.m., they retreated to the bar to pay the bill. Monique insisted on paying and she said Andy could settle up with her tomorrow or whenever.

They wandered around the town and down to the church before entering Monique's house. She offered them a brandy and coffee and they accepted. It seemed as though they were in another world from that which they'd been in for the last few weeks and, in particular, the last four days.

"So, Andy, why are you two in France and in this part of France particularly? Are you involved in something excitingly secret? Why are you in a car that seems to have been hit in the side rather hard and with a bent rear bumper?"

"My dear Monique, you are quite correct, we are involved in something very secret. What I'm going to tell you is very confidential and is for your ears only. You are not to talk to anyone about what I'm going to tell you. If you do and the information gets into the wrong hands, mine and Gerhart's lives are in serious jeopardy. We could be tortured and possibly killed."

"Oh my goodness me! Look, if you don't want to tell me anything then that's fine. I'm just curious, that's all."

"I am in a dilemma, Monique. Somebody, sometime soon, will start asking you why we stayed with you so, at the moment, you are in more danger than we are and we are sorry that we have put you in that position by coming here. As you know nothing, it's possible that whoever asks you about us probably won't believe you when you tell them that you don't know. They'll think you are hiding something from them. Equally, if we do tell you, they will think you do know something and possibly torture you until you tell them more. Does that make sense?"

"As I said a moment ago, oh my goodness me! So what are you proposing to do, Andy? From my point of view, I would rather know something than nothing, don't you agree?"

"Absolutely, Monique, I totally agree with you. You ought to know, however, that Gerhart and I signed the British Official Secrets Act so anything we tell you could be considered treasonable by our government if we were found out. What I will tell you, though, is that, amongst other things, we have been trained to execute acts of sabotage. We have successfully carried out such an act quite recently and we are now escaping through France back to England. Please forgive me for saying this, but we are not in a position to tell you what and where it took place or give you any further details."

"I quite understand. Thank you for telling me."

Artur had been sitting on his own on the sofa, but Monique got up from her chair and went to sit next to him. She put her arm round Artur's neck and brought him towards her and looked him in the eyes.

"We will be very careful during your time here. There are strange people in every village and town in every country that always want to find fault with people they don't know. We even have some here in our small village; we must be very wary and vigilant. What pleases me greatly is that you have come to me in Pesmes looking for a safe haven. I thought I would never see you again after your wedding in 1936, and yet here you are in my house. Even though we have only been together once since 1931, we have had a lot of fun and there's no way that I would want to do or say anything to anyone that might harm you or give any of your exploits away. I need to know no more."

Monique kissed Artur on his cheek; he closed his eyes and grinned.

"Tomorrow is Saturday, just in case you're not sure! I will go out for some shopping and you are welcome to stay in the house, if you would prefer. I suggest we go out on Saturday for lunch and if it's a nice day, we could go for a picnic by the river near Bresilley. It's not far from here, probably less than 15 km. What do you think, boys?"

"It all sounds fine to me," replied Artur, shifting Monique's arm from his neck for a moment and getting a smile of agreement from Gerhart. "But I'm a bit concerned about our car in the square. As you saw when we crossed the square, it's quite badly dented and it is likely to attract attention. Is there anywhere we can put it, Monique?"

Monique thought for a moment and then an idea came to her.

"There's a nice old lady who lives round the back of here who has a large courtyard at the front of her house. The whole property is behind a high wall and there are double gates at the entrance. I'll ask her tomorrow if you can park the car there. I'm sure she'll say yes."

"That sounds great, doesn't it, Gerhart? I would be very happy if we could arrange it before you go shopping, please?"

"Of course, that's no problem. That's settled then. As it's getting quite late, I think we should call it a day and get some sleep."

Chapter 18
Tuesday, 20th of June 1939

Andrew drove quickly away from Bisley and the Woking area and on into Sussex. He was very excited, but he had to try and think of somewhere to go with Anne, somewhere that he wouldn't be known or recognised – that was the problem. The traffic was quite heavy for an early Tuesday evening but he felt he was making good progress – he didn't like being late. He then realised that perhaps he should have phoned her to confirm arrangements.

He came round the corner near to where he had taken her that Saturday several weeks ago, and it was not yet 6 o'clock. He drew up near the bus stop and looked around in case she was sitting somewhere nearby. He stopped the engine and got out of the car. He walked to the bus stop because he assumed she would be coming on the next bus from wherever she lived.

Time went by and so did the one bus but she wasn't on it. Andrew went and studied the bus timetable to see what time the next buses might arrive and thought he would wait till 6:30 p.m. Another bus was due at 6:25 p.m., and he was hopeful she would be on it. He wasn't very good at waiting for people who were already late, but he knew he had to make an exception for Anne, especially if she arrived after he had already left; he would never forgive himself and nor would she.

Someone arrived at the bus stop so Andrew asked him if the buses were usually late and he replied that they weren't. The bus arrived just two minutes late and Anne wasn't on it. He felt very deflated and he had no idea where she lived. He decided to drive off and go to the Red Lion where Anne worked. He was sure she wouldn't be working in the evenings, but she might have been called in for some special function. In any case, if she had a change of plan she'd had no way of getting in touch with him, except to the pub that they met.

It took him till 7:15 p.m. to reach the Red Lion and there were many cars in the car park so perhaps his hunch was correct. He was hopeful that at least he might see her or she might have left a message for him with the barman. He went into the main bar and it was quite a scrum – people calling in after work and before going home probably. He worked his way to the bar and the barman saw him. He went via the till and handed Andrew a slip of paper.

"I think this is for you. Anne phoned in and left this message that my wife took a couple of hours ago."

Andrew took the piece of paper and saw that Anne had apologised for not making it this evening as she wasn't feeling very well. Her phone number was on the paper and she asked him to call her. Andrew rummaged in his pockets for some change and went outside to the phone box on the corner. Nobody was using it so he dialled her number.

"Hallo, Anne? It's Andrew here."

Before he could say anything more, she said how very sorry she was that she couldn't meet him tonight. She explained that she must have eaten something that disagreed with her and that she had been sick. She was glad that he had thought of going to the Red Lion and hoped he hadn't been waiting too long at the bus stop.

Andrew said he felt very sorry for her and hoped she would be feeling better soon, and not to worry about tonight; they could meet up another time.

"I don't know where you live, but would you like me to come round?" asked Andrew.

"It's very sweet of you and I'd love to see you, but as I'm not feeling my best, probably not."

Andrew didn't want to press the point, but she did give him her address which he noted on the piece of paper. He said he hoped to see her before too long and would phone her, or see her at the Red Lion to make another arrangement.

Andrew decided to go back to the bar and order a pint of bitter.

"Is everything alright? I knew Anne was unwell because we had asked her to come in to help us with this evening's supper party but she was unable to," said the barman.

"Thank you," said Andrew, "but, as you say, she's fairly unwell. Hopefully she'll be better in a day or so. A bit of food poisoning, she thinks."

The barman got Andrew's pint and told him it was on the house, for which he thanked him. He was obviously very disappointed, but was able to relax now that he knew the situation. He downed his pint, thanked the barman and went out to his car. *Such a shame*, he thought to himself, *and such a nice warm evening too.*

He arrived home before 8:30 p.m. and left his holdall in the car – he would take it in later when he took Max for his last walk of the day. He found that his wife had already eaten as she had been rather hungry. She seemed in good humour and didn't ask him about his 'after work meeting'.

"If you haven't had anything to eat, there's the last of the pie in the bottom oven that you could warm up, if you like."

"Thank you, dear. I might just do that, but I'll go upstairs and change first."

Andrew went up to his dressing room and changed. As he entered the lounge on the way back to the kitchen, he heard some rattling sounds coming from the kitchen.

"I thought I would warm the oven up while you were changing to save you some time; after all, it is just after 9 o'clock and getting rather late."

"That's very kind of you, dear. How was your day?" said Andrew, hoping that by enquiring after her day, it would keep her in a good mood and not let her ask him about his day.

"It was very good, thank you. I got out with Alfred in the pram and we went to see the ducks in the park. Obviously he's a bit too young to know what is going on, but it was sunny and warm and very pleasant. On the way back, I went to the post office and all the invitations have been sent out."

Andrew didn't have to do anything about his supper because his wife completed all the preparations; she even poured him a glass of wine. After his meal, he insisted on clearing everything away so that she could go and sit down. After about fifteen minutes, he went into the lounge and stated that he ought to give Max his last walk of the day. Andrew went to the hall and Max knew it was his turn for some attention. They were out for about half an hour and as he got to the house, he went to his car and took out his holdall from the passenger seat. When they entered the house, he could hear that his wife was already upstairs. She was probably giving Alfred his last feed and changing him. As he put the holdall in his study, he felt relieved that she hadn't had the chance of seeing him with the holdall and asking some awkward questions.

The rest of the week went by quite normally. He was pleased with himself for turning down an invitation to go to the pub after work on Friday to celebrate the engagement of one of his colleagues. On Saturday, they received the first formal acceptances to Alfred's Baptism; even though they already knew everyone that was asked had already said yes, they enjoyed getting the replies. Earlier in the week, Andrew had suggested that they go for a picnic on Saturday, if the weather was fine. As it was a beautiful day, Andrew reminded his wife of his suggestion and she said she had bought what was required when she had been out on Friday.

"How about driving down to Hove and perhaps having a picnic near the Devil's Dyke?" asked Andrew.

"Excellent idea Andrew, but I think we should go in my car so that Alfred doesn't get too much sun; it will also give us a bit more room."

"Fair enough, I'll prepare your car. I'll take the rugs from mine and put them in yours while you're putting the picnic together. I'll also get what we need for Max."

All was ready in just over half an hour, and even little Alfred looked excited to be going on a jaunt with his parents. It was quite busy on the road south as many other people seemed to have had the same idea. Fortunately, however, most of them went to Brighton whereas Andrew turned right off the Brighton road towards the Dyke.

They had a great day out and Andrew's wife had brought all the things that Andrew enjoyed, including pâté, cold cooked sausages, fresh bread, salted butter, a bottle of red wine and not much rabbit food – as Andrew usually called salad items! Max got a good run into the Dyke with Andrew and they even took a few photos to mark the occasion.

"I meant to finish the film after the picture I took of you with Alfred but I forgot. Looking at the dial, there's now just one left so stand with Alfred and Max next to my car, please."

She took the last picture and would have the reel developed next week. Andrew lay on the rug and fell asleep in the sunshine for about fifteen minutes, thinking of nothing in particular for once. They packed everything up at about 5 o'clock and headed for home so that Alfred wouldn't be too late to bed.

The rest of the weekend was very relaxing, although Andrew did think he ought to attend to the garden for a couple of hours on Sunday morning. He didn't want the gardener to think that he left all the work to him but it probably wasn't far from the truth anyway.

The next week was uneventful, although Andrew had thought of phoning Anne to see if she was feeling better. As an alternative, he decided on Thursday that he'd go to the Red Lion on Saturday lunchtime; hopefully he'd find her on duty. He agreed with his wife that he'd take Max with him to the pub and gave him a good walk for an hour beforehand so that he might sleep when they got there.

The pub was quite busy, but Andrew left Max in the passenger seat well when he went into the bar. Anne was looking out of the window at his car for a brief moment and thought he hadn't seen her. He crept up behind her and gave a slight squeeze to her waist. She squeaked in surprise (or was it delight?) and turned towards him with her smile and bright eyes.

"Well, well, fancy seeing you again," she said. "I'd almost given you up for lost. Look, I'm really sorry about the week before, but I really was very poorly."

"I was on the verge of phoning you," said Andrew, "but I chickened out. I wasn't really sure that you would have wanted me to."

"But I gave you my number and I even gave you my address. I'd have loved you to have contacted me, one way or the other."

"I'm really sorry. I should have stuck to my instincts and not been so cautious."

Anne then shuffled and excused herself for a few moments as she needed to attend to some of her customers; a few were already staring at the two of them and looking at their watches. Andrew let her pass and she quickly disappeared into the kitchen, nearly knocking a tray out of the other waitress' hands as she was coming out. Andrew went to the bar and asked the barman for a pint of best bitter.

"I think you've made a hit there, sir," he said. "Ever since you picked up her message, she's been asking if I had seen you in here each time she has been on duty."

Andrew wasn't sure what to say, so he just smiled, paid for his pint and went out into the garden. He let Max out of the car and they sat at a table in the shade. He mulled over what the barman had said for a while. He knew he had another course to attend the week after next and he didn't see how he could arrange to meet up with Anne any sooner. He thought he could ask her to meet him in London one evening, but that idea should probably be best left for a few weeks later, probably towards the end of July.

As Andrew was thinking to himself and staring into the middle distance, he was aware of someone standing near him.

"Hallo, Andrew," said a woman's voice.

He turned his head, expecting to see Anne, but the voice wasn't quite right somehow. To his surprise, it was Barbara, one of his wife's very close friends. Andrew quickly got to his feet, gave her his customary charming smile and kissed her on her cheek.

"I haven't seen you here before," she said. "Isn't it a bit out of your way to visit this pub?"

"You're right, I don't often come here, but I was here a few weeks back with Brian. You remember Brian, of course?"

"Yes, I do. I've only just arrived with a couple of friends of mine and I don't usually come here either. Is your wife feeling a lot better after her fall a couple of weeks ago?"

"She seems to be fine now, thank you, and little Alfred is growing so quickly. I believe we shall have the pleasure of seeing you at his Baptism on 6th August?"

"Yes, I'm looking forward to it very much. Let's hope the weather is fine and we can be in that beautiful garden of yours. Excuse me, but I really must go as my friends will wonder where I am. Good to see you, Andrew, and love to your wife."

"I will, Barbara, thank you."

As Barbara left, Andrew breathed a big sigh of relief that he hadn't been seen in the bar area with Anne, by Barbara of all people. He reckoned he now needed another pint to calm himself down. He told Max to stay and went into the bar. He looked around to see if he could spot Barbara and just caught sight of her going into the dining room with two friends. He then looked for Anne as he ordered another pint. She came out of the kitchen with yet another tray of lunches and smiled at him as he caught her eye. He indicated to her that he was going into the garden and could she bring him a menu.

After a few minutes, Anne came over with the menu.

"Look," he said. "I don't actually want a meal but it was the easiest way to get you out here. I have to tell you that I've just had one of the biggest frights of my life. As I was gazing into the middle distance and thinking of you, a woman came up to me and said 'hallo'. She was only a very good friend of my wife's, wasn't she! By some good fortune, she had only just arrived here. I was worried she might have seen me with you in the bar area and put two and two together and made seventy! You can't imagine how relieved I am now. Sorry, I'm keeping you from your work. I'll phone you and perhaps we can meet up on Wednesday next week at the place we had arranged to meet ten days ago?"

"I'd love that, Andrew, please do phone. I'll make sure I don't eat anything unusual for two days before," she said with that captivating smile of hers. "I'm already looking forward to it."

Andrew stood up and took her hand and gently squeezed it; he didn't kiss her on the cheek this time, but just said goodbye for the moment. Anne turned on her heel and left Andrew standing by the table. He quickly finished his pint and took Max to the car. He was on cloud nine and as he drove home a bit too quickly, he sang a few songs to himself thinking that, whatever is going on in Europe, I'm alright Jack!

Chapter 19
Saturday, 6th of April 1940

They all slept well that night and awoke to a lovely sunny morning. When Artur and Gerhart came down stairs after each had had a bath, they found that Monique was not around, but after only about ten minutes, she came in through the front door with some wonderfully smelling fresh bread.

"I thought I should treat you to a nice breakfast, in case you hadn't had anything like this for a while. Please sit at the table and I'll make some coffee. I've got some locally made jam as well so just tuck in."

They had some of the fresh bread with the jam and it tasted delicious. The fresh coffee duly arrived and they chatted about various things for over half an hour.

"I know it's nice and quiet in here, but do you have a wireless that we could listen to?" said Artur. "We want to hear about any new developments in Europe. We haven't really heard much for the last few days and we ought to keep up with the changes going on."

"I don't have one in here Andy, but you're welcome to listen to the one in the lounge."

Artur and Gerhart went into the lounge as Monique started to clear the breakfast table. Artur turned the wireless on and after it had warmed up, he tuned it in to a French radio station. It was good timing as it was coming up to 10 o'clock and he was sure there would be a bulletin on the hour. They sat down and waited for the news to start. They then heard that German forces were gathering in large numbers in the eastern region of Schleswig Holstein, as well as armed forces arriving in the major German ports on the Baltic. The newscaster said that the general thinking in Paris and London was that it can only be a matter of time before Denmark was invaded followed by an all-out assault on Norway. Similar numbers of German forces are also moving towards the Ardennes.

Artur turned the radio off; he had heard enough and the news was not good.

"You know, Gerhart, we ought to try and get back to England as soon as possible in case we're needed elsewhere in Europe."

Gerhart nodded his agreement and they went back into the kitchen. Artur told Monique the news and she started to look rather depressed. She was worried that it probably wouldn't be long before the Germans started being a bigger problem for the French than they were already.

"But still, it's a lovely day for early April, so I'll get some special things from the local shops for our picnic. By the way, when I was out getting the bread, I called to see the lady about putting your car there. She said it would be fine and that you can bring the car anytime this morning."

Artur looked very pleased with the information and asked Monique if they could do it straight away – the less time it's in the market place for locals to see, the better was Arthur's hope.

"OK," said Monique. "If you've got the keys, let's go."

Gerhart decided to stay behind as Monique and Artur left the house and went to the market square. The car was still there; it looked very sad with its battered side, but nobody was taking much interest in it at the moment. They got in the car and drove it down towards the church and round to the right past Monique's house. They then turned left into avenue Jean Jaurès and the house was a little way up on the left.

Monique got out and pressed the bell. The house was set quite a way back from the gates, but the lady came out after a few moments and opened both the gates. The lady made a wave movement with her arm and Artur drove the car in. He drove it in on the left hand side where there was more room for it to be parked and the damaged side was out of sight of passers-by.

"Andy, this is Madame Pélissier," said Monique. "And she says your car is fine here till you decide to leave next week."

"That's very kind of you, Madame. If it should be in the way at any time, please let us know and we will be glad to move it elsewhere."

"Thank you, Monsieur, but I'm not expecting anyone till next weekend."

Monique had a little chat with Madame Pélissier and when they had departed, the lady closed and locked the gates.

"She's a very nice lady," said Monique. "And to think that she lives all on her own in that big house. She knew my parents very well.

"Let's get back to my house now and I can go off to do some shopping. By the way, don't you need a few more clothes, or are you happy to use the two changes that you have?"

"No, we're fine, thank you; as long as they don't start to smell!"

Monique gave a little giggle and put her hand to her nose. They walked back to the house. Gerhart had fallen asleep in the armchair in the lounge, but he woke up quite startled when they walked in.

"Oh, so sorry, I fell asleep and I was having a rather disturbing dream when you came in. It was very strange."

Monique had gone upstairs so Gerhart quietly told Artur that he would tell him about it once she had gone out shopping. She came down a few moments later and asked them if there was anything special that they would like and anything that they didn't like. They both told her that they would be very happy with whatever she bought. Artur passed her some money for some wine which she reluctantly accepted. As soon as she had gone, Gerhart told Artur about his dream.

"As you will no doubt recall, the car that we have 'borrowed' from Phillipe was bought with money left to him by his grandmother about a year ago. The registration plate has LJ, denoting Moselle and it's a bit unusual being an olive-green body and black wings and wheels. He also said he had a brother down near Dijon, so maybe he's visited him since he bought it. In my dream, someone in Pesmes thinks they recognise the car because of its colour and the registration letters are not from Haute Saône – QA, QB or QC. They then report the damaged car to the police and they come looking for us in order to question us."

"That's a little bit too near the mark, Gerhart. Are we being careful enough putting the car in Madame Pélissier's driveway? It is rather conspicuous with its damaged side. I'm surprised Madame didn't mention it when I drove in to her courtyard."

They pondered for a while and decided it would make things even more obvious if they moved it again. They would take the risk and leave it where it was until they were ready to leave

After about an hour, Monique returned with lots of food and wine. She smiled happily as she went into the lounge, proudly showing them the things she had bought for the next few days. She went skipping into the kitchen and was singing quietly to herself as she put the items away. She was enjoying having people to stay and was particularly happy to be seeing Andy again.

She joined them in the lounge sometime later, and declared that she'd prepared the picnic and that she was ready to leave whenever they were.

"Excellent, Monique, we'll just get our jackets and we can be on our way. Where do you park your car, Monique, do you have a garage nearby?"

Monique found a couple of rugs in the cupboard under the stairs and gathered her jacket.

"No, I don't have a garage so I park it in the square not far from where you had left yours. OK, are we all ready now? We're not going too far but it is very pretty down by the river."

Monique followed Artur and Gerhart out of the house and locked the front door after her. They walked to the square, and she said good morning to a number of people that she passed and they smiled back politely. Artur looked round at the few cars parked in the square trying to identify the one that might belong to Monique.

Monique noticed him searching and she said, "So, Andy, which one of all these cars do you think is mine?"

"I really don't know and I can't remember what you had when I came here in 1935."

"After my parents died, I sold my father's old Salmson as it was too big for me, and so I bought an Amilcar Pégasse about eighteen months ago. There, Andy, you can just see it over in the corner." Monique pointed to her right.

"Wow! That looks rather special. I've not seen many of those around."

They walked over to the car and Artur walked slowly round the car making complimentary noises. They put the picnic and rugs on the back seat and climbed in, with Artur in the front. As Monique started the car and pulled away, a few people waved at her and smiled. Artur noticed two men out to his right who were close to each other but didn't smile; they seemed to be whispering something to each other and then one pointed at the car, or was it at Artur? He stared back at them as they moved out of the market square and he made sure he would remember them, if he should meet them again.

"This is a beautiful car, Monique. Did you buy it new?"

"Yes, I did. Whenever I get into it, it reminds me of my parents. Some people think that I've been a bit extravagant, but why shouldn't I enjoy myself when I have had such a big loss? It was terrible. They were in Vienna on holiday in March 1938 when Heinrich Himmler and some SS officers arrived – you remember the *Anschluss*? They rounded up tens of thousands of potential political dissenters and my parents seemed to be in the wrong place at the wrong time. They were not in good health, but they both had heart attacks and died before they were taken to the concentration camp at the disused Vienna railway station."

"But that's dreadful, Monique, and only two years ago."

Monique slowed the car and took a handkerchief from her sleeve. She wiped away a tear. Artur put his hand on her arm and squeezed it; she looked back at him with a sad smile. It didn't take them long at all to find Bresilley. They drove through the village towards the river Saône and went left along the embankment. For early April, the temperature was warm, particularly when out of the breeze. They found a spot, or rather Monique found a spot, and she parked the car facing the river and the weir.

After a few minutes admiring the scene, they got out and laid the rugs out in the sunshine.

"I have bought something special to drink so please would you open it, Andy."

Artur fumbled in the basket and brought out a fine bottle of champagne and three glasses.

"Well, well, this looks very special. Shall I open it now, Monique?"

"Yes, please. It won't open by itself will it?" she said with a wink at Gerhart.

The bottle was duly opened and the glasses filled to halfway. They all stood near to each other and touched each other's glass.

"Here's to less troublesome times in Europe and to meeting up again not long from now."

"*A votre santé*," they all said to each other and took a good mouthful of the cool, dry, fizzy wine.

Chapter 20
Saturday, 1ˢᵗ of July 1939

Andrew arrived home to a very agitated wife; she'd put the oven on for the roast lunch about an hour earlier and then realised she hadn't put the meat in it.

"Never mind, dear, we'll just eat a bit later, in the afternoon. Let me get you a drink of something to brighten you up. Would you like a martini or perhaps a medium sherry?"

"Oh, a sherry sounds an excellent idea. Please make it a schooner size – a large one!"

"Are you sure that's alright with you still feeding Alfred? We don't want him getting tipsy, do we?"

Andrew's wife was insistent on a schooner, so Andrew poured one out and said he would lay the table in the dining room for her while she prepared the rest of the meal. He went into the garden to see that Alfred was still asleep and sat down for a few minutes to enjoy his 'G an' T'. There was a call from the lounge window that lunch would be in ten minutes and he should attend to the carving knife if he hadn't already done so.

They had a beautiful piece of beef and he treated himself to a bottle of Bordeaux red – one of his favourites – but his wife declined. They passed the rest of the weekend quietly in the garden with Andrew doing a spot more gardening.

The week went by without any incident or anything different from normal, so Andrew phoned a few of his friends and asked them to meet him, his wife and Alfred for a drink on Saturday lunchtime at the Royal Oak. He managed to get positive responses from Brian, Peter and Harry but all the others were unavailable.

They all arrived around midday and sat in the garden as it was such a nice day; not too hot or too cold. None, except Brian, had seen Alfred before so they all were interested so that the two who were married could report back to their wives what and who he looked like. Alfred was on good form and seemed to smile at anyone who peered into his pram at him and tickled him under the chin. They all thought he looked like his father – poor devil – but he also had some of his wife's features.

Andrew thought his wife was getting a bit tired by 2:30 p.m., so he excused them for leaving a bit earlier than planned. The Watkins said they were looking forward to seeing them all on 6th August for the Baptism, if they didn't see them earlier. They all waved them off from the car park and commented to each other how surprisingly good Andrew was at being a father.

"I really enjoyed that," said Andrew's wife. "It's really nice to get out and meet our friends, just like we used to before Alfred was around."

"Me too dear, but it does help that it's summer time and the weather is warmer."

The outing on Saturday seemed to liven up the rest of the weekend for Andrew's wife, and it helped Andrew to relax and take his mind off the next course that was due to be next Wednesday. This one was at Aldershot for fitness training. He was to meet Anne afterwards, of course. He would phone her beforehand this time – on Monday – on his way back from work. He didn't think she worked on Monday evenings and presumably not on Wednesday evenings either.

During Monday morning at the office, Andrew made an appointment to speak to his manager about his training course on Wednesday. He saw him after lunch at 2:30 p.m., and he was in a very lively mood when Andrew went into his office.

"Well, Williams, I suppose you're going to tell me that you're going on another training course soon; am I not right?"

"Yes, sir, that's quite right. I'm very sorry, but I should have spoken to you last week about it because the course starts the day after tomorrow."

"Yes, you should have but there's not a lot I can do about it now. What are you going to be taught this time: how to chat up twenty year old girls?" he said with a raucous laugh.

"It's funny you should say that sir," said Andrew, going along with his manager's theme. "But no I'm not, not this time as it happens!"

"I don't expect there's much they can teach you about that subject anyway, is there, from what I hear, Williams? You'd be better at being the teacher rather than the student, don't you think?"

"I wouldn't think so, sir. Anyway, I assume you will allow me to attend the fitness training course at Aldershot, sir?"

"Just as long as you don't come in on Thursday on crutches!" Again, he let out an outrageous laugh, so much so that most people heard it in the open office and turned to find out what was going on.

"I'll try not to, sir, but as far as I know, I shall only be shown what exercises I should be doing on a regular basis rather than putting me through some strenuous military course."

Andrew's manager quietened down and agreed for him to attend the course. He wished him well and hoped he would arrange to give him an update once all the training had been completed.

Andrew gave a big sigh of relief once he was back at his desk. One or two of his colleagues wanted to know what all the laughter was about, but he said he would tell them at another time. After work, and before he caught his train home, he phoned Anne. The phone seemed to ring for a long time but was eventually answered.

"Hallo, this is Anne, who is speaking please?"

"This is Andrew here."

"Andrew, I'm really pleased you called. Could you possibly come to my place as I would like to cook a meal for you here?"

"Are you sure you wouldn't like me to take you out? You must be sick and tired of serving food to people."

"I know it's my job, but I really would like to, especially after messing you about last time. You've got my address so can you be here at 6:30 p.m., please?"

"Won't your boyfriend want to know why you are not seeing him on one of your evenings off?"

"No, he won't; in any case, I split up from him a month ago."

"Oh, I'm sorry, he seemed a nice lad to me. Sorry, Anne, my money is going to run out very soon so I'll see you at 6:30 p.m. on Wednesday. Goodbye for now."

The phone went dead before Anne could speak again. Andrew started to think that things were beginning to get out of his control. How was he going to tell his wife that he was to be late on Wednesday – for yet another time! He ran from the phone box hoping to catch his normal train only to find that he'd missed it by a couple of minutes. As the next one wasn't for another twenty minutes, he thought he'd go and have a drink at the pub by the booking offices. He ordered a pint and tried to get his mind in order. He decided to phone his wife and tell her that he'd just missed his usual train as he was a bit later leaving the office than normal. He finished his pint and went back to the telephone kiosks. She said she was pleased he had let her know and said she would wait for supper until he arrived home. *Phew,* he thought to himself, *that's a close shave; I'm back in her good books again for a day or two!*

He got home to a warm welcome from his wife; she'd obviously had a good day, but Andrew waited until she told him. Nothing was said, however, and by the time supper was finished, he'd forgotten to ask her anyway. When he was doing the washing up, he told her that he was likely to be late home on Wednesday; there was some celebration going on that he couldn't avoid attending. She looked at him with a sideways glance, only half believing him, but knowing she had no other option than to accept what he was saying. Andrew detected this perception and it made him feel rather wary.

The following day, he went to work as normal but got home a bit earlier, mainly so he could prepare all that he needed for Aldershot, but also to think what he needed for supper with Anne. As with Bisley, he packed some old clothes and shoes in his holdall as well gym shoes, socks, running shorts, lightweight shirt and towel. The holdall was stuffed almost to bursting, but he took it to his car and placed it in the well in front of the passenger seat.

He went back in doors and loudly called to his wife, who was in the kitchen, if he had time to give Max a bit of a run round the garden before supper, to which the answer was 'yes'.

On his return to the house, he rubbed down Max as it had rained when they were out.

"Are you going to be ready for supper in the kitchen in five minutes, Andrew?"

"Yes, that's fine by me. I'm just rubbing Max down and I'll be with you in a couple of moments, dear."

Andrew joined his wife for supper, but he could tell that one of her moods was starting. She said nothing during the meal and barely mentioned a word afterwards. She said she was rather tired only twenty minutes after finishing her meal and said she was going to bed early. *Oh well,* thought Andy, *I wonder how long this will go on for this time.*

The following morning, Andrew left home at about the same time as usual, but headed for Aldershot. He got to the gate and the sentry saluted, asking him his name. He looked down his list and asked him for some form of identification. He looked through his passport and asked him to sign his name on the list.

"Mr Williams, welcome to Aldershot. Captain Jones is expecting you so please make your way to Hut G, which is just down the road on the left. I will phone Captain Jones to say you are on your way."

"Thank you," said Andrew as he took back his passport.

He had no problem finding Hut G. He saw a figure standing outside the hut and he assumed it was Captain Jones. Andrew got out of his car and took his holdall from the passenger side.

"Mr Williams. Welcome to Aldershot. Did you have a pleasant drive from your home? I assume you had no difficulty in finding us?"

"Thank you, Captain; a very easy journey," said Andrew as he reached forward to shake the Captain's hand.

"Do you mind if I call you Andrew?" said the Captain. "And please call me Jeremy."

"Andrew is fine. Thank you Jeremy."

They exchanged a few pleasantries as they walked towards another building, which turned out to be the gymnasium. Jeremy asked Andrew if he had brought sports gear with him to which he replied 'yes', and directed him to the changing room. He met Jeremy in the gym and he was told what the day would comprise of, what exercises he expected Andrew to do on a regular basis in order to improve his stamina and his general physical fitness. Jeremy demonstrated the exercises on ropes, wall bars, parallel bars, floor mats and so on; Andrew repeated the exercises each time. It was a tiring, exacting morning and Andrew was pleased when they stopped for lunch; he couldn't believe where the time had gone.

After a light lunch, they went to a classroom where Jeremy talked about various other forms of exercise that Andrew could do, even when sitting down at the office. In the middle of the afternoon, Jeremy took Andrew to the athletics ground and he was asked to do some sprinting – 100 and 200 yards – and then three half miles. Andrew was a good sprinter, but didn't enjoy the longer distances.

After each exercise and run, Jeremy had recorded comments and times on a sheet of typed paper. At the end of everything, both Jeremy and Andrew signed the document which would be returned in the stamped addressed envelope to an address not known to either of them.

Andrew had a shower at the end of the sessions and was pleased that it was all over; he thought he was quite a fit man for his age. He was relieved to see it was only 5 o'clock and so he was in good time to get to Anne's. He thanked Jeremy for his instruction and his time with him. He left Aldershot and thought he was going to have a more enjoyable time over the next few hours than what he had endured earlier in the day.

Chapter 21
Saturday, 6ᵗʰ of April 1940

Monique had prepared a simple but very enjoyable picnic. She remembered some of Artur's favourites from his last visit: local pâté, locally cured ham, two fresh bread sticks, salted butter, tomatoes, blue cheese, but no rabbit food! She managed to find some grapes but not many of the other items he liked were available. Along with the champagne, she bought a nice bottle of full-bodied red.

The sun went behind the clouds in the middle of the afternoon that caused the temperature to drop quite markedly. They stayed at the riverside till about 4 o'clock, then packed everything up. Monique thought the two men would enjoy going back to Pesmes through some of the countryside to the east of Pesmes and drove to the XII century Abbaye d'Acey near Vitreux. They parked the car and wandered around the abbey for about half an hour before setting off for a bar that Monique had taken Artur to in 1935 in Ougney. Monique was welcomed very warmly by the barman, and she introduced her two male friends to him without mentioning their names. The time there was very convivial, but Artur was beginning to think that they should get back to Monique's house.

They arrived in the square in Pesmes as it was starting to get dark. The clouds had thickened from the afternoon and it looked as though heavy rain was on the way. They ran to the house just as the rain started and gave a sigh of relief that they would be dry for the rest of the day. Monique had told Artur and Gerhart that she had managed to buy some nice steak for the evening meal and that she would be preparing everything for about 8:30 p.m.

Not long after they had arrived home, Monique opened a bottle of red wine for the men that they were to enjoy as she cooked the meal. There was then a knock at the front door that surprised everyone.

"Andy, can you see who that is please. I'm rather busy at the moment," said Monique from the kitchen.

Artur looked at Gerhart and they both stood up and looked very tense. Artur left Gerhart in the lounge as he went into the hall.

"OK, Monique, don't worry, I'll see who it is," said Artur.

The door was locked so he took the key from the side of the wall cupboard in the hall, switched on the outside light and opened the door. He saw two policemen outside looking very serious.

"We're sorry to bother you at this time on a Saturday evening, Monsieur, but could we please speak to Mademoiselle Monique for a moment?" said the policeman that looked the more senior.

"It isn't very convenient as she's preparing supper for us. Can I possibly help you?"

"Yes, you may be able to help. We have reason to believe that two men drove a Citroën car here late yesterday afternoon. It was noticed by two Pesmes residents as being registered in the Moselle department but, most particularly, it was damaged on the passenger side and the rear bumper. Someone, most likely the owner, has phoned the main police station in Gray and asked if we could find it as it is very likely to have been stolen by these two men from the Nancy area."

"I'm sorry, Monsieur," said Artur. "But why have you come here to Mademoiselle Monique's house? Why should she have anything to do with a stolen car? Have you tried asking any other residents in Pesmes about the car?"

Just at that moment, Monique came to the front door from the kitchen, wiping her hands on a tea towel. She squeezed past Artur and stared at the two policemen.

"I thought I recognised your voice, Pierre. How nice to see you. I don't think I've seen you since the New Year's Eve party at the Mairie's residence. What a wonderful evening that was."

"Monique, I am very sorry, but I have to be serious for a moment. As I was saying to your friend, the police force in Gray has asked us to investigate the disappearance of a Citroën car that was last seen in the Square late yesterday afternoon. We've been to other houses nearby, as well as yours, to ask if anyone has seen it or knows where it is now."

"Oh, I remember seeing it when we went for supper last night at the new restaurant owned by the Vieille family. Do you remember, Andy, we remarked on the dented passenger side of the car as we passed it?"

Artur joined in the story and said that he thought he remembered seeing it too.

"When I went shopping at about 10:30 a.m. today, it had gone," said Monique. "Sorry, I don't know whose it is nor do I know where it is now."

"OK, Monique, I quite understand," said Pierre. "But we would be very grateful if you could phone us at the station should you see it, or hear anyone say where it is. We are very sorry to trouble you."

"Only too pleased to help, Pierre," said Monique and she went down the step and gave him a kiss on his cheek.

The policemen went away. Monique closed and locked the front door. She and Artur went into the lounge where Gerhart had listened to all that had gone on. They looked at each other in silence for a few moments.

"We ought to be OK for tonight; we've been lucky so far," said Artur. "I think we shouldn't do anything hastily but stick to our plan of leaving on Tuesday morning, unless we are forced to. Do you agree?"

"The main problem as I see it," said Gerhart, "is that the car is at Madame Pélissier's. Are the police going to call on her and then notice the car in her driveway?"

"She does have stabling to the right side of the house that is usually empty, as far as I know," Monique pointed out. "She leaves her car in the courtyard. I could go to her now and ask if I could put the Citroën in the empty stables for a couple of days and see what she says?"

"I think we'd be very much more comfortable about the whole situation if we could possibly do that, don't you Artur?"

"I agree entirely. Let's do it right away."

Monique suggested that she should phone Madame Pélissier before going to her house to make sure she was in. She said she'd make up some excuse about it being in her way, or something along those lines.

Monique went to the phone. They could hear her speaking and gathered that the plan was acceptable. Monique returned to the lounge with a smile on her face.

"Madame Pélissier is very much in favour of the car being in the stables. In fact, she was going to ask us if we would do that, especially if it was to be there till Tuesday."

Smiles all round and Monique said she would move the car and that the two men should stay behind at the house while she moved it.

"Monique, is there anything I can do regarding supper while you are out?" enquired Artur.

"Yes, please could you lay the table in the kitchen and check that nothing is still cooking on the stove."

Monique removed her pinafore, put on her light, outdoor coat and took the keys from Artur. He explained that the gear change handle comes out of the dashboard, in case she wasn't familiar with that model of Citroën. The rain had eased off.

"Thanks for telling me, Andy. I'll be as quick as I can, then we can all relax and enjoy the rest of the evening."

Artur and Gerhart set the table for supper and returned to the lounge for a much needed glass of wine. It was half an hour before Monique returned, and they had started to get worried about her. Had the police called at Madame Pélissier's just as Monique was moving the car? All sorts of possibilities went through their minds. There then was the sound of the key going into the lock and Monique came into the house.

"The mission has been successful," she said joyfully. "It took longer than expected because I had to move a few things round in the stables so that the car would fit. It's all locked away now and she didn't even notice the dented side of the car in the dark. Please pour me a glass of wine and bring it to me in the kitchen, Andy, and I'll finish getting the supper. If you are anything like me, you'll be hungry after all that excitement!"

They took a long, deep breath and smiled broadly at each other. Artur thanked Monique for thinking about the stables as she went to the kitchen. He poured her a glass of wine and took it to her in the kitchen. She put the glass on the table, moved close to him and put her arms around his neck. She kissed him full on the lips. He remembered how they had enjoyed each other's company when he last visited her in 1935.

"Enough of that for the moment, Andy," as she slipped away from his arms. "I'd better get on with the meal."

Artur went back into the lounge. Gerhart and he clinked their glasses together and toasted their good luck. They couldn't help thinking about the policemen coming to the house and how that very same thing had appeared in Gerhart's dream. It didn't make sense so they inevitably started to consider 'where do we go from here?' Artur was all in favour of staying until Tuesday, letting things settle down and keeping their ears and eyes open for any snippets of information that might come their way. Gerhart couldn't come up with any better ideas, so that's what they decided to do.

There was a call from the kitchen to say that supper was ready and to bring the bottle of red with them, if there was anything left. They did as they were told and their noses followed the exciting aromas.

"Wow, that smells fantastic Monique," said Gerhart. "What have you created for us?"

"Well, I know that Andy is very partial to a piece of steak; he likes his under done and prepared with a garlic sauce. I've made some mashed potatoes and spinach, which he also enjoys. I hope it meets with your approval, Gerhart, but your meat is cooked *à point*, as we say."

"It all sounds delicious. Fancy remembering so much about me," Artur remarked.

They sat down at the table and Monique served everything from beside the cooker on to warm plates. After she had sat down, they all raised their glasses to the future, whatever that might bring, and their friendship. There was comparative silence as they enjoyed their meal, punctuated with the occasional noise of enjoyment. As the wine was nearly all finished when they had come into the kitchen, Artur was told to open another bottle.

"I'm not sure if you would like some dessert, but I did buy some more blue cheese, if you would like it? We have some bread left from this morning and I can warm it up in the oven to give it some life."

"Bread and cheese would be an excellent way to finish the meal," said Artur. "Look, I hate to spoil things but we need to talk about what Gerhart and I should do after the visit of the policemen. Whilst you were cooking our gorgeous meal, we have come to the conclusion that, if it's still alright with you, Monique, that we stay here till Tuesday as previously planned. We sort of pretend that nothing has happened, but we keep our wits about us when we go into the village. It's probably sensible if Gerhart and I don't go out together because someone might recognise us if we're out as a pair. What do you think, Monique?"

"That seems fine by me. The only thing we have to sort out is when and how we get your car out of Madame Pélissier's stables when you leave."

"I've actually given that some thought already, Monique. As you seem to get on so well with Madame Pélissier, I suggest you tell her that as we shall be leaving very early on Tuesday morning, you ask to borrow her keys so we can get the car out without disturbing her. You can then return them to her a little later in the morning. I'll also get a small gift for you to give her as a thank you. Do you think she will go along with that idea?"

"I'm sure she will; she's a very nice lady and I'm sure she will think we are being very considerate towards her. I'll see her at church tomorrow morning and if nobody else does it, I'll walk her home and tell her of the plan."

"Great idea," says Artur. "It sounds as though it is all working out beautifully. Now, you didn't happen to mention some coffee and some cognac did you, Monique?"

Monique got up from her chair rather begrudgingly and winked at both of them as she walked to the other side of the kitchen. Artur followed her and offered to do the washing up while she was making the coffee. As it happens, it didn't take very long as she was the sort of person who cleared and washed up as she went along. Artur said he would put things away, but apologised if she found things in the wrong place.

When they got back into the lounge and were enjoying their coffee and brandy, Monique suddenly got up from her chair and went to the sideboard. It wasn't really a sideboard; it was a Philips record player that stood about 1.5m high with a built-in speaker at the front. She took out a couple of records and switched on the player and let it warm up.

"It cost a lot of money last year but I had to have something to play records on. Do you remember this one, Andy? You bought it for me in 1935, but I didn't have a player until last year. I play it very often when I'm on my own and I think of you." She played 'Night and Day' sung by Fred Astaire.

She played the record twice and each time it was playing, she sat in her chair and closed her eyes, smiling to herself.

Chapter 22
Wednesday, 12th of July 1939

The drive to Anne's was very straightforward. He found the row of shops near Reigate that had flats above. Andrew went and parked round the back; it was 6:25 p.m., so he was on time. He had stopped on the way to buy some flowers and he took them from the car. He went up the back stairs and found Anne's flat at the end. He knocked on the door and almost immediately the door opened; he nearly fell in. Anne laughed and told Andrew that she had seen him park his car so she was prepared for his knock. Andrew hid the flowers behind his back as he entered the flat. Anne put her arms round his neck, hugged him and kissed him on the cheek.

"I've got something for you, Anne," said Andrew as he handed her the bunch of flowers. "I wasn't sure what you would like so I bought a bit of a mixture."

"They're lovely Andrew, thank you so much," she said as she kissed him again, this time very sweetly on the mouth. "Please go into the lounge, Andrew, while I put these in a vase."

The lounge-cum-dining room was larger than he was expecting and was very comfortably furnished. Andrew looked around at the pictures and the photos in frames, and thought Anne must come from a good background. The table was laid for supper for two and just at that moment Anne reappeared with the flowers nicely arranged in a vase, which she placed in the centre of the table on a mat.

"I know you won't probably have much time this evening so I thought we should eat first," she said with a wink at Andrew. "So please take a seat and I'll bring in the starter."

"Eat first?" said Andrew. "You have something planned for later, do you?" He knew, of course, what she had meant but wanted to play it along a bit.

Anne wasn't in the lounge so she didn't hear his comment, but she came back in with two large prawn cocktails. Andrew didn't repeat his question. They tucked into the prawns and, before too long, Anne was up again clearing the dishes away.

"Will you open the wine please, Andrew. The cork screw is next to the bottle of red. I know you like red so I brought one from the pub."

Andrew opened the bottle just as Anne returned with a steaming steak and kidney pie, mashed potatoes and green vegetables on a tray. Conversation seemed very easy between them. Andrew declined a second helping even though it was one of his favourite main meals. Anne got up from the table and came round behind Andrew's chair, putting her arms round his shoulders and crossing them in front of his chest; she kissed him on the side of his face. With her still behind him, he brought his hands round the back of the chair and ran them up her legs under her loose fitting frock above her knees towards her thighs. Anne didn't resist, but gave a little shudder as he moved his hands round to the front of her panties and to the inside of her thighs.

"Don't you think it would be easier if we went into my room?"

"I'm sure you're right," said Andrew. "If you're sure that's what you want?"

Anne said no more, but took Andrew's left hand and led him into her bedroom. He could feel his blood racing through his body in anticipation of what was to come next. She pushed the door closed, turned to face Andrew and moved him to the side of the bed. As though it was their first time ever, they quickly took off the other's clothes until she was just in underwear and he in underpants.

"My, you are getting very excited Andrew," she said with eyes wide open and a broad smile. She brought her hands down the front of his pants and held the large swelling very gently in her left hand whilst moving her right hand between his legs. He put his right hand behind her back, unhitched the clip of her brassiere and brought both hands round to cup her adequate breasts.

With a sudden but careful movement of her right hand, she slipped her panties down from her narrow waist; she wriggled her legs so that they fell to the floor. In one quick move, she stepped out of her panties, turned Andrew so that she now had her back to the bed and pulled him on top of her as she fell onto the bed. They wormed their way further onto the bed. He easily found his way into her as her legs were now wide apart and her hands were round his back giving him encouragement.

It was a full twenty minutes before Andrew gave a big sigh and his swelling started to shrink. They lay there in each other's arms, trying to get their breath back and smiling at each other in genuine pleasure.

"What did you say was for pudding Anne, or was that it?" said Andrew with a chuckle as he squeezed her breasts very slightly and looked into her eyes. Anne just smiled as she lay beside him for another ten minutes, teasing each other with their hands. She hoped she might make him swell again so she gently rubbed her hands round his groin and testicles. To help him to swell, he moved his right hand between her legs and massaged the damp area with his fingers.

Just when she was getting hopeful of success, the clock on the nearby church struck 9 o'clock. He shot up into a sitting position.

"Oh my goodness, is it really that time already?" said Andrew anxiously. "I don't really want to go, but I ought to be thinking of driving home."

Andrew kissed Anne, slid off the bed and collected his clothes from the floor. He asked her if he could have a quick wash so she led him by the hand to the bathroom and gave him a towel. She looked very disappointed that he felt he couldn't stay any longer, but quite understood.

In almost no time at all, Andrew was dressed and ready to leave. Anne just had her dressing gown on as they embraced in the lounge.

"That really was a great evening Anne, thank you so much. I wish I could stay longer, but I dare not."

"Maybe we could do it again sometime, but start earlier?"

"I'll see what I can arrange and let you know. Thanks again."

Andrew blew Anne a kiss as he went out of the door. He just hoped he hadn't left anything behind that was important. It was a warm, early July evening outside, and strangely enough, he didn't feel too tired after the day's and evening's exercise.

Andrew drove home quickly but carefully, and was in his driveway before 10 o'clock. Max was in the garden and he thought that a bit odd. He came in through the front gate; Max had heard his master's arrival and came bounding towards him. His wife appeared from the end of the garden and looked daggers at Andrew.

"Where on earth have you been? I've been worried sick that something must have happened to you. I phoned the office this afternoon to remind you that we would be eating early this evening, but they said you hadn't been in all day. What's going on, Andrew?"

Andrew knew from experience that he had to say as little as possible in these situations, so for the moment, he said nothing but just let her rant on. In any case, he certainly couldn't tell her about the training course at Aldershot, or his weapon training at Bisley.

"I waited till 7:30 p.m. for you to get home and as you hadn't arrived by then, I had to cancel going over to see Barbara. It is so selfish of you not even to think of phoning me to tell me what was going on."

What with one thing and another, Andrew had completely forgotten about getting home early. He didn't want to make up any old cock and bull story because she'd see straight through it. Max was at his wife's side at this time so he decided to call him over, which he did. Max bounded over to him as he walked down the garden.

"I suppose you've had something to eat, have you? I had kept yours in the oven, but it will be quite ruined by now; not even Max would eat it."

Andrew was beginning to feel that the heat of her anger was waning a bit, so he decided to just say sorry for forgetting to be back early. But explaining to her about where he'd been during the day was more problematic.

"I'm very surprised that my boss' secretary didn't tell you that I had to be elsewhere today; after all, she knew."

"I didn't get through to her, did I. I spoke to one of your colleagues and he hadn't a clue where you were."

"Not everybody knows everything, so I do suggest that when you phone the office in future, you ask to speak to my boss' secretary as she knows most people's activities in the branch."

"It doesn't answer my question about where you were and why I didn't know either," she shouted.

Andrew was beginning to get bored of the conversation, so told his wife that he was going in doors for a drink and Max followed. He told Max to go into his basket and he walked to the corner cupboard for a brandy that he knew he desperately needed. His wife came into the lounge a few minutes later after locking the front door.

"Have we had any more acceptances to Alfred's Baptism?" asked Andrew, trying to introduce a new topic that she might be interested in.

"As it happens, we had one from your mother. She apparently can't now attend as she has been asked to have dinner at the Savoy with her friend, Lord 'whatever his name is', and could we change the Baptism date. Of all the nerve! And what is more outrageous is that she wants us to cancel her booking at the hotel she was due to stay at if we can't change the date! Typical of the bloody woman!"

"I'll call her tomorrow evening dear, and tell her she has to attend. She can have a dinner arrangement any day she likes with little Lord Fontelroy, but Alfred is her first grandchild and a grandson at that."

"I'll happily leave that to you, but I'm certain she won't change her mind," she retorted.

"Anyway, how has the little chap been today?" Andrew enquired.

"Nothing new from him, but I think he might be teething. He's always wanting to put his thumb in his mouth and you know how much I dislike him doing that."

Andrew felt the atmosphere between him and his wife was improving a bit, but he knew it could change at a moment's notice.

"Sorry dear, I completely forgot to ask you if you'd like a drink. What will you have?"

"Oh, perhaps I'll be daring and have a very small gin and it' with a dash of tonic, please, even if it is a bit late in the day."

"Coming up!" said Andrew very jovially.

With the drinks poured, they both relaxed in the lounge for another half an hour before calling it a day and going upstairs to bed. Andrew breathed a great sigh of relief that his late arrival home had not been pursued any further – for the time being, anyway.

Chapter 23
Saturday, 6ᵗʰ of April 1940

It was getting late after Monique had played the record, but for a short while that didn't matter because Artur's and her memories of their time together in 1935 came flooding back to them. Gerhart was feeling rather uncomfortable as he witnessed what must have been a very strong relationship between them for such a short space of time.

Gerhart made a slight cough and stood up. As he started to say that he thought he would retire to bed, Monique and Artur were quickly brought back to the present.

"So sorry Gerhart," said Monique. "I think we got a bit carried away for a while when we heard that record playing."

Monique got up slowly from her chair, put the record back in its cardboard sleeve and turned off the record player. She stood for a short moment looking at the record before putting it in the storage space beside the turntable. There were tears in her eyes, so she wiped them away with her sleeve before turning to face Artur.

"I quite understand Gerhart, if you want to go up to bed," said Monique. "It has been a long but enjoyable day. Good night and I'll see you in the morning. As you know, I shall be going to Mass tomorrow so I shall be leaving the house at 8:45 a.m."

Monique went over to Gerhart and kissed him on both cheeks, but Artur stayed seated. He just said good night to Gerhart and also said he would see him at breakfast, at about 8:30 a.m. Gerhart disappeared upstairs and Monique went and sat beside Artur on the sofa. She put her hand on his knee.

"Life can get very complicated sometimes. I'm sorry for playing the records, but as we are suddenly together again after five years, I just wanted you to share my pleasure in hearing the tunes again. I know this will be a bit of a shock and obviously I know you are a married man, but will you come to my bed tonight and keep me warm?"

"I do have very strong feelings for you Monique, and we've had a lot of fun in 1931 and 1935 but are you really sure it will help? As I have implied, I would like nothing more, but won't it make matters worse?"

"We both realise that the position in Europe is only going to get worse and this might result in us never seeing each other again," said Monique. "At the moment, as far as I understand it, you are on the run for a number of reasons and from a number of different people. You say you will be leaving on Tuesday at the latest, then where do you go? I'm sure you want to get back to England as soon as possible but it won't be as easy as you think. Do you have anyone else, to stay with? Have you got a plan, or are you taking one day at a time? Let's make the most of the small amount of time we have together. Maybe I can help you to get to where you want to."

There was silence for a while.

"What do you mean, have we got anyone else to stay with?" said Artur.

"I know people in various places who would be only too happy to put you up for a night or two, but where do you intend leaving France from, Andy?"

"The original plan was through Denmark for me and the northwest French ports for Gerhart, but this is looking increasingly more difficult as time goes by. We are now thinking of Gerhart going through Spain and me going from Marseille."

"How will you get to Marseille Andy, and how will Gerhart get to Spain and, presumably, to Gibraltar?"

"We are supposed to use our initiative Monique, and any assistance we can get."

They discussed the options for quite a while, but they were both beginning to feel very tired. Eventually, Artur put his arm round Monique and brought her close to him. She didn't resist, but turned her head towards him and brought her lips into contact with his. He gently drew away from her and looked into her eyes.

"You can read my mind in my eyes Andy, can't you, but you are still a little uncertain, aren't you? Don't you remember in 1935, after you'd been down to the Monaco Grand Prix, you arrived here and we spent two days in bed and hardly ventured out of my bedroom, even to get something to eat or drink?"

"Of course I do. I was exhausted after those days together and I still don't know how I drove back to England. I've never experienced anything like it, before or since."

"So why did you get married to that English woman Andy, when you knew there was someone in France who would have you as a husband or a mistress at the drop of a hat?"

"That's why I'm hesitant, ma chérie. I really can't have you as either. Can't you see that? You deserve better than that anyway. You should find a nice young French man to settle down with, have babies with him and have a proper life."

"The situation in Europe doesn't help my position. At the moment, I have to take my pleasures any way I can find them."

"Do you mean, Monique, that you attract yourself to lots of men and that's how you get the pleasures you need?"

"Of course not, Andy, you are twisting my words and reading different meanings into them. What I mean is that the European situation is so unstable that it isn't right to get involved with someone when there is a distinct possibility that tomorrow they will be killed and taken from me."

"But that is exactly why I'm hesitant about us."

"I understand that Andy, but we started all those years ago in 1931. Neither of us will ever forget that weekend. Then, you spent three days with me here in Pesmes. We hardly saw the world outside my bedroom. Can we not just relive a little bit of that, and then you can go and get back to England."

Artur thought Monique put forward a very strong case for spending the night with her and he didn't have anything else to justify not being with her that night. He got up from the sofa and she looked at him with that amazing look that could suggest nothing else. She went upstairs and prepared herself for bed. Artur followed a few moments later and went into the bathroom. When he came out, he noticed that Monique's bedroom door was ajar. He went into her room, closed the door carefully behind him and slipped into her bed and into her arms.

Artur awoke suddenly, but he didn't know what time it was. He slipped out of bed trying not to waken Monique and went to the bathroom. He switched on the light for a brief moment and saw it was 4:30 a.m. *Why have I woken at this hour?* he thought to himself. *Something must have caused me to wake.* He looked out of the bathroom window, but he couldn't see much as it faced the back of the house. He went into his bedroom and without switching the light on, he peered through a narrow gap in the curtains out of the window very carefully. He saw the shape of two men in front of the church in dark clothes. He thought he recognised them as the two who had been in the square the previous day when they went out for their picnic. He couldn't understand what they were doing at this time of the night, nor what it was that had awoken him. He went downstairs very quietly and then into the lounge to see if he could get a better view of the men. The curtains were open so he sidled around the wall towards the window. They weren't there, nor were they further down the road towards the Porte St Hilaire. He waited a few minutes and then decided to go back upstairs to his own bedroom and try and get some sleep – he certainly needed it!

Artur was aware of movement downstairs. He saw it was well after 8 o'clock, so he went down into the kitchen. Monique was already dressed and was having some bread and jam.

"Hallo, Andy," she said. "What time did you leave my bed?"

"I am very sorry, but I suddenly woke at about 4:30 a.m. and went to my bedroom to look out of the window. There were two men standing in front of the church and they looked very much like the ones I'd seen in the square yesterday, when we drove off for our picnic. They were talking and one of them pointed at your house. But I've no idea what woke me. I hope I didn't disturb you at all."

"No, you didn't disturb me but when I turned over I noticed you were no longer there. You were wonderful last night, Andy, I really needed you to be with me. I will always remember this night for the rest of my days. I'm sorry, but I really must dash for Mass. We'll talk more later about how I might help you and Gerhart to get away from France. Help yourself to whatever you want; I'll be back by about 10 o'clock."

Monique went over to Andy and gave him a gentle kiss on the lips. She took her coat from the hall and disappeared out into the fresh, morning air as though she was walking on a cloud.

Gerhart came downstairs and saw Artur in the kitchen. He said he heard movements at about 4:30 a.m., but then went back to sleep.

"It was most probably me," said Artur. "I was woken by something and when I looked out of my bedroom window, I saw the two men that we saw yesterday in the square, standing near the church. One was pointing at Monique's house. I don't think they saw me. I then went down stairs to get a better look from the lounge window, but they weren't there anymore, were they? You must have heard me going down stairs."

"So, if they were the same men, what do you think they were doing at that time of the night?" said Gerhart.

"I asked myself the same question and I have no answer. Do you want some coffee? There's some in the pot."

"Do you think we should leave earlier than Tuesday, Andy, or shall we hang on here and hope for the best?" Gerhart helped himself to a coffee and took the milk from the kitchen table.

"I would be happier if I knew what those men really wanted. I would like to meet them and ask them what interest they have in us. I know it sounds risky, but I really do need to know who they are."

Artur poured himself a coffee, but kept his black. He went to the bread bin and tore off a piece from the rest of the baguette. He spread some butter and jam on the bread and sat at the table to eat it, leaving Gerhart standing by the cooker. Artur was deep in thought as he ate his bread and jam.

"You know what I'm thinking, Gerhart? I think we try to ignore the incident in the early hours of the morning. Once Monique has returned from church, I think we should wander round the village together and into the square. Have a beer in the bar and generally behave as though we have no cares or worries. If the two men are around anywhere, I will go and ask them point blankly what interest they have in our car and us. What do you think, Gerhart?"

"Why not, Artur? I'm up for it, but it's very risky."

Artur finished his coffee and bread, and after putting the dishes in the sink, he told Gerhart that he was going to get shaved and cleaned up before Monique got back from Mass. He asked Gerhart to wash the dishes after he'd had some breakfast, if he wanted anything.

On Monique's return, Artur told her of their plan; she wasn't too sure about it but went along with it anyway. She had another coffee and when she put her mug in the sink, she was surprised that all the washing up had been done and thanked whoever had done it. She said that she had spoken to Madame Pélissier after Mass about the keys and she would gladly let Monique have the spare set whenever she wanted to collect them. They all agreed that they should get the keys sooner rather than later.

Chapter 24
Thursday, 13th of July 1939

Andrew felt rather stiff when he stepped out of bed on Thursday morning, but he wasn't really very surprised after what he'd been through at the gym, and at Anne's place. He still couldn't work out how lucky he'd been with his wife's attitude and how she hadn't really interrogated him – as she'd done in the past

When he arrived at the office, his boss called him in to 'have a little chat', as he said. Andrew closed the door behind him. He wanted to know how he had got on at Aldershot and whether or not he was feeling a bit worn out.

"Thank you for asking, sir, but I feel much better than I expected. I suppose I can consider myself very fortunate in being quite fit anyway. As you well know, I have a dog and that means I get out for walks, particularly at weekends. That all helps to keep me in reasonable trim, as they say."

"Quite so, Williams. Now I'm obviously interested in your training and so on, but I really want to tell you that we would like to transfer you to another branch for about a month. You've developed some good skills within the Foreign Exchange group and we feel you would benefit from a brief spell in Manchester. How would that seem to you? I know your wife has only recently given birth to your firstborn, but could she cope without you?"

"That sounds fine to me, Mr Beckett, but when do you have in mind for me to start? The reason I'm asking, sir, is that my son's Baptism is due on 6th August and I must be at home for that."

"I'm sure that won't be a problem as you'll only be away during the week and back home again at weekends anyway."

"Oh well, that sounds alright."

"Let me just look at my diary a moment," said his boss. "A good start date from our point of view would be in one week from next Monday, the 24th. How does that seem to you?"

"As far as I can tell, that's good timing for me. Shall I be staying at a hotel, or will a colleague be putting me up?"

"We'll pay for you to be in a hotel. I think you'd prefer that wouldn't you?"

"I would, yes sir. Thank you. Shall I be going up by train, or should I drive?"

"By train would be the best. It's a long way to drive, especially if you will be coming home at weekends. There's just one other thing, Williams: all this will coincide with your next course with the Intelligence Service. You will be told in the next few days, but there is a training establishment that they want you to stay at for a couple of days, not far from the main Manchester office, so be prepared."

"Oh I see. Thanks for warning me, sir."

"I think that will be all, Williams, unless you have any questions? The finance man will sort you out with some money for expenses and the hotel bill will be paid by the Manchester office."

"Very good, thank you, sir. No more questions at present."

Andrew left his boss' office and returned to his desk. Some people were looking at him and wondering what was going on. He took the usual train home and arrived in a good mood.

"Hello dear, I'm home," he shouted as he entered the front door. He couldn't see or hear his wife, so he assumed she must either be upstairs putting Alfred to bed or in the garden enjoying the warm, evening sunshine. He went up to his room and changed into some casual clothes. He looked into Alfred's nursery to find that he was already in bed, so returned downstairs and out into the garden. He saw her down at the end of the garden relaxing in a deck chair with Max by her side. Andrew whistled and Max immediately bounded up the garden towards him as his wife looked up from her book.

"Hello Andrew, you're home nice and early tonight!"

"I've got some good news for you, my dear. I've been asked to work at our Manchester branch in a couple of weeks to increase my experience in the Foreign Exchange section. I shall be away for four weeks, but I'll be back at the weekends."

"That sounds exciting. I don't suppose it's anything to do with your possible promotion, is it?"

Oh my goodness, is she still going on about that? he thought to himself. *I suppose I'll just have to go along with it.*

"It could be dear, but nobody's said anything yet. Shall we have a drink in case it might be?" asked Andrew.

"What a good idea, and it's such a nice evening too."

Andrew disappeared into the house and found a bottle of red from the wine rack and a white from the pantry floor. He searched in the kitchen for some cheese and biscuits, and wandered back to the garden with everything on a tray.

"There we are. I assume you'll be having wine or did you want something different this evening?"

"White wine will be just the ticket," she said.

Andrew drew the corks and poured out the wine.

"Cheers, my dear. Here's, to many more sunny days and good surprises," said Andrew.

"I was thinking, when you were getting the drinks, if I might come up with you one of the weeks and go and stay with my brother and his wife – they're not far from Manchester, and they've not seen Alfred yet."

Andrew was wondering when this sort of suggestion was going to come up, especially having now told his wife when he was due to be up north.

"It sounds like a good idea, but we've got the Baptism coming up in a few weeks and, as they'll be coming down for that, there seems little point in you seeing them only a week or so beforehand. Anyway, how will you get from Manchester station to their house? It's a long way. Also, he works and his wife doesn't drive."

"It seems as though you always put an obstacle in the way when I want to do something different, especially if it involves you as well."

"I'm only trying to be helpful and pointing out some of the considerations to be taken into account at this particular time. We could always ask them down in the summer for a few days and I could take a few days holiday to be here too," Andrew suggested.

"I thought you might think it would be nice for me to get away for a short while, instead of being stuck around here all the time," she replied, rather tersely.

Andrew was not prepared to get drawn into a heated discussion, but he had to make a response.

"I'm not saying it's not a nice idea, but the timing is probably not right. After all, there are still some things to arrange for the Baptism. In any case, you have plenty of friends nearby, you have a car and Alfred's now old enough to be taken with you. You are free to do whatever you like, as far as I can see it."

Andrew thought he might have gone a bit too far, but he felt he should remind her of how much freedom she already has.

"I suppose you're right, Andrew, as always. But it would be nice if we could get out together a bit, now that it's summertime. Take a trip to the seaside, or meet some of our friends for lunch somewhere at the weekend."

"I agree entirely, so let's look at arranging something for after the Baptism. Later in August perhaps? Alfred will be that little bit older by then."

Andrew felt he had just about placated his wife; he poured out another glass of wine for each of them and as he touched her glass with his, he toasted her with one of his engaging smiles.

"Do you mind if I call Brian?" asked Andrew, expecting his wife to enquire why.

"No, I don't mind. Are you planning to meet him over the weekend? Make sure he's still got Alfred's Baptism in his diary. After all, he's the main Godfather."

"I'm sure he's not forgotten the date. I'll see if he's free on Saturday before lunch. Talking of food, have you got something in mind for supper? I'm feeling a bit peckish."

"I'll see what I can rustle up, but I'm not going to get it yet, it's so nice to enjoy this summer evening.

Andrew took another swig from his glass, filled it up again and wandered off to the phone in the hall, taking the glass with him. He dialled Brian's number and waited for a few moments as it rang. Brian answered and seemed to be out of breath.

"Are you alright, Brian? You seem to be out of breath."

"Ah, Andrew, how nice to hear from you. Sorry, we were sitting in the garden with a couple of pals having a drink so I ran in when the phone rang. It's such a wonderful evening, isn't it?" Brian took a deep breath.

"Brian, I rang to ask you if we could meet for a beer around Saturday lunchtime. I need to talk to you about something important. Can we meet at the Crooked Billet at about midday?"

"You sound in a very serious mood, Andrew. Is everything alright? You haven't been getting yourself too close to that Anne woman have you? You know, the waitress at the Red Lion?"

"No, Brian, it's nothing to do with her, I promise. By the way, you are still free for the Baptism, aren't you? It's three weeks on Sunday, the 6th of August."

"Of course, how could I forget that very important date? How is Alfred?"

"That's good. I'll reassure my wife. So, meeting on Saturday will be OK? I'll probably bring Max, especially if the weather is like it is now. I'll ring off now as you have friends with you."

"Don't count on the weather being warm and sunny on Saturday. Haven't you seen the forecast in the papers? Rain and thunderstorms are due this weekend, so they say. I'll see you anyway and don't worry about a thing. Cheerio, old chap."

The phone went dead. Andrew returned to the garden and told his wife not to worry about the Baptism: Brian hadn't forgotten. He also told her that he'd be meeting him on Saturday at the Crooked Billet. She finished her wine and said she was going inside to get something for supper.

"If it's alright with you, I'll just take Max for a short walk across the road," he said to her as she stood at the entrance to the house. "I won't be more than twenty minutes."

"That's fine, but no longer please. Anyway, not long ago, you said you felt a bit peckish."

"I think the wine and some of that cheese has reduced my appetite. Whatever you decide to get will be fine by me, thank you."

Andrew fetched Max's lead from the hall stand; Max had already realised that his master meant business. He ran round in circles on the lawn making funny sounds. He came near to Andrew and then rushed off to do another circle. When Andrew was ready, he called Max quite sternly; he came to his side and rubbed his head against his leg.

"I'm going now, dear," shouted Andrew through the front door. There was a mumbled sound in reply that came from the kitchen, but he wasn't certain what she had said. He just needed a bit of space, to clear his mind and think through his four weeks in Manchester.

Andrew arrived back after twenty five minutes and offered his apology for being later than he'd said he would be. It was a simple supper of Welsh rarebit, followed by some of his favourite cheese. They finished the bottles of wine and went to bed before 10:30 p.m.; both of them were in reasonable humour.

Chapter 25
Sunday, 7ᵗʰ of April 1940

They left the house at about 11:30 a.m., and as it was starting to drizzle, Artur and Gerhart wore their 'acquired' jackets. Monique put on her new rain jacket and took an umbrella. They walked casually up Le Grand Rue and left into the square. There weren't too many people around, probably as the two bars in the square weren't open until midday. They decided to go down the stairs towards the restaurant they had been to on Friday evening, then left up the incline past the sign for the centre of the village. After a while, they turned left towards Madame Pélissier's house. Monique didn't need to ring the bell as the gate was ajar.

"That's very strange," Monique said to Artur. "She doesn't usually leave the gate unlocked. I hope everything's alright."

They went with Monique as she walked through the front garden to the front door. She knocked on the door and called her name, but the door was unlocked. She gradually opened the door and they all went in to the large hall, leaving the door open behind them. They were all very concerned and didn't really know where to start looking for her. As they were about to enter her kitchen, they heard someone running from the stable area down the drive. Artur immediately ran to the front door and saw two men going out of the gate, then to the right and down the road. He was too far away to properly identify them, but he was sure they were the same men he had seen in the square and in the middle of the night.

Meanwhile, Monique looked round the kitchen, then into the front lounge. Madame Pélissier was lying on the floor. She seemed unconscious and had probably been hit on the head with something hard; there was blood on the carpet in front of the fireplace. Monique told Gerhart to place the rug that was on the sofa on top of Madame Pélissier and place one of the small cushions under her head very gently in case she had damaged her neck. Monique told Gerhart that she was going to use the phone in the hall to call Madame's doctor. She wasn't sure if she should phone the police yet as they might start asking them some very awkward questions.

Artur came back to the house from the front garden to find Monique and Gerhart attending to Madame Pélissier, who was beginning to come round. He went into the kitchen and brought back a glass of water for Madame. He then went back to the kitchen to find the door that went out to the side area by the stables was open. He exited the kitchen down the steps and strode to the stable where their car was garaged. He examined the doors and saw that the padlock had been forcibly opened. Somehow, the men had known that the car had been put in Madame Pélissier's stable, but where did they get that information from?

As he was racking his brain, a car horn blasted at the gate so he ran over to see who it was.

"It's probably Madame's doctor. If so, please let him in, Andy," shouted Monique from the front door.

Artur ushered the doctor into the drive and greeted him with a handshake. He told the doctor that Madame was in the lounge on the floor being attended to by Monique. He hurried quickly in to the house, followed at a more leisurely pace by Artur. When the doctor got to the lounge, he saw that Madame was sitting up on the floor and drinking a glass of water. She smiled at the doctor.

"What have you been up to, Madame Pélissier?" said the doctor. "Can you tell me what happened?"

"Not really, doctor, it all seemed to happen so quickly really. I hadn't been home from Mass very long when there was a knock on the front door – I must have left the gate unlocked. There were two men there and they insisted on coming in to my house. They pushed me into here and the next thing I knew I was being attended to by Monique."

The doctor examined Madame's head very carefully, then her arms and legs.

"Is any part of your body hurting apart from your head?"

"No, I've just got a bad headache, as if I've had one drink too many!"

They all laughed while the doctor looked more carefully at her head.

"It's a nasty gash, so I'll bathe it and see if it needs some stitches."

Artur excused Gerhart and himself from the room and showed Gerhart through the kitchen and out to the stable doors.

"As you can see, the lock has been forcibly opened by those men. Not sure if they went inside the stable, but we'd better take a look around in any case."

They opened the doors wide so they could see their way inside the stables. Artur remarked that it was fortunate the boot was locked and that they'd left nothing inside the car. It wasn't easy to tell if the men had looked round the car but one thing was certain: they knew where the car was and would have recognised it as the one that had been parked in the square a couple of days ago. This was what really worried them both.

They closed the stable doors and chatted about what they should do next for the best as they went back to the lounge. Madame was now sitting in a chair with her feet up on a stool and the rug around her shoulders. The doctor had given her some painkillers and told her she was lucky that she hadn't been more badly hurt.

"I'm so sorry to have been a nuisance doctor, and having you to visit me on a Sunday too. I usually take better care of myself and won't allow strangers into my house, but they barged their way in."

"It's not a problem. As you know, I only live a short distance away from here. Just take things easy for the rest of the day. Take the painkillers every two hours and I'll come and see you again tomorrow."

Madame Pélissier thanked the doctor again for calling, as did Monique, who showed him to the door. Artur went to the gates and let the doctor out, at the same time giving him a wave. Artur went back to the lounge to join the others who were talking to Madame about the attackers.

"Did you recognise either of them, Madame?" enquired Monique very softly.

"Well, it's very strange but I think I did. I've seen them around over the last few days and they've always been together. I think one of them lives in Pesmes, out on the road to Gray, I believe. He's lived there quite a while. The other man doesn't come from around here and I've not seen him before the end of last week."

"That's very interesting, Madame," said Artur, "because I saw them in the square on Friday afternoon." Artur refrained from mentioning that he saw them at 4:30 a.m. the previous night outside Monique's house.

"Do you happen to know the name of the one from round here?" asked Artur.

"I think his name is Jacques Bouvet, and someone told me he had a brother running a bar in a village east of Nancy."

They all went quiet for a while. Artur looked at Monique and suggested they should leave as Madame needed some rest.

"We think we should be going now, Madame," said Monique. "But I'll call again later this afternoon to see that you are alright, or you can phone me at any time. Is there anything I can get you before I go?"

"No thank you. You've already been most kind and so have your two nice friends. Enjoy the rest of your stay with Monique, messieurs."

Artur went and locked the kitchen door at the same time that Monique was collecting the spare keys so she could let herself back in again later. They all said goodbye and locked the front door and the gates as they left Madame's property.

They decided to go straight back to Monique's house rather than to a bar; they could have a well-earned drink there. Monique fetched a bottle of wine and glasses from the kitchen and joined the men in the lounge.

"Monique, we have to tell you that we are very concerned about this Jacques man and his brother that runs a bar in a village east of Nancy. We need to explain to you why we are so worried, but let's have a drink first, please.

"We need to be absolutely certain that what we're going to tell you will go no further than these four walls. It is very secret and we trust you to tell nobody else."

Artur went through all that Gerhart and he had been involved in; how they got across the border into France; the incident with the barman from Breidenbach; how the car was damaged and who it belonged to and so on. Monique listened to it all very intently and made no interruptions. When Artur had finished, Monique said that she clearly understood why he and Gerhart were so anxious.

"Monique, I firmly believe that we need to draw up a new plan. My suggestion is that we take our car from Madame's stables after dark this evening and park it back in the square. But, before that, we drive yours to the stables and take the things from our boot and put them into yours. We drive our car back to the square and park yours down near your house in Le Grand Rue. We then ask you very kindly to take us to Lyon railway station and I suggest we leave just before dawn. Instead of Lyon, we could go to Chalon-sur-Saône. What do you both think?"

There was silence for a few moments as Monique and Gerhart mulled over what Artur had said.

"I really don't mind doing what you suggest – taking you to Lyon or Chalon-sur-Saône – but what do we do with your things that will be in the boot of my car?"

"That's a good question, Monique," said Gerhart. "That crossed my mind too. I'm sure we should go to Chalon and then take our chances with the train services. Leaving the Citroën in the village square will not give a problem to Madame Pélissier, we hope."

"So, what time do we clear the Citroën's boot and move it to the square?" asked Artur.

"As soon as it's dark," Gerhart reckoned. "Or when Monique pays Madame a visit this afternoon, she can tell her that we will move our car from her stables and put it in the square. She shouldn't then need to worry about any more intruders."

"That's what we'll do then," said Artur, concluding the discussion.

Chapter 26
Saturday, 15th of July 1939

Early on Saturday morning, Andrew was aware that his wife had already got out of bed. He heard some crying sounds coming from Alfred's nursery. *That's very unusual,* he thought to himself, *I hope everything's alright?* He jumped out of bed, put on his dressing gown and went into the nursery.

"Is Alfred alright, dear?" said Andrew.

"Yes, thank you. I think he was uncomfortable in a wet nappy, so I've changed him and I'm also giving him a feed. You go back to bed and get some more sleep."

Andrew did as his wife suggested, but when he got into bed, his mind was churning over the things he would be doing over the next few weeks. He must have fallen asleep for a while because the next thing he knew, his wife had come back into their room with a cup of tea for him.

"That's a very nice surprise, dear. Have I been asleep very long?"

"Probably over an hour as it's now 8 o'clock."

"Goodness gracious me. I mustn't hang about for long as Max will be standing with his legs crossed if he doesn't get out soon."

"It's alright, Andy. I let him out into the garden about half an hour ago, just before I made the tea. He's had a few biscuits and he's back asleep in his basket."

"That's very kind of you, my dear."

Andrew sat up in bed and drank his tea. He patted his wife's side of the bed and suggested she got back in for a short while as she'd had her sleep disturbed by Alfred's waking early. He embraced her and they slid down under the bedclothes together, she in his arms. She mumbled sweet nothings in his ear that surprised him just a little. Andrew's mind strayed for a moment and he thought of the amazing short evening he had spent with Anne.

"It's all very nice, my dear, but I think I should get up," said Andrew, breaking his hold from around his wife's shoulders.

"But it seems to have been such a long time since we have had a time such as this. Do you have to get up now?"

"I really think so, but we'll promise to have a time like this again once the Baptism is over and I'm back from my stint in Manchester. Don't you agree?"

"I suppose so," she said rather reluctantly.

Andrew kissed his wife on the lips for a full two minutes and as he could feel an arousal starting when his wife's hand found its way down under the bedclothes to his crotch, he slithered out of bed.

"You're a spoil-sport, Andy."

Andrew took no further notice and disappeared into the bathroom. He kept wondering why his wife was so friendly all of a sudden. A little while later, he was dressed and down in the kitchen preparing some breakfast; his wife had gone back to sleep. After he'd finished and cleared everything up, he went out with Max to the garage to tinker with his Bugatti in preparation for his meeting with Brian at lunch time. It was turning out to be quite warm and there didn't appear to be any sign of rain, so he was looking forward to going out in the 'Bug' and having a bit of a spin. When he was satisfied that the car was in good working order, he helped Max into the well in front of the passenger seat and backed out into the road. He needed some petrol, so he drove out of the village and down the relatively straight road towards Horsham at speed. He was really enjoying the drive, but had to slow down as he approached the garage. He had the tank filled up and as the tyre pressures were a bit on the low side, he had them inflated just a bit above the recommended pressure – he had been told it was the right thing to do many years ago when he had his first car.

He decided to go the long way back home and eventually brought the car to a halt in front of his garage doors. By this time it was nearly 11 o'clock, so he hurried into the house closely followed by Max. His wife was not to be seen anywhere so he went into the garden and found her in a deckchair with Alfred in his wicker cot next to her.

"I wondered where you had got to," she said. "You didn't tell me you were going out so I was beginning to get worried. You've been out for over an hour."

"Sorry, it was such a nice morning and I didn't want to disturb you. I went to get petrol and then took a long route home. Is everything alright? Can I get you anything?"

"No thank you. What time are you meeting Brian? Where are you meeting him?"

"About midday," Andrew replied, deliberately not giving her any clue as to which pub it would be. "I shouldn't be out for more than a couple of hours or so."

The conversation ended, so Andrew went back into the house to change out of his old clothes and into something casual. He didn't really know how much he should tell Brian; it just depended on how things went and how many people were near them. He knew he was going against all the Service's regulations, but he had to share his thoughts with someone; it would only be Brian, nobody else would know anything.

After changing, Andrew went back into the garden and kissed his wife goodbye. He had agreed to take Max so she would only have Alfred to look after. He enjoyed the Crooked Billet: the beer was good, the landlord was not over friendly and there was a good selection of things to eat. He had a good run to the pub in the warm sunshine and parked his car next to Brian's dark red Alvis – the cars looked good beside each other, their paintwork gleaming in the sunlight. He walked briskly into the main bar where he greeted his friend.

"Sorry I'm a bit late, old boy. Hope you haven't been here too long?"

"I've only just arrived, Andy. What will you have to drink?" Brian bent down and stroked Max who gave him a knowing and welcoming lick on the back of his hand.

"A pint of the best for me," he said to the landlord as they shook hands across the bar.

"Haven't seen you for a while," said the landlord. "Haven't you recently become a father? How's the little chap coming along?"

"You've got a very good memory. He's coming along very well, thank you. It will be his Baptism in a few weeks' time."

"Hope you have a nice day for it, sir," the landlord said as he passed over Andrew's pint, together with Brian's

"What's special on the menu today? You haven't got liver and bacon by any chance? It's one of the best for miles around."

"It's funny you say that because we have."

"Will you have the same, Brian, or do you want the cottage pie, which is also first class?"

Andrew ordered the liver and pie and they retired to a free table in the corner of the bar. They chatted about Andrew's boy and the forthcoming Baptism as well as the situation in Europe, which lead very easily into Brian asking Andrew about his training with the Service.

"Well it's almost going too well," commented Andrew. "I'm being sent up to Manchester by the bank for four weeks and at the same time being asked to attend some short Service training courses. I seriously think the Service hierarchy are keeping in touch with the bank management."

"My goodness, will that interfere with Alfred's Baptism, or will you be allowed home at weekends?"

Andrew went through some details of how it would all work out and he also let Brian know what he had achieved on the other courses.

"Wow, things are moving apace. What do you think your wife would say if she knew the implications of what you are doing?"

At that moment, the food arrived and Andrew ordered two more pints. Not much was said as they tucked into their lunch, and then took a few swigs of the newly arrived pints.

"So, Andy, you go up north on Monday week. Do you need me to call in on your wife during your absence?"

"That would be a really nice idea if you could, especially as the Baptism is only three weeks from tomorrow. I know everything is organised, but she's very likely to get worried about the caterers, last chat with the vicar, people cancelling at the last minute, that sort of thing."

"Not a problem, Andy. Has your mother decided to come or is she still being difficult?"

"She's not coming, which is probably a blessing as she will only be very critical of the food, what my wife's wearing, complain about the standard of the hotel she would be staying in and so on. She's best out of the way."

They talked more about Andy's bank job in Manchester as well as the training course. Then, out of the blue, Brian asked if he'd be interested in a weekend away in August to Wales with just a few of their mutual friends. Did he think his wife would enjoy such a trip? After all, they'd been to Wales before, but that was before Alfred was on the scene.

"I'll put the idea to her. She had said we ought to get away, so mid to late August would be fine as it would be after I'd finished my time in Manchester and the Baptism would be all over and done with. Sounds to me like a brilliant idea, Brian."

Andrew looked at his watch and saw it was nearly 2 o'clock. *Amazing how time flies when you're enjoying yourself!* He thought.

"Brian, I didn't realise the time so I had better be going soon. I didn't want to be out much more than two hours and I should also give Max a bit of a run about, but I'll do that after I get home. It's been really helpful to speak to you about all that is going on in my life. As I've said before, it's highly confidential so not a word to anyone."

"Don't worry, old boy, my lips are sealed. Shall I settle the bill this time?"

"Let me give you a contribution. After all, it was my idea that we should meet up."

Andrew drew out his wallet and gave Brian a crisp, new note which he reluctantly accepted. Brian went up to the bar to pay and Andrew wandered out into the car park with Max and inspected Brian's car.

"Is she running well, Brian?" asked Andrew as Brian came up beside him.

"Can't grumble, old boy, but it could do with a good long run such as going to Wales for the weekend, perhaps," he jibed.

"As I said, I'll need to talk it over and get back to you. Not quite sure how we'll deal with Alfred, if we're going all that way. Anyway, leave it with me. I suppose I might not see you before the Baptism, but let's pray for a fine day."

"You mind how you go up in Manchester, Andy. We'll see you at the church on the 6th."

The two of them shook hands and Brian patted Max on the head. Once each of them was in his car, they started up almost simultaneously with a roar that drew the attention of some admirers in the pub's garden.

The rest of the weekend went by without any issues. Most of Sunday, Andrew spent in the garden attending to the grass and generally tidying up a few of the flower beds. The gardener had been coming in for an extra day each week leading up to the 6th, and so he had been doing most of the heavy work and the trimming of the hedges. He made a list of what clothes he would need for the following week, bearing in mind that he would only be at the office during the day and not be involved in any Service training course until the third week. On the Tuesday, after Andrew had been in the office for about an hour, he was ushered into his manager's office to take a call from Charles, his Service contact. Charles was aware of his transfer to Manchester the following Monday, and so confirmed to Andrew that all was arranged for his next training course near Manchester two weeks after he'd been up there, starting on Tuesday, 8th August for two days. Charles said that he would get all the details to him by post during his first week at the bank's Manchester office and if he had any questions about what he was being asked to do, he should phone him immediately to discuss. When he had finished talking to Charles, his manager came back into his office to check that all was organised.

"Your hotel accommodation has all been booked for the four weeks that you are in Manchester," said Mr Beckett. "Please talk to my secretary and she'll give you all the details you need."

"Thank you very much, sir. Do you want me to buy my own train ticket and claim it back on expenses?"

"No, that won't be necessary, Williams. We will buy the return ticket, first class of course, and give it to you on Friday when you collect your advance towards any incidental expenses. That exercise will be repeated each Friday up north. Are you happy with that?"

"I'm more than happy with that, sir. What time will the bank's office people be expecting me on Monday, or do you want me to travel up on Sunday evening?"

"It would be best for us if you went up late Sunday afternoon so that you could be in the office bright and early on Monday. You then travel back to London on Friday afternoon. This should be repeated the following week, but after you have your son's Baptism, you can travel up on the Monday morning and arrive at about lunch time. Does that sound alright?"

"I'm very pleased with all the arrangements, sir. Thank you."

Andrew shook his manager's hand, gave him a smile and left his office to get back to his work. *All seemed to be going beautifully,* he thought to himself.

The rest of the week seemed to fly past without any difficulties arising. Andrew's wife was very relaxed about his being away the following week and had set up some plans to meet some of her friends during Andrew's absence. On Friday, Andrew got home early and decided he'd change and go and tinker with his car before supper. It wasn't raining, but the weather had definitely cooled down a bit for late July. During supper, he told his wife that he would like to drive out on Saturday morning for an hour or two, to which she agreed.

"I suppose you'll want to meet Brian for a beer, will you?"

"No I don't think so. I think they're away this weekend anyway."

What he really wanted was to go to the pub where Anne worked, the Red Lion, and have a chat with her about the possibility of her coming up to Manchester.

The Saturday morning was rather dull, but Andrew still thought he'd chance going out for a spin so he set off at about midday. He felt very excited about the possibility of seeing Anne, but he wasn't certain that she would be working. He drove into the pub's car park rather too quickly and nearly ran into someone who had just got out of his car. He jumped out and apologised very profusely for not concentrating on what he was doing. Fortunately, the man was not too cross but was more interested in admiring Andrew's car.

"I suppose if I was to be knocked down by any car, a car like yours would be what I would choose," he said jokingly.

Andrew was relieved and after he had parked his car properly, he ran into the pub to try and buy the man a drink. The man was already at the bar ordering his drink. When Andrew offered to buy it, the man politely refused.

Getting his breath back, he looked around for Anne as he ordered his pint, but couldn't see her. He moved away from the bar and sat at a table near the window. He looked at the menu and thought he would like the cottage pie. As he got up from the table, Anne came in from the kitchen with a tray-load of food. She didn't see Andrew as she turned away from where he was to another table at the end of the bar. Andrew's heart jumped when he saw her, but continued towards the bar to give in his order.

"Not got your friend with you today?" said the barman.

"No, he's away this weekend. I'll have the cottage pie, please."

"We're quite busy today so you might have to wait for about fifteen minutes. Will that be alright?"

"No problem, I'm not in a hurry."

Andrew went back to his table and he was aware of a tap on his shoulder before he sat down. He turned round and Anne's eyes stared smilingly at him.

"Not seen you for a while, Andrew. I thought you might be away or found someone else."

"I have missed you too," said Andrew with his engaging smile. "But I am going to be away for four weeks from Monday, up in Manchester on business. I'll be back at weekends though. I was wondering if you had any time off and perhaps could come up and see me during one of my weeks there?"

Andrew knew it was a faint hope but he had to ask her.

"I do have some time off, but are you sure that's a good idea? It's not cheap to get to Manchester and back on the train. Wouldn't it be better if we met at my place again?"

"You are probably right. Sorry, I was getting a bit carried away with the thought of spending a night with you."

At that moment, Anne suddenly realised that she should get on with her work, so she turned on her heel and trotted off to the kitchen. Andrew sat down and took a very large swig of beer. He knew he'd been a bit forward in suggesting that she should come up and see him in Manchester, but it was worth a try. While he was pondering over a few alternatives, he was brought back to reality with Anne bringing his lunch.

"There you are, Andy. Sorry I can't stay to chat but we are rather busy, as you can see. Catch me before you leave. Anything else you need?" she said with a wicked look in her eye, but before Andrew could reply, she had turned and disappeared through the kitchen door.

Before starting his meal, he bought another pint and returned to his table. It was a table for four and as there weren't any other vacant tables available, a young lady came up to him and asked if he would mind sharing his table with her and her two friends, or was he expecting someone to join him.

"No, I should be delighted," he said, standing up and giving the lady one of his engaging smiles. He moved the three chairs away from the table.

"Are the others joining you soon?" said Andrew.

"They're just parking the car and will be here any minute. Please don't stand any longer as your lunch will be getting cold."

Just as he was about to take his seat again, two strikingly attractive young ladies walked in. They looked around and then waved at their friend. A hush seemed to come over all those in the pub as everyone at once saw those entering the bar. Andrew stayed standing and smiled at the one by the table. The two came over and greeted their friend.

"This gentleman has kindly agreed for us to share his table with him as there are no others available. Sorry, I don't know your name but mine is Veronica and these two friends of mine are Penny and Chloe."

They all exchanged pleasantries and Andrew sat down once the three others had taken their seats. Chloe took the drinks order and went to the bar to get what they needed.

"Is this your local pub, Andrew, or are you passing through?" said Veronica.

Andrew finished his mouthful of pie and swilled it down with a good swig of beer. He then wiped his mouth with his napkin and explained that it was one of his favourite pubs, but was not his local. An easy conversation developed and their drinks were brought over by Chloe.

"Where are all you lovely ladies from, Veronica? I've not seen you in here before, if I had I would definitely have remembered you," enquired Andrew, looking around at all three of them and smiling.

"Penny and I are from a village just south of Billingshurst and Chloe is visiting us from the Bolton area for the weekend. She's going back tomorrow on the train, sometime in the late afternoon."

"Is that so? I'm also going to Manchester tomorrow and I'll be there all week on business. Perhaps we could go up together, Chloe?"

Chloe smiled rather sheepishly at Andrew and then looked hard at Veronica.

"Chloe's a bit shy Andrew, and as we've only just met you she probably feels you are still a stranger to her. I'm sure she would enjoy your company on the long journey, wouldn't you Chloe?"

Chloe looked a bit uncomfortable and fidgeted on her chair. She said nothing, but just smiled rather nervously at Andrew.

"I quite understand how Chloe feels, Veronica. I'll mention it no more but if you don't mind I'll continue with my lunch."

The ladies talked quietly amongst themselves and discussed what they should have to eat. Every now and then, Chloe looked over to Andrew; he noticed and gave her a wink that made her blush. Decisions were made about their choices and Chloe offered to go up to the bar and order. As she got up from the table, Andrew thought it was a good time to get another pint. He sidled up to Chloe and touched her on the shoulder. She turned to him and looked him in the eyes.

"Don't tell the others, but I would really enjoy your company on the train tomorrow. It gets very boring on one's own. What time are you intending to travel from Euston? I'm catching the one leaving at 5:35 p.m. It gets in to Manchester just before 8 o'clock."

At this point, the barman interrupted them asking what they would be ordering. Chloe ordered the food and Andrew asked for another pint.

"I was thinking of catching the same train," said Chloe a little excitedly.

"So why don't we meet in front of the booking hall at 5:15p.m?" suggested Andrew.

"Good idea," said Chloe. "I think we ought to return to our table as they will be wondering what we've been up to."

Just as Andrew was turning round, he noticed Anne was waving at him and was looking rather serious. He went over to her and smiled.

"So, you've now got three very attractive young ladies at your table and not taken any notice of me."

"It's all very simple. Let me explain."

But before he could say any more, Anne turned on her heels and headed for the kitchen. *Oh dear, me thinks a little jealousy is creeping into her pretty young head,* Andrew thought. He returned to the table and sat down. He and the three girls saluted each other with 'cheers' all round and he continued with his not very warm cottage pie. The ladies continued to chat until he'd finished eating. Not long afterwards, their meals were brought to them by a rather frosty Anne. Andrew tried to get her attention, but she wouldn't look at him.

"Look, I'm really pleased to have met you, all you lovely people, but I must be going," said Andrew, at the same time standing up. "Enjoy your meal, and I'll look out for you at Euston tomorrow, Chloe."

They all said goodbye and Veronica said she hoped they might meet up again sometime. Chloe smiled at Andrew, but said nothing. Andrew went to the bar to pay for his meal and drinks, but he couldn't see Anne to try and explain why the ladies were at his table. Just as he was about to go out into the garden, Anne came towards him with a loaded tray of used dishes and glasses; he opened the door to let her through. He decided he wasn't going to talk about the ladies at his table but about when they might meet up again.

168

"Anne, as you know, I leave for Manchester tomorrow and I'm not back until early Friday evening. Couldn't I meet you at your home and take you out for a drink?"

"No, I don't think that would be convenient. Phone me and perhaps we can make an arrangement. Sorry, but I must get on, Andrew. As you can see, we are very busy today."

With that, Anne strode through the door into the bar, leaving Andrew muttering to himself. *Oh well, I've at least got Chloe's company on the train tomorrow.*

Chapter 27
Sunday, 7ᵗʰ of April 1940

Monique prepared a light lunch that they ate in the kitchen. She went back to visit Madame Pélissier at about 3:30 p.m., and on her return, she mentioned that Madame was feeling a little better and had been able to get herself some lunch. Madame was very happy with the arrangements for the car in the stables to be taken back to the square.

The afternoon seemed to drag by very slowly, even with all of them having a sleep for about an hour. The light drizzle and the cloud cover made it get dark a little early. Artur suggested that he and Monique should take her car slowly around through the square to Madame's house and that Gerhart should walk via the church to the house. If any of them detected anything untoward then they would discuss matters in Madame's stables.

Monique drove Artur through the square, but nobody was about in the rain. Gerhart met them at Madame's gate and none of them reported anything unusual, to their great relief. Monique reversed her car up to the stable doors that had been opened by Artur. Without unwrapping the armour, Gerhart and Artur transferred everything into Monique's car whilst she was indoors attending to Madame again.

Monique drove her car to Le Grand Rue, parking it near to her house, and Gerhart went with Artur to park the Citroën in a corner of the square, not far from the steps. They all met up again at the front of Monique's house and, after a quick glance up and down the road, went into the kitchen for a cup of coffee. They hadn't noticed two dark figures standing close to the church, watching them enter the house.

They were all relieved that the first part of their plan had been completed. They knew, however, there was a possibility that, even late on a Sunday afternoon, an alert local policeman might notice that the Citroën was back in the square, or someone might tell the police that they had seen it in the square again.

Monique drew all the curtains to stop prying eyes looking into the house. Artur and Gerhart talked over the next steps of their plan with Monique listening in. The favoured route was for them to be taken to

Chalon-sur-Saône station with Artur going to Marseille and Gerhart to Calais via Paris. It was long overdue that they should separate and go their own ways. The only slight snag was that they had no idea of the times of trains from Chalon to the south and that would affect how long they would be waiting at the station.

"Andy, I have an aunt who lives near Tournus," said Monique. "I could phone her and ask her about train times, if you like? She is often going to Paris by train to visit her sister so I'm sure she would be able to help."

"What a good idea, Monique. Do you think you could call her now?"

"I'll be only too pleased to do that. Just wait while I find her number." Monique went upstairs and after a few moments, she came down excitedly saying that she had her aunt's number.

Artur and Gerhart quietly went over a few details together, but could still hear Monique talking on the phone. After the initial introductory chat with her aunt, there was a long pause.

"Andy," said Monique, "I've got through to my aunt and she's trying to find the timetables so I might be a while just waiting."

"That's fine," said Artur. "Gerhart and I have a few things to go through anyway so there's no rush. It's good that she thinks she can help."

After what seemed an age, they heard Monique talking again. It appeared to them that she must be writing down some times on her writing pad by the phone and repeating them to her aunt as she read them to Monique.

"That's really helpful, auntie," she said. "I'll pass all that information over to them and they can decide which trains to catch. Yes, I suppose I could come and see you once I've dropped them at Chalon station, but it probably won't be till the afternoon, if that's alright with you? Yes, I could stay the night if you would like me to. I'll phone you from Chalon so you know what time to expect me. Thanks for your help, auntie. See you tomorrow. Goodbye."

Monique came back into the kitchen and went through the train times that her aunt had given her.

"The only problem that I can see, if it really is a problem, is that there are more trains going to Paris then there are to Marseille and that's because a lot of the ones going south terminate in Lyon. Gerhart can catch a train to Paris at 10:35 a.m. whereas a direct train to Marseille for Andy isn't till 13:46 p.m."

"So, how long will it take to get to Chalon from here?" asked Gerhart.

"Well, I need to look at the map to confirm, but it's a bit less than 100 km away. So, shall we say 2 to 2.5 hours?" said Monique.

"That seems fine to me," said Artur. "So, we leave at 7 o'clock and grab a coffee on the way. Now, there's only one other thing that we need to consider: what do we do with the arsenal of arms that is currently in your car, Monique? You can't be driving around with it in the boot of your car for ever, can you?"

"Oh my God, Andy, I'd completely forgotten about all that stuff," said Monique, and then put her hands to her mouth, as though she was going to be sick.

"Got any ideas, Gerhart?" asked Artur.

"I reckon that when we're on our way to Chalon, we find a side road and dump any of the armour that we no longer require, somewhere in the woods. What do you think, Artur?"

"I agree. We should get rid of all we don't need as soon as possible," said Artur. "How well do you know the road from here, Monique? Do we go near any wooded areas?

"I know it quite well, but I'll get my map from the lounge and we'll have a look."

Monique went to the lounge and after a few minutes, came back with a map and a beam on her face.

"I think this should show us enough detail, Andy." She cleared a few things from the table and spread the map out. They all peered at the map. "There are two possibilities: the woods on each side of the road just after Moissey, and the ones after Pourlans."

"I think we should go for the ones after Moissey," Artur insisted. "As far as I can judge from the scale, Moissey is only about 15 km away and, if we leave at 6 o'clock, or earlier if you like, it might still be dark when we get there. As you said, Gerhart, we should then be able to hide all we don't need without being seen. Do you both agree?"

The others agreed. Monique suggested they should have a drink and some cheese and bread after such an eventful day. They decided to stay in the kitchen rather than move into the lounge. They were confident about their plan, but were still very concerned about the two men who had attacked Madame Pélissier that morning; who were they and what were they really looking for?

The wine went down well, but with another challenging day ahead of them, they decided to get all their things together for an early start in the morning. It wasn't difficult for the men as they hadn't got much anyway, but Monique needed a suitcase as she was going to be staying with her aunt for a day or two after dropping them off at Chalon station. Artur sorted out his satchel and made sure he had the right documents to hand, should they be stopped *en route*. Both men checked their pistols and ensured they had plenty of ammo.

Artur asked Monique if he could use her car keys as he wanted to get a few things from the boot that weren't going to be dumped in the woods the following morning. He went out in to the street and up to Monique's car boot. As he was about to open it, he was aware of someone close to him. He dropped the keys to the floor and as he bent down to pick them up, he looked under his arms and saw two men standing behind him. He didn't know if either of them had a gun, but he had to take a chance. When he was bent down he pushed the keys under the car, quickly rolled over to his left and stood up facing the men.

"Who on earth are you two? I've seen you around the village over the last few days at very odd times of the day and night. What do you want with me?"

They stared at Artur in a way that suggested they hadn't understood him; they didn't appear to have a gun. Artur wasn't sure if he should speak to them in another language, but he thought that would be rather foolish. He fixed his eyes on them and waited for them to say something or make the next move. In the meantime, Gerhart had been wondering what Artur was up to, taking so long to come back from the car. He instinctively picked up his pistol and looked out of the open front door up to the left where the car was. He saw the situation and ran as fast as he could towards the men, pointing his pistol at them and shouting at them in French to put their hands up. As the men looked Gerhart's way, Artur leapt at one of them and put him in an arm lock, forcing him to the ground.

"If you don't tell us what you want with us or who you're working for, we'll tie you up and throw you in the river. Do you understand me?" said Artur threateningly.

There was still no response from the men. The one still standing stood motionless, but with his head turned towards Gerhart, who now had his pistol up against his left temple.

"What is your name?" shouted Gerhart. "We know one of you lives here. Which one of you is Jacques Bouvet?"

For the first time, there was a muttering from one of them, the one being held by Artur. At that moment, Monique came running out to find out what was going on.

"Monique, go and call the police and tell them we have found the two men that they've been looking for regarding the stolen Citroën. Tell them they have been snooping on us for the last few days and that we have captured them near the Mairie."

Monique gave a slight smile and ran back to the house to make the call. The men still said nothing. In less than five minutes, they heard the police van driving down Le Grand Rue towards them. Monique had at this time returned to the scene. It came to a halt and three policemen jumped out of the cab.

"Messieurs, please see that my friends have apprehended these two men. We believe they are the ones you've been looking for in connection with the stolen Citroën. They won't admit it to us, but if you took them to the police station, and kept them in overnight, they will confess under questioning in the morning, we're sure," said Monique.

"But Madame Monique, how do we know you are telling us the truth without any further evidence?" said the senior policeman.

"I suggest you look in the pocket of this man's coat and you'll find something of interest," explained Gerhart.

The senior policeman went forward and put his hands in the pockets of the man that was next to Gerhart. He rummaged for a moment and then drew out his right hand with a bunch of keys.

"I think you'll find those to be the Citroën keys, Monsieur, but don't take my word for it. Take these two up to the square and try the keys for yourself. If they fit, these two are your men," concluded Gerhart.

The two captured men now started to argue and struggle as they were pushed into the police van. They knew that they had been duped, but they didn't know how it had been done. The van turned around and went up towards the square.

Artur recovered the keys to Monique's car and unlocked the boot so he could continue taking out the items that weren't to be discarded in the woods. Once he'd finished, he locked the boot and they all returned to Monique's house.

When they got to the lounge, Artur quizzed Gerhart about his sleight of hand.

"Well, it's like this," explained Gerhart. "When you took so long, I knew something must be wrong. I picked up my pistol and took the Citroën keys from the hall stand. When I was standing next to the man with my pistol at his temple, I slipped the keys into his pocket."

"It was a stroke of genius, Gerhart. Heaven knows what would have happened had you not been so quick thinking. Unfortunately, it's now even more important that we leave early tomorrow. I'm sure we won't get away with this for very long. It does, however, allow us to have a reward for our initiative, but yours in particular, Gerhart."

"Here, here," agreed Monique. "I'll get a bottle of red wine – if I've got any left! Unless of course, you had something else in mind?" Monique looked at Artur and gave him a wink but he made no comment about any alternative; he was still thinking about the incident outside.

"Wine will be fine," said Artur, walking over to Monique and Gerhart and bringing his arms round them in a fond embrace.

"We've been very lucky, but I'm not sure how long our luck will last. Once those two men are at the police station and they tell their side of the story, it might be enough to convince the police that we're really the two they want."

Chapter 28
Sunday, 23rd of July 1939

Andrew spent most of Sunday morning going through his list, sorting out his clothes and packing his suitcase for the following week. He thought it would be best to travel in his suit rather than pack it. He reckoned he'd got enough clothing for more than a fortnight, let alone just a week. The atmosphere at lunch was a bit strained, and he couldn't help thinking how lucky he was to be travelling up with Chloe.

As there were fewer trains on a Sunday, and as they tended to stop at many stations, Andrew decided to catch the one that left just after 4 o'clock. He'd ordered a taxi to take him to the station and was all ready to leave at 3:30 p.m. He lifted Alfred up from his pram and gave him a peck on the top of his head and then embraced his wife. He told her that Brian might contact her during his week away to check if all was OK.

"I'll call you once I've settled in at the hotel. Have a good week, dear, and I'll see you Friday evening."

"Have a good week in the Manchester office, Andrew. Don't get up to any mischief, will you? This could be a very important time towards your promotion."

Andrew guessed this old chestnut would come up again, but he made no further response as the taxi driver hooted outside. He gave a wave as he went through the gate to the driveway, but his wife had already disappeared indoors. It was starting to drizzle again.

He took a taxi from Victoria to Euston and arrived just after 5 o'clock. He made his way to the booking office and sat on a bench outside looking around for Chloe. The rendezvous time came and went. He was thinking he might be travelling up on his own after all when he heard Chloe's distinctive voice mention his name.

"Andrew, so sorry I'm late, but the underground trains were only operating every half an hour to Euston. Anyway, I'm here."

Andrew stood up and smiled broadly at Chloe. He decided not to kiss her, but outstretched his hand and shook her gloved hand gently.

"Presumably you have your ticket, Chloe, so if you're ready, we ought to go to the platform as the train leaves in ten minutes?"

Andrew carried his and Chloe's case and she took his brief case. They went through the barrier and walked up to the first class compartments.

"I'm not in first class, Andrew, so you'll have to come and see me once the train leaves."

"Don't worry, Chloe, I have checked with the booking office and there's a seat next to mine. I've been given a chitty by the clerk and I'll give it to the inspector when he comes round to check people are in the right seats."

"That's very kind of you Andrew, but you really shouldn't have done that. I'll have to reimburse you somehow."

"Don't worry Chloe, we'll sort something out in due course."

They climbed on board and Andrew found the compartment. His information from the booking clerk indicated that there was only one other person in with them. The luggage was stowed away, coats were hung up and they settled into their seats. In next to no time, the engine gave a loud whistle and they were on their way. The door from the corridor opened and in walked a rather harassed old gentleman. He was rather overweight and was very red-faced as he struggled in with his large suitcase.

"Please let me help you with that, sir," said Andrew as he jumped to his feet to help the man.

"Thank you very much. I have always sworn that my wife should not pack my case. She invariably puts far too much in it and then I can't carry it."

"Don't worry. Maybe I'll put it on the seat opposite. Where is your destination?" enquired Andrew.

"I'm going to Crewe, but I won't be in the seat for long as I'm having a meal on the train."

Andrew sat down; he turned to Chloe, gave her a wink and placed his hand on her arm. Eventually, the man sat down, or rather fell down, and let out a long breath from his mouth. He closed his eyes and seemed to be asleep almost immediately. Andrew and Chloe chatted quietly to each other and occasionally Andrew glanced at the man. The inspector knocked on the door and came in to check the tickets. Andrew handed over his and the chitty from the booking clerk, together with Chloe's ticket.

"Thank you, sir, that's all fine," the inspector said. He then shook the man's arm, and he awoke with a start, muttering something completely unintelligible.

"Sir, your ticket, please? I know you're a regular traveller on this service but I still need to see your ticket."

The man fumbled around his inside jacket pocket, pulled a ticket out and handed it to the inspector, who checked it and handed it back.

"Dinner will be starting in fifteen minutes sir, if you would like to make your way to the dining car.

"Will you and your lady be dining tonight?" Andrew was asked.

Andrew smiled.

"Would my lady like dinner tonight?" asked Andrew with a big grin at Chloe as he turned his head and looked into her hazel eyes.

"It sounds like a nice idea, but I'm not sure I can afford it."

"Not to worry Chloe, the first class ticket upgrade included dinner, so it would be a great pity to let it go to waste!"

"Alright then, why not? It will save me getting something when I get back home."

In due course, the man got up and went off to the dining car, followed a few moments later by Chloe and Andrew. Conversation at dinner was very easy and Andrew found himself quite engrossed in hearing some of the details of Chloe's North Country life. As was Andrew's wont, he learnt much more about Chloe than Chloe found out about him. They spent nearly forty-five minutes at dinner and then returned to their compartment. The man was already there and asleep.

The next thing they all knew was an announcement saying that they would be entering Crewe station in ten minutes time, but the man was still asleep. To their surprise, the inspector came in through the door; he gave the man a shove and told him that they would be entering Crewe very soon.

"We always have to make sure he's awake so he can get off at Crewe," said the inspector. "One time he overslept and he gave us a right ticking off!"

The man duly rose from his seat, took his coat from the rack and dragged his case out into the corridor, at the same time saying goodbye to his fellow travellers.

The inspector returned and checked that nothing was left behind.

"That gentleman's a judge, you know, and he travels up to Crewe every fortnight for just a few days."

Chloe and Andrew just smiled and nodded.

"So you say you live in Farnworth, Chloe, and work in Manchester in a bank. Which one might it be?"

Chloe told him and he couldn't believe his ears when she mentioned its name.

"That's amazing Chloe, because I work for that bank and I'm going to be in their foreign exchange department for the next four weeks."

"I had heard someone was coming up from the London office, but I hadn't heard a name. So you'll be staying in the hotel round the corner from the bank. That's where all our visitors from the south stay."

"Goodness me! What a small world. We must have a drink after work one day."

Chloe was uncommitted. Andrew reckoned she would take only a little persuasion, but didn't pursue it any further at this time. He could always ask her when they were in the office.

Before they knew it, the loudspeaker announced that they would be arriving in Manchester in the next seven minutes, only a couple of minutes behind schedule.

"Will someone be meeting you, Chloe?"

"No, I catch a bus that leaves at 8:15 p.m. It doesn't take long and it stops at the end of my road. Hopefully it's not raining."

Andrew took Chloe's and his case down from the luggage rack and opened the door for her to go out into the corridor. The train gave a jolt as it came to a stop and Chloe fell onto Andrew's chest. She looked up at him and kissed him on the cheek.

"Thank you so much for your company and for arranging my ticket upgrade. I'll look out for you in the office tomorrow, but there are three floors. I know someone in foreign exchange so she'll probably call me when she's seen you."

"I've greatly enjoyed being with you, Chloe. Have a good journey back to Farnworth."

After they had got off the train, they entered the concourse; Chloe went to find her bus and Andrew to get a taxi to his hotel. They blew kisses to each other as they parted and smiled. Within fifteen minutes, Andrew had checked in at his hotel and unpacked his clothes in his room. He thought about putting the radio on, but decided he should call his wife first.

"Yes dear, all is well here. I had a very comfortable journey up. Is everything alright your end?"

Apparently all was fine, although the dog had been sick on the lounge carpet; something he'd eaten in the garden. She wasn't sure what it was, but it looked a bit like a toad. Andrew advised that if Max was not eating properly the following day, she should take him to see the vet, just to be on the safe side.

Chapter 29
Sunday, 7ᵗʰ of April 1940

The bottle of red that Monique brought to the lounge was the last one, or so she said. After they toasted each other, and Gerhart in particular, they took a large swig and then sat down. There was silence for a few minutes that seemed to go on for ever. Much was on their minds, especially Artur's. He was wondering if they'd be able to get rid of the excess arms without being seen; he also wondered whether they should take the grenades or not. Last, but not least, when would the three of them see each other again, once the two men had caught their respective trains?

"It really is very good wine, Monique, but I'm not sure I'm in the right mood for it right now," said Artur.

"I'm afraid I feel the same way," agreed Gerhart.

"Well," said Monique, "none of us know when we'll meet again, so let's finish it and get some sleep. Tomorrow is going to be a long day for all of us and we'll need to be very vigilant and careful until you two are safely on the train. Have you checked all your papers and got enough money? I can let you have some if you need it as I can get more for myself when I'm at my auntie's."

"Yes, thank you Mummy," said Artur jokingly and with a smile. "But a few more Francs would be helpful if you could spare them."

Monique went to the drawer of the desk near the window. She pulled the drawer out completely and put her hand into the back of the drawer space. She pulled out a large envelope and broke the seal.

"This is my secret hideaway for emergencies," she said and put the contents on the table in the middle of the room.

"Good Heavens," exclaimed Artur. "That looks like a small fortune. I'm sure we won't need all of that."

"You're not going to get all of it, my dear Andy, but you can certainly have half of it."

Monique counted out the notes and returned about half into the envelope. She placed the envelope at the back of the drawer and replaced the drawer.

"Andy, I suggest you sort out how much you should give Gerhart and you keep the rest," said Monique as she looked at Artur.

"Are you sure that'll be alright? I feel a bit embarrassed taking all this money after you've been so hospitable to us."

"Don't be so silly, Andy. I can't let you try and leave France without anything to cover a few unforeseen eventualities."

Artur gave a handful of notes to Gerhart and put the rest into his satchel.

"I hope you don't mind Monique, but I think we ought to listen to the radio and catch up with the latest news. It's just coming up to 8 o'clock, so there should be another bulletin on the hour."

Monique went to the wireless and turned it on; it was still tuned to the French radio station that Artur had listened to the day before. It took a few moments to warm up and then a noise became louder and louder: it was a man's voice. The newsreader reported that the French and British Governments had announced that their navies were in the process of mining Norwegian waters in anticipation of an imminent invasion of Norway by German warships. It was also reported that German troops had moved to the border with Denmark and that they had been spotted near the north German coast of the Baltic Sea.

"It's quite obvious to me that the Nazis have a plan to enter Denmark and Norway, and very soon too," said Artur in a serious tone.

"Well, at least they're not too interested in France for the time being," said Monique with a sigh of relief.

The newsreader went onto a few other topics so Monique turned the radio off.

"Well, we could be in for a few exciting years of conflict, don't you think?" said Artur.

"I'm not sure it sounds exciting to me, more like nerve-racking," said Monique.

"You're right, of course, Monique. We have no real idea of what scale of war we are about to enter, but Germany certainly has serious expansionist intensions," remarked Gerhart.

"Does either of you want something to eat by any chance? I've still got some things left over from our picnic and I'm sure there are things in the larder, if you'd like me to look?" Monique enquired.

"What a good idea, Monique. We'll come and help you prepare something and we can eat in the kitchen, don't you think?" said Artur.

They all got up and Gerhart followed the other two with the bottle of wine into the kitchen. Monique looked into her store cupboards as well as the larder; she suggested an omelette followed by cheese and bread that was considered very acceptable by the men.

After a while, they all sat at the table and tucked into their meal; conversation seemed to be bit strained. It was nearly 9:30 p.m. by the time they had finished their meal, and Artur suggested it was time to turn in, once the washing up had been completed.

"Does anyone want a coffee?" enquired Monique, looking at both men but they turned the suggestion down. Gerhart said that he was going to bed once he'd sorted his things out in his room.

"What time do you want to leave tomorrow, Artur?" asked Gerhart.

"We should try to be on the road by 6:30 a.m., if that's OK with you both?"

"Sounds good to me," the others said, almost in unison!

"I'll have some coffee ready at 6 o'clock," Monique offered.

"Good night, Gerhart. I hope you get some sleep," said Monique as she walked over to Gerhart and gave him a kiss on each cheek.

Monique and Artur stood and watched Gerhart go out of the kitchen and heard him striding up the stairs.

"Do you think he's feeling alright, Andy?" whispered Monique. "He doesn't say very much and he looks quite solemn."

"I think he's a thinker and he was troubled by the incident with those two men and the car. It's the second time in two days that he's had to challenge someone with his pistol and it's playing on his mind. He's probably thinking about tomorrow and how he'll manage on his own, once he's on the train to Paris. I'm confident he'll reach England, but he could have a few challenges before he gets there."

"And how about you, Andy, will you get back to England in one piece?" asked Monique, looking into his eyes and putting her arms round his waist. "Do you think our paths will ever cross again, or is this our last time together?"

"If our countries enter into a proper all-out war, who knows what will happen, but I do hope we'll meet again."

Artur put his arms around Monique's shoulders and drew her close to him, kissing her lightly on the lips. Her eyes were closed and she wanted this moment to continue for ever. She was warm and felt secure in Artur's arms. After a few moments, Artur pulled his head away from Monique and smiled as he looked into her watery blue eyes. They said nothing but it was obvious to each of them that they didn't want tomorrow to come, for today to last for a very long time.

"It's nearly 10:30 p.m., and we ought to get some sleep," said Artur and they moved away from each other. Monique took her handkerchief from her sleeve and dabbed away her tears.

"This will not do," said Monique. "You go upstairs and I'll put a few things out for tomorrow morning.

"Thank you so much for coming to see me Andy, and for the last two days of real enjoyment. I haven't been as happy since the last time my parents came to visit me before leaving for Austria. Sleep well and see you tomorrow at 6 o'clock."

"Good night, Monique."

Artur turned out of the kitchen and glanced around the lounge to make sure he'd left nothing behind. Once upstairs, he used the bathroom and, when in his bedroom, closed the door and carried out a thorough check of his things. He lay on the bed with his hands behind his head and went through all that had to be done tomorrow. Before he knew it, he was asleep and dreaming about jumping out of the train and hitting the snow-covered ground. He heard the words that the lady said as she ran her fingers through his hair. He felt the sheep skin coat being placed over his chest and the warmth of her breath on his cheek. He could feel the ache of his head as he stretched out for his satchel.

Artur woke with a start. His hands were no longer behind his head, but were holding tightly to his satchel; his light jacket was over his chest.

That's very strange, he said to himself, *I thought I had left my jacket downstairs on the hall stand. I wonder what time it is.* He looked at his watch and saw it was just after 1 o'clock. He decided to climb into bed properly and try to forget about his dream and why his jacket was over his chest. He'd ask Monique if she had put it there in the morning. He fell into a deep sleep.

"Hallo? Andy, are you awake? It's time you were up," said Monique as she opened the door to Artur's bedroom. She stepped inside and went over to the bed. To her great surprise she saw that he wasn't in bed and she just managed to make out that the bed had been tidied and none of his things were in the room. She walked out of the room and knocked on Gerhart's door. There was no reply, so she quietly opened the door and peered inside. Again, the room was empty so she went downstairs to the lounge. The door was closed so she assumed they must be inside; there was light coming from the room under the door. She opened it and went straight in.

"Goodness me, how long have you two been up?" enquired Monique. "I was getting very worried that you might have overslept and when I found both of your rooms were empty, I thought you had run off without me!"

"Why on earth would we have done that, Monique? We couldn't just get up and leave you, could we? We just needed to go over our plans again and make sure we've covered every eventuality. Anyway, will you be ready to leave in five minutes? After all, it's after 6 o'clock and that's near to the time that we should be leaving."

"I'll be as quick as I can, Andy. My bag is already packed. I just have to jump into my clothes."

With those last words, Monique ran out of the lounge and upstairs. Artur and Gerhart looked at each other and smiled.

"She's quite a woman, Artur. Do you think she will drive, or will you persuade her that you should?"

"If I know her as well as I think I do, she'll ask me to drive and she'll want to sit in the back."

Within next to no time, Monique was downstairs again with her overnight bag in her hand. She picked up her shoulder bag from the hall stand and checked the contents. She looked a million dollars as she walked into the lounge.

"Right gentlemen, I'm ready for action," she said with an engaging smile. "But we haven't had any coffee yet."

"Never mind, we'll call into a bar on our way to Chalon. By the way, I've taken the liberty to look in your desk for writing paper and an envelope and I've written a note to Madame Pélissier. When you get back, I'd be pleased if you could give it to her and perhaps give her a small bouquet of flowers. After all, she's been through a tough time recently, and mostly because of our being here."

"Of course I shall, with great pleasure, Andy. That's very thoughtful of you."

"Excellent, Monique! So if we are now ready, we ought to be on our way. We're ten minutes past our departure time."

"I'll just double check the door and windows in the kitchen and we can be off. Would you mind driving please, Andy, and perhaps Gerhart should be in the front so he can help with any map reading?"

"What did I tell you, Gerhart? No problem Monique, a sound suggestion. By the way, did you happen to place my jacket over me in the night because I awoke at 1 o'clock to find it over my torso?"

"Yes, it was me," said Monique. "You were lying on top of the bed, so I put it over you so you wouldn't get cold. You looked so peaceful so I decided not to slip onto the bed beside you, although I was seriously tempted," she said with a smile and a wink at Artur.

They turned out all the lights, gathered up their bags and maps and went into the hall as Monique was coming from the kitchen. The men went out first and Monique locked the front door. It was still dark, just as they had hoped it would be, but there were a couple of street lights on further up Le Grand Rue. They placed their bags in the boot next to the armour and locked it. Once they were in the car, Gerhart and Artur put their pistols on their seats between their legs for easy access. They had earlier decided not to go through the village square, but out of Pesmes using the road past

Madame Pélissier's and then towards the bridge over the river – just in case someone was loitering in the square. Their first task, of course, was to get rid of the armour.

Chapter 30
Monday, 24th of July 1939

Andrew had slept well following his journey up from London, and after a light breakfast, he was in the office by 8:30 a.m. The receptionist was expecting him and directed him to the first floor with a bright smile, where his manager for his duration in Manchester would be waiting for him.

He took the lift and turned right into the foreign exchange office, looking around him as he entered.

"Ah! Mr Williams, thank you for coming in nice and early after your journey up from London yesterday. My name is Alan Griffiths. I trust your hotel is to your liking and that you rested well?"

"Thank you, all is fine, Mr Griffiths. I'm looking forward to the weeks that I shall be here and will no doubt learn a lot."

Once all the pleasantries were over, Andrew spent a large part of the morning being introduced and chatting to others he would be working with, and being shown to a desk that had been set aside for him. When he was getting his tea from the tea lady's trolley around 11 o'clock, he overheard one of the secretaries say that she'd seen the new man from London called Andrew Williams and what a good-looking man he was. He also thought he heard her use the name Chloe.

Andrew got down to some serious work in the afternoon and was quite ready to leave for the hotel when Mr Griffiths asked him if he would like to join him and a few other colleagues for a drink in a nearby pub. He accepted; after all, it had been a long first day.

Going to the pub had been a good idea and Andrew got to know quite a few new people. Even though he was very thirsty, he was very careful not to have more than two pints and not to talk too much about himself. Most of them were Lancastrians and were eager to talk about how much better and cheaper it was to live in the north rather than 'down south'.

Andrew focussed on his work for the remainder of the week and hadn't even tried to contact Chloe. Before he knew it, Friday lunchtime had arrived and he needed to get ready to catch the train to London in the afternoon. He thought he couldn't wait till the following week to call Chloe, so found her number from one of the secretaries.

"Hallo Chloe. I'm so sorry not to have been in touch with you this week, but time seems to have just flown by. How are you anyway?"

"Well, thank you. I was going to call you on Wednesday, but I guessed you would be very busy. Are you going back home today, or shall we have a drink together this evening?" enquired Chloe.

"I'd love to, but I'm catching the train this afternoon. I'm back again on Monday, so let's arrange to go for a meal on Tuesday. Will that be convenient, or have you something else arranged?"

"No, that would be very nice. I'll think of a place and we'll speak again Monday afternoon. Have an enjoyable weekend Andrew, and don't get up to any mischief will you!"

"Who, me, get up to mischief? I should be so lucky! I shall be under orders to complete the planning for my son's Baptism. It's in a few weeks from now. Anyway, good to speak to you. I'll call you on Monday when I get back."

They finished their call and Andrew wished he'd contacted Chloe earlier in the week rather than just as he was about to go home. Just before Andrew was going to leave the office, a man rushed up to him waving an envelope at him. Andrew recognised him as someone who worked in the post room on the ground floor.

"Sorry Mr Williams, sir, but I meant to bring this to you earlier today. It arrived in today's post."

"Thank you very much Dan, I have been expecting something this week, so I'm pleased it has arrived at last."

Andrew looked at the envelope and saw it had a London postmark. There was no other distinguishing mark, but he knew it was from Charles, giving him instructions for his next course in two weeks' time. He put it in his briefcase, he would read through it on the journey back to London. He went back to the hotel. He had arranged with the manager to leave some of his things in his room over the weekend and have a shirt, socks and underwear laundered. He called his wife to tell her he was about to leave and all seemed well at her end. He was back at home just after 7 o'clock, and was able to have a few minutes with Alfred before he was put into his cot. Max was pleased to see his master again and Andrew had had his wife's agreement to take him for a walk after supper.

On Saturday morning, Andrew went through Charles' instructions for his course in his study for a second time, even though it wasn't for another ten days. All seemed quite straightforward: covering map reading, radio communications and Morse code. Andrew always enjoyed maps and was often the one who planned the trips with his friends to Devon, Wales etc.

He thought this part of his training should be far less taxing than the physical training down in Aldershot.

Having to leave home on a Sunday afternoon for Manchester certainly seemed to greatly shorten Andrew's weekend; as a result, he didn't meet any of his friends at the pub this Saturday, but he did think he'd try and meet Chloe during next week; she was quite special.

Andrew went through the same routine on Sunday: catching the train on Sunday afternoon and arriving at the hotel shortly after 8 o'clock. He was greeted warmly by the manager who told him that all his laundry had been placed on his bed in his room. He was beginning to feel quite at home in Manchester after only a week. When he had checked in and collected his key, he was handed an envelope by the clerk, so after unpacking and putting his clothes away, he sat down on the bed and examined the envelope. It said 'Andrew Williams Esq.' on the outside in beautifully formed writing. *Who on earth could this be from?* He said to himself. *Surely Chloe wouldn't be sending this would she?* He carefully opened the envelope and drew out a postcard that had a photo of a place that looked as though it was somewhere in the Lake District. After a few moments, he turned the card over to read the few words on the back.

You probably wonder why I'm sending this to you, Andy, but I thought you might like the picture. It's one of my favourite places up this way. Maybe we could go there for the day sometime. Warmest wishes, Chloe.

Andrew could smell her distinctive perfume on the card and the envelope that brought back memories of their first meeting at the Red Lion pub, and being with her on the train. He placed the card on his bedside table next to his travelling clock and sat looking at the picture wondering how he could arrange to take her there.

After some minutes, Andrew noticed it was well after 9 o'clock and was past the time that he said he would phone his wife. He would phone the following evening and suffer the consequences. He therefore decided to get himself ready for bed and have a good night's sleep, in case the week ahead was going to be busy.

When Andrew arrived at the office, he was greeted warmly by the receptionist. Alan Griffiths saw him come in to the Foreign Exchange area, so he came over to Andrew and asked him if he'd had an enjoyable weekend and a good journey back up to Manchester, to which he replied that he had. He handed a bundle of papers and envelopes to Andrew and told him that if he had difficulties dealing with any of the tasks, he should let him know.

About the time that the tea lady came round, at 11 o'clock, the Foreign Exchange manager's secretary came to Andrew and told him that a Mr Livermore, the branch's main manager, would like to see him in his office about fifteen minutes before lunchtime. When the time arrived, Andrew went over to the secretary, who duly phoned her boss. Andrew knocked on Mr Livermore's door before entering and was ushered to a chair in front of his desk.

"Sorry I haven't spoken to you before now, Williams, but I thought I'd give you a week to settle in. I've had the occasional update from Mr Griffiths and he seems to be well pleased with your work."

"Thank you, sir. I've been made very welcome by everyone here."

"What I really want to talk about is the time you will be away next week and the week after. I don't really need to know all the nitty-gritties, but your manager in London told me before you arrived that you would have to be out of our office for a couple of days for two consecutive weeks. I presume that is still the case?"

"Well, not quite, sir. It's just next week. I hope it won't be too much of an inconvenience to you and those in the department."

"I suppose we'll just have to put up with it, but at least I was given prior notice. Will you be requiring transport to wherever you are going?"

"That's very kind of you, sir but I'm being collected from the hotel and brought back again after the days that I'm away."

"Very good. All very well organised then. Incidentally, Williams, I have been talking to my wife and we've been wondering if you would like to come to our house for supper one evening, instead of suffering in solitude in the dining room of your hotel."

"That's very thoughtful of you, sir, it certainly would make a very nice change. The food at the hotel, by the way, is quite good, but it doesn't vary very much from one day to the next."

"Then how does Thursday suit you? We can go straight from the office, have a pint on the way to my house and have supper at 7:30 p.m."

"That sounds ideal, sir, but how do I get back to my hotel?"

"No problem with that, Williams. We'll get a taxi to take you back. I'll organise it for about 10 o'clock."

With that all organised, Andrew left Mr Livermore's office. He decided to eat lunch in the canteen with some of the other staff, and although he didn't really have anything in common with most of them, he managed to keep them amused with some of his anecdotes. During the afternoon when his workload had reduced a bit, he called Chloe.

"I was just about to call you Andy, when my phone rang. How was your weekend? Did you have a good trip back to Manchester yesterday?"

"It was not nearly as pleasant as it was last weekend; I didn't have you for company."

"You flatter me, Andy. Now, are you still on for tomorrow evening? I've found a really nice place for a meal about midway between the office and my home."

"Why don't we have a drink at my hotel and then go to the restaurant you've chosen? Have you made a booking?"

"No, I haven't, but it doesn't get very busy at this time of the week. It's probably best if I meet you in the bar. I don't want people from the office seeing us together, it will only result in a lot of gossip."

"Agreed. So I'll see you at 6:30 p.m. tomorrow, in the hotel's main bar. Bye for now, Chloe."

The rest of day followed a typical pattern for a Monday. Andrew left the office at the usual time, and because it was quite a warm evening, he walked slowly back to his hotel. Before heading for the bar for a beer, he decided to go to his room, change into something a bit more casual and then ring his wife.

"Hallo, dear, how are you getting on in this rather hot weather?"

"Do you mean it's warm in Manchester too?" she said. "I thought it always rained up there! Anyway, we are just fine and Alfred has been as good as gold during the last two nights. I have been checking the responses to our invitations to Alfred's Baptism and had to phone a few who had not replied. Only two of the six outstanding replies cannot come."

"Well done, dear. So how many people do we now expect?" Andrew enquired.

"We are now at thirty six and unless someone drops out at the last minute, that's the number we will cater for."

"Still no change of mind from my mother, I suppose?" Andrew said.

"I'm sorry, Andrew, I haven't even bothered to phone her and she certainly hasn't called us."

"Never mind. I might call her at the weekend. I'd better ring off now dear. I'll see you on Friday evening. Good bye for now."

Each of them hung up. Andrew thought he sensed a bit of tension in his wife's tone, but he wasn't going to worry about it now. After all, he had a meeting with Chloe to look forward to.

Andrew's evening passed quite calmly and after he had had supper, he decided to turn in shortly after 9:30 p.m. The next day, he thought it would be time to focus on the instructions sent by Charles about his next week's training. Somehow or the other, he found his mind drifting away and thinking about meeting Chloe, so he put the envelope and its contents back into his briefcase. Also, instead of going for lunch in the canteen, he decided to walk for half an hour in the sunshine round a few blocks close to the office.

The afternoon seemed to pass by very slowly, but eventually 6 o'clock arrived. He put away his paperwork, picked up his briefcase and walked back to the hotel. Once in his room, he changed out of his suit into more casual clothing, looked at his watch and saw it was 6:30 p.m.

I'll play it carefully and arrive in the bar about five minutes late, he said to himself. *She'll probably be late anyway; women usually are.*

He walked down the staircase, rather than taking the lift and went towards the bar entrance. Just at that moment, he was aware of someone running behind him.

"Excuse me Mr Williams, sir, but a lady has been asking for you and I've told her to wait in the bar area at a table near the window."

"Thank you John, I have been expecting her. I'll go and find her. Has she been here very long?"

"About fifteen minutes, Mr Williams."

Andrew went in to the bar and looked round to his right and towards the window at the end. There was Chloe, looking absolutely fantastic. When she saw Andrew, she smiled so warmly and gently, and her eyes had a sort of expectant but inviting look that Andrew stopped for a brief moment before going over to her.

"I am so sorry to be so late. You look wonderful. You didn't go to the office in that dress and jacket today, did you?"

"No, I certainly did not. I brought it in with me this morning and changed in the ladies before coming over here."

Andrew put his hands out to Chloe; she took his hands, slowly got to her feet and as she moved towards him she gave him a kiss on his cheek. He could smell her perfume wafting round his head; he thought he was dreaming. As she moved back from him, she stumbled over the leg of the table, but he moved quickly forward and grasped her round the waist to prevent her from falling backwards. She gave a little gasp, but soon regained her composure as he lowered her back into her chair. As she looked up at him, smiling rather embarrassingly, he couldn't remember a time in his life when he wanted to be with a woman more than Chloe.

"Wow, that was close," said Andrew. "I thought you were about to fall between those two chairs. Are you alright?"

"I'm fine Andrew, but it was lucky that you managed to catch me before I fell."

"What would you like to drink so as to calm your nerves?"

"I think a small gin and it', please."

Andrew waved at the barman and sat down next to Chloe. When the barman arrived, Andrew ordered the gin and it' and a pint of bitter for himself. He told him to put it against his room account, which he already knew from previous occasions.

The drinks arrived and Andrew touched Chloe's glass with his; he looked into her smiling eyes as they said 'cheers' to each other. They talked a bit about office work, but mostly about how fortunate they were to have met at the pub a few weekends ago.

"Are you a regular visitor to Sussex to see your friends?" asked Andrew.

"No, only very occasionally do I get down that way," replied Chloe. "It's a long story how we met. Before I was a teenager, my parents used to bring my brother and me down to the South Coast for a week in the summer holidays. My mother's brother lives with his family north of Littlehampton, and we met the other girls on the beach at Climping. We used to come down every other year at the same time in August and we all kept meeting up. We've kept in touch ever since."

"Well I'm blessed," said Andrew. "And I was the lucky one to bump into you all at the Red Lion. So, is it Veronica who lives near Billingshurst, and you and Penny were staying with her?"

"That's right. We hadn't seen each other for nearly two years. We had a great laugh together and caught up with what each of us was doing with our lives. Veronica is married and Penny lives in South London."

The conversation went through topics covering their interests, families plus a bit about work. It transpired that Andrew was nearly ten years older than Chloe and that she nearly got married following a brief romance in Blackpool just over a year ago. *Silly bugger to have let her go,* he thought to himself, *but lucky for me he did – she is stunning.*

Andrew finished his drink and looked at his watch.

"My goodness, it's nearly 7:15 p.m.! What would you like to do now, Chloe? Should we head off for the restaurant, or would you like to eat here?"

"The problem with eating here," she said, "is that we might see people from the bank that are up at the Manchester office, like you are. Let's go out to the restaurant that I had originally chosen."

"That's fine by me. I'll get the receptionist to get us a taxi."

Andrew helped Chloe to her feet and escorted her to the hotel's reception. Before too long, the taxi arrived and as they were getting into it, Chloe described where the restaurant was that they needed to be taken to. The traffic was still rather busy, but they arrived within twenty minutes. Once they were inside, Chloe excused herself to go and powder her nose and Andrew asked to be given a table in the corner near the window.

On Chloe's return, Andrew showed her to her seat and gave her a menu. It was a simple menu with not too many choices, but three courses if they wanted them. They had a bottle of red wine with the meal and conversation was very easy for both of them. Andrew was his very charming and attentive self. Chloe was very relaxed and did wonder where this was all going to lead. She found herself liking Andrew more and more as the evening went on. At the end of the meal, Andrew paid the bill and they discussed what else they could do with their time – it was only just 9 o'clock, after all. Chloe mentioned that she had heard about a place called the Unicorn in Eccles where they sometimes had a dance band and they could get a drink. It wasn't far from here.

"That sounds like a great idea, let's try it."

They went outside and were able to hail a taxi in a few minutes.

"I've heard about this place," said the driver. "I believe it's quite smart, especially for around here."

In next to no time, they were outside and there were people filing in through the front door. Chloe and Andrew followed. Andrew took her hand as they entered and were astounded at how many people were in there. They looked around for a table and managed to see one in the far corner. The dance band was already playing a familiar tune and there were many couples on the dance floor. Occasionally, one or two people looked over at Andrew and Chloe as they passed their table, but soon took more interest in the others at their own table.

"Who would have believed that so many would be here, and on a Tuesday too," Andrew remarked as he led Chloe by the hand to the unoccupied table.

"It looks as though there is waiter service, so I'll try to attract the attention of one of them. What would you like to drink, Chloe?"

"I'll just have a tonic water, please."

Eventually the waiter arrived and Andrew placed his order: one tonic water and one half pint of beer. They both looked around the room but saw nobody they recognised. When the music started up again, Andrew asked Chloe if she would like to have a dance – it was a slow fox-trot.

They left their table with the drinks on it and Andrew took Chloe's hand as he led her to the dance floor. She seemed to float like a swan and Andrew almost felt he was dancing on air. She looked into his eyes and he thought there were some special messages being sent his way.

"It really has been a very special evening, Andrew. I have really enjoyed it. I feel so lucky to have met you and then to find that the two of us should be up here for a few weeks together. Since I split up from my boyfriend earlier in the year, I have felt that nothing has really mattered anymore, until now. I'm very lucky to be living with my parents because they seem to understand. They let me live my life as I please, and yet are still there for me. Do you know what I mean?"

"It has been a very special evening for me too, Chloe. I hope we will have more times together like this. You understand my situation and that I'm only here for a few more weeks. I've also been honest enough to tell you that I have a wife and baby son and that complicates things a bit."

The dance tempo changed, but they still held each other tight, occasionally looking into each other's eyes with a longing for something extra. After a few more dances, Andrew took Chloe's hand and led her back to their table. Once they had finished their drinks, Andrew suggested it might be sensible that he called for a taxi and took her home, to which she reluctantly agreed.

They went hand in hand out of the Unicorn to be greeted by a friendly driver.

"Where to now, sir? Another club maybe?"

Chloe gave her address and they sat very close to each other for the fifteen minutes that it took the driver to reach Chloe's home. They kissed each other fondly on the lips, and to Andrew's surprise her tongue searched its way round the inside of his mouth. He slowly brought his right hand over her left breast and gently caressed it; she moved herself even closer to him. The effect of all this excitement made Andrew aware of his arousal in his loins, but he didn't think Chloe had noticed it. The driver came round and opened the door to let Chloe out.

"Thank you for a wonderful evening, Andrew."

"I too enjoyed it very much. I'll never forget it. I'll probably speak to you tomorrow, Chloe. Good night." He blew her a kiss as she moved away from the taxi.

The driver waited until Chloe had gone through the front door of her house before setting off back towards Manchester and Andrew's hotel. All the way back, Andrew couldn't stop thinking about the evening, and how special a person Chloe was and how lucky he was to have met her.

Chapter 31
Monday, 8th of April 1940

There were no vehicles on the road as they drove past Marpain, and before too long they saw the woods on each side of the road.

"There should be a track off to the right very soon," said Gerhart, looking at the map with his torch.

Artur saw the turning and slowed right down as it was quite sharp and narrow at the entrance. The car bumped around on the uneven surface as they made their way further from the road. Artur braked gently as he saw a small break in the woods with a path going off to the left.

"That looks a possibility," said Artur. "Could you go and do a recce, Gerhart, while we wait here. I'll turn all the lights off for the moment, so you'll have to use your torch."

Gerhart got out of the car and stood for a moment to let his eyes get accustomed to the darkness. He went around the back of the car and stood still to listen for any vehicles, but there was nothing. He switched on his torch and slowly picked his way up the path for about thirty metres. He stopped and slowly turned through 360 degrees, inspecting the ground around for a possible hiding place for the armour. He then noticed a large pile of leaves to the right of the path that looked a possibility. He picked up a stick and stuck it in the path opposite the pile of leaves so he could find it when he came back with Artur. He went back to the car.

"There's a place just up the path, Artur, so come and have a look and judge for yourself."

Artur cut the engine and got out of the car, leaving the door ajar.

"Will you be alright for a few moments, Monique, while I see what Gerhart has found?" enquired Artur.

"I'll be fine Andy, but I'll get out and go back towards the road in case any inquisitive *fouinards* come this way."

Artur followed Gerhart up the path and stopped at the stick. Gerhart shone his torch at the pile of leaves for Artur to inspect. Artur strolled up to the pile and poked it with a stick he'd picked up earlier.

"It looks ideal, Gerhart. It means we won't have to dig a hole. You stay here and I'll go back and bring the arms from the boot."

In less than five minutes, Artur reappeared with the guns wrapped in the rug. The two of them pushed the guns and accessories under the leaves and piled more on top so they were completely concealed from view.

"What do you think, Gerhart? Will someone easily notice something untoward?"

"It's hard to say in this light, but without digging a hole it's probably as good a place as any without spending more time searching elsewhere."

"I agree, Gerhart. As a precaution, we should try and walk backwards towards the car and brush away our footprints as best we can as we go. In addition, I'll drive the car further up the track for about 100 metres, walk off into the woods to the right then back into the car and reverse back to the road."

Artur did as he had suggested, picking up Gerhart on the way and Monique near to the road. He was satisfied that they'd done all that they could to avoid the armour being discovered in a hurry. He looked at his watch and noticed it was already well after 7 o'clock.

"We had better get moving. We don't want you to miss your train Gerhart, or not have enough time for a coffee."

"Here, here!" said a voice from the back seat.

Artur backed into the road very carefully and drove off towards Dole; it was starting to get light. After a few minutes, he saw a car in the rear view mirror that had full lights on and was moving very fast towards them. He suddenly realised that he hadn't put the lights back on, so he immediately did. He slowed and indicated right to let the car pass, which it did at some speed. He looked to his left to see if he recognised any of the occupants.

"Did you see anyone you knew in that car, Monique?" Artur said rather hopefully.

"I'm not sure, Andy. It was going quite quickly and it isn't light enough to clearly identify anyone. I did notice the passenger was looking at us rather interestingly. I don't think we should get too concerned, they were probably wondering why our lights weren't on."

"Gerhart, have a look at the map and see if we go close to anywhere that looks promising and that might have a bar or a café."

"After Dole, we go through the village of Choisey. It is close to the Canal so we should find somewhere near there."

"Sounds like a good idea. Are you familiar with the village of Choisey, Monique?"

"Not really, but as Gerhart has said, it's near the canal. Let's give it a try. I'm sure we could all do with a coffee. It shouldn't take us more than twenty minutes to get there."

They drove carefully through Dole and kept their eyes skinned for any vehicles that might resemble the one that overtook them. Nothing was obvious. Choisey was a small village that was almost connected to Dole. After they had passed the memorial to the Great War dead, Artur saw a sign to the Rhône-Rhine canal and turned left down a narrow street. Just before they reached the road that ran parallel to the canal, Artur saw a café on the right on the corner that was open. He drove around to the right and parked the car next to the pavement. They all got out and Artur looked all around to see if he recognised any of the cars.

"It looks a good choice. Let's go and order some coffee and bread."

Monique led the way and they went into a warm bar that had a friendly feel about it. The man behind the counter greeted them and there was an older lady sat at the far end of the bar; she was reading the paper and smoking. Just as they were about to order their coffees, bread and jam, a large dog of mixed parentage came bounding towards them from the other side of the lady at the bar. For no apparent reason, it jumped at Gerhart, and as he was taken by surprise, it knocked him to the floor. He shouted and swore at the dog in English and then suddenly realised what he had said. The man dashed around from the bar, pulled the dog off Gerhart and dragged it into a room at the far end of the bar. In the meantime, Gerhart picked himself up and restored his composure. The man returned, looked at Gerhart and apologised for his dog's unusual behaviour – in French. Artur realised he should take control of the situation.

"Look, monsieur, it's no problem," said Artur in French. "My brother is over from England staying with me and my girlfriend for a short while, and even though he speaks French like a native, he will occasionally lapse into English, particularly if he feels threatened. He's not a dog lover either."

"Is your brother alright?" said the man. "Perhaps you would all accept a coffee from me to make up for this unfortunate incident?"

"That's very kind of you," replied Artur, "but it isn't really necessary."

"I insist," said the barman. "Can I get you three black coffees?" he said as he looked at each of them in turn and finally back at Gerhart again.

"Thank you very much," said Monique with a broad smile and a fluttering of her eyes. "That would be very kind of you."

The man started to prepare the coffees as the three of them sat at a table next to the window. Artur glanced outside just as a car drove slowly past. He recognised it and his heart jumped for a moment; it was the one that overtook them at speed after they had hidden the armour. For once, he was undecided what to do next. The man was just about to bring them their free coffee so they couldn't make a run for it and he was sure Monique's car would have been noticed.

Their coffees arrived and Monique thanked the man with one of her engaging smiles. At that moment, a man came in through the door. He looked at the lady and the three of them and greeted them all. He walked to the bar and waited for the barman to return before asking him for a coffee. While he was making it, he went back outside and Artur watched him walk past the window and out of sight. The other two had not seen the car and so were unaware of any possible danger.

Artur downed his coffee and gestured to the other two that he was going outside. He got up and went out of the door, hoping the others wouldn't follow him. He peered around the corner, and up and down the road that ran parallel to the canal. He just caught a glimpse of the man leaning on a car further up the road, no doubt talking to other occupants through the window. He was probably telling them that people from Monique's car were in the café. Artur turned and walked up the road that they had driven down. He went a little way up and into an alleyway between the café and a house. He waited for a full five minutes before hearing the café door open, and as it did so, he looked to see if someone was going in or coming out. To his surprise, a man – a different one from the one he'd seen earlier – was standing outside. *He's probably acting as a lookout,* Artur thought. *Who the hell are they anyway?*

Artur was now in a real dilemma: *how many went into the café, are Monique and Gerhart alright, how can I get past the man outside the café?* He decided to walk further up the alleyway and see if there was a back entrance into the café, which there should be. He found a gate into a small courtyard and noticed a door that should go into a back room – probably where the dog was. He checked the door and it was unlocked, so he gently opened it and glanced inside. He couldn't see the dog and so tiptoed into the room, closing the door behind him. He could hear voices coming from the bar, two men were talking to Monique and Gerhart, but he couldn't quite make out what they were saying. He walked towards the door that went into the café and put his ear next to the door.

"You don't seem to know where your friend has gone. Is that right?" said a man. "I find that rather odd, don't you?"

"Look, officer," said Monique. "A few minutes ago, he was here with us and then he went outside, perhaps to look at the canal," she said with a smile.

Officer? said Artur to himself. *What sort of officer could he be: police or military? Either one doesn't sound like good news.*

"Do you know anything about these people?" said the same man that had spoken to Monique, probably to the barman.

"I don't know who they are. They came in here about ten minutes ago, but that man there was knocked over by my dog that had found its way into the bar, and he started swearing at the dog in English. The man who is missing said he was his brother visiting him and his girlfriend. That's all I know except they're not from around here. Why are you interested in them anyway? They seem decent enough people to me."

There was a noise of someone walking to the entrance of the bar and the man outside was asked to come inside. Artur wanted to hear the answer, but thought he now had the opportunity to get round to the front of the café. He crossed the courtyard, went down the alleyway and carefully walked down the road. He passed the bar entrance, went to the right, crouching low as he went past the window so as not to be seen from inside the bar and ran to the men's car. As he reached it, he was relieved to see that there was nobody in it. He quickly went back to Monique's car, took his pistol from under the driver's seat and placed it in his jacket pocket. He returned to the men's car, opened the passenger door, leant across the seat, took out the keys from the ignition and put them in his other pocket. He looked around inside the car and saw jackets, torches and a rifle, but didn't disturb anything.

Artur walked back to the café and went inside in a very nonchalant manner. He had a surprised expression on his face as he greeted everyone. He looked at Monique and then Gerhart, and told them that they ought to thank the barman for the coffee and be on their way.

"Just a minute, monsieur, we have some questions to ask you that we believe you can answer for us," said one of the men. "The two of us are police officers, so just wait a minute."

"I'm sorry, officer, but my brother has a train to catch and we need to get to the station at Chalon." Artur thought it was safer to be reasonably honest with these men rather than make up too many stories.

Gerhart helped Monique to her feet and they made their way towards the door where Artur was standing.

"Do you know anything about a car with a crumpled side that was involved in an accident east of Nancy a few days ago?"

"No, I'm afraid not, officer. That's quite a long way from here anyway, isn't it? Now, we really must be on our way," said Artur as he ushered Monique and Gerhart out into the street.

"Goodbye gentlemen and good luck with your investigations."

Artur went out of the door and they proceeded to Monique's car. They all got in without saying a word and Artur drove off. A short distance down the road, they all started to laugh, and then even louder when Artur waved a set of keys and said he didn't think the men would be going very far for quite a while. Gerhart took the map from the side pocket and tried to focus on where they should be going, but they couldn't stop laughing as they drove on towards Chalon, probably as much in relief as anything else.

Chapter 32
Wednesday, 26ᵗʰ of July 1939

Andrew awoke with a start thinking he had overslept, but it was only 6 o'clock. He'd been dreaming about Chloe. As he was so awake, he decided to have an early breakfast and be in the office by 8 o'clock. When he got there, his boss, Mr Griffiths, was already in his office, but hardly anyone else was there. He called Andrew over and closed the door after Andrew had entered. He thought his boss looked rather serious and wondered what he might want to say to him.

"Good morning, Williams, I'm very glad you decided to come in early. Please take a seat for a minute. Don't worry, there's no bad news, in fact, quite on the contrary. We are really pleased with the work you are doing for us up here, so much so that as some immediate help is required in the Foreign Exchange department at one of our Liverpool branches, we wish to send you there till the end of the week. It means, of course, that supper at Mr Livermore's house on Thursday will have to be postponed to another time. What do you think?"

"I feel very honoured that you think I could be of such help when I would be there for only a few days."

"It's only for a short time because the man that currently runs the department has fallen sick and we need an immediate replacement. We won't bother to move you to a Liverpool hotel, but will provide taxi services at the beginning and end of each day – at our expense, of course. I'm fully aware of your commitments elsewhere for two days next week and we wouldn't alter that arrangement."

"Then I don't see that there will be any problem from my point of view. Will you want me to start today or tomorrow?"

"I believe today would be a good starting point, in other words, the sooner the better. My secretary will organise a taxi for you for 10 o'clock. The person you should ask for when you get there is Mr Blackburn. He's a nice chap and you should get on well with him. Thank you, Williams, for being so flexible. It is much appreciated. I'll make sure my report at the end of your term here fully reflects your commitment and attitude."

"Thank you, sir. Will that be all?"

"Yes, I think so. If you have any outstanding work here, please let my secretary know. She'll pass any unfinished business on to an appropriate person in the department."

"Thank you, sir. I will be ready for the taxi at 10 o'clock downstairs in the entrance hall."

Andrew left Mr Griffith's office and went back to his desk. He took papers from a drawer and searched through for those that he could deal with in the next hour or so. He got on with his work, but couldn't stop thinking about whether or not he should call Chloe. He thought he ought to do as much of his work and then phone her afterwards, if he had enough time.

Just before 10 o'clock, Andrew's phone went. It was Mr Griffith's secretary telling him that his taxi had arrived. He closed his briefcase, gathered up all unfinished business papers, took them to the secretary and walked to the lift. He waited for the lift to arrive and when the doors opened, he was so surprised to see Chloe walk out.

"Chloe, I was going to call you, but I ran out of time. A feeble excuse, I know, but I only heard this morning that I'm to help out at one of the Liverpool branches till the end of the week. How are you anyway?"

Fortunately, there were no other people around so they couldn't see the gleam in Chloe's eyes as she looked at Andrew with some surprise.

"I'm fine, Andrew. Will you be staying over in Liverpool, or can we meet up after work on Thursday?"

"Good idea. I'll phone you later today, once I've got myself sorted and stuck in to this new job. I must rush as the taxi is waiting for me."

Andrew shot into the lift and deliberately touched Chloe's hand on the way. When he reached the entrance hall, he saw that the driver stood with the taxi door open for him; they sped off towards Liverpool. On arrival at the Liverpool branch, he signed in at reception and was told to take the lift to the second floor and ask for Mr Blackburn.

After Andrew had been introduced to his new colleagues, he settled into his duties very quickly and was able to easily help others in the department. He had a light lunch in the canteen and before he knew it, he saw it was 4:30 p.m. He had a few things still to do with one of his new colleagues and he reckoned he would have enough time to phone Chloe once he had finished. Andrew asked the switchboard for the Manchester office number. He was put through quite quickly and he asked for Chloe. The voice he then spoke to told him that she had already left the office and wouldn't be back until tomorrow. Andrew felt completely crestfallen, but there wasn't anything he could do about it now. It was already nearly 5:30 p.m., so he tidied his desk, fastened his briefcase and left the office.

A taxi was already waiting outside the entrance for him, so he set off to return to his hotel. He was very annoyed with himself that he hadn't found time to phone Chloe earlier.

Andrew thanked the driver for taking him back to the hotel and went up to his room. He thought it would be politic if he phoned his wife to tell her of the temporary job change.

"Hello dear, how are things at home?"

"Not too bad. Alfred is still sleeping well through the night. And with you, is the job going well?"

"Well, as it happens I must be doing things right because I've been asked to help out at one of our branches in Liverpool. My boss said he was very pleased with my work, and would I go and help out in Liverpool as a senior chap is off sick. I went there today and I'll be there until I return home on Friday evening."

"That sounds fantastic. Perhaps it will help your possible promotion."

Andrew knew she would interpret things that way; it would help to keep him in her good books – at least for the time being. They chatted on for a few more minutes, until his wife said she would have to deal with the baby. They closed the conversation and rang off.

Now what do I do with myself, thought Andrew. *Pity I don't know how to contact Chloe.*

Andrew decided to change from his suit into more casual clothes. He went down stairs to the bar.

"Good evening, Mr Williams. What would you like me to get you to drink tonight?"

"I think I'll have a pint, please."

The barman duly obliged as Andrew waited at the bar.

"Forgive me for asking sir, but are you not meeting that lovely young lady again tonight?"

"No, I'm sorry to tell you, I have no such arrangement and I have no way of contacting her at home. I only have her office number." Andrew took a large sip of his beer.

"That's a great pity. Forgive me for saying it, but she looked like a very special person. Not many like her around here very often. She seemed quite fond of you too, if I may be so bold."

Andrew took another large swig of his beer and placed the glass on the bar. He thanked the barman, and said he was going to have a light supper and then go to bed early.

He awoke at 6 o'clock, after a very restless night. He wasn't sure what it was that had been on his mind. He washed and dressed and decided to have a hearty breakfast – including the black pudding that was a favourite of his – and was ready for the taxi to take him to the Liverpool office at

8:15 a.m. For some reason that he couldn't quite make out, most of the day was very busy, so Andrew had no time at all to think about anything else, not even Chloe.

By 6 o'clock, Andrew was quite exhausted so the taxi took him straight back to his hotel; he went directly to his room and lay on his bed. *I don't think I can cope with all this; thank goodness I shall be out of banking for a few days next week,* he thought to himself. He fell asleep, woke up in a sweat thinking that he'd missed supper and went swiftly down to the dining room; he was just in time to order.

The following day – it was Friday – he packed what he needed to take home in his suitcase and was in the entrance hall waiting for his taxi exactly at 8:15 a.m. During the morning, he had a meeting with Mr Blackburn who, like Mr Griffiths, complimented him on his work and how helpful he had been to the department. By 4:30 p.m., he was ready to leave and catch his train back to London and on to home. For some strange reason that he couldn't really explain, he was actually looking forward to it.

Andrew arrived home just after 8:30 p.m., and he was greeted very enthusiastically by his wife.

"It's really nice to have you back home, Andy, it's been quite a week. One or two people have cried off from Alfred's Baptism and the caterers are querying the numbers that they should be catering for. Also, my friend Barbara has been off sick, so I haven't been able to discuss much with her."

"I'm sure everything will turn out just fine," said Andrew very reassuringly. "Let's face it, as long as the Godparents are still coming and Alfred isn't suffering from anything nasty and the vicar is expecting us, all will be fine. Perhaps if I got you a drink, you might feel a bit better. I know you don't like drinking on your own so you are probably in need of one. "

Without waiting for an answer, Andrew walked over to the cocktail cabinet and drew out a bottle of gin.

"I'm sure you would like a gin and tonic, wouldn't you, my dear?"

"That's a great idea, Andy. You have read the situation exactly. Sorry, I forgot to ask: how was your week? Are you any nearer to a promotion, or is it still a bit of a long shot?"

Andrew continued with the drinks and thought carefully how he might answer.

"I'm not sure if I told you when I phoned during the week, but I had to stand in for a senior man in the Foreign Exchange department who was sick in the Liverpool office for the last three days. Apparently I did a good job, so much so that it will be highlighted by the Manchester office manager, Mr Griffiths, when he writes his report at the end of my time there."

The conversation at that point died out. Andrew excused himself from his wife's company, went to the hall where his case was and went upstairs. He poked his head round the door of Alfred's nursery and could tell that he was fast asleep. After unpacking his things, he returned to the lounge and took a hearty swig of his drink. It had been quite warm during the second half of the week, according to his wife, and it certainly felt it during the evening.

Andrew spent the weekend with his family that was much appreciated by his wife; he didn't even venture out to meet any of his pals at one of the local pubs. He fussed around in the garden, making sure that it was tidy. From time to time, he spent the occasional hour in his study, reading through Charles' notes about his next course that would start next Tuesday; he really wanted to do well so that he could have the chance of escaping from working in the bank at the earliest opportunity. He also needed to focus on his son's Baptism that was only a week away. He wanted it to go smoothly and for his wife to really enjoy the occasion.

As was the case on the previous Sunday, he caught the late afternoon train to Manchester and took a taxi to his hotel. The manager and the receptionist welcomed him back, and handed him an envelope that had apparently been brought in earlier in the day.

Andrew went up to his room, unpacked his case and put his laundry away in the chest of drawers. He sat down and opened the envelope: it was from Chloe, of course. He recognised the perfume from the envelope as well as her very neat, distinctive hand-writing that was easy to read. She didn't say very much, just that she was sorry he hadn't found time to meet up with her during the last week; she hoped he could find time in the following week, suggesting Wednesday as a possibility. He wasn't sure her suggestion would work: he had two days of his courses and he was concerned that his manager back in the Manchester office might ask him to his house after the previous invitation had been postponed. As he didn't feel hungry, he decided to have an early night.

The Monday in the office went very quickly, but as he had had no invitation from his manager, Mr Griffiths, he phoned Chloe. They arranged to meet at the hotel bar at 7 o'clock later that day, rather than Wednesday. She seemed very excited to be seeing him again and told him she had a surprise for him. This intrigued him and he wondered what it could be all about.

Andrew walked briskly to his hotel and went to his room to change. He wanted to be in the bar before Chloe arrived. Eventually, at just after 7:15 p.m., Chloe flew into the bar and over to Andrew.

"I'm so sorry to have kept you waiting, but my manager wanted to discuss something with our group and it went on a bit."

Andrew leapt to his feet and drew Chloe to him in a warm embrace, but he didn't kiss her – the barman had been watching her entry, as were some of the other residents.

"Don't worry, Chloe. It's very nice to see you again. Come and sit down, I'll get you a drink. Would you like a Gin and It or just a tonic water?"

"Just a tonic water please, Andy."

Andrew gesticulated to the barman what Chloe wanted; he brought it to their table, ignoring others who were waiting at the bar.

"Cheers," they said as they touched their glasses and looked into each other's eyes.

"So, what's this surprise that you said you had for me?" said Andrew with one of his engaging smiles.

"I thought we could go back to my place rather than to a restaurant. I prepared something yesterday and it will be quick to heat up."

"So will we be eating with your parents, as I thought you lived with them?"

"No, we shall have the house to ourselves as they have gone to the Lake District for the week. I hope you won't mind my cooking, it's not up to a chef's standard but it will be very eatable."

"I'm sure it will be just fine. But if we have to get to your place, should we not leave soon?"

"If we take a taxi, we can be there in no time. Let's drink up and we can have a drink while I'm cooking the meal."

They downed their drinks and Andrew went to sign for the drinks at the bar. Once again, the barman gave him a wink and hoped he would have an enjoyable evening.

They didn't have to wait long for a taxi and in less than twenty minutes, they were outside Chloe's home in Farnworth. It was a Victorian end-of-terrace house with a small front garden. Chloe led the way to the front door and Andrew closed it behind him. The stair case was a few yards inside the door and a passageway went to the right of the stairs towards the kitchen, passing the dining room off to the right. Andrew followed Chloe down the steps into the kitchen. She went to the pantry and took out a pie and a few vegetables.

"Shall I take your coat, Andy? Perhaps you would like to open the wine for me, it's in the cupboard at the back of the kitchen. The meal won't take long to cook so I'll lay the table in the kitchen – if you don't mind eating in here – and we can have a drink while I finish things off."

"No problem, Chloe. I'll eat anywhere you suggest."

Andrew brushed past Chloe to reach the cupboard and she gave a little giggle. He opened the bottle of red and poured it into the glasses that she had placed on the table. There was quite a new gas cooker to the right of the range, so Chloe lit the oven and put the pans of vegetables on two of the rings.

"The meal shouldn't take too long Andy. Perhaps you would like to sit at the table while I finish laying it for supper."

Andrew did as he was told and watched Chloe as she went about her business, humming to herself and smiling. He thought he liked what he saw and wondered how the evening would pan out. After a while, she checked the oven and turned the pans down that were now boiling gently; the table was laid to her satisfaction.

"You seem very happy in your work, Chloe. Won't you stop for a drink, or shall I start without you?"

"Oh, I'm so sorry. I got a bit carried away making sure everything was properly laid out for our supper. Cheers, Andy! I am so happy to be entertaining you in my humble home."

Chloe brought her chair next to Andrew's, touching his glass with hers. She sat down and looked into his eyes.

"I want this to be another memorable occasion that we spend together. I am very much aware that you don't have many more weeks in the Manchester office so I want to make the most of it."

Chloe leant over and kissed Andrew firmly on the lips and placed her hand on his leg. Andrew put his wine down on the table and drew Chloe towards him so that she nearly fell off her chair. They laughed at the incident. Chloe excused herself and went to attend to the things that were cooking.

"We'll be eating in about seven minutes, Andy. If you want to use the bathroom, it's upstairs and then to your right."

Andrew left the kitchen for the bathroom and returned in less than five minutes to find that everything was on the square table for the meal. Chloe dished up the meal and they sat next to each other.

"This is absolutely delicious, Chloe. I've not had such a tasty meal like this for a long time," said Andrew with a mouthful and nearly choking.

"You're a real flatterer, Andy," retorted Chloe as she slapped Andrew on the back when he had taken a swig of wine to clear his throat.

They rolled around laughing, but continued with their meal in silence for the next ten minutes.

"As I said before, that was a truly delicious meal. Very many thanks, Chloe. Perhaps you ought to open a restaurant. It could pay better than what you currently earn."

"Once again, Andy, you are flattering me but I do enjoy cooking, especially for someone who appreciates it all, like you."

Chloe got up to clear the dishes, but as she trod on Andrew's foot, she fell into his lap, spilling gravy down the front of his trousers. She quickly retrieved a damp cloth from the draining board and dropped to her knees to wipe away the stain. She undid his belt and the top fly buttons. She slid one hand down inside his trousers and dabbed the stain with the cloth. She asked him to stand up so she could take the trousers off and do a better job. As he stood up, she pulled down his pants as well as his trousers. She dropped the cloth and held his manhood with both hands, gently massaging it as it rapidly grew in size. Much to Andrew's surprise, she pushed as much of him as she could into her mouth. Andrew immediately remembered the only other time this had happened to him: he and a few of his school friends had arranged to meet some girls from the nearby village in the woods on a Sunday afternoon near the school; they were all about sixteen years old.

"Chloe, I really like what you are doing but please stop," Andrew pleaded, "before I embarrass us both. I'm trying like mad to control myself but I'm not sure I can for very much longer."

Chloe drew back and smiled wickedly up at Andrew. She picked up the cloth and attended to the trouser stain again; Andrew drew a deep breath and sat down.

"I suppose that was the dessert course, Chloe?" he said with a smile and some relief in his voice.

"You are probably right, Andy, but that was only a taster! We ought to finish it properly, don't you think?"

Andrew slipped out of his shoes, stood up, and pushed his trousers and pants down his legs; he stepped out of them and lifted Chloe into his arms.

"There is a very comfortable sofa in the lounge, or we could go upstairs to my bedroom, if you would prefer?"

Andrew didn't reply, but carried Chloe to the lounge and placed her gently on the sofa. He lifted her dress and slid her panties down and threw them onto the floor. She opened her legs and guided his hand between them. He felt she was already very moist and ready for him to enter her. He gently lay on top of her. They kissed with their tongues searching far inside each other's mouth. She grasped him and led him inside her. She gave a high-pitched gasp as he went further and further inside her. She wondered if she could take all of him as she grabbed his buttocks with both hands. Andrew rocked backwards and forwards and achieved even greater penetration. Occasionally, he would pause but Chloe would plead for more. Eventually, she arched her back, pulled one more time on his buttocks and let out a squeaky noise just as Andrew gave one more thrust.

Nothing was said for what seemed like ten minutes, as they lay in each other's arms, very happy but quite exhausted.

"Wow! Now that really was quite a dessert, don't you think, Andy?"

Chapter 33
Monday, 8th of April 1940

Artur drove carefully out of Choisey and on to the road that would eventually take them to Chalon. Artur found himself frequently looking at his rear view mirror in case someone might be following them, but he reckoned the men in the bar would be in Choisey for a long time – unless they had duplicate keys.

"According to the map, it shouldn't take us more than an hour and a half to get to the station in Chalon, and it's now 8:30 a.m. already."

"Let's hope we don't have any further delays on the way. We've buried the arms, we've had a coffee, we don't need any petrol and we think we've delayed those officers at the bar. Hope for the best everyone. We need a bit of luck on our side for a change."

There was quiet in the car for quite a while, except for the occasional instruction given by Gerhart. Artur felt confident that they would make Chalon in good time for him to catch the 10:35 a.m. train to Paris. The only problem, as he saw it, was how old was the timetable that indicated there was a train going to Paris on a Monday at that time.

After about an hour, they passed through St Maurice de Rivière without any incident or concern; they were making good time.

"The road will be almost straight for a few kilometres, then there are a few twisty sections before we cross the Saône," said Gerhart. "But just stay on this road. We will turn left into Boulevard de la République."

"Not too many instructions at one time, Gerhart. I'm also trying to concentrate on my driving."

As they got closer to the twisty sections, the traffic was noticeably heavier with buses, cars and people, all of which made Artur focus his attention even more. He needed to take the left turn into the Boulevard, but the traffic was stopped by the policeman in the centre of the intersection. Eventually, they moved forward and turned down towards the station. He turned left in front of the station and looked for somewhere to park.

"Over there," came an instruction from the back.

"Thanks, Monique, I had also seen the space," replied Artur.

"I was only trying to help!" said Monique rather curtly.

Artur steered the car into the space and looked at his watch.

"Not bad timing, Gerhart. Your train leaves in twenty minutes."

They all got out of the car. Gerhart collected his bag from the seat next to where Monique had been sitting.

"Are you certain that you've got all you need, Gerhart?"

"I'll just do a quick check."

Gerhart opened his shoulder bag and went through in his mind what should be in there. He then took out all of his papers and put those that he wouldn't be needing under the few clothes he had in the bag.

"OK, let's go and get my ticket."

They walked inside the station and saw the ticket office. Artur went over to the departures' board to find the time of the train leaving for Paris. To his surprise, it was saying 10:35 a.m., the time they were expecting. It took a good ten minutes for Gerhart to buy his ticket and return to the others.

"I was told by the ticket clerk that the train might be a few minutes late, so all is well."

"Gerhart, have a safe trip to Paris and on to London," said Artur. "We have done what we were asked to do and we've worked well together. I look forward to meeting up with you again in London."

They all walked towards the platform for the Paris train and embraced each other in the typical French way. Gerhart turned and went from their sight.

"I think we should wait until the train has left, Monique, just in case a problem arises."

The two of them found a seat outside the booking office. They said little to each other, and the time seemed to go by slowly. Just after 10:35 a.m., they were aware of a train entering the station and realised it must be the one for Paris. Artur took a deep breath and Monique noticed his slight anxiousness and took his hand in hers.

"Gerhart will be fine," said Monique. "He's strong and will be able to take care of himself. I'm sure he's got contacts in Paris who can help him."

"You are right, Monique, but with what the Germans are likely to do in Scandinavia, so much is out of his control."

There was a shrill whistle from the train's engine that brought them back to the present, followed by a large plume of smoke at the far end of the platform.

"There she goes," remarked Artur. "Shall we go and get a coffee before I think about getting my ticket to Marseille?"

They walked to the station's restaurant; Monique's arm was linked through Artur's. They bought their coffees and stood by the window looking out at all the people hurrying to get to somewhere that only they themselves knew. They looked at each and smiled, but said very little. Out of the corner of his eye, Artur noticed two men running towards the booking office.

"Oh my goodness, I do believe those are two of the men we met at the café. Do you think the third one is in their car, or perhaps he's found ours and is waiting for us to return?"

"You stay here, Andy, I'll go out to the car. I know of another way out to the car park and it comes out at the far end. I should be able to see if anyone is standing by our car."

"Are you sure you want to go? Wouldn't you prefer me to go?"

"I know my way round this station very well, so you wait here. Keep an eye open for them coming out from the booking office and see what they do next."

Very reluctantly, Artur let Monique do as she had suggested. He grabbed a stool and sat close to the window, looking towards the booking office. He didn't see them come out as there was quite a crowd between him and the office entrance. After about ten minutes, he thought it was strange not to have seen them and guessed he must have missed them. He was getting concerned about Monique and so decided to leave the restaurant. He walked in the same direction that Monique had gone, but couldn't help looking behind every few metres in case the men were following him.

"Where are you going, Andy? I asked you to stay in the restaurant."

The sound of Monique's voice nearly made Artur jump out of his skin, but his concern soon changed into a smile.

"Sorry, Andy, I really didn't mean to alarm you. I saw our car and nobody was standing by it, but I couldn't see the men's car. If they are police, they probably parked it right outside the station entrance.

"I'll take you to where I went out to the car park, you wait there while I go and get the car. I have to drive past you to exit the car park and we'll head off towards my aunt's place near Tournus. We can then decide what we should do for the best. Agreed?"

Artur took the keys from his pocket for Monique and they walked to the far end of the station where the way out to the car park was. Artur waited and, after a few minutes, Monique drove up. Artur jumped in and they drove out of the car park into the street.

"I suggest we go towards Tournus and I'll phone my aunt from a bar on the way. You really ought to stay the night at my aunt's and catch a train to Marseille tomorrow. She has three bedrooms in her house so it won't be a problem."

Artur said nothing; it all made sense but he wasn't sure what she would tell her aunt about him. At least Gerhart was well on his way and they seem to have lost the 'officers'– for the time being anyway. After about fifteen minutes, and no conversation occurring between them, Monique said she would stop in a small village called Simandre as she knew a café where she could phone her aunt.

"I think it's called the Café du Commerce. I've been there a few times before and it's very nice."

"Oh good," said Artur. "I could do with stopping quite soon, after all that excitement in Chalon. Just make sure you say nothing about why I'm really in France."

"Of course I won't. We should be there in about ten minutes, Andy. Is that soon enough for you?"

Artur said nothing. Before too long, they were parked outside the bar. Artur got out and followed Monique inside. A friendly barman greeted them warmly and they in turn acknowledged him and the other three people standing at the counter.

"Will you have a coffee or a glass of wine?" enquired Monique.

"That's a good idea. A glass of red please, Monique."

Monique ordered two glasses of red wine and asked the patron if she may use his phone. She was directed to a booth at the far end of the bar. Artur made use of the facilities and returned to take the drinks to a table near the window. He always favoured being near the window so he could keep an eye out for any unusual activity outside.

After a few minutes, Monique returned and said her aunt had invited them to be at her house for a light lunch. She had also agreed to her friend staying the night, if he needed to, but he'd have to sleep in the small single room. Artur smiled and nodded his thanks.

Their conversation was light and relatively inconsequential as they enjoyed their drinks. Monique was rather troubled by Artur's quiet mood, but thought it must be because he was now on his own and still had the tricky part of getting back to England. They finished their drinks and after settling the bill, left the bar.

As they drove out of Simandre, Monique mentioned that her aunt lived near a village called Lugny.

"We have to go through Tournus and go over one of the bridges over the Saône. Her house is just north of Lugny in a place called Collongette."

Monique drove through Tournus and down a narrow road through Chardonnay and Champvent. As they entered Collongette, she turned left.

"Her house is up here on the right," said Monique very excitedly.

"It looks quite a large place," said Artur. "I thought you said it only had three bedrooms?"

"There are more rooms, but she keeps them for storing all her old furniture. She used to live in a large farmhouse with an extensive vineyard until her husband died about seven years ago. She sold that property and moved into here. She's always lived in Collongette and knows most people. She's my mother's sister and is called Vivienne."

They drove into the courtyard, and as they were parking the car, Vivienne walked out of the house to greet them. Artur thought there was a striking similarity between Monique and Vivienne, although Vivienne's hair had turned grey, whereas Monique's was blonde. It was the looks and the smile – not to mention the eyes – that struck him most.

Vivienne opened Monique's door for her. Monique fell into a long embrace with her; they were obviously very fond of each other. Vivienne came round to Artur, who was by this stage standing outside the car. She put both of her hands out to him and they greeted each other warmly.

"Auntie Vivienne, this is Andy, someone I haven't seen for a few years. He's in France on business and looked me up in Pesmes."

Vivienne looked at Artur very hard for a few moments; she seemed to be trying to work out what sort of business he could be involved in. She then broke into a broad smile, took Monique's and Artur's hands and led them into the entrance hall.

Vivienne took Monique and Artur upstairs to their rooms. Monique's room was spacious with a large double bed, and there were fresh flowers in a vase on her bedside table.

"I hope this will be alright for you, Monique? You've been here before so you know the layout of the house and where the bathroom is."

"It's a wonderful room, auntie, looking out over your lovely garden at the back. Thank you."

"Now, your room is a bit smaller at the other end of the corridor, Andy. You follow me while Monique unpacks her case."

Vivienne strode off along the corridor and turned left into a small room that also had a view over the garden.

"I'm so sorry, Andy, but this is the only room I have for you as my other bedrooms are full of my furniture from the large farmhouse."

"Monique told me that you sold the farm not very long ago, so I'm grateful to you for putting me up, especially at such short notice."

Vivienne opened the window of Artur's room and told him he could use the chest of drawers for any of his clothes. She mentioned that she had made lunch for them all and that he should come down when he's ready to the lounge for an aperitif. She left Artur's room having given him a smile that resembled ones that Monique gave him.

After about ten minutes, Monique and Artur went down to the lounge. Vivienne came in from the kitchen with a tray of glasses, a bottle of Pernod and a jug of water.

"I thought you would enjoy a typical French drink, Andy, before we have a light lunch. You can then tell me all about what business you've been up to in France during these very troubling times in Europe."

Artur turned to Monique with a very concerned look and wondered what she was going to say. When Monique had phoned from the bar, she must have told her that he was on business. Artur had already been well briefed by his seniors in London on what he should say if a situation such as this occurred. He felt it was up to him to explain before Monique tried to.

Vivienne poured out the drinks and asked them to add the amount of water they would like. She suggested to Monique that she sit in the chair near the window and beckoned Artur to sit next to her on the sofa.

"*Santé*, Monique and Andy. I'm really delighted that you have come to call on your old aunt, Monique, but it would have been better if you had given me more notice," she said with some firmness in her voice.

Her tone didn't surprise Artur; however much she loved Monique, she was probably a person of routine and liked visitors to give a few days, or even a week when planning to visit.

"We must apologise, Vivienne, for not giving you more notice, but I got myself into some trouble in Germany a few days ago. The company I work for had sent me to collect some debts from a German business that we had traded with. The money had been outstanding from before Britain declared war last September. The situation got nasty between us, and I was chased out of the country into NE France, not too far from Nancy. I stole a car and drove to Monique's house in Pesmes and hoped she would be able to help me. And that's why we are here."

Monique's eyes were fixed on Artur in almost disbelief as he told his story, but she said nothing.

"So presumably you didn't get the money?" said Vivienne, turning her head towards Artur.

"No, I didn't but I did escape with my life."

"You know, Andy, I don't really need to know why you're here in France, but with so many uncertainties in France and elsewhere, I had to ask, as I'm sure you well understand."

There was silence for a few minutes. Artur really didn't know if Vivienne would believe his story; he was not going to be the first to break the silence.

"Don't you think it's time we had some lunch, auntie? We are quite hungry after our travels and you usually have lunch around 1:30 p.m.," said Monique, as she looked at her watch.

"That's a good idea. I'll go and finish setting the table. I'll call you when I'm ready."

Vivienne got up from the sofa and collected her drink from the table in front of her. As she turned to go to the kitchen, she looked into Artur's eyes, as though she was searching his brain for the truth. For the first time in his life, Artur felt nervous about telling this woman anything more, regardless of how he might be interrogated. As she left the room, Artur looked at Monique and put his index finger to his lips. He hoped she understood that she should say nothing more.

Monique joined Artur on the sofa and placed her hand on his knee. They smiled rather nervously at each other. After a few minutes, Artur finished his drink and there was a call from the kitchen that lunch was ready. Monique took Artur's hand and led him through the kitchen to the dining room. Vivienne smiled at them as they went in and gestured to them to sit at the settings each side of the table; she would sit at the end and serve.

The meal was delicious, but the conversation seemed to be rather strained. This made Artur rather nervous and felt more questions were likely to come his way. At the end of lunch, Monique helped her aunt clear the table as Artur sat watching, and thinking. He felt tired and wondered if an afternoon nap might be acceptable to Vivienne, who, at that moment, returned to the dining room.

"Andy, I usually have a rest in the afternoon, for an hour or so. I don't know what you and Monique want to do, maybe wander around the village perhaps?"

Monique returned to the dining room just as Vivienne posed the question and glanced at Artur.

"Would you like a walk or to take a rest, Andy?" Monique enquired with an inviting smile.

"We could go for a walk, if you would like to, Monique. It's up to you."

"While you're trying to decide, I'll bid you *bon après-midi* and see you later."

Vivienne seemed to spin on her heels as she turned to go to the lounge and eventually upstairs. Monique drew close to Artur and took his hand. It was hot and he was perspiring.

"Are you alright, Andy? You don't seem to be your usual self. What is troubling you? If it's my aunt, she has an inquisitive nature, especially now that she's living on her own and has moved from her farm."

Artur was worried about something, but he couldn't put his finger on it. He reflected over the lunchtime conversations, the questions asked in the lounge and his explanations. He felt uncomfortable in Vivienne's presence. He had been warned about such people during his training. He took out his handkerchief and mopped his brow. He knew he shouldn't display himself in this way to Vivienne; there was no way of knowing who she knew or where her allegiances lay.

"I think some fresh air would be a good idea, so let's walk round the village for a while," said Artur with a sigh of relief from having made a decision at last.

Monique led Artur into the hall. They took their jackets from the stand and went out to the spacious driveway. For some reason, Artur turned and looked back at the house to see Vivienne watching them leave from a slightly drawn-back curtain, hoping she wouldn't be seen. Artur thought of smiling and waving, and so he did but there was no response from Vivienne except for the curtain being slowly closed again. Monique hadn't noticed anything, but Artur's suspicions grew.

They set off up the road, not saying anything to each other. Monique tried to take Artur's hand, but he put it into his pocket. They turned right after a few hundred metres and entered the centre of the village, or what there was of it. There was nobody about, not even a child or an old man sitting on the bench with a friend. Artur glanced around and just caught a glimpse of an old lady getting up from her chair in the doorway and going inside. Across the other side of the village square, they turned right again, down a narrow street that contained a large number of derelict terraced houses. What little sun there was had vanished behind a band of clouds rolling in from the southeast. Artur shivered as he felt the temperature dropping; it was only early April after all. There had been a very cold winter.

Monique led the way into the garden at the back of the house. They had hardly exchanged a word during their forty minute walk. They went through the back door that entered a back hallway where there were boots, heavy jackets and hats. They entered the kitchen very quietly so as not to disturb Monique's aunt as her bedroom was above the kitchen. Artur heard a voice that sounded like Vivienne's so he went on tiptoe into the lounge. She appeared to be on the phone and she was speaking German.

Who was she speaking to? Artur asked himself, *and why was she speaking German?*

Artur decided to go into the hall where the phone was and pretend not to have been aware that she was on the phone.

"Oh, I'm so sorry, Vivienne, I didn't know you were on the phone. I expected you to be resting upstairs," Artur said in a surprised tone.

Vivienne put down the phone after saying a few words to whoever it was. She straightened her hair and ran her hands down her skirt. She turned to Artur and was prepared to explain herself when Monique came into the hall.

"Did you have a nice walk, Monique? It's turned a lot colder now so it's best you are back in the house."

"Yes, auntie, it was good to get some fresh air, especially after such a nice lunch. Did you manage to get a rest, or did you come and clean all the dishes?"

"I couldn't really rest, Monique. The news has not been good recently and it seems that Germany is up to something again. A friend of mine called me and she lives in the north of Germany. She said there were large numbers of troops, tanks and planes entering the Baltic coastal area and into Schleswig Holstein. You must have noticed or heard something when you were in Germany, Andy?"

Artur was only feeling a little more relaxed towards Vivienne after what she said about her phone call, but could he really believe her? He thought he had heard Vivienne mention his name and Monique's to whomever she had been talking and that disturbed him. He didn't answer her question and Monique said nothing either. The hallway was silent for what seemed like a long time, until Vivienne said that she would go upstairs and try to get some rest.

"We'll just sit in the lounge for a short while, if that's alright with you, auntie?"

"Of course, Monique, please make yourselves at home. I'll be down again in about an hour and we can decide what to have for supper."

As Vivienne got to the top of the stairs, Monique signalled to Artur for him to join her in the lounge. She sat on the sofa, but he decided to sit in the armchair opposite her. There was a frosty air between them and it seemed that neither wanted to be the first to speak, but Monique could wait no longer.

"I can guess from your behaviour that you have some concerns about my aunt, Andy. Am I right?"

"I think we should talk very quietly, Monique, so that your aunt doesn't hear what we're saying, even if she isn't in the room immediately above the lounge. How well do you know your aunt? Who would have been the person that had called her or was she pretending and it was she who had phoned someone? I think she was speaking to a man," Artur said in a whisper that Monique could hardly hear.

"Obviously I don't know everything about her, Andy," she said rather curtly. "But I am aware that she had some distant cousins living in Germany. I didn't know they lived in Schleswig Holstein."

"I think we have to be very cautious. I really believe that my position could be compromised and my name could be forwarded to the wrong people. Did you overhear her mention your name and mine to the person she was talking to?"

"No, I didn't. Don't you think you're getting a bit paranoid, Andy?"

"I certainly am not. Just remember, Monique, Britain is at war with Germany and I am here as an agent that has carried out sabotage on German soil."

Chapter 34
Tuesday, 1ˢᵗ of August 1939

Andrew overslept after his evening with Chloe. For some reason, he hadn't remembered to ask for a wake-up call from reception. He rushed through his bathroom activities and returned to put on his shirt from yesterday. It smelt strongly of Chloe's perfume, his trousers were still stained with gravy. He decided to wear a clean shirt and a different suit; he would get the soiled items sent to the laundry, even if he didn't get them back till next week.

Andrew walked briskly to the office and arrived over half an hour late; he'd had no breakfast. He didn't look at anyone else in the office as he reached his desk, but he did notice that his boss's office was empty. He tried hard to concentrate, but his mind kept returning to the previous evening and to Chloe. The tea lady brought the trolley round at 11 o'clock, and he couldn't resist having a large tea and a cheese sandwich.

"You 'av a late night and miss your breakfast, Mr Williams? You don't normally 'av anyfink 'uver than a cuppa?" said the lady with a smile.

"For once I overslept, so I missed breakfast," said Andrew, looking at Doris with his usual engaging smile.

Nothing more was said as he returned to his desk and eagerly munched into the sandwich. He started to feel better after a short while, but he thought he had better work through lunch to make up for lost time. He left the office promptly, went straight back to the hotel and up to his room to take a bath. He called room service for an evening meal as he didn't want any sarcastic comments from the barman.

After a good night's sleep, followed by a big breakfast, Andrew felt he was back to almost 100%. Wednesday went past quickly; he was even commended for his work by Mr Livermore, Mr Griffith's boss, as he was about to leave for the hotel.

"Well done, Williams, I'm very impressed at the work you've completed today. It wasn't easy, I know. Sorry we haven't been able to rearrange supper at my house yet, but we'll certainly organise something before you end your time here."

"Don't worry sir, I'll be available whenever you say. By the way, I'm sure you recall that I shall be out of the office for two days next week, Tuesday and Wednesday?"

"Yes, I do remember but thank you for mentioning it. I believe your son is to be christened this weekend, is he not? We've got a small present for you to take him and I'll let you have it tomorrow afternoon."

"That's extremely kind of you, sir, you really shouldn't have troubled yourselves."

"Nonsense, Williams. You've been a great asset to our office and, what with you being away from your home for four weeks as well, it's the least we could do."

Nothing more was said, but Andrew certainly felt very pleased that the Manchester office staff had put their hands in their pockets on his behalf. This time when he returned to the hotel, he went straight to the bar for what he felt was a well-earned pint. He was pleased to find that the usual barman was not on duty, so he didn't expect any comments or questions about him and Chloe.

After his second pint, Andrew went to his room to change and decided he would phone his wife to make sure everything was alright at home.

"Hallo dear," Andrew said. "How are you and is everything still on course for Sunday?"

"I'm pleased to say that no more people have cancelled. I did think you might have called me a day or two ago. After all, you don't know anybody up there so you could easily have phoned me yesterday."

"Sorry dear, but I will be home the day after tomorrow and you will probably remember that I have been allowed to return to the Manchester office by Monday lunchtime," Andrew replied, hoping to console his wife a little.

"I should hope so. We have a very busy day on Sunday and I'm not sure the weather forecast is very good either."

Andrew and his wife went over a few more details about Sunday's event; he then rang off. He was pleased he had spoken to her, even if she was worried about the weather for Sunday. He enjoyed his dinner in the main dining room and went to the bar for a nightcap: a good French brandy – a double. He entered into light conversation with a couple – probably in their early twenties, Andrew reckoned – and found they were up for a long weekend to celebrate his parents thirtieth wedding anniversary to be held in Bolton. In his usual manner, Andrew said not very much about himself, why he was in Manchester or about having relatives near Bolton. He was already training himself to extract information from other people and limiting what he said about himself.

After about an hour, and having bought drinks for the couple, Andrew was ready to retire. He bade them goodnight and went up to his room. As it was nearing 9 o'clock, he turned the wireless on to hear the news and the weekend's weather forecast. It was apparently going to be on the cool side for August, with the chance of an occasional shower. Andrew was pleased that he'd arranged for a marquee to be erected in the garden near the French doors; people could move in and out of the house without getting wet. He decided to get a good night's sleep in preparation for the weekend's activities.

Andrew woke up on Friday feeling refreshed, and enjoyed a full breakfast. He was very busy in the morning at the office, but managed to complete all his tasks before leaving for the railway station and his trip back to London. Mr Livermore presented him with the gift for Alfred in front of the staff and hoped all would go well on the day. He looked forward to seeing him back around lunchtime on Monday, or early afternoon.

The taxi got Andrew to the station in good time to catch his train and he was back home by 8:30 p.m. His wife was pleased to see him although she was still concerned about the weather for Sunday. The marquee had been put up, so having poured drinks for his wife and himself, they went outside to see if it was firmly fixed.

"I'm so glad you decided to go for a marquee, it certainly means we don't have to worry about what the weather will be like," his wife remarked. "It would be nice if the sun shone for the photos."

"The photographer is a very experienced chap," said Andrew reassuringly. "I'm sure we will not be disappointed with his results, whatever the weather."

They both felt quite relaxed with the arrangements, and so decided to go to bed just after 10 o'clock.

On the Saturday, Andrew was busy sorting out tables and chairs in the marquee, his wife was fussing over Alfred and the family christening outfit that had been sent by Andrew's mother shortly after Alfred was born – she didn't like it but felt she had to use it, even if she was not coming now.

It was a little warmer in the afternoon, so they had tea in the garden but not in the marquee. Alfred was gurgling away in his pram and both his parents hoped he would behave as well as this at his christening.

After a restful night for all of them, the advance party of the catering team arrived around midday. Andrew's sisters-in-law, brothers-in-law and his father-in-law arrived from London shortly after the caterers, and they all had a light lunch together. The atmosphere seemed very jovial and

Alfred was in good form. The weather was bright and sunny which made everyone quite relaxed, particularly Andrew's wife.

They all left for the local church and arrived fifteen minutes before the service was due to start. The vicar and the churchwarden had set everything up around the font. Just before 3 o'clock, all who were expected had arrived. Alfred didn't enjoy having water poured on his head and let out a loud squeal that made everyone smile.

Back at the house, Alfred was passed from one person to another and the photographer took lots of pictures to record the occasion. All seemed to be going well and with a lot of laughter, until Andrew's father-in-law slumped to the ground, spilling his tea all over his suit; he had apparently fainted. Everyone was very concerned for him, and Andrew's in-laws thought they should leave early and get father-in-law back to his home in Twickenham as he might be feeling the heat.

Most guests had left by 6:30 p.m. The caterers had cleared everything away, so Andrew and his wife sat down with a glass of champagne with a few locals, such as Brian and his wife, and congratulated each other on a memorable event, although Andrew's wife was understandably still concerned about her father. She phoned her sister during the evening and she was reassured to hear that their father was feeling much better; he was just annoyed for making such a spectacle of himself.

The following day, Andrew caught a train from London that arrived in Manchester just after 2 o'clock. All those working in the Foreign Exchange department wanted to hear how the christening had gone, and Andrew had remembered to bring enough cake back with him to have with their afternoon tea. He managed to get away from the office by 5:30 p.m., and once again reminded his manager that he wouldn't be in again until Thursday morning.

Andrew went back to his room and sorted out the clothes he needed for the following day. After a long time of searching, to his relief, he found the envelope from Charles giving instructions for the next two days' courses. He sat on the bed and read through all the pages. He felt relaxed, so after changing, he decided to have some supper in the hotel dining room. Later that evening, he returned to his room, laid out his clothes for the following day and read through the instructions once again before retiring to bed.

Chapter 35
Monday, 8th of April 1940

"I hope you don't mind, Monique, but I am going to my room. I need to review my plans. Did you happen to mention to your aunt that you and I will be leaving tomorrow and that you will be taking me to catch a train to the south?"

"When I phoned her from the bar in Simandre, I don't think I told her where we were going, Andy, but I did say that we would only be staying one night."

"OK. Let's hope I'm overreacting, but I still can't be too careful. Your aunt mentioned earlier that the news was not good, so presumably she has a wireless? Perhaps we could ask to listen to the news at 6 o'clock this evening. There might be an update on the situation in the north of Germany."

"I'm sure that could be arranged. You go and have a rest for a while, by which time it will be close to 6 o'clock."

Artur went from the lounge to his room upstairs and closed the door behind him. His brain was in a bit of a spin. He lay on the bed with his hands behind his head, staring at the ceiling. He started to think about Gerhart and hoped he hadn't run into any trouble on his way to Paris. He wished he was with him now so he could discuss the various options that had come into his mind. In the end, Artur reckoned it would be best to stick to the original plan and catch a train in Mâcon and head south.

The next thing he knew was a knocking on the door. He shot up on the bed and looked at his watch. He had obviously fallen asleep.

"Who is it?" he shouted.

"It's me, Monique. Are you alright? Can I come in? It's nearly 6 o'clock and auntie is downstairs with the wireless on."

"Come in, Monique. I must have dozed off."

Monique entered the bedroom and smiled broadly at Artur as she walked towards his bed. She sat down beside him and put her arm round his shoulders. She pulled herself towards him, but he suddenly leapt to his feet and rubbed his eyes.

"Sorry, Monique, but I must go to the bathroom and freshen up. I'll see you downstairs in a few minutes. Make sure you listen very carefully to the news, if it starts before I get down."

Artur walked quickly out into the corridor without even a glance at Monique and along to the bathroom. Meanwhile, Monique went downstairs and joined her aunt next to the wireless.

"Andy was fast asleep, auntie, but he'll be down in a minute or two, after he's been to the bathroom."

Auntie Vivienne said nothing, but turned the wireless volume up a little so she could hear it more clearly. The newsreader started with the headlines and mentioned that there were reports of significant troop movements into the north and north-eastern part of Germany. People on the ground had telephoned in to the radio stations in northern France that tanks and heavy artillery accompanied the troops. It was suggested that the Germans might be heading for Belgium or the Netherlands, with an outside possibility of going into Denmark.

"Oh my goodness," said auntie. "It would seem that my friends in northern Germany were right. At least those nasty Nazis will be leaving France alone for the time being. I wonder what they are really up to."

Nobody else said anything, but just listened to the newsreader as he went into more details. As soon as he went onto other topics, auntie turned the wireless off and glanced round at Monique and Artur, who were standing away from each other on the other side of the lounge.

"I think we need a drink after that news, don't you, Monique? I'll fetch some glasses and a bottle of red wine. Would that suit the two of you?"

"A very good idea, auntie. You don't happen to have some olives as well do you?"

"I certainly do. You two make yourself comfortable and I'll fetch everything from the kitchen."

As Vivienne left the lounge, Monique looked at Artur with a smile, but he didn't respond with one; he turned away and sat in the armchair. He was starting to think that this auntie of Monique's was rather clever and needed to be treated very carefully, with kid gloves. Before too long, Vivienne was back in the lounge with a tray full of goodies and a smile on her face.

"Here we are, my lovelies. Andy, would you kindly open the bottle while I get some serviettes."

Artur raised himself from his chair and briefly gave a half-hearted smile at Vivienne. In no time, they were clinking each other's glasses and muttering a few pleasant remarks. The atmosphere was, however, rather tense and there was little mention of the events unfolding in northern Germany.

"I thought we should have a light supper, if that's alright with you?" said Vivienne. "I have a few lamb chops and I can prepare a salad. We'll plan to eat about 7:30 p.m."

There were nods of approval from Monique and Artur. Vivienne topped up her glass and mentioned that she would start preparing supper. Monique offered to help, but was told to remain in the lounge and look after Andy.

"So, Andy, what do you make of the news about northern Germany?" enquired Monique.

"It's obviously very worrying, but what their real intentions are is uncertain. Fortunately, it doesn't really affect us here at present, but what does concern me is the next step of my journey back to England. If it's alright with you, I would like you to take me to Lyon station so I can take a train south. Would you be happy to oblige, Monique?"

"Of course Andy, to where ever you choose. What sort of time should we leave in the morning?"

"Soon after 8:30 a.m., if that will be alright with your auntie. It might take us about one and a half hours, but it will give me plenty of time to find a train. You had better tell her our plans and see what she says."

Monique went into the kitchen and Artur could hear her talking to Vivienne about the time they were proposing to leave. It didn't appear to be an issue.

Supper was served soon after 7:30 p.m. Conversation at table was still a bit strained, but Artur managed to lighten the atmosphere with a few anecdotes. Before anyone knew it, the clock in the hall struck 9 o'clock.

"Would anyone like a coffee?" asked Vivienne.

Artur and Monique both replied in the affirmative, with Artur preferring black. Monique helped clear the table and Artur was told to make his way to the lounge where they would join him shortly.

Just before 10 o'clock, Artur asked if he could be excused from further conversation and make his way to bed as he had some travelling to do. As it happens, he wasn't tired, but he just wanted to sort out what he was to do the next day. He made his way upstairs and could hear Vivienne saying what a nice man he was and that she hoped he would get back to England before any more troubles start. Artur then closed his bedroom door and put his small suitcase on the bed. There weren't many clothes in it, but he unfastened a strap and pulled up a section that revealed a small, secret compartment in the bottom of the case. He took out all the contents and checked through what he might be requiring the next day, placing them on the bed. He replaced the strap, closed the suitcase and sat on the bed. He went through in his mind how the following day would probably pan out.

Artur slept well for a few hours, but the remaining hours were spent very fitfully. By 6:30 a.m., he decided to go and use the bathroom and freshen up. On his return to his room, he saw Monique coming out of her room towards him.

"Did you sleep well, Andy? I stayed up with auntie for about an hour after you had gone to your room, chatting about family matters and what the war might do to France. I told her that I would be taking you to Lyon to catch a train, but I said nothing else. She's planning a breakfast of bread and coffee at 7:30 a.m., if that's OK with your timings?"

"That's fine, Monique. Please ask her to switch on the wireless so we can hear the 8 o'clock news, just in case there have been some further developments in northern Germany. Please don't say that it is for my interest, but more for her knowing what might lie ahead for hers and your relatives."

"Fine, understood, Andy. I'll see you downstairs in the kitchen a bit later."

Monique passed Artur as he went back into his room. He looked into her eyes, but didn't smile. His demeanour was serious; he wasn't sure where he would be by the evening. He closed his door, placed everything except the clothes he would be wearing neatly back in the case. He went through his papers and selected those that he would be wanting. After dressing, tidying his room and checking that he had left nothing behind, he went down stairs and put his case near the front door. He could smell the coffee being prepared and so went into the kitchen. He greeted Vivienne warmly and thanked her for allowing him to stay.

A few minutes later, Monique appeared and they all sat at the kitchen table for breakfast. Vivienne then mentioned that she was very concerned about her relatives in northern Germany, and would listen to the 8 o'clock news to hear about any possible developments. Monique felt a little relieved that she now didn't have to raise the subject.

Just before 8 o'clock, Vivienne got up and went into the lounge, the others following on behind. She turned the wireless on and, after a few moments, musical sounds came out that preceded the news, as a sort of time filler.

None of them could really believe what they were hearing:

'*Reports have been coming in from our contacts in northern Germany for the past four hours that German troops and tanks have invaded Denmark. They have entered from Schleswig Holstein and are swiftly moving north into Jutland towards Aalborg. At the same time, ferries and ships carrying heavily armed troops, supported by bombers dropping paratroopers, have arrived in southern Sjaelland and are heading for the*

Danish capital, Copenhagen. The German invasion armies have encountered only limited resistance so far.'

"Oh my goodness," exclaimed Vivienne. "So that's why the German troops were all assembling on the Baltic Coast and in Schleswig Holstein, just as my relative said. I shall have to call him and find out if they are all still alright."

Artur showed little concern, but he knew he was pleased that he'd been right about the sex of the person Vivienne had been speaking to the day before. Monique said nothing either, but held her hand hard against her mouth for fear of shouting or saying something inappropriate. Vivienne turned off the wireless. They stood for a few minutes, not saying anything, but Artur felt he had to break the silence.

"I am very sorry to say it, but I think Monique and I ought to be leaving for Lyon, Vivienne. Once we've gone, you will be free to call your relatives and find out how they are."

Monique rushed upstairs and quickly returned to the hallway with her case. She and Artur took their jackets from the stand and embraced Vivienne.

"I'm sure the Germans are not really interested in Denmark," said Artur, "except to control the movement of ships through the Straits. I think they will use Denmark as a stepping stone into Norway. With all the hilly countryside and the fjords, they will encounter much greater resistance from the Norwegians, but they will eventually conquer Norway and be able to control the North Sea."

With these rather troubling statements, Monique and Artur went to the car in the courtyard. As they got into the car, Vivienne waved at them and went back into the house. Artur wondered again about her and where her allegiances really lay and what she would say to her relatives in northern Germany. He just knew he had to get away, and fast. Just as Artur had predicted, Vivienne went into the hall and made a phone call to her relatives in northern Germany.

Chapter 36
Tuesday, 8ᵗʰ of August 1939

Andrew woke early, had a good breakfast and was down in the hotel's reception with his brief case by 8:20 a.m. At precisely 8:30 a.m., a very attractive young lady in RAF uniform came through the doors.

"Mr Williams?" she enquired.

Andrew stood up and smiled in his usual way.

"That's me."

"Are you ready to leave, Mr Williams?"

"Indeed I am."

Andrew followed the lady out of the hotel to the RAF staff car. She opened the back door and to Andrew's surprise, a voice he recognised greeted him.

"Good morning Charles. This is a very pleasant surprise," said Andrew as he slid into the seat next to Charles and they shook hands.

"Please take us to Manchester Airport at Ringway, Corporal Wade," said Charles. He looked back at Andrew and, with a grin, he told Andrew that he wanted to be present during this part of his training, but he also said quite loudly that he didn't want him to be alone with Corporal Wade, even in an RAF staff car; he knew his reputation with the ladies. During the drive to Ringway, Andrew positioned himself so that he and Corporal Wade could see each other in the rear-view mirror. They frequently smiled at each other without Charles being aware.

They arrived at Ringway, showed the guard their identification papers and stopped outside the main administration building. Corporal Wade came around to open Andrew's door, but Charles was expected to open his door for himself. Just as he was leaving the car, Corporal Wade told Andrew that she would be back at 5 o'clock to return him to his hotel. He turned to her, gave her a wink and thanked her for her kind attention.

Just as they were about to enter the building, Charles turned and pointed towards the planes outside the hangar.

"Not sure if you know about those biplanes, Andrew, but they are called Swordfish and are built by Fairey Aviation down in Middlesex.

Their primary use is in despatching aerial torpedoes at enemy naval convoys. Its ingenious design enables the wings to fold so it takes up much less space on an aircraft carrier. Anyway, enough of that, let's go and meet your instructors."

They went upstairs into the communications room, and Sergeant Thwaites was ready and waiting. After the usual pleasantries had been exchanged, Charles said he would leave and meet them for lunch in the canteen at about midday. Andrew explained to the sergeant that he had learnt the Morse code and it surprised him a bit, so he asked Andrew to sit at the table and familiarise himself with the operation of the Buzzer Military training key. They talked for a while about Morse code and training keys and the various types that can be found in military establishments. Andrew was then given a text that he should send in code; he could refer to the conversion chart if he needed to but Andrew declined.

The instruction and testing of Andrew went on until 11:30 a.m., with a few breaks for coffee. The sergeant didn't say much to Andrew after each test, but he was very impressed with his knowledge of the codes and the speed that he could transmit and receive. As Andrew had progressed so well, they all took a longer time over lunch and the sergeant reckoned Andrew would be finished with the section of the course on map reading by 4 o'clock. Charles returned to the instruction room and was handed the envelope with the completed results and comments' forms for posting off to the Service.

"Well then, Andrew, you seem to have had a very successful day, according to the instructor. He was impressed with your preparation for the course. Why don't we have a drink in the officers' mess before taking you back to your hotel?"

"I certainly could do with one, Charles, especially after being in a classroom all day."

Charles used the phone and asked if Corporal Wade could come a bit earlier than had been arranged to take them to the officer's mess for a drink. There was a brief pause and then Charles was told that it wouldn't be Corporal Wade, but Lance Corporal Sutcliffe as Wade hadn't returned from a previous duty.

Andrew thanked Sergeant Thwaites for all his help and instruction. They then went down to the main entrance and waited for the car, which arrived after a few minutes and drove them across to the other side of the airfield. They had a couple of pints and were duly driven back to Andrew's hotel at about 6:30 p.m. by Lance Corporal Sutcliffe.

"The Lance Corporal was a nice enough chap," remarked Andrew as they bade their farewells. "But what happened to Corporal Wade?"

"She was unfortunately called away to take the Group Captain to an urgent meeting in Stockport. She'll be back tomorrow to collect you from your hotel at 8:30 a.m., and I'll be with her too," said Charles with a wry smile.

"Fair enough," replied Andrew. "Thanks for today and I'll see you tomorrow."

Andrew went to his room and decided to have an early night after taking supper in the restaurant. Seeing Chloe was quite out of the question – even if he hadn't had too taxing a day.

The following morning, he was up bright and early. He was collected from the hotel at 8:30 a.m. by Corporal Wade.

"Good morning, Corporal," said Andrew as he walked through the door that was held open for him. Just as he got outside, he stopped and turned. Corporal Wade didn't expect him to do that so she marched right into him; the peak of her cap knocked into his chin and it slid upwards. He could feel her breath on his mouth as she straightened her cap and apologised for not seeing him stop.

"It's my pleasure, Corporal."

There was a shout from the car as Charles noticed the position of the two outside the hotel door.

"For Heaven's sake, Andrew, can we please get a move on? We have no time to waste."

Andrew gave the Corporal a big smile, turned and went to the rear door that Charles had opened for him. Once inside, Charles reprimanded him for trying to get friendly with Corporal Wade, but in a gentle way. They were soon through the gates of the airfield and then to the admin building. The two men had said nothing more during the journey, but once out of the car and walking to the building's entrance, Charles turned to Andrew.

"Today's exercises are probably more important than all that you've completed so far. You will be introduced to a two-way short-wave radio. You will be given a text which you must codify using a novel and you will send it using a particular frequency. After a while, you will receive a reply with some instructions that you will decode using the same book."

By this time, they were in a classroom on the first floor; the bespectacled instructor stood behind a desk but came round to greet them.

"This is Mr Andrew Williams," said Charles. "Flight Officer Digby will be taking you through the morning's course," he said as they all shook hands.

Charles excused himself as he had a meeting to attend and said he would be back at 12:30 p.m. to take them to lunch.

Digby told Andrew to call him Stephen, whereupon they sat down and he went through the workings of the wireless and the details of the first

231

exercise. Most of what happened over the next three hours – with a tea break at 11 o'clock – involved Digby being in another room. They would communicate with each other over the radio and using the code books. By the end of the morning, Andrew had made very good progress and everything was written up on the forms that were given to Charles when he returned at 12:30 p.m.

After lunch in the officers' mess, Charles had a surprise for Andrew.

"As you know, this is a fully operational RAF station," said Charles. "And I've managed to arrange for you to take a flight in one of the Swordfish biplanes for about an hour. What have you got to say about that, Andrew?"

"Wow, what a fantastic surprise Charles, and a wonderful experience too. What I've never told you though is that I did pass my pilot's licence at Croydon airport in the early '30s, but couldn't afford the time to keep the licence going."

"My goodness, Andrew, I had no idea! What did you learn to fly on?"

"I flew a Tiger Moth and had quite a few flights in the south of England over a two-year period."

"Well here's your chance to be in a Swordfish, it has greater speed and versatility. I'm quite sure you will really enjoy it."

They were driven over to one of the hangars where a pilot was standing by one of the planes that stood outside. Andrew was introduced to the pilot and after explaining a few details of what they would be doing, he took him inside to change into some flying gear. After about ten minutes, they reappeared all kitted out.

"Do I look the part, Charles?"

"You certainly do, Andrew. Enjoy the flight."

They wandered over to the plane and the pilot went through all the pre-flight checks with Andrew both outside and inside the plane. Once on board and belted, the plane was started and they taxied to the end of the runway, having first had clearance from the tower and being given the wind speed and direction. The pilot engaged full power and before too long they were airborne. Andrew's memories of his flying days came flooding back; he felt he was in a different world and wished he'd kept his licence. They flew to a nearby training area south of the Lake District where the pilot carried out some aerobatics and low level, precision flying over Lake Windermere. After gaining a reasonable height and levelling out, the pilot asked Andrew over the intercom if he would like to take control of the plane.

"Yes, sir!" he said with great eagerness.

"Just don't try anything silly, old chap. Do some nice turns then climb steeply to 5,000ft and do a stall turn. I take it you did these when you were learning?"

"Yes, I used to love doing them."

"OK, Andrew, you have control."

Andrew took over and completed a near perfect rate two turn followed by a stall turn that he turned into a spin on the way down, coming out of it with ease well above the water surface.

"That was rather foolish of you, Andrew, especially as you don't know much about these planes. I have control now, we'll return to Ringway."

There was complete silence in the plane until the pilot contacted the tower for landing instructions. They touched down on the grass runway, taxied to the hangar and cut the engine. Andrew got out first, closely followed by the pilot, and walked over to Charles, who had been joined by Corporal Wade.

"Mr Compton-Browne, I don't know what sort of jobs Mr Williams might be involved in after his training, but I suggest you keep tabs on him as he's very likely to take matters into his own hands. He displayed excellent control of the plane, but he then became very reckless when he took the plane into a spin after a stall turn when he knew very little about the plane's capabilities."

"I apologise to you, sir," said Andrew. "But you did pass control over to me. I thought it was time for a bit of fun!"

"Fun indeed! I am the chief flying instructor here and you don't exercise initiative like that when you are out with me without first telling me. Do I make myself clear?"

"Yes sir, very clear. Thank you for the flight in a remarkable plane."

"I have noted your comments," said Charles. "But thank you for the opportunity of allowing Andrew to display a characteristic that we were not aware of."

They all then shook hands, leaving the pilot to complete the post flight checks and fill in the log book. They walked to the car and this time Corporal Wade opened the door for Charles and not Andrew. Not much was said until they arrived at Andrew's hotel.

"I think I should treat you to a drink, Andrew. I'm sure you could do with one after today's activities and experience. Corporal Wade, would you please stay with the car for about half an hour?"

"Of course, sir, I'll be in the hotel car park awaiting your arrival."

Charles and Andrew walked in to the hotel bar where Charles ordered two pints. They chose a table at the far end of the bar and sat down. Andrew knew Charles wanted to start the conversation, so he waited after he had taken a good swig of his beer.

"As you are no doubt aware, old boy, your training has now been completed, but only for the time being. The reason I say 'for the time being' is that war is very likely to be declared in the next few weeks. There's no point in saying this in confidence because everyone can see that Hitler will continue to cause mayhem in Europe by invading more countries. No threats from us or France will stop him. I and C clearly recognise that a person with your skills and training will be invaluable to the Service once war is declared. I know we have said this before, but we now see more significant roles for you. Before the end of the year, we may well want to send you to Europe on a sort of test run. The location and timing will be dependent on the state of Britain and Europe at the time. Obviously I can't be specific at the moment, but what is your reaction to this?"

"I am not very surprised by your statement," said Andrew with a serious look on his face. He took another mouthful of beer. "So you think I might need additional training for some of the jobs you'll be getting me to do in the future?"

"Most certainly, Andrew. You'll most likely need training in unarmed combat, fighting with knives, the setting and laying of booby-traps plus the handling and use of explosives, such as dynamite."

"All sounds very exciting, Charles, but for the moment, no more courses are planned?"

"Correct. I will say that we are extremely pleased with your progress and your attitude towards the tasks given to you. You could, however, have behaved a bit less recklessly during the flying exercise."

"I just couldn't help myself, Charles. A plane like the Fairey Swordfish is also made for aerobatics, so there was no real risk involved. The instructor could have taken control at any time, should he have needed to, but he didn't. He must have felt the plane was in good hands."

"I don't think we need to talk about it anymore, Andrew. I can see you enjoyed the moment."

Charles looked at his watch, downed the rest of the pint and stood up, followed immediately by Andrew. They shook hands and walked out of the hotel. Charles waved to Corporal Wade, who drove to where Charles was waiting.

"That's all for the time being, Andrew. I'll contact you sometime during the week beginning the 20th, once you are working back at the London branch. Keep an eye on the news."

Andrew waited until the car had disappeared from sight and strolled back in to the bar. It had been a very good day and he needed another pint before having some dinner and phoning his wife.

Chapter 37
Tuesday, 9th of April 1940

As soon as they were out of Collongette, Artur told Monique that he didn't need her to take him to Lyon, but only as far as Mâcon station.

"Why the change, Andy? I don't mind taking you to Lyon? Don't change the destination just for my sake."

"I have what I believe is a very good reason for the change. Perhaps I should call it a hunch. I'll explain when we get a bit nearer, and it'll only take about forty minutes to get there instead of just under two hours to get to Lyon."

They were soon travelling down the road that ran parallel to the river Saône. Artur suggested they should stop at a café for a coffee before getting to the station. Monique saw a sign for a hotel-restaurant and pulled into the car park at the rear. They went round the front of the hotel and inside to the bar area where quite a few other people were standing or sitting on stools. There wasn't much conversation as the wireless was on and they were listening to the latest news reports of the German invasion of Denmark.

"*Café au lait* for two, please," Monique said.

When the coffees were ready, they moved over to a table away from the other people. They spoke little to each other; the situation was serious. Neither of them knew if they would ever see each other again.

"Do you happen to know the frequency of the trains from Mâcon to Marseille," Artur asked Monique in a whisper that she barely heard.

"I believe they are usually every two hours, but you'll have to check when you get to the station. We should have asked auntie before we left her house."

"I did have a quick look around for a timetable near the telephone, but saw nothing."

They finished their coffees, said farewell to the others in the bar and went back round to the car. Monique said that they were probably only a little over five minutes away from the station.

"When we get to the front of the station, Monique, I just want you to drop me off and not come in to the station with me. I know it will be very hard for us both after all that you've done for me, but I'm now going back into my agent mode of operation."

Monique said nothing; she could feel tears beginning to blur her vision, but she knew Artur was right. She pulled up outside the station entrance. They both got out of the car and Artur took out his suitcase. They embraced each other for a few moments. Artur asked Monique that, when she got back to Pesmes, to thank Madame Pélissier for all her help and hopefully she will find her well on the road to recovery. Monique said it would be the first thing she would do and she would ring her aunt to thank her for putting them up. Then Artur was gone from her side. Monique watched until he had gone through the doors and was out of view. She got into her car and wiped her eyes with her handkerchief. She drove north out of the station and was now looking forward to getting back home. She had no idea if or when she might see him again.

As Artur went into the station, he looked at the departures board and saw there was a train going to Marseille in just over an hour. The train would be stopping at Lyon, Avignon and Aix and other stations in between, but he wouldn't have to change although it did seem to suggest that it would be waiting for ten minutes before proceeding further south from Lyon. He had plenty of time.

He set off for the toilets and put some centimes into the slot to use the closet and closed the door behind him. He took off his shirt and trousers, placed them in the suitcase and put on some different ones that he had taken from the compartment at the base of the case. He checked that the labels still said that they were made in Denmark. He had some special dark cream that he massaged into his hair and scalp and stuck a dark moustache onto his top lip. He swapped his passport and other documents over so that he now appeared to be a genuine, Danish businessman. He placed them in his inside jacket pocket. He also found some Danish kroners that he put into his trouser pocket. He put on his jacket and was now ready to leave the closet. He inspected his handiwork in the mirror over the wash basin and washed the dark cream from his hands just as someone came in.

Artur was as satisfied as he could be with his new identity, and he went out into the main concourse. The only thing that remained the same was his name: Artur Selmer. That was his name in all his passports and on his documents. He double-checked the time of the train and bought himself a single 3rd class ticket to Marseille. By this time, there were only fifteen minutes left before his train would arrive, so he passed the time by looking through a few magazines at the news stand.

There was an announcement over the station loudspeaker that was barely audible, but which seemed to herald the arrival of the train from Paris that was bound for Marseille. Artur walked towards the gate to the platform and presented his ticket.

"May I see your identification card, monsieur," asked the station official.

Artur pretended not to understand for a few moments and then produced his passport from his inside pocket. The official scanned through the passport for the entry visa, looked at the photo and up at Artur, and back again at the photo. He mumbled something that Artur couldn't quite hear and handed it back to him.

"*Merci, monsieur, bon voyage.*"

Artur placed the passport back in his jacket pocket and walked down the platform to the 3rd class compartments. He wanted to sit on the platform side so he found a carriage that had the corridor on the far side. He got onto the train, placed his suitcase on the rack and sat in the seat facing the engine. There was a high-pitched whistle, the train gave a slight lurch forward and then it was moving. Artur gave a sigh of relief; he was the only person in the compartment, but he expected more passengers to get on in Lyon. As the train gathered speed, he took down his case and made sure that all the items that he had taken off were now in the concealed part at the bottom of the case. He snapped the lid of the secret section closed and arranged all other items above it so the lid was now not visible. He replaced the suitcase in the overhead rack, sat back and closed his eyes.

So far so good, he thought to himself. *I wonder how far Monique has driven by now. Will I be right about Vivienne and her relatives in northern Germany?*

Before Artur knew it, the train started to slow down. He unhitched the window's leather strap and looked out towards the passing buildings and houses as they entered the city of Lyon, one of the largest French cities after Paris. The train came slowly into the station; he looked out of the window towards the front of the train. Other passengers were leaning out and there were quite a number of new passengers waiting on the platform. The carriage that he was in was nearer the front than the back, so he looked carefully but not too obviously at those on the platform as he passed them. The train stopped. He looked up and down the platform a couple of times, then sat back down in his seat again in case some passengers wanted to get into his compartment. He had noticed some policemen walking up the platform, looking intently at the passengers waiting to board.

The door of Artur's compartment opened and two elderly ladies got in and greeted him in the usual French manner, but Artur just nodded his head and mumbled something to them. He saw them struggling with their cases so he got up and put the cases on the rack. They thanked him, but he just nodded his head again and sat back in his seat.

"Did you see the two sets of police, those at the platform entrance and the others walking up and down the platform?" said one of the ladies who was overheard by Artur. "What do you think that was all about?"

"I have no idea," said the second lady. "But it must be important for so many to be there."

Artur tried to compose himself by looking out of the window at the passers-by on the platform whilst the ladies continued to chatter about the police. The next thing he knew was the door into his compartment being opened from the corridor by a ticket inspector. He entered the compartment followed by two police officers. Artur knew immediately that he had been right about Vivienne all along. She must have contacted the police as soon as they had left Collongette and alerted them of a suspicious person catching the train at Lyon bound for Marseille.

"Please may I see your tickets and either your identity cards or passports," said the inspector to everyone in the compartment.

He examined the ladies' documents, passed them to the police, who returned them saying they were fine. The inspector took Artur's passport and passed it to the police. They looked at the photo, then at Artur and back at the photo.

"What is the nature of your business in France?" said one of the officers.

Artur pretended not to understand and said he was Danish and spoke very little French.

"So why are you on this train to Marseille?" said the second officer very slowly with a few nondescript gestures.

Artur decided to speak to them in broken English which he knew they would not like.

"I 'ave finished business in ze Nort' and wis ze problems on de Danish border I find new way 'ome."

"If you have been working in France, why do you not speak better French?"

Artur repeated what he had said before without answering the officer's last question. This irritated the police officers and when the description of who they were looking for clearly didn't match his passport, nor to what Artur actually looked like in the flesh, they all left the compartment and moved on further down the train. The two ladies talked in low voices to each other, hoping Artur couldn't hear them or wouldn't understand them, but of course he could and he did.

The train was due to stop for only ten minutes in Lyon, but it was nearly another fifteen minutes later that the whistle went. The inspector and the police officers passed all of the carriages on their way back to the front of the train; they glanced into each compartment in case they had missed the person they were looking for. When they reached Artur's window, they saw him looking out at them, but his expression was no different from when they had seen him earlier. They were satisfied with the examination of all the passengers and would report back that it must have been a false alarm. But, unknown to Artur, one of the policemen got back on the train at the front; he was not convinced that he had missed the person he was looking for.

The train gathered speed and was soon on its way out of Lyon. After about half an hour, Artur decided to go to the buffet bar for a drink and possibly something to eat – he felt he needed it and certainly deserved it. He had a long journey ahead of him.

Chapter 38
Thursday, 10ᵗʰ of August 1939

The morning was bright and sunny when Andrew woke at about 7 o'clock, and it made him feel good about life. After a healthy breakfast, he walked briskly to the office and was greeted by M. Griffiths, who asked him to have a talk in his office.

"It's good to have you back, Williams. Did everything go well for the two days you were away?"

"Yes, all seemed to go very well, thank you sir."

"We have certainly missed you and you now only have one more week with us before you return to the London office. I arranged while you were away for some of your colleagues and one or two of the management team to have a farewell drink next Thursday in a pub not far from here. We would like to take the opportunity of thanking you for your contribution to the Foreign Exchange department, your general friendliness and helpfulness towards other members of my team. Would that be alright with you?"

"That's a very kind gesture, sir. After all, I was only doing my job to the best of my ability and I have really enjoyed my time here too."

"Good, that's settled then. Is there anything you want to discuss with me?"

"No thank you, sir. If that's all, I'll go and get on with my work as I'm sure there'll be many things waiting for me to attend to."

Andrew spent the rest of the day catching up on his paper work and left the office just after 5:30 p.m. He had phoned Chloe during the lunchtime, hoping to see her after work, but could only arrange to meet her the following Tuesday. When he arrived back at his hotel, he had a beer in the bar and returned to his room to call his wife. For some reason, she was in a foul mood, but Andrew raised her spirits a bit by suggesting they go for a drive somewhere on Saturday and have some lunch as the weather was expected to be fine and a little warmer than it had been of late. The call only lasted a few minutes, probably because she was having difficulty with Alfred.

The next day was unusually busy in the office as most clients were hedging their bets on investments because of the situation in Europe. Although Andrew had been unaware of it, a large proportion of England had been dark for four hours from midnight to test how the country could shroud itself from enemy planes. Everyone was very much more pessimistic about the future.

Andrew managed to leave the office in good time to catch the train back to London and was home by 8:30 p.m., much to his wife's surprise.

"You know, Andrew, that the newspapers and the radio are reporting that war in Europe is imminent?" said his wife with a great deal of concern. "You are still a young man, so will you join one of the services when war is declared?"

Andrew knew very well what he would do, but he couldn't tell his wife. He thought he ought to placate her so he suggested he got a drink for the two of them, but he tried to avoid her question.

"Don't you have any thoughts about what your son and I should do under the circumstances of a war? For the last few months, families have been evacuated out of London and the large cities to the countryside. We've even had a few arrive not far from here. That piece of paper that Chamberlain brought back from Munich last year is obviously totally useless."

Andrew could hear all that his wife was saying as he was getting the drinks; it all made sense and was exactly what Charles had been saying when they first met.

"Do you want any cheese and biscuits with the drinks, dear?" asked Andrew.

"That's a good idea. There's plenty in the larder."

After handing his wife her drink, Andrew went to the kitchen for the snacks. Whilst he was gathering everything together on the tray, he pondered over what his wife had asked him and how he should reply if she pressed him for an answer. He returned to the lounge and placed the tray on the coffee table.

"That all looks very nice, Andrew, thank you. Now about tomorrow. You probably noticed when you were coming home from the station that it's got rather cloudy and the temperature is quite low for August. Wouldn't it be better if we planned something for next weekend and celebrate the end of your time at the Manchester office?"

"Excellent idea! Whilst I'm away next week, perhaps you would like to plan something for the Saturday or the Sunday. Actually, that reminds me. Brian had been suggesting some time ago about going to Wales for the weekend. Wouldn't that be of more interest to you for next weekend, or should we look at the following one, the 26th and 27th?"

"Oh going to Wales would be a lovely idea," she said as she got to her feet and put her arm round his shoulder. "We haven't been there for ages. Perhaps we could stay at the Lake Vyrnwy Hotel, where we used to stay? Give Brian a call tomorrow and discuss it with him," she said as she kissed him on the cheek.

For the rest of the evening, they chatted and laughed about the times they had spent at the Lake Hotel over the years. It pleased Andrew that he had remembered Brian's suggestion as it took the spotlight off his wife's questions. They retired to bed well after 11 o'clock in a very happy mood, especially with the prospect of a weekend away.

Andrew phoned Brian on Saturday morning, and they agreed to go away for the weekend in a fortnight's time. Brian said he would contact the hotel and arrange for them to stay Saturday night and have a cot for Alfred. He also asked if he wanted his brother-in-law and sister-in-law to go as well, to which Andrew said yes.

The Williams' household was in very good spirits for the rest of the weekend, until Andrew left on Sunday afternoon to return to Manchester for his last week. He arrived at his hotel in the early evening, and went straight to the bar for a pint.

"You seem to be in a very good mood this evening, Mr Williams. Did you have an enjoyable weekend?" said the barman.

"All went well, thank you. I shall, however, be sorry to be leaving here on Friday. I've really enjoyed my time up here and met some very nice people."

"We shall be sad to see you go, sir, it's been a pleasure to have you at our hotel."

Andrew thanked the barman for his kind words, downed his pint, bade him goodnight and went to his room to unpack and go to bed.

He was in the office bright and early the next morning, and everyone commented on how chirpy and happy he seemed to be. He called Chloe in the afternoon and they arranged to meet in the hotel bar at 6 o'clock the next day. This made Andrew even more light-hearted and he suspected some of the secretaries knew that he'd been seeing Chloe. He could tell from the way they whispered to each other and giggled when they looked at him, but he tried not to let it affect him. He didn't know if Chloe had anything planned, especially after their last evening together at her house.

The day ended and Andrew decided to get an early night after a light supper at the hotel. He was in early again the next day, and kept his head down with his work until most people left the office at 5:30 p.m. He walked briskly to the hotel and just had enough time to change before heading for the bar, but he was a little late arriving, after the time he had arranged to meet Chloe. He glanced around but couldn't see her, so he bought a pint and sat at the table they had used before. Time went by and she hadn't arrived by 6:45 p.m. He hoped all was well with Chloe as she was usually very punctual.

"Mr Williams?" said the voice of the hotel manager as he came over to Andrew. "I have just received a message for you," he continued and he handed over a piece of paper. Andrew opened it and it was from Chloe.

So sorry to mess up our arrangements for this evening, but I had a call from my father just before I was about to leave work to tell me that my mother had fallen down stairs at home and had been taken to hospital. As I'm sure you will understand, I have had to go straight home. I hope to see you at your farewell party on Thursday. Love, Chloe.

Andrew was worried for Chloe, but he had no way of contacting her; in any case, she would probably be at the hospital. He ordered another pint and went to the dining room for supper feeling rather deflated.

On both Wednesday and Thursday morning, Andrew tried to contact Chloe during office hours, but he was told that she hadn't come to work because of an accident to her mother.

On Thursday evening, all of Andrew's colleagues and some of the management team escorted him to the nearby pub where a private room had been prepared for his farewell party. Drinks were provided as were an assortment of sandwiches and some cakes. Some of the girls got rather giggly and started to flirt with Andrew. Suddenly, his manager raised his hand and asked for quiet in the room.

"As you will all know, we have been very fortunate to have had Andrew Williams working for us in the Foreign Exchange department for the last four weeks."

"*Here, here,*" they all said, with some of the girls nudging each other and smiling at Andrew.

"He has made a significant contribution to the way we work and even agreed to spend a few days in our Liverpool office. His manager in London will receive a very favourable report on his contribution and we wish him well for the future. Let's face it, the future does seem very bleak with what is happening in Europe. Please raise your glasses to wish all good wishes to ANDREW WILLIAMS."

Everybody responded very noisily: "*ANDREW WILLIAMS.*"

Andrew knew he had to say a few words of thanks, but just as he was about to speak, in walked Chloe looking as pretty as ever. As the door closed behind her, everyone turned to see who it was. She blushed a bit and went up to the drinks' table for a glass of white wine. She turned, raised her glass to Andrew and smiled the most beautiful smile that only she could do. Andrew continued with his response, and at the end everyone applauded. He went over to his manager and shook his hand, then went to Chloe and gave her a light kiss on her cheek at which everyone cheered.

"It's really good to see you, Chloe. I trust your mother is comfortable? Is she still in hospital? Did she break anything?"

"No, she didn't break anything, it was just a precautionary measure. She'll be back home tomorrow evening, I'm pleased to say."

"Are you able to have dinner with me once we finish here, or do you have other plans?" asked Andrew; he held her hand and everyone was watching them.

"I'd like that very much, Andrew, but we won't be able to eat at my house this time," she said with a twinkle in her eye.

Andrew let go of her hand and excused himself to go and chat to some of the other people. After about an hour, Mr Griffiths came up to him and shook his hand. He wished him well again, and said he thought Andrew would have a good future in the bank and would do great things for his country, once war was declared. Andrew frequently pondered over his words for many months to come. People started to leave and eventually only Chloe and Andrew were left.

"Where shall we go to eat?" asked Chloe.

"I'll take you to my hotel and we'll have a very good meal there. I really have no concern about what anyone might say or think about my being with you."

Chloe smiled and took Andrew's hand. Andrew thanked the staff for looking after them all, and the two of them walked out of the pub and to Andrew's hotel.

The dining room manager welcomed them and showed them to a table in the corner of the room. During dinner, Chloe asked Andrew about his view of the European situation, to which he answered very vaguely. At the end of dinner, Andrew said he would love to take her to his room, but felt she had to go back home to her father.

"I'm sure we will meet again sometime," said Andrew philosophically, as he took her hand that was close to his and looked longingly into her eyes.

Chloe just couldn't stop smiling at Andrew and bent her head to kiss him on the cheek. They gave their thanks to the waiters and walked arm in arm to the bus stop. Just as the bus arrived, they embraced and she waved from her seat as the bus drove off.

In the morning, Andrew packed all his clothes and checked out of his hotel before leaving for the Manchester office for the last time. Those who saw him mentioned how much they had enjoyed the evening. As he entered the Foreign Exchange department, his manager called him over and said he wanted a quick word. He repeated what he had mentioned the previous evening and told him that if he wanted to leave on an earlier train for London, he was free to do so.

The day seemed to pass by very quickly, and just before he was due to leave for an earlier train, Chloe phoned to thank him for taking her to dinner. They chatted for a few minutes, but Andrew had to cut the call short after explaining that he was catching an earlier train.

Andrew was home by 7 o'clock, and he was welcomed with open arms by his wife, who expressed great pleasure that he was no longer having to travel up to Manchester on a Sunday afternoon.

The weekend was spent peacefully at home and Andrew noticed how quickly Alfred seemed to be growing, even though he was only three months old. They worked out what they needed to take to Wales for the next weekend and Andrew phoned Brian to ask him if all had been organised, even though he knew the answer. He had to tell him, however, that his bother-in-law wouldn't be able to make it, so Brian said he would call the hotel and let them know. On Sunday, Andrew checked over his wife's car to make sure it was fit for the long journey; he really wanted to take the 'Bug' but it was not practical with Alfred and Max coming as well.

On the Monday, he went to his London office and was greeted warmly by management and his work colleagues. He quickly set about his work following a brief chat with his manager in his office.

By the time Friday came, he thought he might have received a call or a letter from Charles; neither happened, but he didn't feel inclined to be the one to make the contact.

There was great excitement on Saturday morning, as they filled the car for their trip. They had arranged to meet Brian and his wife near Cheltenham at a pub they knew just after midday, so they left home just after 8 o'clock. They made good time and arrived a few minutes before the scheduled arrival time and just before Brian and his wife. They had a light lunch, fed Alfred and gave Max a brief walk – they knew they would get an excellent dinner at the hotel. After leaving the pub, they decided to go in convoy for the rest of the route to the hotel and arrived before 4 o'clock. They all agreed it was a long way, but it was worth it: they got a very warm welcome and they didn't know when they would be able to make the trip again.

They each had a room overlooking the Lake and went down for afternoon tea on the terrace looking out over the lake as it was warm and sunny. They were all in good humour and the manager was very pleased to see them as the hotel was less than half full. They changed for dinner and were given a gratis drink by the management out on the terrace. Needless to say, the conversation amongst the guests was about what might happen next in Europe. Andrew would not be drawn into saying what he would do in the event of war being declared, nor did he say anything about which arm of the services he might join. There was a suggestion that all sixteen of them might like to sit at one table, but it was turned down. Just before going in to dinner, Andrew's wife went to check on Alfred to make sure he was asleep.

The evening became quite lively as wine was flowing freely and there was a pianist playing many of the popular tunes of the 30s, to which some people sang the words, including Andrew, rather raucously, much to his wife's embarrassment. At the end of dinner, they all went off to the bar, but as Andrew's wife excused herself of any more drinks, she decided to go and check on Alfred and take to her bed, followed by Brian's wife.

The following morning was fine, so Andrew and Brian took Max for a good walk along the lake. Brian asked how things had gone in Manchester and wondered if he'd heard from Charles recently. Andrew said all had gone well and that he expected to hear from Charles sometime in the week. They returned to join the rest for a good breakfast, but some of the guests were complaining about suffering from sore heads!

Andrew and Brian were not in a hurry to leave, but felt they ought to be on the road by 11 o'clock. One or two couples were staying for an extra night, but everyone said their goodbyes with most appearing rather glum about what the situation might be in a few months' time. They had a good run home with a welcome stop for a snack and a quick walk for Max. Not far from Andrew's home, Brian took off towards his house with the Williams family arriving home shortly after 6 o'clock.

"Well that was a great time away, Andrew," said his wife. "It's such a pity it's so far away."

"So glad you enjoyed it, my dear, and we met one or two very interesting people too. I'll give Brian a call in about an hour and thank him for organising it all."

Everything was unpacked, Alfred was back in his cot, Max had had a walk and they sat down with a drink to listen to the news. They listened with alarm when the news reader mentioned that Hitler had ordered the invasion of Poland on Saturday only to postpone it on Sunday. The news cast also referred to the agreement between Britain and Poland that stated clearly that Britain would stand by its obligations to Poland, especially in the event of an invasion.

"My goodness," said Andrew's wife as she finished her drink. "It sounds to me that we could be waging war against Germany in the next few days, if they invade Poland, alongside France, that has a similar attitude to Britain."

Andrew didn't say anything for quite a few minutes, but mulled over what his wife had just said and remained looking serious. He was sure he would be called by Charles early in the week so his future might be a little clearer.

"Would you like a nightcap, dear? The news is very grim, of course, but there's not much we can do that will alter the probable outcome."

Andrew got up, switched off the wireless and took his wife's glass to be refilled. He returned with her drink and as he handed it to her, he kissed her on the forehead.

"What troubles me is that if we go to war, are we really ready? Have we got enough fighter planes and bombers? Do we have enough tanks and trained army personnel? Do we have enough fighting ships and armour? I strongly suspect not, especially when one hears that the Germans have been rearming themselves since Hitler became Chancellor, totally against the Treaty of Versailles."

"Oh dear, you paint an even worse picture, Andrew, suggesting that even if we went to support Poland and declared war with Germany, we wouldn't stand a chance. It could be all over in a matter of months. The German forces would take over Britain and we would be run as a fascist state. We would all have to learn German. It's a very frightening prospect."

Silence then filled the room. They jumped out of their skin when the telephone rang.

"Who could that be at this time of the evening?" said Andrew's wife rather angrily as Andrew rose to his feet and went to the hall.

"Good evening. Who's that calling please?" said Andrew as calmly as he could.

It was his brother-in-law from Lancashire. He wanted to know if they had heard the news this evening, to which Andrew replied that they had. The conversation went on for a further few minutes before Andrew rang off. He went back into the lounge.

"It was your brother from Lancashire asking if we had heard the news this evening, which of course we had. He declared he was going to be a conscientious objector, if war is declared; not if but when. He's never had the stomach for a fight, has he?"

"That's not very fair. He's a good ten years older than you and he's certainly not as fit either. Anyway, were they all well up there, or didn't you ask?"

Andrew hadn't asked; he did say they sounded alright but worried. He was tempted to have another drink but decided against.

"I think that after the weekend and all that excitement on the news, we ought to retire to bed. I'll let Max out for a few minutes and then lock up the house."

Andrew cleared away the glasses to the kitchen and let Max out into the garden; his wife went upstairs still in a bit of a trance after the news.

The following morning, Andrew went to the office as usual and the papers were all full of gloom and doom. When the tea lady came round at 11 o'clock, Andrew's manager called him into his office.

"How are you settling back into the London office, Williams? You seem to be a bit preoccupied this morning. Is everything alright? How is your young son?"

"Everything is fine, thank you sir, except for the slightly worrying things going on in Europe," said Andrew, trying to play the situation down a bit. "Young Alfred Williams is well and over three months old now so we've really got used to him being around."

"Good, I'm glad to hear it as I am pleased to tell you that I have some good news for you. The management have had agreement from the Board to promote you to the level of Senior Clerk. As you know, this is only one level away from being Head of Department. It is richly deserved and it has been endorsed by the management team in Manchester after their glowing report to us."

Andrew could hardly believe his ears; he had been working so hard in an attempt to achieve this promotion.

"That's fantastic news, sir. I am deeply grateful to you for putting my name forward and to the Board for acknowledging your recommendation."

They shook hands and both of them appeared to be pleased with the outcome. Andrew was told that a notice will be placed on the branch noticeboard and it will take immediate effect. In addition, the pay increase will be backdated to commence from 20th August, that is to say, from last Monday.

Andrew went out into the main office feeling very pleased with himself; he knew very well that these promotions were not awarded lightly. He found it quite difficult to settle back to work, so he left the office about half an hour earlier than usual. On the way from the station to home, he bought a bunch of flowers for his wife and a bottle of champagne from the off-licence.

"Hello dear, I'm home."

"Gosh, you are nice and early today."

Andrew handed the flowers to his wife, gave her a kiss and told her that his promotion had come through.

She was ecstatic and after giving Andrew a big hug, she went and put the flowers in a vase that she placed on the coffee table.

"I thought we should celebrate with some fizzy stuff," said Andrew as he went to the cocktail cabinet for some glasses.

They stood there cheering each other over and over, and before long half the bottle was finished. Andrew asked if there were any biscuits and cheese and his wife literally ran to the kitchen and brought some to him.

"You have no idea how pleased I am for you, Andrew. You certainly do deserve it, especially after all these late nights and working in the Manchester office. Let's face it, you have worked at the bank for a long time and been very loyal to the London City branch."

Andrew couldn't help but agree with her, even if the late nights over the last six months were mainly to do with Charles and the Service.

"Do you want to celebrate this event with some friends and have them round for dinner at the weekend?"

"No, I don't think so, thank you. So many of my friends run their own businesses, it would seem very trivial to me to tell them that I'm now a Senior Clerk at the bank. It wouldn't mean much to them and I'm not normally the sort of person that shows off about my work. I just do my job to the best of my ability and occasionally I get an award. Thanks for the idea, but no thanks."

His wife looked rather disappointed and crestfallen; she thought she had found another chance to entertain and was thwarted. She slid out of the lounge, followed by Andrew's eyes, having said she would sort something out for supper. They finished the champagne with the sandwiches and not much more was said about a celebration party for the rest of the evening.

The following morning, Andrew arrived at the office not feeling any different from the way he felt before his promotion, except for a few of his colleagues coming up and congratulating him.

"How do you know?" he asked.

"There's a notice on the office board announcing your elevation to Senior Clerk," said one of the office secretaries. "Everyone knows and is very happy for you."

"Thanks for your good wishes," Andrew replied.

The next two days seemed to fly past, but on Thursday afternoon his manager called him to his office and said that someone needed to speak to him; he could only think it was Charles.

"Hello, Williams speaking."

"Hello Andrew, Charles here. How are you? Have you got a few minutes for us to talk?"

"Charles, good to speak to you again. Do we need to meet up soon?"

"Yes we do; it is very important that we meet tomorrow; can we have a snack tomorrow lunchtime at the pub just round the corner from your office?"

"I don't see why not; I'll be there by 12:30 p.m. if that's alright with you?"

"Great, see you tomorrow."

Andrew knew the situation with Germany and Poland had reached an impasse and that things could only get worse.

Chapter 39
Tuesday, 9th of April 1940

Artur went back to his compartment after a much needed coffee and a croissant, but not before visiting the lavatory to relieve himself and to make sure his disguise still resembled his passport photo. As he entered his compartment, he smiled and nodded to the ladies; they smiled back at him before continuing with their conversation and him to his seat. He thought about the police on the platform at Lyon and the ones that came on the train with the inspector. He also thought about the situation in Denmark, and how France and Britain might respond to Germany's invasion. He couldn't work out the reason for going into Denmark, unless it was to take over Norway next, acquire the iron ore mines in the north and have control of the North Atlantic.

When Artur was at Mâcon station, he noticed there was another train to Marseille about one and a half hours after the one he was catching. He thought carefully about the attention that the police had shown to him and his passport. For once he felt very nervous and isolated, especially without Gerhart, and Monique of course. He decided he would get off the train at Avignon and wait for the next one to Marseille. Having made the decision, he felt more relaxed, closed his eyes and slept. He awoke with a start and realised the train was slowing. He looked out of the window to see what was going on, but there was no hint of a town or station to give him a clue. He overheard the ladies mention something about it possibly being an unscheduled stop, but nothing about where they were. There was then a rather crackly voice on the intercom that apologised for the stop and the slight delay – it was apparently due to a signalling problem. *That's a relief,* Artur mumbled to himself in Danish.

Within ten minutes, the train proceeded again. Artur was aware of some passengers moving down the corridor towards the bar. He glanced at his watch: it was after 1:40 p.m. He had more than two and a half hours to go to Avignon; no wonder he was feeling hungry. He was just about to get out of his seat and go to the buffet car when he saw a police officer walk along the corridor. It wasn't any old officer, but Artur noticed it was one of the two who had been inspecting everyone's papers whilst the train was in Lyon station. He turned away from the corridor window, got up from his seat and brought his case down from the rack onto the seat next to him. He looked carefully to his left as he opened the case; the officer had stopped and was looking at him quizzically.

Artur opened the case to about halfway and brought some papers out of the section in the lid. He took out a file, closed the case and replaced it on the rack. He deliberately looked towards the corridor; the officer was no longer there. He sat down again and opened the file. It contained papers relating to the business meetings that he had had in France; they had been typed in Danish by one of the Services secretaries back in London in early February. He flicked through the papers and found the page that referred to two trusted contacts: one in Avignon and the other in Béziers, should he need them.

After about half an hour, Artur replaced the papers in his case and ventured out into the corridor. He thought he would go to the buffet carriage, and if the officer was there, acknowledge his presence. He wanted to be in control and not suddenly be surprised by the officer's arrival at his carriage and be asked questions in front of the ladies. He reached the bar and ordered a black coffee. He looked around and into the dining area. The officer was having a meal and was talking animatedly to a man in a suit who turned his head and looked straight at Artur. Their eyes met for a brief moment; Artur nodded and smiled. The man did not smile back, but turned to the officer and continued his conversation. Artur placed himself by the window, half facing the restaurant, so he could keep an eye on the two men without making it too obvious. He sipped at his coffee and smiled. *This is exactly the sort of situation that we covered during my training*, he said to himself. *What I must do now is walk slowly through the buffet car and down to the back of the train.*

Artur entered the restaurant carriage and walked past the table that the two men sat at. As he did so, he nudged the other man's shoulder and he turned to look up at Artur.

"So sorry," said Artur in Danish, loud enough for both men to hear. "The carriage swayed a little as I passed by your table," he continued in Danish. Of course, the men didn't understand what Artur had said, but they got a rough idea. Artur exited the carriage into the next one and glanced over his shoulder as he closed the door. The officer was looking towards Artur and he pointed to a piece of paper that he had shown the other man. Words were exchanged but Artur couldn't tell what had been said. He walked slowly through the carriages passing people standing in the corridors and into the guards van. The guard greeted him, but Artur responded in Danish and then in broken French after an apology.

There were many parcels and packages in the van, as well as bicycles and travelling trunks. The guard looked anxiously at Artur; it wasn't usual for passengers to enter the van, especially when the train was between stations.

"Can I help you?" said the guard. "Do you have a parcel or a package in here?"

Artur didn't reply, but just searched the parcels looking at the names of the recipients. It was helping him to pass the time of the journey.

"Do you have anything for Avignon?" asked Artur in a very broken French accent.

"Sorry, I don't understand," said the guard quite slowly.

"Avignon?" said Artur very clearly, just to make conversation.

"No, most for Aix and Marseille," said the guard rather slowly.

Artur continued his search for a few minutes and then moved back towards the door to the passenger carriages. He went into the first carriage where there were no passengers. He drew all three blinds down to obscure the view into his compartment and sat down with his back to the engine on the corridor side. He looked at his watch: there was still more than an hour to go. He watched the countryside go by; it was starting to rain. His mind drifted back to his home in England, to his wife and his young son, Alfred. He wondered how they were coping, especially with not knowing where he was and what he was really doing.

Artur was suddenly brought back to the present as he was aware of footsteps coming down the corridor and the voices of two men. He recognised the officer's voice; he just caught a glimpse of them as he carefully peered through the small gap between the blind and the window. They went into the guard's van and closed the door behind them. Artur decided to quickly leave the compartment; he opened and closed the door as quietly as he could. He walked with purpose through two carriages and into the lavatory. He didn't lock the door, but stood with his foot against it to prevent entry; that way they wouldn't know if anyone would be in there. He drew his pistol from his trouser pocket and cocked it. He looked at his watch – nearly another quarter of an hour had passed.

I wonder if the officer is going all the way to Marseille, or will he be getting off at Aix, or even Avignon? Artur thought.

Artur knew he would have to get back to his compartment before too long to collect his case. He waited another ten minutes. He had not heard anyone walking past the lavatory; he assumed the two men were still in the guard's van, probably quizzing the guard. He decided it was time to leave so he locked the door and flushed the lavatory. He put his pistol into safe mode and placed it in his pocket. He stood for a moment with his ear to the door but could hear nothing. He opened the door and walked directly to the left towards his carriage.

"Monsieur," said a voice behind Artur. "May I have a word with you please?"

Artur pretended not to hear, or understand the French being spoken, and carried on walking through to the next carriage, which was the buffet car. The men caught up with him at the far end of the carriage and tapped Artur on the shoulder. He stopped and turned to face the two men with a smile.

"We have reason to believe that you were in the guard's van. What was the purpose of that?" asked the officer.

Once again, Artur pretended not to understand and spoke some words of nonsense to the men in Danish. The men clearly didn't like Artur's attitude and were about to take hold of his arms when the two ladies from his compartment came through the doors into the buffet car.

"What are you doing to this poor man?" one of the ladies said, with a fierce look at the officer. The other lady then took Artur's hand.

"You leave him alone. He's coming to have a cup of coffee with us."

The two ladies led Artur by the hands and brushed past the two men without saying another word. The men stared after the three of them as they walked to an empty table, not really knowing if they should apprehend Artur or leave him with the ladies. They chose the latter; they seemed quite a formidable pair and thought there might be another opportunity at a later stage. After all, he couldn't get off the train until the next stop even if he was booked through to Marseille.

When their coffees arrived, Artur continued in his very broken French accent. They asked him a few questions which he vaguely answered, but they were more interested in talking about themselves, their life and their experiences. After a while, Artur looked at his watch; the time had flown, only ten minutes before the train was due at Avignon. He thanked them for the coffee and their company and excused himself. He went back to his compartment, hoping that the officer hadn't been inquisitive enough to have looked in his case. He took down the case, looked inside and carefully searched through the few belongings inside. He breathed a sigh of relief; he was satisfied that all was in order and closed the case again.

A half discernible announcement came over the speaker system: they were about to enter Avignon station. The ladies had not returned to their seats yet. Artur had decided he was going to get off here anyway.

The train came to a halt. Artur had opened the window and was looking out at the waiting passengers, but he couldn't see any police or anybody of a suspicious nature. He stepped down from the carriage; he jostled and mingled with the people on the platform. He decided to go to the toilet and wait for the train to leave. He heard the train's whistle and came out onto the platform. He stood with others as the train disappeared into the distance. The station master then allowed people to jump down and cross the railway lines to the other side. Artur went into the booking hall and looked around for the left luggage cabinets. He saw a room with a man standing outside who he assumed must be in charge of the cabinet area. The man took his small suit case, placed it in a cabinet and returned to give him a ticket and a numbered key. Artur was told that he should pay the fee when he came to collect the case.

Artur then looked for a public phone. He took some papers out of his jacket pocket and dialled a number.

"Hello!" said Artur. "May I speak to Monsieur Harmel please?" Artur tried to appear calm when he spoke to the lady, but was concerned when Pierre hadn't answered the phone himself.

"Just a moment please. Who shall I say is calling?" the lady said.

"Please tell him that it's a friend."

There was silence for what seemed like many minutes. There was then the unmistakable voice of Pierre.

"Hello?"

"The Pope is ill," said Artur.

"Tell him to call for Doctor Renée," Pierre gave the expected, coded response. Artur knew he was speaking to his local contact; he was certain he would be able to help him.

The two men spoke very briefly and arranged to meet at one of the tables outside the Hôtel de Palais des Papes, on the opposite side of the square from the main entrance to the Palais des Papes. Pierre said he hoped to be there in about twenty five minutes, and rang off. Artur looked for a newspaper but they were all sold out. Even though it was quite a nice afternoon, he thought it might be too risky to walk so he took a taxi to the hotel. He knew Pierre wouldn't recognise him in his disguise, but he wasn't going to change out of it yet.

Just as Artur was thinking of ordering a second coffee, he saw a car arriving and being parked further along the road from the hotel entrance. A man got out. He was wearing a heavy coat and he had a furled newspaper under his arm, just as he had said he would on the phone. When Pierre reached the tables outside, Artur stood up and handed him a piece of paper, but there was nothing written on it. Pierre studied the paper, looked at Artur and smiled. They were satisfied that each was the one they were expecting to meet and shook hands.

Artur called the waiter over and ordered a black coffee for each of them. There were very few people at tables near them so they could talk reasonably freely, but still with some care.

"Have you been updated by control with why I'm in France?" asked Artur.

"I have heard that you and Gerhart were involved in sabotaging a train in Germany. They thought you would be returning to England through Denmark. They were concerned for your safety when their informants told them about developments in Schleswig Holstein. They guessed you might have heard about these developments and would return via France. They alerted me in case you came south but nothing else."

"I hoped you might have heard about the operation, but I'm a wanted man by the French police as well as the German SS."

Artur explained briefly about the escape from Germany, the car crash, the shooting, his change of identity, his encounter with French police on the train and his decision to get out at Avignon. Pierre was expressionless and listened intently; he knew why Artur had contacted him.

"I have to say that I was quite confused by your appearance as I walked up to the hotel tables, but I now understand. How long do you think you should stay with me, Artur? As you know, I live in a town called Aramon not many kilometres southwest of Avignon. You can lie low for a week or two at my place, if you wish. You may not be aware that I live alone so you will only have me to contend with. When you decide to leave me, have you worked out what route you will take from here?"

Pierre was about the same height as Artur but was nearly in his fifties. He looked in good physical shape. His dark hair was going grey at the temples and he had a large, black moustache. He was a good-looking man who took care of his appearance. Artur couldn't work out why he hadn't got a wife, but he might hear about that later.

"Tell me, Pierre, have you heard what's going on in Denmark?"

"By all accounts, the Germans have now entered Jutland with very little resistance and they've also sent ships and planes into Sjaelland. It has apparently taken the British and the French a bit by surprise. I don't think the Germans are too interested in Denmark, but are using it as a way of getting to Norway – the Germans need to gain access to the iron ore on the Norwegian-Swedish border."

"That's more or less what I heard on the wireless early this morning."

They continued to discuss the general situation and what the Allies might do for a further twenty minutes. Pierre then called the waiter, paid for the coffees and led Artur to his car.

"I do have a small case, Pierre, but I put it in a left-luggage cabinet at the station. We can collect it later, if that's alright with you?"

"That's fine," said Pierre. "We can come back this evening to pick it up and have a bite to eat on our way back home in a little restaurant in Les Angles. I know the owners very well."

Artur gave no reply; he was just pleased to be in the company of someone he could trust.

They arrived at Pierre's house that was down a side street off the main Boulevard in Aramon. He showed Artur to his upstairs room and the simple bathroom. He said he would make up the bed later. They went down into the small kitchen that overlooked a very small, tidy back garden. The kitchen was clean and tidy; Artur thought it rather unusual for a man living on his own. Pierre went to a small pantry and retrieved a bottle of red and two very fine wine glasses.

"I take it you would like a glass of wine, Artur? I have a Châteauneuf-du-Pape. As you probably know, the main vineyard is just north of Avignon so I buy a few cases every now and again."

"That really does sound an excellent choice, thank you."

They chatted about various topics for well over an hour, including the possible routes that Artur could take to return to England. Pierre poured the last of the wine into Artur's glass and looked at his watch to find that it was coming up to 7:30 p.m.

"I think we should be making a move fairly soon, Artur. We have to collect your suitcase from the station and then return to the restaurant. It might be wise to drop in and book a table as we're passing through Les Angles. It's not a very large place."

"Good idea. I'll just freshen up a bit. I feel a little light-headed after that beautiful wine and not much food during the day."

They got up and Pierre cleared away the glasses into the kitchen. Artur went upstairs to the bathroom and examined himself in the mirror to check that his disguise still looked acceptable. He also made sure that he still had all his Danish papers in his jacket pocket and then joined Pierre down in the hallway. Pierre drove to the restaurant, booked a table for just after 8:30 p.m. They then set off for Avignon station.

As they arrived at the station car park, Artur noticed there were a couple of police cars by the main entrance.

"What do you think the police are doing here at this time of the evening?" asked Artur.

"They're probably looking for you," said Pierre in a light-hearted way.

"I'm not sure that's a very funny thing to say," Artur retorted sternly. "I would like you to go and fetch my case, Pierre, and here's the key and the ticket."

As Artur handed him the key, he decided to slide down into the passenger seat well as far as he could so he wouldn't be seen.

Pierre took the key, got out of the car and walked to the station entrance. As he walked inside, he saw there were four policemen: two of them were talking to the man in the ticket office, the other two turned and watched Pierre enter the hallway; he recognised one of those looking at him.

"Hello, Jean. How are you? You're not usually on evening duties. What's up?"

"We are of the impression that someone, who was on an earlier train, got out here instead of proceeding to Marseille," replied Jean.

Pierre thought carefully; he decided he wouldn't try to get in too deeply with these policemen.

"Sorry, can't help you Jean. I've just come in to look at the timetable of trains going north to Lyon. As you may remember, my sister lives in a village northeast of Lyon and I'm planning to visit her sometime soon."

Pierre walked over to inspect the timetable that was next to the ticket office; he said nothing more to Jean and ignored the other three. He took out a piece of paper and a pencil from his pocket. He wrote down a few times, said farewell to Jean and walked out of the station towards his car. He knew not to look behind him, but as he reached the driver's door, he took a quick glance and saw Jean standing in the entrance writing something down.

"Stay down where you are, Artur. I think the police are looking for you, so I didn't collect your case. I'll get it tomorrow morning."

Pierre drove off. He noticed that Jean was looking hard at his number plate, probably writing it down against his name and the time of day.

Once they were near the bridge over the Rhône, Pierre told Artur that it was safe to get back on the seat. Artur smoothed his hair and straightened his moustache.

"Pierre, do you think it will be wise to go to the restaurant, or should we choose somewhere else?"

"I really don't think the police will follow us tonight but Jean might come to my house tomorrow and ask some questions. Let's have a good supper and talk about what we should do when we get back home."

Chapter 40
Friday, 1ˢᵗ of September 1939

Andrew was on time for his meeting with Charles. They greeted each other like long lost friends.

"What will you be having, Andrew, the usual?"

"Yes please. It seems particularly busy in here today. Is there something going on that I should know about?"

"I think you'll find that we are just about to go to war with Germany over the Poland issue. Germany invaded Poland earlier this morning. The French and British ambassadors will no doubt submit an ultimatum to Germany for an immediate withdrawal. Otherwise the two governments will have no option than to fulfil their obligation to support Poland and declare war on Germany."

"So we have arrived at the point that everyone thought was imminent, Charles. Does this mean that you will soon be needing my services?"

"It certainly does. You have mentioned before that you favour being linked to the Royal Navy. Is that still your wish?"

Andrew agreed that he felt strongly about the Navy and Charles recommended that he be in Naval Intelligence. He also mentioned that he might not be on a ship for some time, but he would be acting on their behalf.

"With your agreement, Andrew, I will write a letter today recommending that you be recruited into the SIS with immediate effect. Your manager at the bank will also be put in the picture as you might be called upon to carry out an important assignment late next month."

Charles paused to take several mouthfuls of his beer, as did Andrew.

"Are you still up for this, Andrew, or have you got second thoughts?"

"I'm as ready as I ever could be, Charles. Let me buy another beer for the two of us."

Andrew pushed his way to the bar and was served quite quickly. He gave Charles his pint and they toasted each other: "To the future, and to a successful outcome for Britain and its allies."

"Even though these letters will be written and received by the various parties, you should continue to work at the bank as usual until you are contacted by a senior SIS officer to go and meet your superiors. Are you feeling hungry as we could skip round the corner for a snack?"

"That's a good idea," replied Andrew. They quickly downed their beer and pushed their way out of the pub. Andrew thought he knew where they were going, but he let Charles lead the way. The small restaurant was almost empty.

"I think everyone's drinking today rather than eating," said Charles. The manager was pleased to see them and took them to a table. He brought a menu and they ordered a bottle of red wine as they looked at the choices. They both chose steak pie. Charles was just about to say something to Andrew when Andrew told him that he had been promoted to Senior Clerk.

"That's good news. Let's hope that position will stay open for you during and after the war."

"I certainly hope so, Charles, as I need some money to keep my family going while I'm away on active service."

They talked about various things as they were eating, but they decided just a main course was sufficient. Charles paid the bill and they parted amicably outside Andrew's office.

"You would be advised to listen to the wireless over the weekend, Andrew, just so you are kept in the picture regarding hostilities. I realise that your wife will be very anxious and might ask some very searching questions, particularly about what part you might play in the event of a war with Germany. You will have to deal with them in the best way you can. I can't really give you any specific advice."

"I understand. I will wait to be contacted by the SIS. Should I contact you when I hear something?"

"No, that will not be necessary as I will be kept in the loop and will be asked to be present when you meet them."

With that, they shook hands and parted. Andrew finished his work at the office and arrived home to a very anxious wife. She had had the wireless on most of the day and was pleased to have Andrew back home to discuss things. She hadn't been out with Max since mid-afternoon, so Andrew suggested he should take him for a walk before supper, to which she agreed. He found it helped him to think things over, although he wouldn't be able to predict all his wife's questions.

Andrew tried to say very little over supper and just let her prattle on. She was obviously very nervous and had already phoned her sister to find out if her husband might be joining up. They decided not to listen to the news anymore, so they retired to bed quite early. In the early hours of the morning, they were woken by heavy rain and a thunderstorm that seemed to shake the whole house. They both went to see if Alfred was alright, but he slept through it all. Max had come upstairs but wasn't too frightened. Andrew went downstairs and put Max in his basket; he made a cup of tea which he brought back up to their room.

"My goodness, that thunder was loud. The lightening must have struck a tree quite near to here," said Andrew, "I'll have a look in the morning."

They listened to the wireless on and off during Saturday, and they thought they should go to church on Sunday morning. There was a full congregation and the sermon was very stirring. They chatted to the vicar after the service and he tried to reassure everyone, but not very convincingly.

They returned home just in time to hear Mr Chamberlain addressing the nation on the wireless: Britain was now at war with Germany. The deadline given to Germany had passed with no response and that the Government's struggle for peace had failed. They spent much of the day very quietly but pensively. Some phone calls came from friends who had heard that the Government was to enforce full conscription on males between the ages of 18 and 41; they wanted to talk over the options available. Brian said he would join the RAF, but others were still undecided. They listened to the 6 o'clock news and to King George talking about the dark days ahead and that with God's help, Britain will prevail.

On Monday, the train to London was very full and, unusually for English people in public, they all talked about how the war would work out for Britain and the Empire. When Andrew arrived at his office, people were in a very glum mood and found it difficult to concentrate on their work. On Wednesday morning, Andrew's manager told him there was a phone call for him in his office. It was Charles and he asked him if he could come to C's office on Friday at midday, to which Andrew agreed. He was given directions and he had it cleared with his manager that he could attend. He was very excited and hoped it wouldn't be too long before he was given an assignment.

Andrew left the office on Friday morning, and took a taxi; he was in good time for his appointment. He entered the building and was greeted by Charles, who took him up in the lift to the office where the meeting was to take place. He introduced Andrew to the other three people in the room – C was a different man from the one he had met earlier in the year. They talked about the recent declaration of war and how much more important the role of the SIS will be. C said that he had read all the reports of Andrew's training courses as well as the letter of recommendation submitted by Charles. It all made very interesting reading and they all agreed that he had a great part to play within the Service. After about forty minutes, there was a knock on the door and a lady came in with some sandwiches, snacks and wine that she put on the large table in the corner of the room. Once she had gone, Andrew was asked to help himself to what he wanted and Charles poured out the wine.

"Now that war has officially been declared, we will have particular missions that we think would be suitable for someone with your sort of talents," said C. "But you would be advised to have some training in unarmed combat before we release you into the real world of espionage," he said with a grin and a wink. "There's a chap working for us down in the New Forest near Beaulieu who deals with this sort of training. Charles will organise it all for you in a few weeks. Two days should be enough, don't you think?" he said as he looked at Charles, who nodded in agreement.

"Just before the course, we suggest you move into a flat up here in London for the foreseeable future. You are likely to be with two or three others. Again, Charles will give you all the details nearer the time. We're probably looking towards the end of September. You will need to tell your wife that you are joining the Royal Navy and that you will be required to go away on training for a considerable period of time. The bank will still pay your salary until you become one of our permanent agents at the end of October. How does that sound, Williams?"

"It's all fine by me, but my wife will need a lot of convincing for sure. As I shall be staying in a Service's flat, I shall need to bring quite a lot of clothes and my wife will notice that they will have gone…"

"We will give you an allowance," said C, butting in. "So only bring the bare minimum. Again, Charles will go through the details."

"Will I be in contact with my wife at all once I'm in the flat?"

"Yes, you can write to her just in general non-specific terms about every three or four weeks and we will have it posted from somewhere far from here. All being well, we will try to get you home for Christmas, but it will depend on the assignments, how long they might be, where you might be and so on. Do you still have concerns about joining us or are you happy to continue?"

Andrew agreed that he was keen to continue. In fact, he said he couldn't wait to give the Service and the Country his full support to rid the world of the Nazis.

Over the next few weeks, Andrew continued to work at the bank as usual, but his mind was looking forward to some action. He completed his training course near Beaulieu with flying colours and he felt he was equipped for any challenge that might arise. He had told his wife only what she needed to know, but she was highly suspicious of there being much else that she should know. On Saturday, 23rd September, Andrew had drinks with Brian, who had already signed on with the RAF; he was starting his pilot training in ten days' time. Charles contacted Andrew during the week beginning 25th and took him to the flat he would be moving into, where he was introduced to his flatmates. He went to the SIS HQ at Broadway in London and met some of the people he would be working with. He had had a meeting with C in the presence of Charles and he had explained that because his wife had felt she knew little about what he was to be doing in the war, she could be a problem to the Service. C reassured Andrew.

The days went by and Andrew moved into the flat on Friday 29th September, but still worked at the bank for the next couple of weeks. During the week beginning 16th October, Andrew was summoned to C's office; as usual, Charles was present.

"We are reliably informed, Williams, that Hitler is planning to make a speech in Munich to mark the anniversary of the Beer Hall Putsch in November 1923. Did you hear about this event?"

"No sir, I was still at school," said Andrew with a smile.

"Of course, how silly of me! Anyway, we want you to take a trip to Munich and observe the event. We'll have you ready for leaving England by the end of the month. Charles will give you all the necessary papers and set up your new identity. You will, of course, be a German and you will be accompanied by another agent that we've not yet finalised on. Assuming the speech goes ahead, the two of you are to return to London for the debriefing. How does that sound?"

"I can't wait, sir. When will I know who will be accompanying me?"

"You'll know by the end of this week," said Charles. "And you will be in charge, Andrew."

The meeting came to an end following a few light-hearted comments about Hitler and the Beer Hall incident. Andrew returned to his room at the flat and contemplated his first assignment. He also wondered who his companion was to be: a man, or a woman perhaps.

On Friday evening, Charles came to Andrew's flat to find all the flatmates playing cards.

"Sorry to interrupt your evening, gentlemen, but I need to borrow Andrew for about an hour or two."

Charles led Andrew out and took him to the O&C Club. Drinks were ordered and they sat at a corner table; the Club was quiet for a Friday. After about ten minutes, Charles turned to Andrew.

"We have the name of your companion: her name is Maggie Pearce. She is a highly intelligent and an attractive brunette, has been part of the Service for five years and been on many missions. She speaks fluent German and French and is expected to be in a senior position within the

Service by the end of the war – so long as she survives, of course. I will come to collect you tomorrow at 11 o'clock and I will take you to meet her at a pub out of London where we will have lunch together. Will those arrangements be alright with you, Andrew?"

"Of course, Charles. How much does she know about me?"

"Much more than I have told you about her!"

They talked over the situation in Europe and after finishing their drinks, Charles took Andrew into the restaurant for some supper.

Andrew slept fitfully that night, but arose at 8:30 a.m. to make a light breakfast for himself – the others were still asleep. Just before 11:15 a.m., he was ready. He looked smart in his newly acquired sports jacket and trousers and had even polished his shoes. He was sitting in the lounge when there was a knock on the door. He was prepared but it still startled him. He opened the door and greeted Charles warmly.

"I won't come in as we shouldn't keep Maggie waiting."

Andrew didn't lock up as the other flatmates were now up and they knew he was going out for several hours. Charles' car was on the road and as they drove north towards Barnet, conversation was rather limited. They arrived at the Waggon and Horses at Elstree.

"Why are we coming out this way?" asked Andrew with some annoyance in his tone.

"Maggie lives out this way and so I thought it would be a polite gesture for us to travel rather than her."

Andrew said nothing but grunted quietly.

Charles parked the car. They walked in through the front door and into the saloon bar. Andrew looked around and immediately saw who he knew must be Maggie. She stood up as they walked towards her. Charles introduced them, but Maggie did not put out her hand to Andrew's. She smiled at Charles but was stern-faced towards Andrew. *How am I ever going to get on with this woman?* he said to himself.

They sat with drinks bought by Charles and chatted about various things, including the state of Europe, and what the Nazis might do next. Meals were ordered, but Andrew did more listening than talking, trying to pick up as much as he could of Maggie's character and what might make her tick. The food arrived and still Maggie directed most of her conversation to Charles. Andrew thought he would try and get involved.

"So, Maggie," he said in his best French, "how did you come to speak such fluent French?"

She looked rather astounded at Andrew's question, but she turned to him and looked him straight in the eyes with just a glimmer of a smile:

"My mother is French, Andrew. I studied languages at the Sorbonne in the early thirties. My elder sister is married to a Frenchman, so there's a lot that is French in my life. You're very new to the Service, aren't you?"

Just at that moment, their meals arrived; conversation was very limited. Charles noticed the rather frosty air between Maggie and Andrew so at an appropriate moment, he thought he should talk business.

"As you both are aware, we have an assignment for you. We want you to come to my office in St James' on Tuesday at 10:30 a.m. for a briefing and to discuss the best approach."

Charles looked at both of them; they nodded in agreement, said nothing but continued eating. Charles began to think that these two agents might not be the best to work together on the job to be assigned to them, but the decision was made by someone two levels higher than him.

They finished their lunch, said their goodbyes and Charles looked forward to seeing Maggie again on Tuesday, as did Andrew. They drove off back towards London

"So, Andrew, do you think you'll be able to work with Maggie? You didn't seem to want to say much to her during our lunch," said Charles in a concerned tone.

"I don't see any concerns, Charles, but she seems rather nervous. Has she had any narrow escapes on any of her recent assignments?"

"It's very interesting you say that because on the one before last, her fellow agent disappeared and hasn't been seen or heard of since. That was also in Germany."

"Are there any similarities between him and me?"

"It's funny you should say that too. There are, but we all thought she had got over that incident. Do you think you can handle it?"

"Of course, but can she?"

Little more was said about Maggie as they entered London. Charles dropped Andrew off at his flat and wished him a pleasant rest of the weekend.

Andrew was up bright and early on Tuesday morning, and after a light breakfast, he took a taxi to St James' and Charles' office. He knocked with the brass knocker and the door was opened.

"Hello, Helen," said Andrew with his best smile. "I hoped you might still be working here. You are looking very lovely. I'm not too early am I?"

"No, you are in good time, Mr Williams. In fact, Mr Compton-Browne's other visitor is already here."

Andrew was disappointed not to have arrived first, but there was nothing he could do about it now.

"I think you know your way, Mr Williams. I will phone to say you are on your way up."

Andrew smiled engagingly at Helen and skipped up the stairs two at a time. He knocked on Charles' office door and went straight in. He saw Maggie, who had turned round to greet him; this time she had a warm, friendly smile on her face and she looked amazing. They all greeted each other like long lost friends; *quite a different atmosphere from only a few days ago,* Andrew thought to himself, *long may it continue.* When a lady came in with coffee and biscuits, Charles asked her to change the notice outside that said 'Meeting in Progress, DO NOT Disturb'.

"I've already been through the assignment with C and apart from a few changes that he insisted upon, I can describe what we are asking you to do."

Charles told them that they had to make their way to Munich together and be in the *Bürgerbräukeller* where Hitler is due to make his annual speech on Wednesday, 8th November. They will have all the necessary papers and documents identifying them as Baron Albert von Schwartzman and his younger sister, Magdalene. He said there was information from the Service's contact that an assassination attempt is to be carried out by a man called Georg during Hitler's speech.

"Georg is not working for the Service, but we have known about the possible attempt for many weeks. One of our people, known as 'Sparks', knows Georg and has been giving him guidance. Your job is to be at the event as it is likely to be attended by many senior members of the Nazi Party."

"How do you want us to get there, and when do you expect us to set off for Munich?" Andrew asked.

"We recommend you catch a ferry to Calais on Friday, 3rd November and travel to Munich by train via Paris. You should arrive in Munich by Sunday, the 5th, and make yourselves familiar with the *bräukeller* in the days before the scheduled speech. We have identified suitable hotels for you to stay in."

"What is the real objective of our trip?" asked Maggie.

"To give whatever help is required by Georg and 'Sparks' to successfully fulfil the assassination attempt. It could bring the war to an abrupt end. We will meet again here next Wednesday at 10:30 a.m. to collect all your documents, tickets and money. We cannot stress how important this mission is. Are there any further questions?"

There were none.

"All I can say then is thank you and have a safe trip."

Maggie and Andrew left Charles' office and decided to have a coffee before going their separate ways.

"So," said Andrew, in a whisper, as they sipped their coffee, "here we are, not many days away from helping someone to change the world. Do you think he could be successful?"

"It won't be from a lack of trying and good planning, but Hitler's henchmen are always on the alert. It is a highly risky assignment but we will do our best to see it through."

After a few minutes, they paid and left the café.

Chapter 41
Monday, 22nd of April 1940

Pierre hosted Artur for nearly two weeks. During that time, Artur discarded his Danish disguise, after Pierre had collected his suitcase, and even though he felt a little more relaxed and enjoyed being with Pierre in Aramon, he still stayed on full alert, especially when they occasionally went out to a local bar. During the first few days, they talked at length about where Artur should go next and how he should get back to England; they came up with a couple of options but the favourite was to get on a ship in Marseille.

Artur managed to send a coded telegram to his contact in London saying that he hoped to be back in England before too long, but nothing more specific. They listened to Pierre's wireless so as to keep up to speed with the situation in Denmark and Norway. Artur's hunch about the Germans being more interested in Norway and the ports of Trondheim and Narvik proved correct. He also reckoned that it would only be a matter of time before the Germans invaded Belgium, the Netherlands and probably France.

Early in the evening of the 26th, they sat down with a bottle of wine to talk over the details of Artur's move to Marseille. Pierre strongly recommended that he take Artur to Arles – rather than Avignon or Aix – where he can catch a train to Marseille. He told Artur that he had an old friend named Claude who lived in the rue de Forbin. Claude had contacts in the port and he would get him on a ship going back to England.

"If you agree with this plan," said Pierre, "I will phone Claude this evening to make the arrangements."

"Can this Claude chap really be trusted?"

"I would not be suggesting we use him unless I was confident of his willingness to help and that he will keep your mission a secret."

"Fine," said Artur. "I probably can't see there is any real alternative and I certainly trust your advice. I fccl I ought to catch a train on Wednesday morning and hopefully might get on a ship within a week."

"I agree totally, Artur. I'll go and call Claude now before it gets too late."

Pierre went into the hallway and after a few moments, Artur heard him dialling a number. There was quite a long pause then Pierre started talking in a friendly manner for nearly ten minutes. Pierre returned to the lounge and filled up the two glasses.

"Well, Artur, that's all arranged with Claude for Wednesday. I will take you to catch the train at Arles in the morning. Once your train leaves, I will phone Claude and he will meet you at Marseille station. He will be in the main bar next to the newsagents. I strongly suggest you don't use your German identity, but revert to your Danish disguise and use the Danish passport. With the German invasion of Denmark, your wish to leave France will be all the more credible."

"That all sounds very sensible, but how will I recognise Claude?"

"He will be wearing a beret and smoking Gaulloises cigarettes – there will be a packet on his table to the left of his glass of red wine. He will also be reading a copy of the *Le Figaro* newspaper."

"How will he know that it's me when I find him?"

"You will say to Claude in broken French: Is it far from here to rue de Forbin? Claude will reply: Have a coffee and I will take you there. The exchange must be precise, as I'm sure you will appreciate."

Artur agreed with Pierre's plan. They refilled their glasses, smiled at each other across the table and Pierre toasted Artur for a successful return to England. After they had chatted and laughed for about the next half an hour, they went to the kitchen where Pierre prepared a light supper of bread and cheese and they opened another bottle of wine.

"I will go to Arles tomorrow," said Pierre, "to buy your ticket. Can you let me have some money, Artur, as I'm running a bit short?"

"Of course, old man, I'll give you some tomorrow morning, and a bit extra for letting me stay here."

The time passed quickly as they ate and talked. They drifted off to bed just before midnight feeling a bit light-headed from the very special wine that Pierre had provided.

Artur awoke after 9 o'clock to find that Pierre had gone out; the note on the kitchen table mentioned that he'd gone to Arles and would be back shortly after 11 o'clock. Artur decided to get washed and dressed and sort out his clothes for the following morning. He found the bread and jam in the kitchen, made himself some coffee and wiled away the time by looking through his notes and papers that had been in the 'secret' compartment of his suitcase. After so many days at Pierre's, he knew he had to be very well prepared for the next part of his escape from France.

Pierre returned to his house just after 11:20 a.m. with Artur's ticket. He recommended Artur catch the train that left at 11:48 a.m. It would stop at a few stations and arrive at Gare de Marseille Saint-Charles at ten minutes past 1 o'clock. Artur gave Pierre the money for the ticket and several more notes towards his keep.

"Thanks for the money, but are you happy with the arrangements that I've set up for you, Artur?"

"Yes, I am, but it just remains for Claude to be at the bar in the station. I suppose I do have some apprehension as I have relaxed a lot during my stay here and got out of the habit of being an escapee in a foreign land. The sooner I get on the train, the better."

"I quite understand, Artur, but I'm as sure as I can be that all will work out satisfactorily for you. Claude is a very trustworthy person and he will help you all he can."

They decided to go to a local bar for a drink and a snack at lunchtime, and would eat out at a restaurant in Tarascon that Pierre was very familiar with in the evening. After a really enjoyable meal, they were back at Pierre's before 10:30 p.m. and went to bed without being tempted to have a nightcap.

Artur slept very fitfully that night, tossing and turning, dreaming that he was followed from the train by two policemen, who apprehended him just before he reached the bar and Claude. He woke up suddenly and found himself sweating profusely. He went to the bathroom and threw cold water onto his face and noticed he was shaking. *I hope this isn't a portent of things to come,* he said to his image in the mirror. He took some deep breaths and told himself to pull himself together and not to be so anxious and panicky; after all, he had been selected by the Service for his resilience, courage and clear-headedness under pressure. He went back to his room – hoping he hadn't woken Pierre – slipped under the bedclothes and counted sheep to get himself back to sleep.

The next thing he knew, Pierre was knocking on Artur's door.

"It's 7 o'clock, Artur. You ought to be getting up and changing into a Dane!" said Pierre with a chuckle.

"Thanks, Pierre, I'll be up in two shakes," he said with a half Danish half French accent.

Artur felt better than he expected after his disturbed night. After returning from the bathroom, he selected the clothes he needed, darkened his hair and checked that he had packed the rest of his belongings in his case. He went downstairs and was greeted by the smell of coffee and warm bread.

"How do you feel, Artur? You look refreshed, but where's your moustache?"

"I thought I would leave it until after breakfast."

"Good idea. Do you want black coffee as usual?"

Artur said yes. He didn't feel hungry, but he knew he would perform better with some food inside him. They talked little at breakfast as the wireless was on; the news came through at 8 o'clock. Even though the reports mentioned that the Germans had been forced to retreat during the Battle of Gratangen, with the Norwegian and Allied forces, it was not always easy to believe the broadcasts as they may just be propaganda to boost morale.

With the train due to leave at 11:48 a.m., they had agreed to leave at 10:15 a.m. in case there might be delays on the roads. Artur finished his packing and checked he had all his papers. He then attached his moustache. They left the house at the appointed time and took the route that went to the west of the Rhône towards Beaucaire. Just as they exited the village, there was a loud noise from the front of the car; it lurched to the left and hit the kerb as it came to a stop.

"I think we might have a puncture," exclaimed Pierre. "I didn't check the spare so I hope it will be alright."

They got out of the car and inspected the damage: it was a puncture as they thought initially.

"Have you got the jack, Pierre? I'll get the damaged wheel off while you get the spare out."

Before doing anything, Artur took off his moustache and put it on the passenger seat. Pierre passed the jack and brace to Artur, who got to work on getting the wheel off. Pierre had the spare ready for Artur. Just as the spare was going on, a police car stopped in front of the car. Two men got out and came over to Pierre's car.

"Hallo, Pierre," said one of them. Artur recognised him as the one at Avignon station whose name was Jean. "Did you get to see your sister?"

"No," said Pierre. "I had to postpone my trip when my friend arrived."

"You are just a bit too late to help us, Jean," said Pierre with a smile. "But you could carry the damaged wheel to the boot for me."

Jean did no such thing but just stared at Artur, who by now had quickly replaced his moustache.

"I've not seen you around here before have I, monsieur?" said Jean to Artur. "Which part of France are you from?"

"He's a Dane, Jean, and he's been staying with me for a few days. He wants to get back to Denmark, but the Nazis got there first, as you probably have heard."

"Can I see your papers, monsieur?" Jean asked.

Artur put his hand into his pocket inside his jacket and drew some documents out. He quickly glanced at them, selected the correct ones and handed them to Jean.

"Do you realise that your visa for temporary residence in France expires in two weeks' time?" said Jean.

"That's why I'm catching the train today and getting out of France," said Artur rather cheekily in very broken French.

"No need to take that tone with me, monsieur."

"I've fixed the spare on so we ought to be going now," said Pierre, mainly for Jean's ears.

"Please could I have my papers back?" said Artur rather anxiously to Jean.

"On one condition, monsieur. Whichever station you are going to, find the nearest police station and they will write your details down. You are to tell them to send them to the main police station in Avignon, just in case we need to find you again."

"You have my word he'll do that, Jean," said Pierre, who was now pushing Artur in through the passenger door. Pierre shook Jean's hand and the other policeman's. He ran round and got into the car. As he went round the police car and into the traffic, Artur looked at his watch.

"Do we have enough time, Pierre, because it's 11:05 a.m.?"

"Hold on tight, Artur, we should get there in time."

Pierre drove very fast and made it to the station by 11:35 a.m. Artur got out, grabbed his case, checked his moustache and gave a bear hug to Pierre. He thanked him for all his help and hospitality.

"I'll phone Claude once I know the train has left. *Bonne chance, mon ami.*"

Artur didn't say any more, but walked quickly into the station, found the platform and waited only a few minutes for the train to arrive.

Chapter 42
Wednesday, 1ˢᵗ of November 1939

Andrew hadn't contacted Maggie since the last meeting, but he knew she would be staying in London until they left for Dover on Friday. He hurried to Charles' office as he was a little behind time for the meeting. He knocked and Helen let him in with her usual engaging smile and welcome.

"I know I'm a bit late and I presume I'm the last to arrive?"

"Miss Pearce is not here yet, but she phoned in to say she had been delayed: problems on her railway line. Go straight up please, Mr Williams."

Andrew knocked, went into Charles' office and apologised for his late arrival. Charles smiled and said Maggie was delayed on the train. They each took a coffee and sat down just as the phone rang; Maggie had arrived, Charles was told. She came into the office, and they greeted one another and sat down to discuss the assignment. Charles went through the documents, gave a list of hotels in Munich and handed to Andrew two envelopes containing Francs and Marks. Just before they were to enter Germany, they were to be Magdalene and Albert and should then only speak German. They each examined their German passports and Maggie made some amusing comment about her photo not looking like her but some girl off the street; they also had false British passports. Andrew was handed a third envelope that contained information about Georg and 'Sparks', plus their photos. Charles went through everything in great detail which each was asked to repeat, just to make sure the overall plan was quite clear.

"You are now agents of His Majesty's Service. Mr Chamberlain and his cabinet are fully aware of you and your assignment. They back you 100%. It's up to you if you want to meet up before you catch the train to Dover, but I recommend you arrange to meet at the station about twenty minutes before the train departs. You may not be aware that there is only one ferry operating from Dover as the rest have been requisitioned by the Navy. There is a change of plan for security reasons. You are not to catch a train from Calais to Paris but go to Brussels and Utrecht. I hope you are good sailors because the sea might be quite rough on this rather small ferry."

They nodded in agreement and smiled. They all rose from their chairs; Charles wished them well and told them to use 'Sparks' if there was an emergency and they needed to contact London.

Andrew walked out of the St James' building with Maggie and they shook hands as they went on their own way: Maggie to her hotel and Andrew to his flat. He still thought Maggie was rather nervous and it alarmed him that she showed it. He arrived back at his flat and decided to lay out the clothes he would need and the ones he had been given to make him look more Germanic by the Service. He went out for a snack at about 7 o'clock to a café round the corner and, on his return, he went through the information given to him, particularly about Georg. He read that he was a carpenter and that he had been planning the assassination for many months. He had been going to the Keller for a late meal, hiding until the place closed and working during the night. Andrew read everything in almost disbelief. *What a man and what a huge risk,* Andrew said to himself, *we must help him succeed.*

Andrew walked around London the next day, thinking through everything. When it started to rain in the late afternoon, he returned to his flat and lay down on his bed in his room. There was a knock on the door; one of his flatmates wanted to know if he would like to join them for a meal but he politely declined. They knew he was due to go on a mission the next day, but nothing more. He was relaxed and slept well until 6 o'clock. He was ready to leave by 9 o'clock, but he still double checked his suitcase and his trusty satchel with the documents and money. He met up with Maggie and the train arrived on time at Dover. For some reason, the captain of the ship had been looking out for them and showed them to his private cabin. He told them they could stay there for the duration of the crossing if they wished, but they both said they would rather be out on the deck, especially if was to be rough.

They arrived in Calais and the sea had not been too choppy; they didn't have long to wait before the train left for Brussels. They would catch another train to Utrecht where they would stay overnight, not far from the station. For both these legs they would have false British documents: he was Andrew Black and she was Margaret (Maggie) Black, his sister. The next morning, they took a bus to the border and after going through the Dutch controls, they changed their papers for those of Baron Albert von Schwartzman and his sister, Magdalene (Maggie); both of their passports had false stamps showing their entry and departure from Belgium and the Netherlands. On entering German passport control, they were asked about the nature of their visit to Germany.

"We have been living in Brussels and we are returning to Germany as our mother lives in Heidelberg and she is very sick," said Albert in fluent German.

"Don't you have any papers or documents to confirm that you were in Brussels?"

Albert fiddled inside his satchel and brought out a letter; it had the address of where Baron Albert von Schwartzman had been staying and it had been sent from Heidelberg only two weeks before. He passed the envelope and letter to the officer who examined it carefully.

"That all seems to be in order, Baron von Schwartzman. We wish you a safe journey to Heidelberg."

The officer returned the passports, clicked his heels together and raised his arm in a Nazi salute as he said, "Heil Hitler."

Albert and Maggie just repeated the two words without the salute.

They walked out of passport control to the barrier where they had to show their passports again.

"Is there a bus going to Münster?" Albert enquired.

"No but there is one going to Düsseldorf in ten minutes," said the guard as he pointed to a bus about forty metres away.

"Thank you very much, Düsseldorf will be fine."

They boarded the almost empty bus, paid the conductor, sat on the right side and waited. At precisely 10:30 a.m., the bus left and to their surprise was going to Düsseldorf station. The journey was incident free, but they did notice a lot of troop movement and armoured vehicles. At the station, they bought first class tickets for Munich; the train was due to leave in fifteen minutes. Not many words had been exchanged between Albert and Maggie since leaving the Netherlands but they did now express their pleasure that everything seemed to be going well so far. The train was expected to arrive in Munich station at 7:15 p.m.; they were relieved that they wouldn't have to change.

Their tickets included a typical German meal on the train and they only had to show their passports and tickets twice to the inspector; each time he ended with the Nazi salute. Some ten minutes before they were due to arrive, Albert brought out the list of hotels that the Service had given him. He suggested to Maggie that they should try the Eden Hotel Wolff as it was not too far from the station.

Once off the train, they walked out of the station and took a taxi to the hotel, even if it wasn't far away. Luck was again on their side as two single rooms were still available. They showed their passports, but refused courteously not to leave them with reception. They arranged to meet back down in the bar at 8 o'clock, have a drink then a light supper in the dining room.

"Well, Albert, this is certainly quite a smart hotel. How far is the Beer Keller from here?" asked Maggie in a low whisper.

"Not far, Maggie. I think we should pay it a visit tomorrow evening after we've walked around town getting our bearings."

Maggie agreed.

After supper, they decided to retire to their rooms and try to get some sleep; it had been a very long day and they had plenty to focus on over the next few days. They would meet for breakfast at 8:30 a.m.

Albert slept very soundly, but Maggie couldn't get comfortable in her bed. She woke several times and had to walk round her room trying to tire herself out but it didn't work. In the morning, she looked in the bathroom' mirror and she thought she looked dreadful; she felt dreadful too. She entered the dining room for breakfast and went straight over to Albert.

"I'm sorry to say it, Maggie, but you don't look your best. Did you not sleep well?"

"You could say that again. I'm sorry but I think I'll have a light breakfast and go back to my bed. You don't mind, do you?"

Albert commiserated with Maggie and said he would wander around Munich on his own; they could meet again in the late afternoon, if she felt well enough, but they did need to be at the Beer Keller this evening.

Albert passed the day going around the city; he found the Beer Keller and there seemed to be a lot of activity, presumably in preparation for Hitler's visit. Munich was bedecked in swastikas and Nazi banners, and there were many SS and soldiers wandering the streets. He arrived back at the hotel in the late afternoon and found Maggie in the residents lounge with a cup of tea.

"My goodness, you hardly look like the same person that I saw at breakfast. You must have had a well-earned rest."

"I did, thank you. How was your day?"

Albert explained what he'd been up to and that he had found the Beer Keller. Security was tight all over town and particularly near the Beer Keller. He suggested they should meet up in the hotel's reception at 7 o'clock and then go to the Beer Keller for a meal.

After meeting in the reception area, they wandered round to the Beer Keller. As they went under the bricked archway, a security man asked for their papers. Albert produced their identity cards and Nazi party membership cards, all made by the Service experts. They were allowed through but asked again by more guards at the main entrance to the hall. They walked into the vast hall that was laid out with tables for dinner. Albert spoke to one of the waiters that he wanted to be near the front on the right. As they were escorted to their table, Albert noticed a man sitting on his own on the opposite side of the hall. After the waiter had left, Albert pulled out a photo of Georg; he looked at the man and then the photo several times. He was convinced and quietly spoke to Maggie without pointing at Georg. She seemed to tense but tried to smile.

"Oh my goodness," she said. "Do you think 'Sparks' is here yet?"

Albert looked around after he'd examined the photo and he wasn't there yet. They ordered a couple of drinks and a main course from the menu. Albert changed places with Maggie so he could watch Georg more easily without making it obvious.

"Albert, do you have a contact number for 'Sparks' or do we hope he'll just turn up?"

"Yes, I do, but I only want to use it in an emergency."

Maggie looked rather disappointed.

Their drinks arrived followed by their meal; by this time, it was well after 8:30 p.m. and apparently the hall closed at 10:30 p.m. during the week of Hitler's speech. Every now and then, Albert noticed that Georg ordered a drink, but he didn't think it was alcoholic; he obviously needed to keep a clear head. Just then a man walked up to Georg's table and shook his hand. *That must be 'Sparks',* said Albert to himself. *I must find a way of saying something to him, let him know I'm here.* He excused himself, stood up and walked to the toilets but went via Georg's table. He bumped in to 'Sparks' and as he did so, he placed a card into his pocket with his name and hotel number on it, insisting that he phone him any time. On his return to his table, he noticed 'Sparks' looking at him and he gave Albert a wink. That's all the recognition he needed; he knew he would phone him. The next morning at breakfast, a bellboy came to Albert's table and said he was wanted on the phone. He went to the kiosk in the hall and lifted the receiver. They exchanged a few coded words and knew that each was the right person. They arranged to meet in the Hofbräuhaus am Platzl at 11 o'clock about 1500 metres from the hotel. Albert returned to Maggie and said that they had an appointment later with 'Sparks'.

They took a taxi near to Platzl and then walked. Albert had told 'Sparks' that he would be arm in arm with a lady and he would be wearing his German hat with a large pheasant feather in it. They walked into the main concourse; it didn't take long for a man to nudge into Albert and indicate he should follow him into a nearby bar. They exchanged coded messages to ensure each was who the other thought he was. 'Sparks' ordered three *steins* and moved to a nearby table. He carefully looked about him and they raised their glasses with a smile. 'Sparks' spoke first.

"I take it you understand what is happening on Wednesday evening?"

"Your leader's visit and a speech in the evening," replied Albert. "But it is due to be cut short."

"That's what we hope, but nothing is certain when *he* and his cohorts are due in town. I know you were in the Beer Keller yesterday but I suggest you don't go in again until Wednesday at 6:30 p.m. He is due to make his speech at 8 o'clock. Usually he speaks for half an hour, but we are now in war mode so it might be shorter or longer, but it always starts at 8 o'clock."

Albert thought he would get straight to the point.

"Has Georg done all he can to ensure success? What I have heard is that the bomb is due to be set off by a timing device inside one of the pillars as Hitler is giving his speech."

"That's correct, and Georg has worked all on his own for many months. Security will be very tight, as you can imagine, so make sure you have all the right papers with you when you come on Wednesday."

They drank some of their beer. Albert looked around the bar and asked some more questions.

"Will Georg be in the beer hall when the bomb goes off? Will you be there 'Sparks'?"

"Georg will be on his way out of Munich when the bomb goes off, but I will be there with you and Maggie to witness the explosion and the mayhem that will follow."

They finished their drinks and 'Sparks' departed.

"I think we should go back to our hotel separately. I'll meet you in my room this evening at 6:30 p.m. and we'll have dinner together later on."

In Albert's room, they discussed how they should escape from Munich the day after the explosion: through Switzerland seemed the best way. They had an enjoyable dinner and agreed to go round Munich and its parks for most of the next day.

Fortunately, it was a fine day although quite chilly for the walk. They were both anxious about what the evening might bring. They agreed to meet at 7 o'clock in the reception and take a taxi to the beer hall. Outside the hall, there were many Mercedes cars for Hitler, his entourage and security guards. It took ten minutes to go through the checks at the entrance due to the interest in the annual speech. At 7:55 p.m., Himmler stood on the platform and welcomed the senior officials plus all other supporters in the hall. The national anthem was played and to a great roar from the assembled crowd, Hitler came to the platform.

He mocked his international enemies and proudly spoke about Germany ruling Europe. He continued in his usual manner for only fifteen-twenty minutes shorter than in all previous years. He and his top brass left to tumultuous applause for the exit to return to Berlin. Ten minutes later, there was a huge explosion near where the Nazi leader had been speaking. There was destruction and panic all around. Albert and

'Sparks' had become separated from Maggie. They thought she had ventured nearer to the platform and one of the pillars. People were screaming and surging towards the exit doors. Albert then saw Maggie on the ground covered in blood; she looked unconscious and one of her legs was bent at a crazy angle. 'Sparks' called a few people over to help him carry Maggie through the emergency exit. She didn't look in good shape but she had quite a strong pulse.

Outside, a few ambulances had already arrived and 'Sparks' waved one of them over towards him. She was put on a stretcher and pushed into the back of the vehicle. 'Sparks' said he would go with the ambulance, but it would be best if Albert went back to the hotel. He told Albert he would get a message through to London later that evening, once he knew the extent of Maggie's injuries. Very reluctantly, Albert returned to the hotel and prepared himself for an escape from Germany and into Switzerland.

The following morning, Albert checked out of the hotel and explained that Fraulein Schwarzman would be leaving separately later in the day. He took a taxi to the bus station and found a bus going to Zürich in half an hour's time. He had no way of knowing how badly injured Maggie was, but leaving on his own was the instruction given to him by the Service – if it was really necessary. It made him feel sick to be doing it.

Albert reached Zürich late afternoon and checked in to a hotel overlooking the lake. He now needed to get back to England but he hoped 'Sparks' had given London good news about Maggie, even if Georg had failed in assassinating Hitler.

Albert reached London nearly two weeks later via west France and a boat from Bordeaux. He phoned Charles once he was on English soil. Charles was pleased to hear Andrew's voice, but he had to break the news gently to him that Maggie had died on the operating table in Munich's main hospital. 'Sparks' had taken charge of the funeral and she was buried locally. He also said that the German press had reported that Georg had been captured by the SS.

Andrew got back to his flat in London and met Charles the following day at his office in St James' for a full debriefing. He explained to Charles that even with all her experience, Maggie had displayed an unusual amount of nervousness during the whole trip; a sort of premonition perhaps? They both agreed that it was a very sad day for the Service and for Maggie's family.

Chapter 43
Wednesday, 23rd of April 1940

Artur stepped onto the train at Arles, and as usual sat facing the engine on the platform side. Just as the train was about to leave, a middle-aged man wrenched open the door and jumped into the compartment as the guard blew his whistle. Artur managed to tuck his feet under his seat but the sudden movement of the train sent the man into Artur's lap. He scrambled to his feet and expressed his apologies to Artur who nodded and mumbled a nonsensical noise in response. The man went into the corridor and walked towards the back of the train. There were two other passengers in Artur's compartment but nothing was said by either of them, nor did they look at Artur, and continued to read their newspapers.

The train stopped at nearly all the minor stations before Aix where the two passengers got off. Artur felt more comfortable being on his own. The inspector came in to see Artur's ticket after the train had left Aix; he wished him a good rest of the journey, but Artur just grunted a response and didn't look him in the eye.

After what seemed only a short time, Artur realised he was entering Marseille as the train started to slow down. He got his case down from the rack, straightened his clothes and moustache and waited for the train to come to a halt. He walked through the barrier towards the café next to the station's main newsagents, but couldn't see anyone that resembled Claude from the description given to him by Pierre. He chose an empty table and sat where he could easily see any new people arriving. The waitress came over to him and he ordered a black coffee. He looked at his watch and wondered if Claude had been given the correct time of arrival, or perhaps he had been delayed for some other reason.

A half hour passed; Artur was beginning to get concerned. He had no information about Claude except a phone number. He wondered if he should phone Pierre to find out if he had made contact with Claude. The waitress came over again and he decided to have another coffee while he put his thoughts together. He finished his second coffee, paid the waitress and went over to the phone boxes. He phoned Claude and there was no reply. He phoned Pierre and there was no reply there either. *I'm now definitely on my own*, he said quietly to himself. Artur walked out of the station to the taxi rank. He had already decided not to go to the police station as the policeman had told him to do. He talked to the driver of the first taxi in broken French, which the driver barely understood:

"Excuse me, can you take me to the main Customs Office in the port?"

The driver asked him to repeat his request which he did and this time the driver repeated Artur's request back to him; he had understood correctly. Artur put his case on the back seat and indicated that he would prefer to be in the front seat next to him rather than the back; the driver said it would be fine with him. It only took about fifteen minutes to get to the dock entrance. The guard spoke to the driver and looked at Artur. He ushered them in and turned left so the quay was on the right. Artur looked around and indicated where he wanted to be dropped off and paid the driver. He took his case from the back seat and waited for the taxi to depart before walking towards the Immigration Office.

Inside the office, he asked for the man in charge and was shown to an office in the corner where he could see there was a man on the phone. Artur decided he would keep to his Danish disguise and speak in broken, but clear French. He knocked on the door and the man waved Artur in, even though he was still speaking on the phone. The man was looking out of the window while he was talking; Artur was waiting for only a few minutes before he was asked to sit down.

"How can I help you, Monsieur?" said the man.

"I'm a Dane and I'm appealing to you to help me catch a ship to England," Artur said in broken French. "As you may know, my country has been invaded by the Nazis and I cannot safely go back to Jutland."

"I understand your situation. Please, could I see your papers?"

Artur took his Danish passport and other relevant documents out of his pocket and handed them to the man. There was silence for a few minutes before the man spoke and handed back the papers to Artur.

"There are no ships leaving for the next two days and the one that goes on Friday is only going as far as Gibraltar. Also, it's not a passenger ship, but a merchant vessel."

The man looked at his wall calendar.

"The next passenger ship leaves in a week's time. Oh, just a moment, I've just remembered, there is one in port now that leaves tonight at 10 o'clock I will help you if I can."

The man lifted his phone and dialled a number. After a pause, he started speaking and listening to the responses. He cupped the phone with his left hand.

"Do you have money? The captain of the ship says he will take you to England if you have enough money."

"How much does he need?" said Artur, trying not to get excited.

The man spoke into the phone again and then put it down on the receiver.

"The captain says if you go and see him now, he might be able to sort something out. He is in an office further along the quay to the left as you go out of our offices. His name is Captain Hansen. I think he has some Scandinavian blood in him, hence his name."

Artur shook the man by the hand, thanked him for his help and went out of the office. He walked along the quay looking for the office that the captain might be in. He asked a man who was walking towards him and he pointed to the second small building about forty metres away. Artur reached the building, knocked on the door and walked in. Several people were inside, so he asked if he could speak to Captain Hansen in his broken French accent.

"He's in the office in the corner," said one man, who laughed at Artur's accent.

Artur knocked on the office door.

"Come in," said the man inside, in French.

Artur entered; the captain smiled at him, put out his large hand and gave Artur a very firm handshake.

"I hear you want to go to England, so please tell me why I should let you come on my ship tonight?"

The captain spoke French in a strange way and Artur thought he would try his luck with Danish.

"I have Danish papers but, as you know, the Germans have invaded my country and I would be in serious danger if I tried to get back to Jutland via Schleswig Holstein. I would be obliged if you will allow me passage on your ship back to England."

"Well I never," said the captain in Danish, "but your accent isn't from Jutland, so why do you want to go back to Jutland when you seem to come from Sjaelland?"

"It's a long story. Here, have a look at my papers, please. I have to tell you something in the strictest confidence, so please don't tell anyone else."

"All very fascinating, Artur," the captain said as he looked through the documents. "You can rely on me."

"I have been on a secret mission in Germany for the British Government. I have successfully completed the task and am escaping from the Nazis and the French police through France and wish to get back to England."

"I understand, Artur, you have told me enough for me to want to help you, but you'll need money. I can't let you on my ship as a stowaway," said the captain with a loud chuckle.

The captain told Artur how much money was needed and Artur fished around in his satchel for a moment or two.

"Here is the amount you asked for," said Artur as he handed a bundle of notes to the captain.

"Sorry, you don't pay me, but the purser. He is outside so let me introduce you to him."

The two men went out of the captain's office and the purser was introduced to Artur. He didn't question why Artur should be allowed on the ship; after all, it was the captain's decision. The purser counted the money and prepared a ticket for Artur.

"Please be ready to board the ship by 7:30 p.m. at the latest as we will be leaving harbour at 10 o'clock. By the way, you don't mind going to Liverpool, do you?"

"I couldn't be more pleased to be returning to England. Liverpool will be fine," said Artur, but this time in English and with a broad grin as he shook the man's hand.

"Well, that's all fixed," said the captain to Artur in Danish. "There aren't too many passengers on board, but they are rather subdued, what with the state Europe's in at present. You'll be very comfortable in your cabin."

The time seemed to have flown by as Artur looked at his watch: it was already well past 4 o'clock. He thanked the captain and the purser again and left the building. He decided to walk out of the main dock gate and find a café as he felt in need of some food and a coffee. He showed his ticket to the guard as he went out of the gate and explained that he would be back again by 6:30 p.m. to board the ship. He asked if there was a café nearby and he was told there was one up the main road about 100 metres on the right.

Artur entered the café to find that it was surprisingly full for this time of the afternoon. It seemed to be quite a cosmopolitan place with many choices of dishes, but he ordered a large black coffee and two chocolate croissants. There were no empty tables so he asked if he could sit at one with only one person at it. It was near the window so he sat where he could see clearly out to the road. The waitress brought what he had ordered and said she hoped he would enjoy them; he nodded and smiled at her.

Artur wanted the time to pass quickly; he felt he still could be in danger. He wondered what had happened to Claude and Pierre and why their phones hadn't been answered. He thought he might be getting a bit paranoid but it was better to be safe than sorry. He looked at his watch and found to his pleasure that it was after 5:15 p.m. At that moment, a car travelling very fast went down towards the docks; he was fairly sure it was a police car. He waited a few moments before getting to his feet and going off to the toilet that was past the bar and through a door. There was nobody else in there so he went in and closed the door behind him. He put his case down against the door as there was no lock on it. It was a typical smelly French toilet with just a hole in the ground; there were flies near the hole and the person before hadn't used the flush, or maybe it didn't work.

After about ten minutes, Artur used the facility and came out through the door. There was another door leading to a courtyard, but he noticed that it looked locked. He had no option, but to go back through the café to the main road. He thanked the barman and the waitress and went out to the road. He went straight across and down a narrow street until he reached another street going to his left towards the docks. At the end, he found himself on a road that ran all the way along the outside of the dock wall. He stopped before turning left to the main entrance and listened very carefully; he tried to keep out of sight of the main gates. He wasn't sure if the police car was still in the dock area but he carefully walked towards the gates. He was about forty metres away from the gates when the barrier went up. It was a police car and the driver was talking to the guard. The guard pointed up the road and seemed to be pointing to somewhere. Artur could only think he was telling the driver about the café that he had just come from. The car drove off, but not before Artur caught a glimpse of the person in the back seat behind the driver: it was Pierre.

Gosh, I wouldn't have expected Pierre to tell the police of my plans, said Artur to himself. *They must have tortured him. They must be the ones who spoke to us when we had to change the wheel on the way to Arles.*

Artur struggled with what he should do next for the best; time was not on his side, especially if the people in the café told them which way he had left. He believed that he should make haste for the dock gates and get inside. He covered the forty or so metres quite quickly and ushered the guard from his hut. He presented his ticket and asked, in his broken French, if he could come through and find a room in which to wait.

"There was someone looking for you rather urgently a few moments ago," said the guard, "but they've driven to the café up the road." He pointed to the one Artur had been to.

"Did you notice if the people in the car were police?" asked Artur.

"I couldn't really tell," said the guard. "But the driver seemed very keen to find you. As you have a ticket for the ship leaving at 10 o'clock, I'll let you in. There's a Passenger Waiting Room a little way down to the right."

Artur slipped the man some money and asked him to tell the driver that he hadn't seen him. The guard nodded and smiled in approval. Artur turned right and walked smartly towards the waiting room just as the noise of a car on the other side of the wall went towards the gate. Artur went quickly into the waiting room and looked around; nobody else there. He headed for the toilets and went inside. *A bit better than the one at the café*, he mumbled to himself. He didn't lock the door but sat on the toilet with his foot against the door. He listened carefully for anyone entering the waiting room.

He sat quietly for what seemed like a long time so he looked at his watch: it was nearly 6:30 p.m. *Not too long now*, he said to himself. He wondered if the captain would let him sit in his office until the time of boarding. He opened the door slowly and looked into the waiting room; there were three people in there now and they looked at Artur as he came from the toilet. He smiled at them and nodded as he went to the main door. As he exited, he looked left and right but he didn't see the police car – if that's what it was. He knew he had to pass the dock gates to get to the captain's office and that could be risky. He walked quickly and tried to look confident as he reached the guard's sentry box. The guard was in there and he noticed Artur going past. He came out and greeted him, but Artur smiled and walked on, determined to get to the building where Captain Hansen might be as soon as possible.

Just as he passed the gates, a car sped along the road towards them. Artur decided to break into a run. He reached the building's door and went inside. There was only one person there: a middle aged woman in uniform who looked up as he entered. He showed her his ticket and his Danish passport.

"Ah, yes, Captain Hansen said you might be here early. He, his crew and the purser are on board carrying out the final checks before allowing passengers to board. He said you could go onto the ship whenever you arrived. Please follow me, Monsieur, and I'll take you."

Artur couldn't believe his luck. The two of them walked along the quay and the woman ushered Artur up the gangway and into the ship. One of the crew welcomed him on board, examined his ticket and papers and told another crew member to tell the captain that Monsieur Selmer had arrived. While Artur was waiting, he turned and saw two policemen on the quay arguing with the woman and gesticulating towards the ship.

"Don't worry, Monsieur Selmer, you are safe now. The police will not have the correct papers authorising us to hand you over to them."

Just at that moment, the captain arrived and spoke to him in Danish.

"Let me take you to your cabin, Artur, where you can relax till we sail. We will have a drink and a talk later, once we are under way."

"Thank you, Captain Hansen, for everything."

THE END